LOST
GROUND

The true paradises are the paradises we have lost.

Gustave Flaubert

LOST GROUND

A NOVEL

MICHIEL HEYNS

JONATHAN BALL PUBLISHERS
JOHANNESBURG & CAPE TOWN

The moral right of the author has been asserted.
All the characters in this book are fictitious.
Any resemblance to persons living or dead is purely coincidental.

First published in South Africa in trade paperback in 2011 by
JONATHAN BALL PUBLISHERS (PTY) LTD
P O Box 33977
Jeppestown
2043

ISBN 978-1-86842-416-0

Reprinted once in 2011

Cover design by Michiel Botha, Cape Town
Text by Alinea Studio, Cape Town
Printed and bound by Paarl Media Paarl
Set in 11 n 14 pt Palatino

CHAPTER 1

Tuesday 19 January 2010

The Queen's Hotel has clung onto its name, but, like a widow cutting loose in middle age, has in every other respect gaily abandoned its former identity.

I remember it as a respectably gloomy establishment, surviving on its Bar and Lounge, the latter later gentrified into a Ladies Bar (without apostrophe). Round the back was a decidedly ungentrified Non-European Bar, really only a counter from behind which Nathan Friedman's wife, Joyce, dispensed boxed sweet wine and half-jacks of brandy. The hotel sported, next to its front door, one little champagne glass, indicating its classification as a one-star establishment by the unexacting standards of the time.

The hospitality of the Queen's was enjoyed or at any rate employed by the odd commercial traveller whose territory covered this part of the Little Karoo, known as the Ghanta, of which Alfredville is the main centre. Calling it a metropolis would be stretching things, but when I lived here, Alfredville did rather lord it over neighbours like Barrydale and Riversdal. This was the seat of the Ghanta Co-op, where the wine farmers (really just grape farmers) brought their grapes to be processed – the Ghanta Pinotage enjoyed a brief period of fame, after John Platter's Wine Guide pronounced it a 'best value wine' for 1988. The area's municipal offices, including the all-important Traffic Department that issued tractor licences, were also here, occupying the second most imposing building in the main street, Victoria Street – the most venerable by far being the large white Dutch Reformed church, defended or at least surrounded by cannon from the Boer War, whether Boer cannon pillaged by the British or British cannon pillaged by the Boers I never did know. Alfredville was the site of the annual Mosbolletjiefees, when the region's wives competed hotly and often crossly for the title of the best mosbolletjie baker. (The dictionary says a mosbolletjie is a sweetish rusk made with unfermented grape juice, but that's like saying haggis is ground-up intestine boiled inside a stomach –accurate enough, but some-how missing the cultural *je ne sais quoi* of the thing.)

The Queen's Hotel, then, used to preside demurely, not to say dourly, over this rather earnest town. If, on a Saturday evening after a victory on the school's rugby field against Barrydale or Robertson, things got a bit raucous in the Queen's Bar, by Sunday morning, as the revellers of the previous night took their places in church, by common and unspoken agreement all was forgotten, and each repentant paterfamilias, stoutly buttressed by corseted spouse and bored children, suffered his hangover in solitude, exchanging at most a shamefaced smirk with a fellow-sufferer.

I never saw the inside of the old Queen's Bar, though my best friend Bennie and I did on one occasion, after writing our matric exams, try to take our dates for the evening, Elrina Potgieter and Gladys Schoonees, to the Ladies Bar for a 'shandy'. The Ladies Bar was really only the old 'Lounge' vamped up to Nathan Friedman's concept of elegant standards. One half of the room was occupied by a massive bar counter, the top of which was copper-plated; around this edifice perched some over-stuffed bar stools with revolving seats. Behind the bar counter was a multi-hued display of liqueurs and other exotic liquors that, judging by the dust on the bottles, served more as decoration than refresh-ment. The other half of the room was scattered half-heartedly with uneasy-looking easy chairs uncompanionably assembled around little amoeba-shaped tables on spindly legs. On the walls were virulent oil paintings of nature scenes, of a lushness and ver-dancy never witnessed in the Ghanta.

I thought at the time that it was all in all rather a larney place for a date. (Bennie and I had put on jackets and ties in deference to the dress code, ascertained in advance, displayed on a gold-coloured perspex sign at the door: Dress: Strictly Smart Casual.)

Gladys, indeed, commented, 'It's really spiff, hey?' Elrina, however, who regarded herself as a cut above the rest of us because her mother was the sister of the wife of some disgraced and now defunct prime minister, let it be known after we had sat down on the sticky leatherette easy chairs that she didn't think it was right to 'hang around in a place like this'. She had evidently caught sight of Doris Vermaas and Joy Duvenhage on their own at a table, knocking back something viscous and yellow, and guffawing loudly – at, I suspected uncomfortably, the four of us. Doris worked in the Standard Bank, and was assumed to be respectable, but Joy had no known regular occupation and was the subject of heated speculation among the schoolboys, and tight-lipped allusion among the matrons of the town.

It was clear that it was Joy's presence that was discomfiting Elrina, but such were the reticences of our youth that nobody mentioned this; we simply trooped out even more gawkishly than we'd entered, to the raucous amusement of Joy and Doris. Instead of the long-anticipated shandies, our over-dressed little party settled for cream soda floats in the Welcome Café and T Room's 'Dining Area', a comfortless collection of tables and chairs behind the sweets-and-cool-drink counter and the magazine shelves. There was a smell of rancid oil in the air, and meticulously executed embroideries of proteas and springboks on the wall; also, I remember, one that proclaimed JESUS LIVES HERE, which reminded me of those signs on garden gates featuring crop-eared Dobermanns declaring I AM ON GUARD. Gladys, it soon transpired, was sulking: she maintained a dignified but deafening silence for ten minutes, then, deciding that silence was golden but lacked impact, said abruptly, 'I can't see that this café is any better than the Ladies Bar, and it doesn't even have air conditioning.' Air conditioning, not being common in Alfredville, was one of the attractions of the Ladies Bar.

Elrina replied with monumental dignity: 'It would need more than air conditioning to *purify* the air in that place.' She pursed her lips genteelly around *purify*, to embody, as it were, the concept while enunciating it.

'At least it didn't smell of vrot fish and chips,' Gladys said, sounding her 'vrot' with all the inelegant force of her ungenteel nature. This set Bennie off giggling, it being one of the more puerile of our schoolboy articles of belief that Joy Duvenhage smelt of fish. Elrina fixed first Bennie then Gladys with her Stare, a basilisk-like glare that she used to devastating effect in netball, where as goal attack she had been known to reduce her opposite number on goal defence to jelly and, occasionally, tears.

'There is vrot fish, Gladys,' she declared, 'and then there are vrot people. I prefer the fish.'

Such was the Queen's Hotel in 1988. Now, twenty-odd years later, it has been transfigured, if that's the term I want. For a start, it's painted a colour I once heard referred to as *puce* in a trendy bar in Camden Town, and which was overpowering even in that setting. Amidst the whitewashed rectitude of Alfredville, it's like a scream in a nunnery. The Victorian veranda – the hotel was built in the late 1890s, largely frequented by British officers on adulterous furlough from Cape Town, and then, during the Boer War, requisitioned as troop headquarters – has been left intact, except for the addition of large flower boxes cascading pink and white petunias. The ensemble escapes any attempt to classify it as to period or style, unless Retro Camp counts as a category.

I park my rental car in the street outside the hotel. Parking was never a problem in Alfredville, and now, at two o'clock on a Tuesday afternoon, there's hardly a soul in sight.

Hardly a soul – but as I step out of the car, flinching from the midsummer heat, and take my case out of the boot of the car, a figure appears from behind one of the syringa trees lining the street (the Queen, the previous one, for whom the hotel was renamed from the Drostdy Inn, planted one of these trees during the Royal Visit of 1947, but the commemorative plaque has since been stolen, so nobody is quite sure which tree it was). A voice says, 'I look after your car, monsieur?'

Another new development: French car guards in Alfredville. The man's very dark colour marks him as foreign as decidedly as his accent: presumably a refugee from Francophone Africa. 'Is it necessary?' I ask the man. In place of the combination of servility and swagger that I associate with beggars all over the world, ready to modulate into either gratitude or abuse at the drop of a coin, he has the bearing of someone consciously lowering himself.

'But yes, monsieur,' he says. 'Lots of crime in the streets.'

I've heard of crime on the streets of South Africa, but didn't imagine it would have reached Alfredville. I suspect that in fact I'm being accosted by its main representative, and I'm being gently blackmailed: you can have your car looked after or suffer the consequences, monsieur. So I say, 'Yes, thank you.'

'That is good, monsieur,' says my new employee. 'Just ask for Vincent.'

I'm not sure where I should ask for Vincent – does he have an office somewhere down the street? – but I leave the matter there, and my car under the the man's dignified regard, and I enter the hotel.

Here, too, things have changed. The lobby, as modernised by Nathan Friedman, used to have a half-hearted fifties look, a flimsy plywood reception desk stuck awkwardly into a corner of the rather grand room, the old double swing doors with their bevelled glass replaced with an automatic glass sliding door bearing a handwritten warning, Automatic door, Don't pull or push/ Outomaties deur, Moet nie trek of stoot, testifying to Nathan Friedman's somewhat makeshift Afrikaans, and occasioning much ribaldry among schoolboys, to whom both *trek* and *stoot* (of which the vernacular connotations may be roughly translated as pull and poke) were hilarious concepts.

Now the old doors have been retrieved from wherever they'd been dumped, and the plywood desk has been replaced with something infinitely grander, resembling a Victorian shop counter, complete with an old-fashioned cash register, its pop-up panel registering 2s 6d in its scratched glass window. The walls sport various comic 'Rules of the House' period posters ('No more than three per bed, all footwear to be removed first'). A fringed curtain covers a doorway presumably leading to some inner office. The

9

floor, freshly sanded and varnished, is probably the original hard-wood boards, the smelly 'wall-to-wall' that used to be a feature of the lobby mercifully consigned to the dust heap of ill-conceived decorating schemes.

The effect, though considerably more solid than the old ticky-tack, is rather oppressive, like a heavy joke after dinner: you can see what was aimed at, but can somehow not enter into the spirit. This effect is intensified by the extreme heat: there seems to be no ventilation in the lobby.

The room is empty, silent and dark, the reception desk un-staffed. There is, however, a large bell on the counter, one of those that are set off by tapping a little knob. I tap it, producing a deaf-ening clang: clearly also a relic of more robust days.

The curtain is swept aside so briskly that one might think that the man now appearing in the doorway had been lurking in wait for the bell to ring. He looks rather fretful, as if put out by my arrival. He is stoutish, in his late thirties. In his Burt Reynolds moustache, black shirt and tight trousers, he looks like a seventies throwback. He's sweating, his forehead damp, the black shirt imperfectly camouflaging the wet patches under his arms.

'Excuse the dungeon effect,' he says, waving an un-Burt Reynolds-like wrist at the gloomy lobby. I get a whiff of sweat with an overlay of something that smells like the ubiquitous Old Spice of my youth. 'Bloody Eskom. No lights, no air condition-ing.'

I've read about the country's power crisis, but this is my first experience of it.

'Load-shedding?' I ask, pleased to know the buzzword for this phenomenon.

'Load-shedding, my arse,' the man says, enunciating the cru-dity primly, as if handling it with gloves. 'That was last year, *kamtig*. This year it's just a normal fuck-up.'

'I suppose so,' I say, not wanting to get involved in a discus-sion that seems, like most South African discussions, on the point of turning political. 'I have a reservation,' I say, in an attempt to deflect the conversation.

The man is staring at me as if registering me for the first time. 'Are you Mr Jacobs?' he asks.

'Yes, Peter Jacobs.'

'Jakes!' he exclaims, and extends his hand, a somewhat pudgy and, on contact, damp appendage. 'Don't you remember me? Joachim Ferreira!'

He clearly expects me to be as thrilled to see him as he appears to be to see me, but search my memory as I may, no Joachim Ferreira surfaces.

Then light dawns. 'Ah!' I exclaim, in my relief rather more loudly than I intended, '*Fairy* Ferreira!' When last I saw Fairy Ferreira, he was some thirty kilograms lighter, but I refrain from mentioning this.

His joy evaporates as suddenly as it erupted. 'Please,' he says. 'I haven't been called … *that* for twenty years.'

'I'm terribly sorry, er … Joachim,' I say, 'but you know, these nicknames … I mean, nobody calls me Jakes any more, either.'

'You didn't *mind* being called Jakes,' he mutters, unmollified. 'People called you that because they *liked* you.'

I can't in all conscience suggest that he was called Fairy in affectionate badinage, and am casting around for some kind of reply, when to my relief the curtain is pushed aside again, and a young man insinuates himself into the room. He is very slim, and dressed to emphasise the fact, in low-slung jeans and a cotton top that scantily covers his midriff. He looks at me without curiosity, nods briefly, then says to Fairy/Joachim, 'What's up, boss?'

'Nothing's *up*, Boris,' Joachim snaps, 'except that the electricity's *down* and I seem to be handling Reception as well as Admin again.'

'Sorry, boss,' the young man says unapologetically, 'but when I was here ten minutes ago there was nobody in sight.'

'Well, there's somebody now. This is Mr Jacobs. Please check him in.'

'Can't, boss. Power's off.'

'I've noticed, thank you. You can still take his details and show him to his room. And stop calling me boss.' He turns to me. 'I'm sorry for the performance. Our normal receptionist is on holiday in Margate. We have a reciprocal arrangement with a hotel there, but they refuse to send us a substitute receptionist, so we have to make do.' His enunciation of 'receptionist' and 'reciprocal' has a viperish sibilance I associate with old BBC radio comedies. He glances sourly at Boris, who remains impervious to the innuendo. 'But so anyway, Boris will take your details and show you to your room,' he explains, as if I've not just witnessed their exchange. 'Room 23,' he says to Boris. 'See you later for a catch-up,' he says to me.

After a somewhat perfunctory check-in, Boris leads the way to Room 23 on the first floor. The lift, of course, is out of commission, but he does not offer to carry my case, of which I am glad: I would rather lug my 22 kilograms up two flights of stairs than be beholden to this supercilious young man.

The room is quite pleasant, with a double door leading out onto the veranda. It's murderously hot; a ceiling fan promises some relief once Eskom relents. The interior decoration is more restrained than I'd expected, though still more chintzy than I find congenial, and cluttered with ornaments of vague provenance and uncertain function – small hand-painted dishes (for bon-bons, perhaps?), cottagey little crocheted squares (samplers?) against the wall, a ceramic dog's head that seems to be a string dispenser, a small pair of scissors gruesomely impaled in its nostrils. There's a replica of an old-fashioned candlestick on the bed-side table, with a candle jammed into it by force, judging by the wax shavings on the table. Next to it are three candles tied together with a red ribbon. A neat hand-printed card nearby warns guests that 'Candles are for use in case of need only.' The bed is volumi-nously draped in mosquito netting.

Boris fusses with the curtains and netting, pointing out the controls of the TV and the fan, opening the door to the bathroom as if to demonstrate that it contains all amenities, and then hover-ing by the door in that deferentially coercive way that hotel porters have. I'm not sure whether he'll be insulted if I tip him or indignant if I don't. I take out a five-rand coin anyway and if it's resented it's at any rate not refused: it disappears smoothly into the pocket of the form-fitting jeans without registering on his face. He still makes no effort to leave, though.

'Thank you, Boris,' I say. 'I think I'll be all right now.'

He doesn't move. 'You know Joe from before?' he asks abruptly.

'Joe?'

'Jo-*a*-chim to you,' he says. 'Also known as Fairy in the kitchen, but don't tell him I said so.'

So poor Fairy hasn't managed to shake off the sobriquet. 'We were at school together,' I say, reluctant to be drawn into a discussion of Boris's employer: there is clearly a certain antipathy, or perhaps a fraught affinity, between the two of them. And Boris is establishing for my benefit the power dynamic in the hotel.

'Old pals, hey,' he says with a smile that somehow fails of cordiality.

'We didn't know each other all that well,' I reply awkwardly, not wanting to seem to be denying Ferreira, yet also not wishing lamely to confirm Boris's innuendo.

'You never know, do you?' he says cryptically, and leaves.

I knew that Alfredville in January would be hot, but I'd forgotten exactly how hot. The candle in the candlestick is slowly tilting over. I try to straighten it out, but it abjectly wilts again as soon as I release it. I open the door onto the veranda and go out. Here it is even hotter than inside, though not quite as stifling. The petunias smell like marshmallows melting in a campfire. There's also a faint smell of paint from the iron railing of the veranda. I look down at my car in the street. Vincent is nowhere to be seen. The only activity is a police van speeding down Victoria Street and slamming to a halt in front of the police station. Two policemen get out, open the back door, and drag out a bedraggled but unbowed man shouting scatological abuse. They manhandle him into the police station. Silence descends once more on Alfredville. I look out over the empty street, trying for an emotion, a sense of recovering a lost past, but nothing presents itself. Proust himself would have had a hard time with Alfredville.

13

I take off my shoes and socks. I'd been looking forward to a nap, after the living death of an all-night flight from London, but now that I'm here, a strange restlessness takes hold of me and I decide to unpack first. There is a bad moment as I fumble in my trouser pocket for the key to my case, my customary travel funk that so exasperated James – it was one of the items in the inventory of grievances cited as grounds for separation – then I extricate the little object from under my handkerchief and snap open the lock.

Odd, to find things that I packed in London now here, like a separate identity on a parallel trajectory across the world. In one corner, jumbled together, all the electronic equipment without which life has become incomplete: a charger for my laptop computer, a charger for my mobile phone (now redundant, since the phone itself has remained behind in England); a charger for my camera, a charger for my iPod; a charger for my toothbrush – it seems that most of one's functions are now rechargeable, except the bodily ones. I untangle the various cords and wind them around their various pronged chunks; I place them in a drawer of the bedside table, together with two adaptors to convert the clumsy British squared three-prongs into the even clumsier South African rounded three-prong. I take my laptop from my carry-on bag; it will need recharging, but that will have to wait till Eskom sees fit to come back on-line. I look around for signs of an internet connection but find none. Wi-fi? I'll have to ask at the desk. The hotel's website claimed internet access in all rooms, but I have learnt to distrust the promises made on hotel websites.

In another corner of the case is a largish toiletry bag containing all the gels and liquids and pastes deemed potential explosives on airlines: gels (Wet Look styling gel, Olivier et Cie Bath and Shower Gel), also shaving gear (Gillette Mach III, shaving brush, Palmolive Foam Shaving Cream, Diesel Aftershave Balm), toothpaste, Disprin and antacid tablets. Sunscreen factor 25. (How *lubricated* modern man is.) Then the hardware: nail clippers, both toe-nail and fingernail. A small torch. And the software: *Country of My Skull* by Antjie Krog, *My Traitor's Heart* by Rian Malan. Five pairs of cotton socks. A pair a walking shoes, a pair of flip-flops, a pair of running shoes. Running shorts and singlets. One pair of shorts, one pair of jeans, one pair of chinos. Five shirts, two of them white. Five T-shirts, two of them white. Three pairs of scants, three pairs of boxer shorts. A light cotton jacket, a tie, just in case. A needle and thread, spare buttons. A spare pair of shoelaces. ('Aren't there shoelaces in South Africa?' James asked, dropping in to say goodbye, he said, but really just to collect some more of his possessions.) What has happened to unaccommodated man, that poor bare forked animal?

Having unpacked and stowed my stuff in the awkward old-fashioned wardrobe, I go into the bathroom, run some water into the basin. I catch sight of myself in the round mirror above it. The last time I looked in the mirror was in London, before leaving, fresh from a shower and a shave. ('Is that my aftershave you're wearing?' James asked, giving me a platonic little peck on the cheek as he left.) Now, after a night on the plane, a two-hundred-kilometre drive and the heat of Alfredville, I'm looking both bloated and desiccated, if that's possible.

My short blond hair, which I normally gel lightly to give it body, is hanging limply. I peer at my day's growth of beard. The stubble is interspersed here and there with grey. I inspect my hair: no grey discernible there yet. My mother, a blonde herself, always said: 'Blond hair doesn't turn grey, it just fades.'

My eyes, which I like to think of as green, look almost colourless, the whites blood-shot and dull. I look like one of those freaked-out survivors one sees on TV after natural disasters, desperate to retrieve some part of their lives.

I take off my trousers. My ankles are slightly swollen from the flight; normally I pride myself on my slim ankles. I take off my shirt. I'll have to watch my weight here; after the inactivity of the flight, my belly seems a bit slack. James forced me to join a gym: 'I don't want some bulging-bicep Adonis, but not a tub of lard either.' James is naturally fit, or his routine as an actor keeps him fit. With my more sedentary occupation as a freelance writer, I have to run almost every day not to subside into obesity. Not that it matters any more, I suppose; certainly not to James.

I wash my face, hoping to freshen it up somewhat, and then lie down in my underpants. I drop off to sleep almost instantly.

The electricity comes on at four o'clock and with it some ghastly 'reality' show on TV, waking me up from an uncomfortable nap, sticky with sweat, my crotch itching. I switch off the set, have a shower and a shave – the water is lukewarm – and go downstairs. Boris is at the desk, peering at his computer screen. He doesn't look up as I approach the desk, though he can hardly not have noticed the only moving object in sight.

'Is there internet access in the rooms?' I ask.

'You got a wi-fi modem?'

'Yes.'

Without looking up, he stretches out his hand, finds a sheet of paper under the counter and places it in front of me. 'Fill that in and bring it down and we'll give you the password. There's a charge of R10 a day.'

'Thank you,' I say, and remain standing, determined to make him notice me. He continues staring at the screen for a calculated five seconds before lifting his eyes. He has very long eyelashes; it is possible that the languid eye movements are designed to bring this fact to prominence. 'Was there anything else?' he asks, as if I'd been plaguing him with unreasonable requests all afternoon.

'Yes. Is there off-street parking for my car?' I ask.

He visibly suppresses a sigh. 'R25 a night,' he says.

This seems steep: no square metre of Alfredville real estate was ever worth R25 per night – but then, in those days there was no reason not to park on the street.

'Where is it?' I ask.

He gestures with his head. 'Behind the hotel. You drive round the block and turn in by the bottle store.'

'Right,' I say, 'I'll go and park.'

'Payable in advance,' he says, and holds out his hand.

'That's ridiculous,' I say.

'Hotel policy,' he says.

16

'Oh, all right,' I say, take out my wallet, and give him my credit card.

'Cash,' he says, his hand still extended.

'Nonsense,' I say, pointing to a sign on the desk. 'It says All credit cards accepted.' It actually says All Credit Cards Excepted, but I don't think Boris will challenge me on the basis of a mis-spelling.

He shrugs. 'If you say so, boss,' he says, the moral victory his, and returns his sullen gaze to his computer screen. 'You can pay when you leave.'

'Thank you very much,' I say, and go out to my car. I have hardly zapped the locking system when Vincent appears as if from nowhere.

'Hello, monsieur,' he says. 'I watched your car very well.'

'I looked from up there,' I tell him, pointing at the balcony, 'and I didn't see you.'

'No, monsieur,' he says, 'but just because you couldn't see me doesn't mean I couldn't see your car.'

This seems philosophically sound albeit dubious on other grounds, and I give him a five-rand coin and drive my car round the block. The forbiddingly designated Queens Hotel Strictly Resident's Only Parking Area Violator's Will Be Towed is, for such an exclusive facility, unprepossessing, consisting of a back yard the hotel shares with the Queen's Hotel Off-sales and Groenewald's Butcher. It seems, if anything, less safe than the street. As I get out of the car, Vincent materialises.

'I watch your car, monsieur,' he says.

CHAPTER 2

Tuesday evening
I manage to wangle a wi-fi username and password out of Boris by not seeming over-eager for it – I've figured out that he operates on the principle that whatever anybody wants from him is by that token too valuable to surrender – and then I power up my laptop. I call up Skype and try James. There's the pulsating purr of the electronic miracle doing its thing in London, but the call is dropped without being answered. I could send an e-mail – not that I imagine James is hankering after news from me, but he did say to keep in touch. 'We don't want you disappearing in the middle of Africa without a trace, do we?'

'This isn't the middle of Africa, James,' I pretended to object, though pleased at the concern. 'This is *South* Africa.'

'Well, that's worse, isn't it? South Africa? Crime capital of the world and all that?'

'That's *Johannesburg*, for Pete's sake. I'm going to Alfredville, in the middle of nowhere. They haven't had a crime since the baker slept with the candlestickmaker.'

'So if they don't have any crime, remind me what exactly you'll be doing there, then?'

'Oops. But don't you see, it's exactly *because* crime's so rare there that this one's newsworthy?'

'Sophistry, pure sophistry. But keep me posted in any case. Ex-partners are supposed to look out for each other. It's a tribal thing.'

'*Dear James*,' I write, wincing at the formality of it – but we have yet to fix an acceptable level of intimacy. Breakups can be as complicated as relationships.

I've been wondering how you are, catching glimpses in passing on

18

the odd TV screen of London all snowed up and people stranded next to the road. Well, I know or hope you won't be stranded next to the road, not having a car to get stranded in, but just generally, I've been thinking of you freezing your ass off, as our American friends say, while I've been frying mine here in Africa. So hope you're okay, and that the audition will go – has gone? – well.

So far, I'm fine. I've survived my first day in Africa without getting mugged or raped. The main mishap, in fact, was at the other end: my mobile got stolen on the Heathrow Express. I know, because I tried to phone you from Paddington just before leaving, and then, when I wanted to try again from Heathrow, discovered it had disappeared. Drat. You'd think pickpockets would stick to the Tube – though I suppose pickings are richer on the Express. And then I thought I'd rent a phone at Cape Town International, but somehow, with the fuss of collecting a rental car, and the general chaos of an airport being, apparently, rebuilt from the basement up for the World Cup later this year, I forgot about it.

South Africa – what does one say? It seems to be muddling along, the roads are in reasonable shape, those that aren't being dug up for said World Cup, though the drivers are still terrible. Judging by the conversation of the chap next to me on the plane, a corporate type from Stellenbosch, an upmarket university town that rather fancies itself, any hitch in any arrangement confirms the whites in their none-too-covert conviction that blacks (or they as they are elliptically but pregnantly called) can't run a country. Not, I seem to remember, that they (the other them!) did a much better job when they (we!) had the opportunity. Heavens, the very pronouns are confused in this place.

And Alfredville – well, it's still a dorp, which is Afrikaans for a village, except that village makes you think of cricket on the village green and cream teas in the village tea room, whereas dorp has connotations of dust and windmills and donkeys and hand-cranked petrol pumps. So no change here as far as I could make out from an admittedly cursory examination, it being too hot at midday for anything more extensive. But I'm not here for the night life or the cultural attractions – I must just get this story written and then bugger off.

The Queen's Hotel, where I'm staying (every town in South Africa has, or used to have, a Royal Hotel or a Queen's Hotel), has been gaudily

19

redecorated and is run by, as it happens, a queen and – if I read the signs correctly – his black consort. So there are some changes after all. Heaven knows how extensive they are, but I'm hoping I'll find out in the course of my – research? investigation? poking about?

I must go to supper. I haven't eaten since BA's attempt at a breakfast this morning. Air travel: the least convenient distance between any two points.

Hope you're keeping well. Button up your overcoat. I'm keeping fingers crossed for the audition. Best, Peter.

Before dinner in the hotel restaurant (The Klein Karoo Kitchen – Regional Specials), I have a drink at the Ladies Bar of old, refurbished to the cornice in heavy wooden panelling and dusty-looking plush upholstery colour-coded to the puce exterior of the hotel. It is now called The Purple Penguin. Joachim Ferreira himself is managing the bar, looking less fretful than this afternoon. There are few people in the bar – three farmers, I guess, sharing a bottle of Chateau Libertas; a young couple carefully dressed, painfully sunburnt, possibly honeymooners on their way through from the coast; two black businessmen – as I assume from their suits and ties – drinking what seems like whisky on the rocks.

I order a glass of Ghanta Sauvignon Blanc. The three farmers are telling jokes, or one is telling a joke and the others are listening.

'So Mandela says to De Klerk, So Mr de Klerk' – the raconteur goes into an imitation of the famous Mandela chest-voice – 'so, Mr de Klerk, you white people know more about dogs, so what shall I call my new little Jack Russell?'

He looks at his audience, as if inviting them to propose names. Meeting only their expectant stares, he carries on, now in the heavily-accented English of De Klerk, '*Nee wat*, Madiba, I suggest you call him Tuck Shop.'

Again he looks at his audience. One man says, 'Why Tuck Shop?'

'Exactly, why Tuck shop, that's what Mandela also asks himself. So when he gets home, his daughter, Zinzi, she's there, and he says to her, Zinzi my girl, look up the meaning of Tuck Shop in the dictionary. So Zinzi looks up tuck shop in the dictionary and she says, Madiba, here it is, tuck shop: a small cafeteria.'

The raconteur leans back, revealing a substantial paunch, waiting for his audience to respond, but they only look at each other in puzzlement.

'Shit, you're slow,' the joker says. 'A small cafeteria, don't you get it, *a small kaffir terrier*!' and he guffaws like a hippopotamus. His auditors join in but with less gusto, not liking to have the joke explained to them.

I groan inwardly – I'd forgotten that South African men celebrate their togetherness by ritual clowning for one another's benefit. And racist jokes, I'd hoped, would at least have gone underground under the new dispensation. I look at the black businessmen: it's not impossible that the joke was partly aimed at them. But if they've heard it, they make a good show of not having done so, and carry on their discussion unperturbed.

Joachim has been listening. He shakes his head. 'That's an old one, Kobus!' he shouts across as he fills my glass. He dawdles, apparently inclined to engage me in conversation. I was entirely truthful in telling Boris that I'd not been close to Fairy Ferreira at school – I remember him as a loner, perhaps perforce – but country pubs have their rules, and one of them is that you speak when spoken to. Besides, Fairy could be useful to me in my enquiries.

'You still have folks around here?' Fairy – or Joachim, as I now remind myself to think of him – asks. 'I suppose not, otherwise you wouldn't be staying here, hey?'

'My parents moved to Knysna more than ten years ago,' I say, choosing to interpret the question as pertaining only to my immediate family.

'Yeah,' he says, 'I remember. Your old man was the chemist, wasn't he?'

I nod. 'Jacobs Pharmacy. Is it still there?'

'Naw,' he says. 'Didn't last long after your old man left. There's a Pep Stores there now. Medicine they buy at Clicks. There's no class anywhere any more, just chain stores. Except here,' he adds, surveying his domain complacently.

'But how come you're running this hotel now, Joachim? Your folks farmed, didn't they?' From nowhere I've dredged up a memory of Fairy Ferreira being dropped at school by a scowling behatted man in a dusty bakkie, usually with a farm labourer in the back to open the gates.

'Ja, and I was supposed to go farming after school and army, but while I was in the army the old man got kicked by a horse, *morsdood*, not surprising, the way he treated his animals, so I asked for compassionate leave, that's a fucking joke hey, and came home and sold the farm lock stock and longdrop to Coenraad Stofberg, who was always nagging my father to sell so he could graze his sheep there.'

'And your mother?'

'I bought her a flat in Worcester. She'd had enough of sheep and flies, and to be honest with you I'd had enough of her, and I sure as sherbet didn't want to go back to the farm. My aunts and uncles carried on like the Mormon fucking Tabernacle Choir about the fucking Ferreira family farm, seventh generation and all that bullshit, bloodline and all, you'd think we were royalty, so I tuned them, right, I can get three million from Coenraad Stofberg tomorrow, but seeing as how you're family and blood is thicker than water, you can have it for two and a half, but that bunch of *bywoners*, the Knersvlakte Ferreiras, haven't got a hundred rand note to wipe their arses, they just wanted me to hang onto the farm so they could come and visit for six weeks every Christmas and do nothing except eat my sheep and drink my witblits, *vreet en suip en snotpik* on the front stoep. So I sold, and when Nathan Friedman dropped dead, some said from an overdose of something because the hotel wasn't doing that well, you remember what a dump it was, I bought it on auction for next to fuck-all. The only other bidder was old Gert Schoeman who wanted to turn the place into a casino, but to get a casino licence like any other licence or concession or tender or fucking *bus ticket* in this country you have to be a previously disadvantaged or designated group or whatever, there are just as many names for being black as ever, only they're different names, so Gert dropped out and I got the place.'

'So *you* refurbished it?'

'Who else? And bloody class too, you must admit. It was mentioned in *Getaway* magazine under Country Hotels with a Difference, said there was nothing like it from Cape to Cairo. Mind you, I must admit, I didn't do it all myself. I got in an interior designer from Cape Town, Ivan Abrahams, he's doing all the cabinet ministers now, a Coloured, but he knows what he's doing, he's on *Top Billing* all the time and even that Afrikaans show *Tuine en Tossels*, so I got him in and haven't regretted it. In the New South Africa, I say, you must fit in or fuck off.'

His patriotic encomium seems to have ignited a suspicion in his mind, because he looks at me as if wondering whether I'm a fitter-in or a fucker-off.

'So where do you live now?' he asks me.

'London.'

'London England?'

'Yes.'

'So you fucked off, eh? Shit-scared of majority rule?'

'I left in '88, before majority rule,' I say somewhat stiffly, not liking to have to justify myself to this self-appointed tribunal.

'Saw it coming, eh?' he says. 'Lots of people buggered off that year. I remember Koot Vosloo packed up his whole family to Perth. Said Western Australia was the last white homeland. He's running a shop now, importing Mrs Ball's chutney and Aromat for the other South Africans down there. And Nik-Naks. Coining it big-time, I'm told, just bitching about the Abos.'

I do not relish being classed with Koot Vosloo, a farmer notorious for feeding his workers prison rations, but I don't think it worth trying to bring home to Joachim the distinction between *buggering off* and principled emigration.

'So what are you doing here?' he continues. 'Heading back?'

I know from chance encounters in London that South Africans who stayed put tend to assume that all ex-South Africans would really rather be living in South Africa, and are somehow slumming it in London because they can't make it back to their biltong and sunshine.

'Actually, no,' I accordingly say. 'I find that London has quite enough to offer.'

To my surprise, he laughs in genuine amusement. 'More than Alfredville? You must be fucking joking! You just haven't been shown the sights!'

I laugh too, relieved to be spared the acrimonious exchange which for a moment seemed imminent.

'Well, if that's an offer, I may take you up on it some day.'

'Just say when,' he says, all affability now. 'How long you staying for?'

'I'm afraid I can't tell you exactly. Is it okay if I give you twenty-four hours' notice?'

'Six hours if you like. Bookings are as scarce as dinosaur droppings at the moment. The credit crunch's got us all by the short and curlies.'

He looks at my glass, which I've drained rather more quickly than I intended, under the barrage of his discourse. 'Good little wine, wouldn't you say, this Sauvignon Blank? The Co-op's been taken over – transformed they call it – by the so-called workers, not that working is what they're best at, and for a while there was nothing a white man could drink, people were saying they'd gone back to pressing the grapes with their feet, but then this new guy moved in, Coloured and all but really jacked-up, Mervyn Jantjies, and he got them going again, threw out the whole so-called top structure and brought in his people from Worcester and Cape Town and now it's running much better and as you can taste the wine's as good as anything from larney places like Stellenbosch and Paarl, all the fancy farms with their gables and their overseas owners, can I get you another glass?'

'Yes, thank you,' I say, 'and then I think I'll have my supper.'

'Any time you're ready,' he says, pouring me a hefty glass of Sauvignon Blanc. 'But if you'll excuse me now I must go and see if the okes need another bottle.'

'Of course,' I say, watching him pad off to the three farmers.

The Klein Karoo Kitchen is empty except for me and the honey-moon couple, whispering intently to each other, and one other person, a woman. I can't see much of her, because she is sitting with her back to me and reading a book, a fact which in itself piques my interest – people who read books not being, in my time, that plentiful in these parts. But then, by definition she isn't from these parts.

Her soup arrives, and she puts down her book. It is JM Coet-zee's *Diary of a Bad Year*. That, too, marks her for me as excep-tional – whereas it's no great event on the London Tube to be reading the same book as the person opposite you (the one who's not reading the *Sun*), in Alfredville it is, in my experience, un-precedented. And, I recognise to my dismay, I am still racist enough to be surprised at seeing a black woman reading Coetzee.

So the meal, pleasant enough in a hearty sort of way (though I avoid the ostrich fillet, ubiquitous in these parts: it strikes me as too much like eating cat or giraffe), passes with my speculating idly about the young woman over the rest of my Sauvignon Blanc and a glass of Ghanta Pinotage. Hotels are, notoriously, docking places for ships that pass in the night, but that's hardly the level of my interest; rather, I reflect over my rack of Karoo lamb, what might a young black woman possibly find to occupy herself in Alfredville? But then, this is not the Alfredville of my youth, of Doris Vermaas and Joy Duvenhage: this is Alfredville with a gay hotel owner and his black partner and, until recently, a black chief of police.

The young woman leaves, self-possessed, self-contained, walking with an easy grace. My mother used to say that black women had such good posture because they grew up carrying pails of water on their heads, but this one doesn't look as if she's ever carried a pail of water on her head. She is dressed smartly, in a bright yellow linen skirt and white blouse, her hair swept back and plaited in a sophisticated adaptation of the traditional corn-rows. I guess her to be in her early thirties, a professional woman. She seems not to have registered my presence. Why should she?

After supper I return to the Purple Penguin. The three farmers are still sitting over their bottle of wine, though it's probably not the same bottle. The businessmen have left. Joachim is nowhere to be seen; Boris is languidly presiding over the bar.

The young woman is sitting at the bar, a glass of red wine in front of her. She is reading her book. I take the stool next to her. One of the farmers passes a comment I can't hear but suspect to be a racist slur, and they all three laugh with the joyless hilarity of the inebriated.

Boris saunters over, and I order another glass of Ghanta Pinotage – in truth a rather callow wine, but since that's what I've been drinking over dinner, I'd better stick to it. As Boris puts the glass down he splashes on the counter, but doesn't bother to wipe the spill, and goes back to his station at the other end of the bar. The woman looks up from her book, notices the spill and catches my eye. I grimace, but she doesn't respond.

'Hello,' I nevertheless say.

'Hi,' she says, her tone committing her to nothing other than the barest civility.

'Enjoying that?' I ask, gesturing at her book.

'I am not sure that enjoyment is what it aims at,' she replies. 'I assume you have not read it.'

'Actually, I have. Okay, I should have found another term. Do you *admire* it?'

'Do you?' she asks, but without much evident interest in my reply. She does, though, put down her book, marking her place with a toothpick she's probably brought from the restaurant.

'That's a second question you've not answered,' I say. 'What happened to my original question?'

'Wasn't that just an opening line?'

'Actually, no,' I say. 'An opening line is, Quiet here tonight, isn't it? or Are you just passing through? But when I ask you about what you're reading I'm interested in what you're reading.'

'You mean you're interested in my mind?' she asks, her flatness of tone allowing a range of interpretations, none of them encouraging.

26

'Well, insofar as it's capable of producing discussible opinions, yes. I think I should tell you that I'm not trying to pick you up.'

'That does simplify things, thank you, and I am flattered by your honesty if by nothing else.' She takes a sip of her drink. Then she turns to me again. 'If you are not trying to pick me up,' she asks, 'why are you persisting in talking to me?'

'Is that the only reason for talking to someone?'

'In my experience it is one of the few reasons for a white man to talk to a black woman.'

I'm disappointed at this response. I had hoped human relations in South Africa had evolved beyond the racial impasse. 'Your experience has presumably been confined to South Africa,' I say.

She looks at me. Her eyes are enormous, with something of the wariness of an antelope; for the first time, she seems affronted. 'If that is a question, then the answer is no. I have travelled. I do not think it is very much different elsewhere.'

'Elsewhere is a big place,' I say.

'You are not South African, then,' she replies, uninterrogatively.

'If that's a question, then the answer is yes and no. I was actually born here, but I've lived in the UK for the last twenty-odd years.'

'You were born here in Alfredville?'

'Yes, as it happens.'

'As it happens? Or is that why you are back? To revisit the native soil?'

'No, not really. I'm here on … well, call it business.'

'What kind of business would you call it?' she asks, but before I can reply, she holds up a hand. It's a shapely hand, slender but strong. 'No, wait, let me guess. You are a writer.'

'Correct. How did you know that?'

'You are here on something that you hesitate to call business and yet cannot call anything else. Your time seems to be your own and your dress is' – she checks quickly – 'casual. You are not a tourist, because that cannot be called business by any stretch of the imagination, not to mention that you are not wearing sneakers and a sunhat.'

27

'Okay, so you got the general category: I'm a writer. But what kind of writer?'

She looks at me. Her face, with its high cheekbones, prominent lips and long jaw, has something of the elongated elegance of the carved mask, of uncertain provenance, I bought on an impulse from a market stall in Camden. 'Peter's totem,' James said to visitors.

'Not a travel writer,' she says, 'because you do not seem to be trailing cameras and notebooks. Not a journalist either, you do not seem driven enough, and as far as I can tell you are not an alcoholic – you have been downing that glass of wine out of nervousness rather than addiction, I think. Clearly, then, you are … a novelist.' She glances at me to check the accuracy of her guess, but I say nothing, and she warms to her theory. She has put down her glass and her long-fingered hands nimbly accentuate her points. 'You are a novelist who is having trouble finding a subject in England, and now you have come out here to write a novel about an ex-South African coming back, let me guess, to be by the bedside of a dying parent – yes, the dying parent is obligatory, like a necklacing in the novels of the eighties – a man who is forced to revisit the past, or *confront* the past, more particularly his own tortured past, the torture usually figurative, sometimes literal, involving the Truth and Reconciliation Commission. At the end of the novel he will go back to England vaguely defeated and strongly relieved.'

'You seem to have the plot off pretty pat.'

'Oh, the plot is standard ex-pat. We have had about twenty of those, treating us to their momentous return to the mother country and the examination of their own entrails and consciences. The details may differ but the essence is the same: a mixture of self-examination and self-congratulation, with poor tired old South Africa serving as both punch bag and security blanket. Your novel, like the others before it, will sell reasonably well and be commended in the press. The Brits like being reminded that South Africa is after all as backward as they always suspected before they were obliged, for a short while, to profess admiration.'

28

'Heavens, how glad I am that I'm not in fact a novelist.'

'You are not?' she exclaims with exaggerated disappointment. 'So you are not here to write the great ex-pat novel?'

I shake my head.

'But you *are* a writer?'

'Of sorts. I had higher ambitions once – to write, yes, a novel, to write screenplays – but now I write for periodicals.'

'A journalist after all?'

'Of sorts.'

'So you are a writer of sorts and a journalist of sorts. What kind of identity is that?'

'I didn't claim an identity. But call me then a freelance feature writer if you insist on a label.'

'Are there features in Alfredville?'

'Possibly,' I say evasively. 'There are features everywhere.'

She makes a face. 'Oh, bullshit! You haven't come here on the off-chance that there may be a story hiding somewhere behind a koppie. You know what you are looking for.'

'Let's say I have a hunch, then.'

'And can you share the hunch?'

I look at my watch. 'How long have you got?'

She glances at her wrist. 'Ten minutes.'

'Not enough.' Somewhat to my own surprise, I ask, 'Why don't we have supper tomorrow night, then I'll tell you all about it?'

'Assuming I am interested.'

'Well, you did ask.'

She laughs, for the first time, showing an array of astonishingly white teeth, with an interesting gap between the two front ones. I don't know her well enough to gauge the tone of the laugh, whether it's amused or derisive. 'Yes, but do I want to spend an evening listening to the answer?' she asks.

'I'll pay for the meal.'

'Now that *is* irresistible. Meet me here at seven?' She takes a card out of her purse and hands it to me. 'You can practise saying my name in the meantime.'

I look at the card. It says:

Nonyameko Mhlabeni BA (Fort Hare) MA (UCT) PhD (Boston) Director, Institute of Women's Mental Health, University of the Witwatersrand.

'Non-ya-meko,' I try out the name.

'Yes, tricky, is it not?' she says. 'It was so much easier when we were all called Doris and Agnes.'

Oh hell, watch your step, booby-traps about. I suppress the urge to snort rudely and ask instead, 'So your PhD is in psychology?'

'Yes. I am a psychologist.'

Ah. I should have guessed. All those confident generalisations. 'And what is a psychologist doing in Alfredville?'

'You think Alfredville does not need psychologists? In fact, I am involved in a project to help impoverished women deal with pregnancy. We want to open a clinic here with a full-time psychologist in attendance.'

'And will you be the full-time psychologist?'

'No, I am stationed in Johannesburg. I do some work for an NGO there. My job is to assess the need here and to set up a clinic.'

'And do you think that's what an impoverished pregnant woman needs? A shrink?'

'Please,' she says. 'I am not a shrink. I am a therapist. And yes, the poorer the woman, the more she needs therapy in order to help her cope with conditions you cannot imagine.'

I can see I've riled her, and I don't necessarily mind. 'Perhaps you can enlighten me on those conditions, as an aid to my impoverished imagination.'

'Perhaps. There is no harm in trying. We can put that on the agenda for tomorrow evening as well.'

'Let's. We may even find that we have some common ground.'

'We must keep an open mind,' she says, not hiding her scepticism.

'Yes, we must. And by the way, in case you were wondering, my name is Peter Jacobs.'

'I was not in fact wondering,' she says, 'but I am sure in due course I will want to know. I am pleased to meet you.'

She extends her hand, and I shake it. It's cool and dry, the skin rougher than I'd have thought from her velvety complexion. I'm not sure that the handshake isn't ironical, but then, irony may not be one of the potentials of her grave manner. It's possible that she is simply profoundly humourless.

We both finish our drinks and I go to my room. I'm strangely irked by the woman's manner, and not quite sure that I really want to spend a whole evening in her company. And then again, I'm not quite sure that I don't.

CHAPTER 3

Tuesday evening

Once in my room, I switch on the television and flick through the available programmes, the whole garbage dump of cable television, from the black-and-white passions of Turner Classics, through the moronic mirth of a sitcom laugh track, the earnest explanation of some overfed and probably overpaid government bigwig as to why there isn't really a service delivery crisis, to Barack Obama trying to get an idiocracy to grow up ... it's a big world out there, in the dark fields beyond Alfredville.

I phone my mother.

'Peter! You sound so close!'

'I'm closer than you think. I'm in Alfredville.'

There's a moment's silence. 'What on earth are you doing there?'

'It's a long story, Mom. Call it an assignment.'

'For a newspaper?'

'Yes. Or a journal, depending on who I can sell it to.'

'But how long have you been there?'

'Only since this afternoon. I arrived in the country this morning.'

'Cape Town?'

'Yes.'

'And you didn't come here first?' My mother tries unsuccessfully to keep the hurt out of her voice.

'I'm sorry, Mom, that's why I'm phoning. I was going to surprise you, but then I thought, well, Alfredville is on the way to Knysna, and I don't know, I just thought I should get this ... assignment behind me first before seeing you.'

'Why? What does it have to do with us?'

'Nothing, really. Not directly. But it's all muddled in my mind, the fact that the assignment is here where I grew up, so I'm trying to keep my personal history out of it.' I can't explain to her that somehow it is important for me to see Alfredville unmediated by their parental concern.

'Is it about Desirée?' she asks.

I hesitate. 'Yes, it is. Sort of. I don't really want to talk about it here, because for the time being I'm not letting on what I'm doing here. It's difficult to explain, but I'll tell you all about it when I get to Knysna.'

'That would be nice, dear.' She pauses. My mother has a kind of maternal stoicism that prevents her from putting pressure on me. She nevertheless asks, 'When will that be?'

'I can't say for sure, Mom; as I say, I want to get this assignment out of the way. To be honest, it's not strictly speaking an assignment, in that nobody's assigned me to do it. It's more of a ... *project*.'

'Your father will be so worried. I don't know if I must tell him you're here.'

Your father will be so worried, my mother's mantra, the gentle blackmail of my childhood. 'What's to be worried about, Mom?' I ask. 'He doesn't worry about my living in London, but he'll be worried because I'm in Alfredville?'

'You know your father, Peter. He worries when I cross the road to buy a newspaper. And it's got worse since we moved to Knysna. He says there are more drug addicts per square mile here than anywhere on earth. The Rotarians have done a survey.'

'Is he there?'

'No, this is his bridge evening. But I suppose I'd better tell him you're here. I can't lie to him. I sometimes think it would save us all a lot of fuss if I could.'

'No, I don't want you to lie to him, Mom. Just tell him I'm writing a story but I'll get away as soon as I can.'

'I'll do that. Where are you staying?'

'At the Queen's Hotel.'

'I'm told it's quite posh now.'

33

'That's one way of putting it. It has certainly been refurbished.'

'Aunt Dolly will feel slighted that you're not staying with them.'

'Aunt Dolly will feel slighted if I do stay with them. It's Aunt Dolly's vocation in life to feel slighted.'

'Shame, darling, she's had a hard time.'

'I suppose so, Mom, but it's not as if staying with them is going to compensate for that.'

'I suppose not. But you will go and see them, won't you?'

'Of course, Mom.'

'Soon?'

'Tomorrow. I promise.'

'Then I suppose that's all right, dear.'

'Of course it is, Mom. And Mom ...?

'Yes, dear?'

'Whatever you do, don't tell Aunt Dolly what I'm doing here.'

'I won't if you don't want me to, dear, but I don't like lying to my own sister.'

'You needn't lie, Mom. Just don't say anything.'

'I suppose I can do that, dear.' She sighs heavily. 'Well, be careful darling.'

'I will, Mom, but what can happen to me?'

'I don't know, dear, but there's been one murder already.'

'Okay, Mom, I'll make sure I don't get murdered.'

'Don't even joke.' She hesitates, and I know what's coming. 'And are you on your own?'

'Yes, Mom.'

She sighs. 'I'm worried about you, always on your own.'

'You'd worry about me if I had a partner, too. This way you get more of me.'

'It's not as if we have that much of you,' she says, without any rancour.

'Well, I promise you my undiluted presence in a few days' time.'

'That'll be nice, dear.'

I ring off, relieved to have got that over with. I've not really taken my parents into my confidence regarding my personal life: there's never seemed to be an opportune time. They met James once, when they came to London, but if they wondered about him, about the tall, elegant Jamaican who seemed to share my life on an undeclared basis, they didn't say so, and I didn't volunteer any information. And now that he's no longer there, as it were, there's little point in mentioning him.

Trying to keep my personal history out of it, I think – have I even *got* one? Of course I have a personal history, in the sense that everyone has one, certain things have happened to me since birth, other things haven't, and sometimes I think the ones that haven't are more significant than the ones that have, a kind of negative history, then. My dear parents, whom I love with a kind of exasperation bordering on despair, saw to it that nothing ever happened to me, even at the price of shipping me off to England: that ultimate act of parental concern and renunciation that has sent generations of young South Africans to seek security and opportunity elsewhere. But had I stayed in Alfredville, would I have had a more eventful existence? What was Alfredville but a very small town in a very small country on a backward continent? Did anything ever really *happen* to me here? Can anything *really* happen to anyone here? Except, of course, something did happen to poor Desirée.

I open the door of my room and go out onto the balcony. Victoria Street is empty at this hour, but the sullen air is teeming with the smells of a summer night – exhausted vegetation, wilting flowers, wet soil from the gardens being watered, heated asphalt. The blend hasn't changed in twenty years. To smell it again is to remember not so much individual incident as the tonal value of those summer nights, the vague ache of an imperfectly articulated desire.

I am tired from last night's flight, but too restless to sleep. I switch on the ceiling fan; it starts up with a creak that bodes no well for my night's sleep, then settles into a steady hum, though wobbling alarmingly. I'm not sure I'm going to sleep soundly with a rotating scythe overhead. I go downstairs to the deserted bar. I ring the bell on the counter and wait for Boris to make his leisurely appearance. When eventually he does, he gives no indication of recognising me; he pours me the glass of Ghanta Pinotage I've ordered, then asks me for my room number.

I swallow my irritation along with my first mouthful of pinotage. The bell, I'm sure, is the same one as was in the old Ladies Bar. Looking at it, I find, after all, a memory, if not a personal history: the aftermath of Bennie's and my unfortunate evening out with Gladys and Elrina.

After the debacle in the Ladies Bar and the Welcome Café, we walked our partners home as fast as we decently could. Neither Elrina nor Gladys was making an effort to be civil – indeed, it would be true to say that they were doing their best to be disagreeable. Bennie was never very good at small talk, and it didn't help that he audibly stifled a giggle every few minutes – a giggle all too evidently traceable to Elrina's defence of fish. I tried as best I might, aided by such props to conversation as Victoria Street provided, to keep alive the semblance of a conversation, in desperation launching into a long story my mother had told me about the mysterious disappearance of the flower arrangement Stienie Pepler had made for the previous Sunday's church service. Stienie had made the arrangement on the Saturday morning, and in the afternoon there was a wedding in the church – Jacoba Munting, the postmaster's daughter, was marrying a telephone technician from Porterville – so the obvious explanation was that Stienie's arrangement had by mistake or even design been removed along with such flowers as had been provided for the wedding. This, however, was hotly denied by the Munting clan; indeed, they maintained that there had been no such arrangement in the church when they arrived. The dominee had tried to intervene, arguing that the flowers would smell sweet in the nostrils of God wherever they were, but Stienie was not to be placated: 'The nostrils of God belong in the House of God, otherwise why don't we just leave the flowers in the garden for Him to sniff?'

Gladys and Elrina heard out the story without comment. Then

36

Elrina said, 'That's what's wrong with this place. A pile of human garbage.'

'And vrot fish,' Bennie added, and he and I both broke down in uncontrollable mirth.

The rest of the walk took place in indignant silence, except for the odd guffaw from Bennie and me. We saw the girls off – Gladys and Elrina were next-door-neighbours – with no attempt by either of them to even pretend to have enjoyed the evening, and Bennie and I hared off in ill-suppressed hilarity.

'Jeez, what a bum evening,' Bennie said as we walked back down Victoria Street. 'What princesses, hey?'

'Only because you started giggling,' I said, 'and pissed them off.'

'Hell, if they piss off that easily we weren't exactly going to get very far, hey?'

'So how far did you think we'd get ?'

He leered at me. 'All the way, of course. I've finished with playing around, I'm ready to move on to the big stuff.'

'And you thought Elrina was going to be the big stuff?' I asked, and we subsided in crude mirth again, with me laughing mainly because Bennie was laughing; he had a lunatic cackle that was at first alarming and then infectious.

'So what are we going to do now?' he asked. 'There's no way I'm going home.'

'Well, if you're really ready for the big stuff,' I said, 'there's Doris Vermaas and Joy Duvenhage.'

My suggestion was intended as a joke, but he narrowed his eyes in that way that marked his moments of intense thought. 'Hey, *there*'s an idea,' he said. 'Car*a*mba.'

'But ...' I said, dismayed. The notion of chatting up Doris Vermaas or Joy Duvenhage filled me with terror.

'But what?' he said. 'It's the first good idea you've had all week, don't spoil it now.' He took out the packet of condoms he'd made me steal from my father's pharmacy months before, and held it up. 'There's one for you and one for me and seconds for the bugger who comes first.'

37

'Thanks,' I said, 'but you can come three times. I'm not going to nail Joy Duvenhage.'

'So? If you're so fussy, you can have Doris Vermaas.'

'Oh come on, Bennie, they'll laugh at us! Didn't you hear them in the bar? They were howling like hyenas.'

'Like hyenas on heat, yes,' he smirked. 'They were pissed off because we were with those two losers. They wanted us for themselves.'

'But where will we take them?' I asked, taking refuge in practicalities. 'To your bedroom?'

This was an unkind cut, because Bennie, to his chagrin, shared a bedroom with his ten-year-old brother.

'No,' he said, with a grin like Dracula making a first appearance in the virginal bower. 'Yours.'

'You must be fucking mad,' I said.

'I'm not mad, but I'll be fucking soon. We can use the back door, your parents won't know.'

'And are all four of us supposed to hump away on my single bed?'

'Love will find a way. I'll use the floor.'

I could see that objection was futile: Bennie had set his mind on Joy Duvenhage and Doris Vermaas, and nothing was going to deter him.

'I don't feel like it,' I said. 'You go alone.'

'And who's going to entertain Doris while I'm doing Joy?'

'You're such a stud, you can do both.'

'Sure I can, so what are you going to do while I'm at it? Sit and read a book?'

'I don't want to do it in front of you. It's private. I won't get it up with you watching.'

'Oh, don't talk shit. You've pulled your wire in front of me, you can poke a woman in front of me. Anyway, don't flatter yourself, I won't be watching you, I'll have my own horse to tame. Come, you're wasting good poking-time. Let's get back to the ladies in the Ladies Bar.'

We walked back through a deserted Victoria Street, the air thick with the scent of syringa. It was only just past half past nine, but Alfredville went to bed early. I placed my hope on the not unlikely possibility that Joy and Doris had found other company or had given up and gone home.

But I'd overestimated their social skills and underestimated their tenacity. When we got to the bar, there they were, in sole possession of the place.

As we entered, I saw Joy kicking Doris under the table, its spindly legs imperfectly concealing the transaction. Both of them assumed very serious expressions and started an animated conversation intended to demonstrate that they were entirely unaware of our entrance. It seemed to be about the Christmas decorations in Osrin's shop window.

'What now?' I asked Bennie.

'We have a drink,' he said. 'That's why we're here.'

He led the way to the bar. There was no barman in sight.

'I think they're closed,' I said. 'Let's get out of here.'

'Sit down and shut up,' he hissed at me. 'I'll handle this.'

Abjectly, I obeyed, sitting down on a bar stool. Bennie remained standing, making a show of peering behind the partition – there was a law, those days, against pouring drinks in front of a woman – and then, with devastating nonchalance, said to the two women, who were now watching with undisguised interest, 'Excuse me, but how do you get serviced here?'

'You want to get serviced, you go to Blik van Blerk's garage,' Joy said, which totally cracked up the two of them.

'I mean *served*,' said Bennie, and I was maliciously pleased to see him blush deep scarlet. 'Where's the barman?'

'There's a bell on the counter, there by the till,' Doris said. She giggled. 'It says Ring for Service.'

Bennie had retrieved something of his savoir faire. He pushed the bell with exaggerated emphasis. 'Normally I don't have to ring for service,' he said. Then he turned to the two women. 'Do you need service?' he asked.

'Oh my, a gentleman,' said Joy. 'Are you offering?'

'Sure,' Bennie said with an appalling leer. 'I'm offering service. *And* a drink.'

'Let's start with a drink,' she said. 'I'll have a Tia Maria.' She pronounced it *Ty*-ah Mar-*y*-ah.

'I'll just have a vodka and lime,' Doris said demurely. 'Double vodka. On the rocks.'

'Coming up,' Bennie said, and banged the bell again. 'Have you got money?' he whispered to me.

'A bit,' I said, 'but don't offer them seconds. Those cream soda floats were expensive.'

A sleepy barman appeared from somewhere. He looked at his watch pointedly. 'We close at ten on weekdays,' he said.

Bennie pointed at the clock behind the bar. 'It's ten to ten.'

'You going to drink up in ten minutes?'

'Sure. Give us two Castles and a ... double vodka and lime and a ... Mia Maria.'

'With cream?'

'No, on the rocks.'

'You want a Tia Maria *on the rocks*?'

Bennie recovered his aplomb with admirable dexterity. 'No, of course not. The vodka and lime on the rocks.'

The barman got the drinks, first the women's drinks, then two bottles of beer.

'You want glasses for the Castle?'

Bennie looked at me for guidance, but I was as much at a loss as he. 'Does it cost the same?' he asked.

The barman surveyed him critically. 'How old are you?' he asked.

'I'm eighteen,' Bennie said. 'Today's my eighteenth birthday.'

The barman looked at him impassively. 'Happy birthday,' he said morosely, and reached for two glasses. 'For you the glasses are free, birthday boy.'

Doris and Joy accepted their drinks with equanimity but without thanks. We stood around awkwardly; they did not invite us to sit down.

'Hey, mind if we join you?' Bennie asked and sat down.

'Suit yourself,' Joy said. I was still standing, feeling unwelcome. 'You too, big boy,' Doris said.

I sat down. 'How tall are you?' Doris asked.

'About six three, I think,' I said.

'You think?' Joy asked. 'Haven't you measured? I thought boys were forever measuring themselves.' She and Doris exploded.

Bennie gulped at his beer. I saw him gagging slightly: he was in general quite puritanical about liquor, having a father who regularly and brutally overdid it. He'd had beer only once before, when he and I had slipped into the town hall after a wedding reception looking for food and found a full bottle of beer on one of the tables. We'd shared it and pretended to be drunk.

'You don't measure pleasure with a tape measure,' he said. 'Hey, that rhymes,' he added, pleased. 'You don't measure pleasure with a tape measure.'

'Sure,' said Joy, 'if that's your motto. Me, I measure pleasure by the clock, and I'm sorry if that comes as a shock. You see, I can rhyme too.'

'Clock? Shock?' said Bennie. 'I could find you a rhyme for that.'

'I'm not interested in writing a poem, Shakespeare. I'm telling you that for me time is money.'

'You mean ...' Bennie looked at her, then at Doris; but Doris wasn't going to get involved. 'I've got to be getting home,' she said, draining her glass with alarming dispatch, and getting up, but not leaving. 'Work tomorrow.'

'I mean it'll cost you sixty rand, if that's what you were wondering,' Joy said, ignoring Doris. 'Special schoolboy rate.' Then she looked at me, shifting her gaze from my face to my feet with some lingering in the mid-section. 'Your friend here I'll entertain for free. I like *big* blond men.'

'Thanks,' I said, horribly embarrassed. 'But it's okay. He can have my turn.'

Bennie glared at me, and Joy seemed less than pleased. 'No, he can't, wise guy. I say who gets what. I'm not a merry-go-round you take turns on. He wants me, he pays, and I do you for free. Low season special.'

'Okay, then, I'll leave you to your negotiations,' said Doris. 'Bye, Joy, spot you around. Bye, loverboys,' and she carefully picked her way among the empty tables.

'See you some more, Doris,' said Joy, without looking at her retreating back. 'So, what do you say?' she asked me.

'Bugger what *he* says,' Bennie interrupted. 'I'm not going to pay so *he* can have a free screw. We both pay thirty rand.'

'What do you take me for? For thirty rand you get a blow job from Malie Spies behind the Co-op. I charge sixty rand minimum or I do it for free for people I like. I'm not some bargain-basement has-been.'

'But what's the fucking difference?' Bennie shouted.

'Hey, watch your language,' the barman said from behind the bar. 'This is a ladies' bar, okay?'

'Oh fuck off, Solly,' Joy shouted good-humouredly. 'Buy yourself a drink. These gentlemen will pay.'

Bennie, paying no heed to this transaction, continued at undiminished volume. 'But what I want to know is, what does it matter to you, long as you get sixty rand, who pays what?'

Joy crossed her legs primly. 'It matters to my professional principles. I don't do thirty-randers.'

'And I don't pay sixty rand so some other bugger can bang you for free just because he's got blond hair. He doesn't even *want* you,' he added spitefully.

'How would you know, boetie?' she asked, not at all put out. 'I can tell he wants me. A woman can tell. Not so, big boy?' she asked, smirking at me.

I sat paralysed, as small rodents are said to be by a snake. There were few things I wanted less than Joy Duvenhage at that moment, and if I'd had the courage of my aversion I'd have said so. I muttered instead, 'Sure. But you heard my friend. He's also got his self-respect.'

But Bennie had a bloodhound's nose for a phoney gesture. 'Hey, thanks, my friend. But I can look after my own self-respect, thank you, so stuff you too.'

'I second that,' Joy said. 'What about *my* fucking self-respect? He'll be wanting *me* to pay *him* next,' she said to Bennie.

'Oh, yes,' he said, 'he charges people fifty cents just to *see* his dick.' Suddenly the two of them, who a minute previously had been ready to spit in each other's eye, were united against me.

'Fifty cents?' she bellowed. 'That's ten cents an inch! You can buy best quality boerewors for that!'

Bennie roared. 'Never mind best quality, this isn't even boerewors, it's pure soutpiel, been hanging in the Atlantic for the last eighteen years.'

'Hey!' I said, 'So what have *I* done wrong?

'I told you, watch your language,' the barman said. 'We're closing now, it's ten o'clock.'

I got to my feet, highly relieved. The other two remained sitting, both of them giving me dirty looks. 'Time to get going, I reckon,' I said, looking at my watch.

'Okay, *big boy*,' Bennie said with killing sarcasm. 'Do you think you can get home on your own?'

'Yes, thank you,' I said. 'I think I might just make it.'

'I notice nobody's worried about whether *I* can get home,' Joy said petulantly. 'And here I thought you were gentlemen.'

'At sixty rand a shot you're not exactly a lady either,' Bennie said.

'I'm not staying here to be insulted by schoolboys,' she said, wobbling onto her stiletto heels. 'Why don't you two Casanovas go off and screw each other? That way it's free for both of you.'

She left with such dignity as she could muster, grabbing a handful of peanuts from the bar as she passed by. The barman watched impassively.

Bennie looked at me with the resentment of unslaked lust.

'Well, you fucked up *that* one, didn't you?'

'Hey!' I said, incensed. 'What did *I* do? So she wanted sixty rand for a poke and you didn't have sixty rand, so now it's my fault?'

'She'd have done it for me for nothing if you hadn't been here. You embarrassed her with your snooty attitude.'

'I *embarrassed* Joy Duvenhage? Embarrass *her*? I might as well try to embarrass a … a charging hippopotamus cow.'

We had both recently seen a nature programme on TV – the SABC was strong on apolitical nature documentaries – about hippopotami, 'Africa's Deadliest Mammal', and been suitably overawed at the speed and determination of an irritated hippo-potamus cow.

Bennie looked at me, clearly honing a devastating reply; then his upper lip twitched in a way I recognised as imminent hilarity. 'Hey, that's not bad,' he said. 'Joy Duvenhage, the Hyped-up Hippo.'

'Yeah,' I said, 'the Hippo Hooker!'

We spluttered the remains of our beer all over the table. The barman, after charging us for the drink Joy had invited him to have at our expense, summoned 'Security' – a sleepy nightwatch-man – to eject us from the premises, which the poor man did so apologetically that we offered no resistance.

'You finished?' Boris asks, pointing at my glass, which is in fact still half full. 'We close at ten weekdays.'

So that at least has not changed. 'I know,' I say, and leave.

When I get back to my room, I check my e-mail, but there's no reply from James. He must be out somewhere. In London, the evening has just begun.

CHAPTER 4

Wednesday morning 20 January

I wake up with a start. It's still dark, though through the open door a glimmering is visible. It's very quiet – I have forgotten what total silence is – and I can't figure out what woke me up until there, again, the cock crows. A sound I haven't heard for twenty years, a memory I didn't know I had. Through the drapes of the mosquito net I reach for my watch next to my bed and, after some fumbling, switch on the bedside lamp. It's just after four. I curse the cock and try to get back to sleep. It crows again and then, having apparently asserted its status or its territory or its bloody *identity*, it shuts up. I switch off the light, change position, remind myself that in London it's only 2 am and freezing. I lie awake, hoping the mosquito I can hear is outside the net rather than inside, and trying unsuccessfully to cool myself with thoughts of freezing. I do this for what feels like hours but probably isn't because the next thing I'm aware of is the sunlight beating into the room. I have forgotten how brutally day blunders into the open in Alfredville, without preliminary or overture; no rosy fingers or shy blushes of dawn, just the sudden blaze of sun. My room faces east, and as I did not draw the curtains last night – I'd opened the French doors for the fresh night air – I am startled awake by an unmitigated glare of sunlight.

The relentless drizzle and early dusks of a London January had lent allure to the prospect of wide bright open spaces and dry radiant heat – but hell, fourteen hours a day is a bit excessive, I protest as I burrow my head under the pillow. But then, welcome back to Africa, where *a bit excessive* is the norm. For moderation there's England, there's Holland, there's Scandinavia, the safe, mature, spongy, cheese-producing Northern democracies who've

45

made their bargain with history and now have nothing to fear other than the delinquency of their bored young and the crabbed resentment of their disregarded old. This is Africa, still negotiating its bargain or settling its score with history, dealing with heat and drought, flood and famine as stoically and inefficiently as with all its other tribulations.

I'm feeling groggy, with a dull, morose pressure behind my temples – the effect, probably, of the Ghanta Sauvignon Blanc followed by the Pinotage; no doubt too much sulphur in it, as my London friends tell me South African wine is prone to have. In London, feeling like this would warrant another couple of hours of sleep, but here the sheets – 100% polyester, I've checked – feel sticky and slippery on my bare skin as the heat pumps up outside. I yawn my way out of bed and into a cold – or lukewarm – shower. If I'm going to keep to my resolve to run every day, this is the time for it. I try to persuade myself that going running now is an excess of zeal, that I'm entitled, for Christ's sake, to a day of rest, that I shouldn't subject my system to so many shocks in such a short time, that it's probably *bad* for me … but my live-in lifestyle monitor, stand-in for a conscience, hybrid offspring of my mother's Calvinist work ethic and my father's manic Jewish energy, isn't having any of that. Get out there and get running, is the message from the monitor, it's not going to be any easier tomorrow if you don't go today.

I obey; I know from experience that the moral discomfort attendant upon disregarding these promptings outweighs the short-term gratification. I tug on my running gear and go downstairs, avoiding the lift in case Eskom decides to pull the plug again. Downstairs there's little going on: somebody left the television on in the Residents Lounge (the apostrophe a lost cause here, as in the rest of the English-speaking world), and an abrasively cheerful – or perhaps desperate – interviewer is dragging mumbled replies out of a taciturn octogenarian who's just published his first novel, apparently dealing with soil erosion.

The front door is still locked, but a side door, though also locked, has its key on the inside, and I let myself out. As I step out into the street, Vincent materialises by my side. 'Morning, monsieur!' he says. 'I have been watching monsieur's car!'

'Thanks, Vincent,' I say, as I start running. 'When do you sleep?'

'Sleep?' he shouts after me. 'Who needs sleep?'

Once on the road, the moral self-approval combines with the first trickle of endorphins to induce a mild feeling of well-being. The early morning light, though harsh after the watery tints of London, is flattering to the near-universal whitewash of Alfredville's houses, most of them built in the early years of the last century, when it was the fashion for English visitors from Cape Town to come here by train for the 'air' – the famously clean Ghanta air, deemed therapeutic for consumptives and asthmatics – and for the hot springs, deemed beneficial for everything else. Alfredville was spared the boom that devastated the surrounding villages in the 1960s, causing whole streets to be demolished in the name of progress. I drove through several such blighted towns on my way here; the buildings erected during the Gadarene sixties now drably persist – banks attempting to look modern and succeeding only in looking insubstantial; garages designed to be as eye-catching, which is to say hideous, as possible; co-ops that seem intent on demonstrating the futility of cooperation; lurid furniture stores with boom boxes thudding hip-hop on the pavement; threadbare clothing stores offering children's panties at R2.99; oxymoronic 'mini-supermarkets' and 'superettes' – the boom no longer booming, the plyboard facades peeling and warping in the sun and rain, their crass colour schemes fading into a universal dun, ticky-tack rampant and triumphant.

By contrast, Alfredville seems almost spruce. Capetonian weekenders have evidently been buying up houses vacated by city-bound locals, the two-way traffic overseen by Pam Golding Properties, ubiquitous sign of upward mobility even in my day. Next door to the Pam Golding offices there is an art gallery – inevitably, The Ghanta Gallery – a tea-room (Time-for-T), a restaurant (The Old Mill – not that I can recall a mill in Alfredville), a café (The Country Pumpkin): all of them, with their carefully-preserved or faux period features, tastefully deflecting the tourist gaze from the blank functionality of the Clicks and Pep that Joachim mentioned. The Welcome Café and T-Room is no more; in its place an antiques shop called Memory Lane has established itself. For the practically-minded home owner there is a hardware store, another hardy relic of earlier days, though now doubling as a Vodacom outlet. Also unchanged, except for the addition of security doors, is the neo-classical edifice of the Standard Bank, though its rival, Volkskas, financial arm of the apartheid regime, has now been repackaged as ABSA, and rehoused in a facebrick structure bereft of character or style. To deal with the needs of a chronically cash-strapped populace, those without the means to be exploited by Standard or ABSA, a number of cash loan offices have opened up, their generic shop fronts converted from failed enterprises – I remember Betty's Bower, a twee florist's shop, and The Bookworm, a courageous but ill-starred attempt by a retired teacher called Koos Lotter to waken Alfredville to the glories or consolations of literature. Down the side streets things look much as they did twenty years ago, modest houses with wire fences and Cape honeysuckle and plumbago hedges; but little brown boards bearing the universal mummy-on-a-bier logo point down most of these streets, signalling a rash of guest houses. No wonder the Queen's Hotel is not attracting the crowds.

I slow down as I run past our old home, Number 68 Victoria Street. The heady scent of the huge magnolia in front of the house catches me unawares, releasing a flood of memories, undifferentiated but powerful.

When my parents left, my Oom Blik bought the house from them, at a bargain price, the old skinflint, my mother wrote. He gave it to his daughter, Desirée, as a wedding present. It's a pleasantly eccentric old house, its off-kilter gable determinedly avoiding the conscientious symmetry of its neighbours. It has a companionable stoep set back from the street, where, in the days before streets were killing fields, the people of the house would sit in the late afternoon, exchanging pleasantries and platitudes with such passers-by as had a few minutes to spare. My own father and mother did not continue the tradition: he was held up in his pharmacy till long after the sociable hour, and my mother did not want to sit there on her own, looking, she said, like Koba Vermaak, the undertaker's spinster daughter who was always to be seen on the stoep of her father's house, waiting, people said, for her fiancé, Willie Lotriet, who had absconded days before their wedding with most of the wedding presents and his prospective father-in-law's hearse.

I'm pleased to see that our old stoep is still open to the street, unlike many others of its kind that have been enclosed in a grim variety of grilles and meshes and bars, rendering them, I should think, unusable for their original purpose: I can't imagine that anybody would willingly sit inside a cage like a parrot, staring at the world outside. But number 68, though the stoep is open to the street, is shut up: the wooden window shutters, which would normally be wide open at this hour to let in a last gasp of morning air, are closed. The stoep has not been swept: dead leaves, sweet papers and a copy of the *Ghanta Herald* have accumulated in one corner. I remember my mother saying to Angelina, our 'domestic': 'If you leave it for one day it looks like a dump, and encourages more people to throw their rubbish there.'

My room used to be round the side, overlooking a long narrow garden stretching from the street to a large back garden. The garden looks better tended than one would expect, given the condition of the stoep. Somebody has been watering and weeding.

There is little traffic. Victoria Street has the deserted look I associate with the tedium of Sunday afternoons, the absence of any sign of human endeavour or initiative, though the morning light has a more hopeful edge to it than the flat glare of afternoon. The street still has a semi-rural look, with many of the plots as large as smallholdings; windmills, static in the morning calm, peer over the houses and trees, and farm animals stand and lie awaiting the day: sheep, goats, a few cows even. It's a compromise between town and country on the part of an agricultural people driven off their farms by circumstance or ill-judged ambition. Here and there a lamppost still supports a Christmas decoration, a sparse near-abstract arrangement of coloured lights. Is there anything more depressing than left-over Christmas lights in broad daylight?

A police van drives past slowly, the driver casting a curious glance at me. I run out of the village – all ten blocks of it – past the high school, Ghanta High, on the outskirts of the village. The only change here is the razor-wire fence hideously surrounding the school grounds. School must have reopened for the new year – the windows are open, the gates unlocked – but it's too early yet for any activity.

As I run past I inspect the dusty playground, the parched rugby field behind the school, the outhouses – the boys' toilets placed at a hygienic distance from the school itself. I try to people the place with memories, summon up the figures that then seemed the arbiters of my happiness, that in some sense must have contributed to making me what I am. But they present themselves as inchoate, amorphous, blurred by time into a slightly resentful, muttering crowd, asserting vague claims that I don't know how to meet. The only one that emerges from the haze with any clarity or individuality is Bennie, who stands before my mind's eye with his insouciance undiminished by time.

Bennie came to Alfredville in Standard Six, that is, when we were both about thirteen years old. Having grown up in Alfredville, I'd long since waged whatever battles of status or precedence were necessary, and my place in the hierarchy of my coevals was fairly firmly established. I was, if not a leader, then at least one of the more prominent members of my class: not spectacular at sport, but good enough not to be derided as a wimp; academically strong, without being suspected of being a swot. I was careful not to know the answer to too many of the teacher's questions, having discovered early in my school career the painful consequences of being perceived to be 'a smart-arse'. I'd learnt to tolerate with good humour even the most puerile of schoolboy pranks: by laughing with the perpetrators you deprived them of the pleasure of laughing at you. My Jewish ancestry exposed me to some mild anti-Semitism, but by and large the few Jews in the dorp, as in many other country villages, were part of the social fabric. The fact that my father had married a boere-meisie from the district, one of the Visagies of Sondereind, also eased his assimilation into the community. I was sent to the Dutch Reformed Sunday school and grew up a nominal Christian, though only very briefly an avid one, when I mistook the onset of puberty for spiritual hunger. Thanks to my mother's resistance, I had not been circumcised at birth, so in that respect I conformed to my fully-prepuced coevals.

Thus, by the time Bennie arrived, I was securely settled in my little world. At first I was not inclined to take much notice of the newcomer – he was a late developer and small for his age, the predestined victim of the class bullies, Pudding Theron and Wolf Schoeman, a year older than the rest of us through being 'held back' the previous year. At thirteen, a year is crucial, the difference between boyhood and adolescence, between at most a theoretical knowledge of physical processes and hard evidence.

So Pudding and Wolf picked on Bennie, and the rest of us prudently accepted this as part of the natural order of things. But one morning during break I went to the boys' toilets, in those days a rather insalubrious facility. The urinal was really only a shallow furrow inside a paved enclosure open to the sky, with beyond it four cubicles swathed in a miasma of flies and Jeyes Fluid. Bennie was standing at the furrow with Pudding and Wolf on either side of him. Lying in the furrow in front of Bennie was a sandwich, rapidly turning soggy from the contents of the urinal.

'Come on, Nienaber,' Pudding was saying, 'take out your little prick and piss.'

'And then you can eat your sandwich like you said,' Wolf added.

Bennie said nothing, did nothing, just stood staring at the wall in front of him. As I entered, he turned his head and looked at me in dumb appeal. I have never been a brave person, and I had no authority to assert over Pudding and Wolf, but I was, if nothing else, an accepted member of the school, immune to their bullying.

'Is there a problem?' I asked.

51

'Fucking sure there's a problem,' Wolf said. 'This little shit tells us he wants to eat his sandwich in peace, so now we're giving him his chance to eat his sandwich in peace.'

'In *piss*,' Pudding said, highly pleased with his own verbal agility.

'You shouldn't waste food,' I said, feebly didactic to the last.

'We're not wasting it,' Pudding pointed out, 'we're making him eat it.'

'I'm not going to piss on my own sandwich,' Bennie declared. 'And I'm not going to eat it after it's been lying in the piss either.'

'Watch it, short-arse,' Wolf said. 'You'll do what we tell you to do.'

Feeling vaguely reproached for my own unvaliant performance by Bennie's stand, I scraped together my meagre resources of courage and said, 'I don't think he has to do what you tell him to do.'

'And why not, Jew-boy?' Pudding sneered. 'Because you say so?'

'No,' I said, 'because ... because he's ... because he's one of us.'

I hadn't imagined my egalitarian argument would carry weight with Pudding and Wolf, and it didn't. But somehow it emboldened Bennie to step back from the urinal and say, 'Yes, I have just as much right as you.'

He turned his back on his tormentors and walked out. 'You can eat my sandwich if you like,' he said as he left. Pudding and Wolf looked at each other. Though cowed, they needed to save face.

'Let's go get him,' said Wolf, 'and fuck him up.'

'Naw,' said Pudding, 'I'm not going to dirty my hands on a piece of shit like that. We'll get him next time.'

'Ja,' said Wolf, 'and next time we're getting you too, Jew-boy.'

'Sure,' I said. 'You and which kaffir army?' which was the standard reply, then, to such a threat. When I left they were stomping on Bennie's sandwich.

Fortunately for Bennie, the annual interschool athletics meeting took place soon after this, in fact on the very next Saturday. We were up against our traditional rivals, Barrydale High – not exactly an Olympic contest, but a big enough event on the calendar of Ghanta High to allow at least a spurious sort of enthusiasm to flare for a week or so.

It transpired that the newcomer, Bennie Nienaber, could run faster than anybody else in either school. How he did this wasn't quite clear: his short, somewhat bandy legs were hardly a match for the straight-limbed stride of the older boys. But match them he did, and ended up winning all the sprint events he took part in, becoming an instant hero, even being singled out for praise at Monday's assembly by Mr Brink, the school principal. After this the group's invisible aegis was extended over him, and further victimisation was unthinkable. He was nicknamed Rabbit Nienaber, and left alone.

Bennie took his success as laconically as he'd handled his brief trial period. He never alluded to my intervention, such as it was, in the sandwich episode, but he did on occasion initiate a conversation with me – guardedly, clearly apprehensive for fear of rejection; but as I was quite flattered by the overtures of the new star athlete, I responded more warmly than I might have had he been merely an undistinguished newcomer.

How do school friendships happen? Often they are alliances, strategic groupings against a common enemy; and sometimes they are the outcome of a common need, two lonelinesses merging into a more robust social unit, two losers looking for strength in numbers. In the case of Bennie and me, there may have been an element of this neediness, but there was also, though I could not have explicated it at the time, something else: a recognition by each of a quality in the other that he lacked. As I became more aware of Bennie physically, I found a fascination in his animal vitality, furtive and sinuous, like that of a mongoose or a stoat, a likeness reinforced by his thick hair, densely packed on his head like fur, and by his pointed nose and round, shiny dark eyes. His face was too irregular to be good-looking: his front teeth were somehow misaligned, which gave his smile a lopsidedness that in time I came to find irresistible. He was small, wiry and lithe, whereas I was tall, gangling and clumsy.

I saw in Bennie's quickness, his darting quality not only of body but of mind, a directness of response that I, with my more ruminative habits, could not emulate. Bennie acted instinctively; I acted reflectively. By the same token, I think, he found my lack of hurry calming, though no doubt frustrating at times. I admired his tough street cred – his family had lived in a poor area of Johannesburg before coming to Alfredville – his self-sufficiency, his devil-may-care attitude to most things. I think he was attracted to the stability and tranquillity of my home and my family, even while he resented it. As one of four boys, he thought our one-child family an aberration, though quite an enviable one.

'What's it like to have first go at everything?' he asked.

'Like what?'

'Like getting food first and like using the bathroom first and like having new clothes instead of somebody else's hand-me-downs.'

'I don't know. I've never really thought about it.'

'Does you father never beat you?' he asked me in wonder once, after I'd unthinkingly spoken of somebody, the father of one of our classmates, as 'the kind of guy who beats his children'.

'No,' I said, 'he doesn't believe in it.'

'Not even when you've been naughty?' he asked. I could sense that it would make him feel better if I said yes, that my father did after all *sometimes* beat me, but I couldn't bring myself to say it, whether from an ignoble desire to reinforce his sense of my superior privileges, or from an admirable refusal to sacrifice my gentle father for the sake of Bennie's feelings. For whatever reason, I said, 'No, *never* means never.'

'Jeez,' he said, 'no wonder you're such a fucking mess.'

I often brought Bennie home with me to lunch. It was tacitly accepted between us that my mother's lunches were better than his mother's. I never did put this to the test, because in all the years of our friendship he never invited me home for a meal, but from what I saw of the house at other times I gathered that the Nienabers, with their four children, Mr Nienaber's railway job and Mrs Nienaber's dressmaking, were poor: in the white community in those days being *poor* was an absolute category, like being *retarded* or *crippled*. I knew also that on Friday evenings Bennie was reluctant to go home and yet scared to be late, from which I deduced that on those evenings Mr Nienaber asserted his paternal authority, presumably after stopping in at the Queen's Hotel. This latter deduction I made from Bennie's reluctance to pass by the Queen's late on Friday afternoons. I sometimes saw him, at lunch time, looking at my father in a kind of wondering wistfulness, evidently puzzled by his absent-minded kindliness.

Bennie was also mystified by the fact that my father listened to music. 'Hey, that's *weird*, man,' he'd whisper to me when he visited in the evenings while my father was sitting in his chair, a glass of wine next to him, his eyes closed, listening, almost invariably, to the Bach cello suites, as he unwound at the end of a day. 'Does he just sit there?' he'd ask. 'Why doesn't he *do* something?'

'So watching some moronic TV show is doing something, but listening to sublime music isn't?' I'd challenge him.

'Oh *sublime* my arse,' he'd mock. 'What the fuck's that?'

But in time he seemed to settle into if not appreciation then at least toleration of my father's eccentricity, and at times I even caught him whistling, not very accurately, snatches from the cello suites under his breath.

It is on the strength of a single incident that I suspect he resented the security of my home. One Saturday afternoon he had to collect his sports kit from home, and I went with him. As we opened the front door we heard a loud altercation in the kitchen, then a dull thump and a moan of pain. Bennie and I paused just inside the front door, frozen. Then he took me by the arm, opened the front door again and pushed me out, following me and shutting the door behind us.

'But ...' I said, 'what was ... shouldn't we *do* something?'

'So what do you want to do? Go and stop them?'

'Yes, couldn't we ... you know ...?'

We were out in the street by now, and he stopped and turned on me. 'You know *what*?' he almost shouted at me. 'You know *nothing* in that bloody palace of yours with your mother and

55

father all over you and all lovey-dovey with each other. *Nothing*, I tell you, *nothing.*'

I stood staring at him, flabbergasted at this unprovoked attack. He started walking again, furiously, and I trotted to catch up with him. 'But Bennie ...' I began. I could see that he was close to tears.

'You don't know what it is to try to stop your own father from donnering your mother and donnering your little brothers and donnering you, and to stop your own mother from drinking herself paralytic because that way it hurts less. You don't know what it is not to have food to eat because your parents have drunk up the household money. You think the whole world is so fucking nice because your little family is so fucking nice.' He stopped, caught his breath, wiped his nose on his sleeve, and carried on. 'And then to be donnered because I spend time with you and to be told I think I'm too good for my family because the Jew chemist is feeding me and his moffie son wants to get into my pants ...'

'Is *that* what they think?'

'It's what they say, I don't know what the fuck they think, I think they've stopped thinking, they just ... *bounce* from one idea to the next.'

'So why are you still hanging around with me?'

He looked at me then, and I could see his anger had been displaced from me to his parents. 'Do you think,' he asked, 'do you really think I'm going to let them fuck up the one thing I've achieved for myself?'

I was too overawed by the new perspective opening up before me – seeing my family as an *achievement* – to reply to this, but some instinct, for which I have since been grateful, made me put my hand on Bennie's shoulder and squeeze it, hard enough so that it could be taken for aggression if he chose to. To my surprise he put his hand on mine, briefly but decisively.

At about this time the Nienaber family finances received an injection from somewhere – Bennie didn't tell me from where, and I knew better than to pry – and his father, in an access of conspicuous generosity, bought Bennie the Mosquito Garelli buzz-bike he'd been coveting, without much hope, for years. It was noisy for its 50 ccs, but also robust and, by the standards of that kind of thing, fast. Best of all, as far as I was concerned, was its long seat that could carry two, and the footrests for the passenger on the back wheel.

But my joy was cut short when my father, with his obsessive solicitude for my safety, refused me permission to ride with Bennie.

'I want you to promise me you won't go on that thing with your friend,' he said when Bennie, flushed with pride, first drew up outside our gate.

I looked at my father in disbelief. 'But, Dad ... it's a *Mosquito Garelli.*'

'I don't care if it's a ... Lamborghini, I don't want you falling off and killing yourself. So I want you to promise. Will you promise?'

'I'll promise you I won't fall off and kill myself,' I offered.

'Yes, yes, easy to promise that, but that's not something you have any control over. The only way you won't fall off is if you don't get on.'

I looked at Bennie, who was mutely witnessing this scene, and rolled my eyes. To my father I said, 'What if Bennie promises to drive safely?'

'Don't get me wrong,' my father said, now addressing himself to Bennie as well, 'it's not that I don't trust Bennie's driving. But there are crazy people out there, and on that little bike you don't have a chance against their big cars and lorries. I don't want you killed or maimed for life. Those things have no protection.'

'Nor does a bicycle,' I pointed out. 'And you don't have a problem with that.'

'A bicycle doesn't go at sixty kilometres an hour,' he said. 'And you don't sit on the back with somebody else driving.'

And there, for a while, it seemed we would stick, and the Mosquito, which I'd envisaged as cementing – as well as mobilising – my friendship with Bennie, seemed destined instead to separate us. There were, I knew, any number of other contenders for the privilege of travelling on the Mosquito, boys whose fathers were less solicitous than mine, and Bennie could not be expected to spend his spare time in pedestrian pursuits with me when he could be making a joyful noise around Alfredville on the Mosquito. He even once or twice took Wikus Scheepers, one of his more obsequious admirers, to the dam, leaving me fretting and furious at home.

In the end, I think it was my manifest misery that persuaded my father that the danger of being killed or maimed was the lesser of two evils, and, after a lengthy interview with Bennie, in which all kinds of conditions were laid down and accepted, I was granted permission to assume what I regarded as my rightful place on the back of the Mosquito.

Sitting behind Bennie, I enjoyed the closeness of the physical contact, without pondering the significance of my enjoyment. There were plenty of jokes around about 'bunnies', but it was, I suppose, part of the function of such jokes to make one feel indemnified. Indeed, I instinctively shied away from giving a name to my feelings for Bennie; even *friendship* seemed too solemn a term to be used unironically. I just thought that I liked his company and enjoyed his closeness; and in spite of his parents' slur upon my motives, Bennie himself seemed not to harbour any untoward suspicions. He was entirely comfortable with being naked in front of me, and when we went swimming late at night in the school swimming pool, laughed at me when I wanted to bring my bathing costume.

'Who's going to see you?' he'd say. 'Do you think Emmerentia's going to sneak out of the hostel to come and perv your dick?'

It was agreed between us at the time that I had the hots for Emmerentia Meiring, a demure, sweet-faced farm girl, who would have been horrified at the lurid fantasies Bennie and I concocted about her – Bennie because he was given to lurid fantasies, me because I enjoyed fantasising with Bennie.

'I just want to spare you the embarrassment if she does come,' I said. 'I mean, what with you being undersized and all.'

Bennie was probably proportionately quite as well endowed as I, but I was taller, and in those days it was inches that counted, not proportions.

'Embarrassed, no fucking way,' he said. 'I punch above my weight.'

So we clambered over the wall of the school swimming pool and took off our clothes and drifted in the water, careful not to splash and attract the attention of the hostel staff. Floating in the darkness, or in the light of half a moon or a full moon in the still heat of a Karoo summer night heavy with the scent of syringa, Bennie's body flashing luminously next to me, I thought I couldn't ask for more from life.

Once, while we were fantasising about our supposed conquests – Bennie about Dorothy Nel, a sturdy netball player in the class below ours, and me about Emmerentia – we both got erections.

He giggled. 'Do you think anybody's ever shot a wad in the school swimming pool?'

'I shouldn't think so,' I said. 'Except if Mr Wagner comes here to pull his wire.'

Mr Wagner, our Physical Education teacher, was famous for the size of his equipment, which he didn't mind displaying in the change rooms, and schoolboy lore had it that size was a result of regular exercise.

'I can see you want to do it, you pig,' he said, pointing at my erection.

'And you,' I said.

'Action stations,' he said. 'First one there gets the cream doughnut.'

It was a chaste business, each attending to his own needs according to his own abilities, but it was curiously intense. We came within seconds of each other, and pretended to be disgusted at the strings of semen floating around us.

'You've come like a horse,' he said, pointing at the stringy blobs around me. 'You'll have all the standard six girls pregnant after their swim tomorrow.'

This thought so convulsed us that we started choking and had to get out of the water. I levered myself out of the pool and hopped on one leg to get the water out of my ear. 'Here,' he said, 'give us a hand.'

I reached out, grabbed his wrist, and pulled him out. He held back for a moment, then seemed to bounce out of the water, landing half on top of me. We balanced precariously face to face, then he put his arm around me and briefly leant back to break his momentum. He swung upright again, and we stood like that, clenched together, for a long moment, in a sudden tense silence.

Then Bennie laughed, 'Shit, we almost ended up on our arses there,' and let go. In silence we put on our clothes.

Bennie was known to be a smoker, which in those days in that place was the extreme of juvenile delinquency. I had been sufficiently brainwashed by my parents to be immune to his example, but I happily went along on the Mosquito to Kanonkop – named for the cannon mounted there during the Boer War – on his smoking excursions. I liked the intimacy of the clandestine situation, the restfulness of just sitting – it was of the essence of Bennie's kind of smoking that one gave it one's undivided attention: it was never for him something one did while doing something else. So we sat staring at the horizon – we faced away from the village, on the theory that otherwise someone might spot us through binoculars – talking about whatever presented itself. He used to chew peppermints afterwards, then blow in my face: 'Can you smell I've been smoking?' As his guinea pig, his canary in the coal mine, I felt pleasantly indispensable, and loved the smell of his smoky-minty breath.

As we moved into our senior years, it was generally accepted that I was 'clever' (another absolute category of my youth). I was given to understand by Mr Brink that Ghanta High expected great things from me, that is, several distinctions in matric. 'And if you are going to do your best for the school, you will have to be careful, very careful, in choosing your associates,' he said to me one afternoon at the beginning of our Standard Nine year, having summoned me to his office.

'Yes, Mr Brink,' I said.

'I take it you know what I mean,' he said, peering at me meaningfully over his specs.

'Yes, Mr Brink,' I said. I knew he meant Bennie.

'And you will be careful, will you?'

'Yes, Mr Brink,' I said.

Evidently I wasn't careful enough, because a month after this Mr Brink and the vice-principal, Mr Muller, paid my mother a visit to warn her against the influence of Bennie Nienaber on her son.

'I told him,' she told me afterwards, 'that I was capable of deciding who was and who was not a suitable friend for my son. I also told him that I didn't care if Bennie smoked, he was a pleasure to have around and I think it's been good for you having him as a friend. I'm not asking you whether he smokes or not, because I know you're too sensible to be misled by a bad example.'

After this it became a matter of honour for me not to smoke – as, I realised later, my mother might well have counted on. I didn't tell Bennie about the visit, but I think he guessed, and our joint determination to prove Mr Brink wrong meant that we both studied much harder for the matric exam than we would otherwise have done. I got a respectable number of distinctions and Bennie got a First Class pass, which was more than anybody had expected for him.

I stop to catch my breath and gaze at the deserted school. It has changed little over the years. The rock garden, never very abundant, seems to be straggling on, its succulents enduring their chronically water-deprived state. The tennis courts have a few more cracks than I remember, and the rugby fields are showing the effects of a hot summer; but if the South African educational system has collapsed, as ex-South Africans in London have assured me it has, this hasn't yet manifested physically in Alfredville. No broken windows, no missing doors; just the vacancy of any school anywhere destitute of pupils. On the gable of the building the school crest, newly done up, still proclaims the school's symbolic representation of its identity – an arrangement of aloes, an open book, and hands extended over a scroll, enjoining the eager young to *Gryp Jou Geleentheid*, a somewhat inelegant rendering of *Carpe Diem*, which we used to translate as Grab What You Can, often while grabbing at each other's persons in crude hilarity.

I spit on the ground and run on. Just beyond the school the tarred road turns into a dirt track leading to farmland. The landscape is starting to shimmer in the heat, the sheep clustering under the few trees for shade. It's a stony landscape, making few concessions to conventional ideas of beauty: some hills, shading off into distant mountains, a riverbed almost dry at this time of year; the great blue bowl of sky already blanching under the rising sun. I was too unaware, when I lived here, to form any conscious or coherent response to this landscape: it was simply the place where we lived and played, and we didn't ask ourselves, and certainly not one another, whether it was beautiful or ugly. Now, running through the empty morning, I feel a certain appeal in the very emptiness, something melancholy in its meagreness and yet comforting in its permanence. It's a landscape without clutter, without noise, without much ambition, neutral, perhaps even negative. It's not a landscape that conforms readily to a formula: it refuses to be reduced to a cliché or even a meaning. What must it be like to live here? An eternity of tedium or a tranquil refuge from a more purpose-obsessed world? Could I return to its stony comfort?

I grin inwardly at my dramatisation of the landscape, really just my self-dramatisation projecting itself upon insentient soil and sky. Having returned after twenty-two years of self-imposed exile, I'm trying for an emotion; the truth may be that I don't feel anything in particular other than the heat and dust. James would say it's the ex-pat syndrome; he's sat through enough evenings of maudlin ex-South Africans sentimentalising over a country that they have no intention of returning to except for the annual family get-together at somebody's beach house. 'So you've left – so deal with it,' was his take on ex-pat nostalgia. 'We live in the age of emigration.' He himself seemed to feel nothing for his native Jamaica, though that may be because he left it when he was twelve, and claims to have had a witch for a grandmother.

I stop running and stretch. I haven't run as far as I'd intended, but I convince myself, without too much back-chat from my conscience, that this is probably far enough for a first day. As I turn around, I see a police van some distance behind me. It's possible that it's been following me, but I shake off the suspicion as vestigial paranoia. As I watch, it does a U-turn and speeds back towards the village, leaving me choking in a cloud of dust.

CHAPTER 5

Wednesday morning
I run back to the hotel, have a shower and go down to breakfast.
I half hope that Nonyameko will be there, but there's no sign of
her: I suppose her rigorous duties don't allow for leisurely break-
fasts.

After breakfast I try to create an opportunity to speak to Joachim without seeming to make a point of it; I'm counting on his
natural garrulousness to render questions redundant once I've
engaged him in conversation. This turns out to be tricky. The
Queen's Hotel is a busy place in the mornings, generating a surprising amount of activity for such a sparsely-frequented establishment: the bar being restocked, orders being placed for food,
linen being changed, all of which apparently requires Joachim's
presence, or the joint presence of Joachim and Boris, the latter a
sulkily ineffectual quasi-supporting act to Joachim's histrionic
performance.

'No, not there, *here*, I said *here*, Jesus Christ you're going to
scratch that counter if you put that box on top, no not on the chair
either, oh my *God*, you're going to drop it, Boris help him for
fuck's sake, yes, yes, over there, just put it *down* and fuck *off*. Yes,
yes, give me the invoice, what do you mean you want the money
now, I always pay at the end of the month, it works out the same,
no it's not the end of the month yet, there's more than a fucking
week to go, what's happened to the regular driver, yes, I *know* it
says terms strictly cash but I've got an arrangement with your
manager, yes, with Mr Kleinbooi, I pay once a month, I can't pay
piddling little amounts every time you deliver a fucking can of
Coke, okay, *okay*, I'll phone Mr Kleinbooi myself, you won't get
into trouble, oh for Christ's sake, what do you mean *now*, can't

64

you see how busy I am? Oh okay, *okay*, Boris, you take over here while I phone Mr Kleinbooi to make this gentleman's day, get the tablecloths from the restaurant the laundry will be collecting in five minutes and you know how pissed off they get if they have to wait two minutes, and don't forget it's Wednesday, we've got the fucking Rotarians today ...'

It seems futile to hope for Joachim's attention in the midst of the various crises he's not so much dealing with as creating. So I go to my room, brush my teeth, sit down in the lone armchair and take up *My Traitor's Heart*, but only get as far as the sub-title – *A South African Exile Returns to Face His Country, His Tribe and His Conscience*. I am put off by the self-consciousness of it all. *My Traitor's Heart, Country of My Skull* – why this solipsistic appropriation? Can't I write the country's story without first making it mine?

I put down the book and go downstairs again. Here things have settled somewhat. Boris is nowhere to be seen, and Joachim is at the reception desk, tidying the pamphlets and leaflets displayed for the use of the guests. The pamphlets give me a pretext to go up to the counter. I select one offering *To Hell and Back: Mountain Biking in the Ghanta.*

'You a mountain biker?' Joachim asks.

'I've done a bit,' I lie. 'But this looks rather strenuous for me.'

'You look fit enough,' he says sourly, my fitness evidently a slight to his self-esteem, 'though I must tell you' – he brightens, finding consolation in the caveat – 'it's not a trip for just anyone, up and down every bloody hill and mountain in the Klein Karoo, ending up in Die Hel – you know the Hell?'

'I remember hearing about it. I've never been there. I didn't know there was a road to it.'

'There wasn't, way back. There's one now so all the inhabitants have fucked off and it's more of a tourist destination, but mind you, if I say there's a road you'll get the wrong idea, it's really just a track full of rocks that carries on for ever until you think you're never going to get there, in any case not something you want to do in January, it really is like hell down there now.'

'I think I'll give it a miss, then,' I say, replacing the pamphlet.

He looks at me quizzically. 'But what are you doing here, really?'

'Just looking up the old spots,' I say as nonchalantly as possible. 'And I still have family here, of course.'

'Do you? Jacobs family?' He means Jewish family, but probably thinks it would be rude to ask.

'No, my mother's family.' I pause for a moment, hoping this will pique his curiosity. 'Dolly van Blerk is her sister,' I say.

He opens his eyes very wide. 'So Dolly van Blerk is your aunt … and Desirée …'

'Was my cousin, yes.'

'Phew,' he whistles, 'no jokes hey, that's a shit shot. I mean I'm sorry of course but bugger it, it must have been a helluva shock …'

'I had rather lost touch with Desirée, actually. But yes, it is a shocking story.'

He shakes his head sombrely. 'Terrible, terrible. She was such a beautiful woman. Of course, there are people who say … Well,' he collects himself, 'there'll always be people who talk and here in Alfredville people talk more than anywhere else because there's bugger-all else to do.'

'What is it that they say, these people?' I ask.

'You don't want to take any notice of it,' he says, but can't resist the opportunity to be indiscreet. He tidies the pile of pamphlets. 'But yes, there was a lot of talk when she married Hector Williams, as you can imagine, people weren't used to that kind of thing, a white woman marrying a black man, or a Coloured man, it's supposed to be all the same thing nowadays, there were people who wanted to run him out of town, only how do you run the town's chief cop out of town?'

'Is there still a lot of prejudice against that kind of thing here?' I ask. 'I'd have imagined that by now …'

He snorts, getting moisture on his moustache. He wipes it with a thumb and index finger. 'I can see you haven't been home for a while, boetie,' he says, 'if you think *that kind of thing* goes down any better with most people than it used to, maybe in the big cities, but here, no chance, they're still as verkramp as ever. Do you know the shit I've picked up because Boris lives in the hotel, in a proper bedroom rather than in servants' quarters behind the hotel? Hey, tell me, can you see Boris in servants' quarters?'

'No, I really can't,' I say, truthfully enough.

'Exactly, but I have people coming in here, especially the ones coming to the bar, first they complain that Boris isn't wearing a uniform when he serves at the bar, they say he doesn't look neat, but it's not that he doesn't look neat, it's that he doesn't look like a servant. Do they complain if *I* serve at the bar without a uniform?' He asks this as if he really expects an answer, so I oblige and say, 'I suppose not.'

'Bloody right not, because I'm white that's okay, but just because Boris is black, and I won't even tell you the stories they tell about him, but I wipe my arse on them, I know I've got the best pub in town, if they'd rather go and drink in that so-called Wine Bar those two letties from Cape Town've opened on the main road they're welcome and I can tell them those two aren't going to put up with their shit, they're a match for any man any day, they threw Tol Prinsloo out on his ear for using bad language in their place, and I mean *physically* threw him so he hit the tar and he's still got the scars to show for it except he's ashamed to. So as I say I'm not hard-up for their custom, as I've told you, I scheme this is the New South Africa, they must fit in or fuck off.'

This seems to offer me an opportunity to get the conversation back on track. 'But it doesn't sound as if the rest of the town is fitting in – I mean, you were saying, the comments when Desirée married Hector Williams ...'

'The comments?' He throws up his pudgy hands in a little ecstasy of outrage. 'It was more than comments, I can tell you, it was a pack of lies what they said about the two of them, especially Desirée, about how you know – I mean why she went for a black man, especially because Cassie Carstens was also after her with the biggest farm in the district and gold taps in his bathroom and Cassie – well I won't go into detail, but he's a big boy in every

67

way and then for Desirée to prefer a *black policeman* didn't make sense for lots of people, and an ex-ANC terrorist just to rub it in and they said she'd picked up all sorts of ideas from studying English at Stellenbosch which everyone knows is a nest of liberalism, anyway, you get the idea, the kind of total crap people talk in a place like this, so everybody said, when this happened, how they weren't at all surprised.'

'But why is everyone assuming that Williams is guilty?'

He looks at me quizzically. 'Yeah, well, for the same reason everyone assumes the cat's eaten the cream when you find it in the kitchen with an empty saucer. It's possible that a ... bloody *camel* slipped in and ate the cream, but just not all that probable, if you know what I mean? Or have you got a different theory?'

'No, er no, I don't really have any theory, I've only just arrived.'

'Well, it seems open and shut, if you ask me. Williams was supposed to be on duty on the evening of the murder, but phoned in to say he'd been called out about a cattle theft on a farm, except nobody can find a record of a cattle theft being reported that night. He comes back on duty looking upset according to the constable on duty and then Desirée is found dead, the doctor says killed in the last half hour.'

'Isn't it possible that somebody phoned him on purpose to get him away from town so as to incriminate him?'

'Sure it is, anything's possible, except the police station's exchange hasn't got any record of a call coming then. And then, the police found blood on Williams's shoe, the police issue one he was wearing on the night of the murder, that matched a stain on the floor. And his fingerprints were on a glass that Desirée drank from. I don't know what more you want.'

All this I know from my own reading on the case, but I'm interested in the town's response to the murder. And if Joachim is anything to go by, the case was followed with interest by the inhabitants of Alfredville.

'So most people think Williams did it?'

'Bloody sure. Except of course the brown and black people. They can't think outside the race box, you know? Boris says there's a story going round the township that it's all a pack of lies to get rid of Hector Williams.'

'Even the murder?'

'Ja. Even the murder.' He looks around the lobby to make sure we're not being overheard, then says in a low voice, 'I tell you, these people are paranoid.'

I decide to test Joachim's certainties. 'But is it completely impossible that someone … ' I begin. 'I mean, if people really feel as strongly as you say about Williams being police chief and Desirée marrying him – this way they'd be getting rid of both of them.'

He laughs derisively. 'Shit, man, five minutes ago you thought Alfredville was okay with mixed marriages, now you think somebody murdered your cousin because she married a black man. Try for an in-between position, man. It's called moderation.'

'As far as I can make out,' I retort, trying not to show that his manner has riled me, '*moderation* dictates that I believe Hector Williams killed his own wife, of whom by all reports he was very fond, for no apparent reason.'

'Who says for no apparent reason? Which reports?' he demands truculently.

'Well,' I flounder, not wanting to let on that I've been reading up on the matter, 'I haven't seen any reason suggested.'

But he spots the hole in my case. 'You wouldn't, in London, would you?' he asks. 'You say yourself you've just arrived, and already you know more than the rest of us?'

My first instinct is to yield to irritation at his tone and to retort in kind, but I remind myself of the journalist's adage that an arse-hole with information is by that token a deep throat, so instead of telling him to stuff off, I ask, trying not to sound too avid, 'So what reason is being suggested in Alfredville?'

'Well,' he says with an affected coyness that doesn't go well with his physical type, 'I don't want to speak out of turn, you know, Desirée's mos your cousin.'

Again I have to resist an impulse to poke my finger in his eye. I say merely, 'As I've said, I'd lost touch with her, in fact.'

My betrayal of Desirée liberates Joachim's worst instincts. He rocks slightly on his heels as he launches into his account. 'It depends on who you talk to,' he says, 'or should I say who you listen to, because I can tell you, standing behind the bar when it gets late and the tongues are well oiled I get to hear some things …' He rolls his eyes at me portentously.

'Such as?' I ask.

He smiles unpleasantly. 'Such as?' he repeats. 'Well, such as that Williams was driven bonkers by jealousy … with good reason, too.'

'Do you mean she was seeing somebody else?'

'*Seeing* – if you want to call it that, but you could also call it something else. The thing is, she was always sociable, liked parties, that kind of thing, with Williams not much of a mixer except for the tennis club, where he first met Desirée, so they say. So she sometimes went to parties, dinners, that kind of shit, on her own when he was on duty and sometimes even when he wasn't, and there are always buggers who'll try their luck with any woman who hasn't got a man with her.'

'But Williams should have known that, surely.'

'Maybe he knew it, but in a general sort of way. I mean, if your wife spends the night talking shit to twenty different guys, that's not really a big deal is it, it's when she spends all night talking to one oke, that's when you know she's got an itch.'

'And Desirée?'

'Let's just say that she started talking more to one oke than to the others, and the others noticed.'

'And who was this one oke?'

'Not somebody you'd know. He hasn't been in town for very long, only arrived a few years ago. Henk Pretorius. He's the vet, took over from Albie Wessels, maybe you remember him?'

I nod. 'Yes, his surgery was in the main street, on the way to the dam. I remember taking our dog there.'

'That's it. Same place, new guy. He's okay, the farmers like him, he's good with horses, and the women take their dogs and cats to him much more than they ever did to Albie Wessels, which is nice for the cats and dogs and also for Henk Pretorius, I'm sure.'

'So he's a bit of a ladies' man?'

'The ladies like him, if that's what you mean, but what they see in him I don't know, quite an ordinary-looking bugger, I think.' Joachim steals a glance in the mirror on the wall beside him to reassure himself that he's not ordinary looking. 'Very quiet, hasn't got much to say for himself, a bit up his own arse if you ask me. Goes for long walks on his own in the veld with his dog, out towards the dam, does bird-watching, they say. He goes off every evening straight after work, like clockwork. So when he started hanging around Desirée at parties and things, the women were the first to start jabbering, especially the ones who'd spent a fortune on fancy cat food just so they could pass the time of day with Dr Pretorius. But the men also started talking, some of them just repeating what their wives were saying, but others, the ones who'd been hoping to shall we say make a personal impression on Desirée, were pissed off, so you can imagine they made the most of the story. Cassie Carstens became a bit of an expert on the movements of Henk Pretorius –'

'This is the Cassie Carstens with the golden taps?'

'Ja, the same, and I'm not saying he's the most reliable of witnesses, but he had plenty of stories to tell Saturday evenings in the pub here, still has in fact, though people are getting a bit *gatvol* of his stories now that Desirée's gone.'

'Does he come here every Saturday?'

'Just about. Not much to do for an unmarried oke on a Saturday evening in Alfredville, so they get together here and drink too much and talk shit. I don't care, it pays the rent and aside from getting a bit loud and having to be told when to piss off home, they don't break the place down or anything. But the point I'm making,' he says, placing a plump finger on the counter, 'the point I'm making is that all this talk in the end got to Hector Williams …'

'How?' I interject.

'How what?'

'How did the talk get to Hector Williams?'

'Hell, I don't know, and anyway who knows?' he asks, then

71

modulates into the more informative mode. 'Mind you, if you're asking me, I think Cassie Carstens *may* have whispered something in Hector's ear, friendly-like.'

'Surely Hector would know better than to listen to a man whispering in his ear if that man was his rival for his wife's affections?'

'Ja, you'd think so. But who's to say Hector knew Cassie was his rival for his wife's affections? Anyway, once a guy's jealous he doesn't stop to ask himself who's spinning him the story, he just goes off the plank. And Cassie Carstens has a kind of farm-charm about him, gets on well with most people ... but I'm not saying that he *did* say anything to Hector, just that some people are saying he did, and that that was why Hector killed Desirée. Pure jealousy.'

'Is jealousy ever pure?' I ask. I realise when I've asked it that I'm not sure what I mean by my question, and that Joachim is even less likely to know.

He surprises me, however, by nodding solemnly. 'You can ask *that* again,' he says. 'All sorts of things mixed up in it. But jealousy's what it's called for short.'

We stand facing each other in silence for a moment, pondering this profundity. Then he shrugs. 'It's a shit sandwich, whichever way you butter it. The only one who made something by it, far as I can tell, is Bennie Nienaber.'

The name is so unexpected that for a moment I think I must have misheard. 'Bennie *Nienaber?*' I ask.

'Yes,' he says, 'you remember him, don't you? Yes of course you do – you were always together, I remember.' There is something wistful in his tone, affording me a sudden glimpse of the loneliness of the young Fairy Ferreira, excluded from the vivid companionships of boyhood.

'Yes, we were,' I say mechanically, still trying to figure out why Bennie's name should leap from the past into the here and now. 'But we lost touch,' I continue, with an effort. 'I didn't know he was still here.'

Joachim is looking at me curiously, as if he has picked up my perturbation. 'You really wiped your arse on Alfredville, didn't you?' he asks. 'Anyway, no, not *still* here – here again. Went away after school for quite a while, then turned up again just like that, as a policeman.'

'Bennie a policeman?'

'Sure, quite high up, or as high up as he's likely to get as a white man in the force, and higher than he would have got if Hector Williams hadn't stuffed up.'

'So he's ...?'

'He's Captain Nienaber now, acting station commander while the Williams case is pending, as they say. I suppose once Williams has been found guilty they'll post some other black guy here over Bennie Nienaber's head.'

I stand there stupidly, trying to work Bennie into a scheme of things that I thought I'd worked out pretty well before I arrived. Fortunately Joachim's attention is now claimed by Boris for some complication involving, apparently, a disagreement between the chef and the housekeeper. I thank Joachim and walk out into the morning.

As I step into the street, I'm not entirely surprised when Vincent appears at my elbow.

'Bonjour, monsieur,' he says, though less ebulliently than usual.

'Morning, Vincent,' I say.

A black Mercedes comes down the street. There is little traffic at this hour, in spite of which the blue light incongruously mounted on the roof of the Merc is flashing, and the siren burps every fifty metres or so. As this sound-and-light show passes us, Vincent takes off his hat in mock obeisance in the direction of the tinted windows.

'And who's that?' I ask.

'That is a very important person,' Vincent tells me solemnly. 'His name is Goodwill Mzweni.'

'What makes him so important?'

'He is the mayor of Alfredville. Alfredville is his ... how do you say? *Royaume.*'

'Kingdom.'

'*C'est ça.* Kingdom. And for us *étrangers* ... strangers ... how you say, foreigners, it is important to be on the good side of the important people. We can easily be deported. Or chased away. It is the same thing.'

'Why should they chase you away, Vincent?'

'Because they say I take their jobs away, and their houses.'

What job? What house? I'm inclined to ask, but refrain. Instead I ask, 'Where exactly are you from, Vincent?'

'I am from Brazzaville in the DRC, monsieur.'

'And what did you do in Brazzaville, Vincent, before you came here?'

'I was an *avocat*,' he says. I look at him in perplexity. My rudimentary French tells me that he was either an advocate or an avocado, and whereas the latter seems impossible, the former seems hardly more probable. But Vincent is clearly used to this kind of reaction. 'An *avocat* in the court,' he says factually, patiently; an advocate then, but he doesn't offer to explain how an advocate in court came to be a car guard in Alfredville. Another African story, incomprehensible and unthinkable.

'I see,' I say lamely, and give Vincent a five rand coin. He accepts it without laughing in my face, and I proceed on my mission, which has recently redefined itself. I'm going to find Bennie.

The police station is where it's always been, in Victoria Street. The small whitewashed building with the steep steps leading up to the charge office still has a blue lamp mounted outside the front door – front doors, really, because in the old days there were two, one for 'Europeans' and one for 'Non-Europeans'. The only other change is a facebrick extension with small barred windows, testifying to the expanding needs of law and order in Alfredville.

The charge office is surprisingly spacious. A break in the pattern of the wooden flooring marks the traces of the old partition between the two sections. There is little activity here. A junior policewoman, Constable Hendrickse a tag on her chest informs the world, is talking on the telephone, and two policemen are looking at a report in this morning's *Burger*.

They glance up without curiosity when I come in. The younger of the two men, Constable Mkathini, comes over to the counter and looks at me enquiringly.

'Good morning,' I say. 'Would it be possible to see Captain Nienaber?'

'What is the nature of your business?' he asks in a flat official tone.

'It's … private, really. I'm an old friend of Captain Nienaber's.'

He pushes an official notepad towards me.

'Please furnish your name and address on that.'

I write *Peter Jacobs, Queen's Hotel (visitor)* and pass the pad back to Constable Mkathini. He scrutinises it as if I've written a message of some complexity, then pushes it back to me. 'Furnish your signature and the date.'

I supply the required information and watch while he slams a massive rubber stamp on the page, tears the sheet out of the pad, and bears it off weightily to some inner sanctum.

He is gone for so long that I wonder whether my identity is being checked on a police database. Constable Hendrickse terminates her call and immediately dials another number. 'Hello, Mavis? This is Chantal. You won't believe what Doreen's just told me …' But I am fated never to find out what Doreen told Chantal. Constable Mkathini appears from the inner reaches. In his deliberate way he marches to the counter and lifts a flap.

'You can go through now,' he says. 'The Captain has been alerted to your presence.'

'Thank you,' I say. 'Where do I go?'

'You proceed straight ahead,' he says. 'You will find his office self-evidently at the end of the corridor.'

The door of Bennie's office is open, and, approaching, I can see Bennie sitting at his desk, apparently absorbed in a file, his forehead supported on the heel of his left hand, a position I recall with a small shock of recognition: that is how he used to sit over his books when we studied together in my bedroom for the matric exams. He is bareheaded – his cap hanging from a hook on the wall – and his hair is as thick as ever.

75

He doesn't look up, though he must have heard my footsteps on the wooden floor. I knock softly. 'Bennie?' I say.

He looks up. He's changed, of course, his mouth more firmly set, the features stronger, but he's disconcertingly like the eighteen-year-old boy I last saw, which makes the uniform all the more incongruous.

'Peter,' he says – not an exclamation, not a question, just a simple statement of fact. Except he used to call me Jakes.

'Yes,' I say. 'I'm pleased you still recognise me.'

'Oh, I recognise you all right,' he says, with no inflection or affect.

I put out my hand; he looks at it for a moment as if considering his options, then gets to his feet and shakes it. Odd, I think, I've known him all these years and this is the first time we've shaken hands. Handshakes weren't part of our schoolboy code.

'I'm … pleased to find you here,' I say lamely. 'I didn't realise that you … you …'

'That I was still stuck in Alfredville?' he asks, without a smile.

'Well, that you'd returned.' I look around the office as if seeking in it a reason for his return.

'Yes,' Bennie says. 'I asked to be stationed here because my mother wasn't well.'

'Your father …?'

'Died. In 1995. Stroke.'

'Oh,' I say. 'I'm sorry.'

'You needn't be. Not for my sake, anyway. He treated me badly. But my mother missed him.' He's not giving anything away, not even an opportunity for sympathy.

'And she …?'

'She died two years later.' There is a pause. I feel a fool, not wanting to say 'I'm sorry' again, and yet not knowing what else to say.

'Your parents?' Bennie asks, the question devoid of interrogative energy.

'Still alive, both of them, in reasonably good health. They retired to Knysna.'

'Yes, I remember. I think they left just before I came back.'

There's a silence, broken only by the sound of a vacuum cleaner in some other office and a loud altercation in the charge office between Constable Hendrickse and Constable Mkathini. I hear the phrase 'languishing on the telephone'.

'So if your parents are in Knysna,' Bennie asks, 'what brings you here?'

'I don't know. I was just curious to see the old place.'

He nods. 'Yes. And …?'

'And?'

'How do you find the old place?'

'Oh, I don't know. The same and not the same, if you know what I mean.'

He nods again. 'And you? Still in England?'

'Yes. London.'

'Mm. Nice,' he says, without conviction.

'It's all right.' I'm not going to volunteer more information than he asks for, and he's clearly not going to ask for much.

'You're staying at the Queen's,' he says, a flat statement of fact.

'Yes. How did you know?'

'It was on that,' he says, pointing at the note I signed.

'Of course.'

'And I saw you coming out of it this morning.'

'Oh. When?' Then I remember. 'Oh, when I went running. Was that you in the police vehicle?'

'Yes.'

'You could have stopped and said hello.' I almost ask him if he was in the van that followed me out of town, but decide against it.

'You were running, and I was on duty. And I wasn't sure it was you. I wasn't expecting to see you.'

'Right. I see.' I try to infuse a more personal note into the conversation. 'And how are you, Bennie?' I ask.

'As you can see. I'm a captain of police.'

'And acting station commander, I'm told.'

'Yes. But that will change,' he says, matter-of-factly. 'They'll

post someone else here. You can't have a white station commander.'

'Is it that bad?'

'I'm not saying it's bad, I'm saying that's the way it is.'

His tone does not invite a rejoinder. We're both still standing in
the middle of his office. He does not seem to be on the point of
offering me a chair.

'You haven't been back?' he asks. 'I mean since you left.'

'Not to Alfredville, no. I did come back a couple of times to
visit my folks in Knysna, but I didn't manage to get here.'

'Yeah, so it's a long time. But I take it you heard about Desirée,'
he says.

'Oh, yes. My mother told me.'

'Of course.'

'Yes. She keeps me informed of what happens here. Not everything, though. I didn't know you were here, for instance.'

'Yes, so you've said.'

Another silence yawns.

'Well,' I say, 'you're a busy man. I mustn't keep you.'

'I'm not really that busy,' he says, but still does not offer me a
chair.

'I'll be around for a while,' I say. 'It would be nice to see you
again.'

He nods, hesitates. Then, 'You can come to supper,' he says.
'Meet my family.'

'Of course,' I say. 'You must be married by now.' I have somehow not imagined Bennie married, though if I'd thought about it
I'd have realised it was more than likely.

'Yes,' he says. 'Been married for ten years. To Chrisna Rabie.'

The name is faintly familiar, but I can't place it. 'Should I
remember her?'

'Not necessarily. She was four years behind us. Friend of
Desirée's, in fact. Her mother was the matron of the school hostel.'

'Of course,' I say. 'That is, I remember Mrs Rabie – the board-
ers called her Mrs Rabies.' Mrs Rabies was notorious for once, in

78

an onset of rage, stunning a misbehaving boarder with a loaf of wholewheat bread.

Bennie nods. 'Yes, and her temper hasn't improved with age. She lives with us. But Chrisna's okay.'

'I'm pleased for you,' I say. 'Children?'

'A boy and a girl, nine and seven. They're okay.'

He does not ask me about my life, my family, my circumstances. We stand in silence. Then, abruptly, he says, 'So do you want to come?'

'Do I ...?'

'Yes. I invited you to supper.'

'Oh. Of course. I'm sorry, I was thinking about your family. Yes, thank you, of course, I'd love to come to supper.'

'Tonight?'

'That would be ...' I begin, then recall Nonyameko. 'Actually, I've made another arrangement for tonight. But any other night would be great.'

'Tomorrow night, then?'

'Great.'

'About seven thirty? We eat a bit later on Thursdays, because I only come off duty at six.'

'I'll be there – but where exactly?'

'It's in Milner Street, if you remember where that is. Number 23.'

'I'll find it,' I say. I stand for a moment, irresolutely, then put out my hand. 'It's good to see you again, Bennie.'

'Yeah,' he says, shaking my hand without warmth.

CHAPTER 6

Wednesday morning

My promise to my mother recurs to me as I leave the police station. Ten o'clock: probably a good time for the visit. Anything much later will be taken amiss. Oom Blik and Aunt Dolly are of the generation or perhaps just temperament that is quick to take offence at what they take to be neglect on the part of family members, however little they have in common. Indeed, they seem to cherish family mainly as a potential source of affront. My mother told me often enough, in my youth, 'Aunt Dolly asked after you,' her tone never quite avoiding a tinge of gentle rebuke. So my visit should be prompt enough to suggest a proper degree of familial piety. But then, I also know that a proper degree of familial piety is a theoretical abstraction never to be attained in an imperfect world, at least not by the stringent standards of Blik and Dolly.

I ponder for a moment whether to call ahead to announce my visit. But then, I recall that such refinements are regarded as citified affectation in Alfredville: the assumption is that one is always ready to be visited, at a convenient hour of course, provided one is at home; and friends and family know each other's movements well enough not to turn up when one is not at home.

Ten o'clock has the further advantage, by my reckoning, that Oom Blik is unlikely to be home at that hour. Aunt Dolly was always easier to handle when not fortified by Blik's presence. On her own she was merely fretful; with his authority to back her she was prone to become querulous.

So it is that I present myself shortly after ten at the heavy teak door of the Van Blerk residence – one of the grander of the old homes in Alfredville, built in the nineteenth century by a local farmer, Isaak Retief, as a town house for his wife, Rachel, reputedly

80

for their mutual convenience, she hating the blood, guts and dung of farm life, he preferring the company of his 'boss boy', one Frederik Stoffels, who duly inherited the farm after Isaak's death, though Stoffels could never take transfer, owing to the passing of the Natives Land Act in 1913, the year of Isaak's death. The farm reverted to Rachel Retief. After her death – she lived to be a hundred and two, ascribing her longevity to 'a restful life' – Blik bought the house from her only son, Ephraim, who is on record as saying that Alfredville was a town of morons and bigots and who went off to San Francisco on the proceeds of the house and the farm, though he was himself almost eighty by this time. He was reported, with satisfaction, as having squandered his fortune in riotous living, and dying of an overdose of mescaline in the bed of his Mexican catamite. Nobody knew what became of Frederik Stoffels.

I am on the point of lifting the heavy brass knocker (a clenched fist holding a cudgel), when the door is opened by an elderly Coloured woman. A small white dog is standing slightly behind her, venturing the odd bark, more exploratory than challenging.

'Good morning,' I say. 'Is Mrs van Blerk at home?'

The woman looks at me, apparently not registering my question.

'Is ...?' I begin again, but she interrupts me.

'Master Peter!' she exclaims. 'Have you come back?'

For a moment I stare at her blankly, then I recollect that my mother told me that Angelina, our servant for as long as I could remember, had gone to work for the Van Blerks when my parents left.

'Angelina!' I say, giving her an awkward hug. 'And you're still here?'

'And where would I go?' she asks. 'Everything I have is right here.'

'You're a lucky woman, Angelina,' I say. 'Some of us are still looking.'

'Ney, I know, Master Peter. The Lord's been good to me – and the missis too,' she adds conscientiously.

'So you're well, Angelina?'

'As you see, Master Peter,' and she indicates her generous proportions.

'Angelina, I wish you wouldn't call me Master,' I say. 'Those days are over.'

'Ney, Master Peter,' she says. 'I don't know what's changed. I always worked six days a week and I still work six days a week and I always had too little money and I still have too little money. So if I call you Master or I call you Mister or I call you Peter, I don't see the difference.'

Angelina, I now recall, was always a great debater, sometimes to my mother's exasperation. Ostensibly the most servile of servants, she could, under cover of investigating the merits of a situation, effectively reverse the power relation, leaving my mother apologetic without quite knowing why.

'This is too complicated for me, Angelina,' I say. 'Is my aunt at home?'

'The missis is at home, yes,' she says. 'And the baas too.'

My heart sinks. 'Is it too early to visit them?' I ask, hoping that I'll be granted a reprieve; perhaps, I catch myself thinking, Oom Blik has some minor ailment that prohibits visiting. Aunt Dolly was always a great hypochondriac, on behalf of her whole family.

But Angelina is relentless in her hospitality. 'Ney *wat*, Master Peter,' she says, 'You're mos family. They're having coffee on the back stoep.'

And she turns round and leads the way at a brisk pace through the front room, the dog following, down the long, cool corridor of the old house, to a vine-shaded veranda at the back.

Oom Blik and Aunt Dolly are sitting at a little table, a pot of coffee and a bowl of rusks between them. Oom Blik is reading the newspaper – *Die Burger* – and Aunt Dolly is crocheting a shapeless object. Her house is full of crocheted creations of vague function and identity; my mother used to say Dolly crocheted on the wait-and-see principle.

They don't look up as Angelina marches me out onto the stoep: she has become an invisible ministrant to their needs. But when

82

she announces 'Master Peter!' in a voice to raise the dead, they look up, startled.

Aunt Dolly stares at me as if I were an apparition. In truth I, too, am taken aback at the ravages of time: Aunt Dolly's wispy blonde prettiness has trickled away into insipidity; the hair, though carefully styled, clearly owes such colour and elasticity as it has to chemical aids, and the baby-blue eyes have lost the sparkle that used to animate them. She looks wan and worn.

Oom Blik gets to his feet. 'My God, Peter,' he says, 'and where do you come from now?' Oom Blik, too, has aged, but with less of an effect of sagging, more a kind of desiccation; his tall, lean figure has if anything lost flesh, and his colour, never very good, owing to a liver condition, has a yellowish-grey tinge.

'No, from London, Oom Blik,' I say, extending my hand. He looks at it as if wondering what I'm offering him, then shakes it, a dry, cold, bony shake.

I go to Aunt Dolly, who is still staring at me, and bend to kiss her. She offers me her cheek in a half-hearted tilt of the head. Bending over her, I smell her cologne – something floral, and too strong for the early morning. She submits to my kiss without enthusiasm. Then the instincts of the hostess take over.

'Angelina, don't just stand there, fetch another cup for Master Pieter,' she says. She has always called me *Pieter*, I suspect as a rear-guard action against her sister's defection from the volk.

'Yes, missis,' Angelina says; behind Aunt Dolly's back she rolls her eyes at me, as if to say, 'You see.' She leaves, the dog trotting after her.

'Sit down, sit down,' says Oom Blik, resuming his own seat.

I look around me. The only available chair is occupied by a huge black cat with white paws. It opens one eye to look at me, but shows no intention of vacating the seat.

'Socks, you're impossible,' says Aunt Dolly in a voice of fond indulgence. 'Jeremiah, fetch Pieter another chair.' Aunt Dolly is the only person I know who calls Oom Blik by his baptismal name.

'It's all right,' I say, 'tell me where it is, and I'll get it myself.'

83

'No, your uncle will get it,' Aunt Dolly says placidly, although Oom Blik does not seem over-eager to oblige. I am left standing awkwardly, until Aunt Dolly darts Oom Blik a pale look, and he gets to his feet. He disappears into the house and reappears with a dining-room chair. I thank him and sit down, the uncomfortable upright chair sharpening my sense of being an unwelcome guest.

'And what brings you to Alfredville?' Oom Blik asks as I try as best I can to adjust my frame to the right angles of the chair.

This is the question that more than any other I anticipated, and I have decided to take refuge in vagueness, leaving my interlocutors to place their own constructions on my motives. 'No, Oom Blik,' I say, 'just looking up the old place.'

'And you didn't come to stay with us?' Aunt Dolly asks, in exactly the reproachful tone I'd dreaded. But I have prepared a reply.

'No, Aunt Dolly,' I say, 'I know how busy Aunt Dolly always is with the Child Welfare and the church and the crèche and the night shelter.'

She nods. 'And I'm on the board of the Old People's Home, too, now,' she says, pride vying with plaintiveness, and winning by a short head. 'But that doesn't mean I don't have a bed for my only sister's only child.' The formula trips off her tongue with the practice of years: I don't think she ever thinks of me in any other capacity. Her only sister's only child has long been a disappointment to her.

'Thank you, I appreciate that,' I say. I suspect that Aunt Dolly doesn't really want to put me up, but needs to sustain the pretence that she does, so that she can be slighted by my failure to rise to her hospitality. For a moment I'm tempted to call her bluff and pretend to accept her implied offer; but it would be too awful if she in turn called my bluff and I found myself staying with the Van Blerks.

Fortunately Oom Blik decides to intervene, I guess from no other motive than inherent meddlesomeness. 'No, Dolly, let him be,' he says. 'A young man like him wants to have a good time, not hang around a pair of old fogies like us.'

Aunt Dolly sighs. 'I suppose so,' she says. 'I suppose after London we must seem very dull to you.'

Actually, they seemed very dull to me even before London, but I can't really say so, so I say instead, 'Oh, London can be very dull too.'

I realise too late that my comment could be taken amiss, and Aunt Dolly doesn't miss the opportunity. 'Well, it's good to know that we're not the only dull people on earth,' she says. 'So, are you thinking of coming back?'

'Not in the near future,' I equivocate. 'I'm quite … *settled* in London at the moment.'

'Got a girlfriend, eh?' Oom Blik asks. 'Marriage plans?' He smiles insincerely, baring shrunken gums. His archness has something macabre about it, like an undertaker cracking a joke at the expense of the corpse.

Aunt Dolly darts him another look. I'm pretty sure that my unmarried state has been the subject of frequent speculation in the family.

'No,' I say. 'I have got a partner, but we're not considering marriage.' Never mind that I no longer have a partner and that we never considered marriage: if they want gossip fodder, I'm willing to provide it.

'Well,' Aunt Dolly says, 'things have changed so much since our day …' She sighs plumply and shakes her head.

This is an unpropitious moment at which to introduce the purpose of my visit, even in the watered-down version that I intend to present to them, but then, the longer I postpone it, the more awkward it's likely to become. So I say, in what I hope is a decently tentative manner, 'I know this can't be an easy subject for you, but I do want to offer you my condolences on your sad loss.'

There is a moment of fraught silence, and I wonder if I have breached some taboo in even alluding to Desirée's death. To discomfit me further, Angelina now appears with the extra cup and places it in front of me. Noticing the silence, she cocks an interrogative eyebrow at me. 'Thank you, Angelina,' I say. The little dog, perhaps sensing the tension, starts barking at the cat; the cat is ostentatiously unperturbed, but Aunt Dolly says, 'Angelina, take Cedric with you. He's making a nuisance of himself.'

'Yes, missis,' Angelina says, and leaves with the offending Cedric. Another silence ensues.

'Ja,' Oom Blik says at length. 'Ja.'

And 'Ja,' Aunt Dolly says. 'Ja.'

Silence descends again.

'It must have been a terrible shock for you,' I venture.

'I don't know,' Oom Blik says, an expression of universal incomprehension rather than a rejoinder to my lame comment.

Aunt Dolly sighs and says, 'Yes, I don't know.'

Silence, while I sit and wonder what follow-up their response can possibly allow. I pour myself a cup of coffee to cover my quandary.

'Help yourself to a rusk,' says Dolly. 'They're home-made.'

'Thank you,' I say, and do so, thankful for some activity to fill the conversational vacuum. But eating a rusk is at the best of times a delicate operation, requiring years of practice or perhaps even inbred ability. Either way, I've lost the knack of dunking an irregularly-shaped rock-hard object in hot coffee for long enough to render it edible, but not so long that it dissolves into mush; then stuffing it into my mouth fast enough to prevent it from dropping gobbets of soggy rusk into the coffee, but not so fast as to burn my mouth. I get the timing wrong, leave the rusk in the coffee for too long, and half of it sags into the cup. I retrieve the sludgy remnant with my teaspoon and put it in my saucer. It lies there in a shapeless puddle.

'Good rusks,' I say.

'They're aniseed,' says Aunt Dolly.

I rack my brains for a convincing transition from the subject of aniseed rusks to Desirée, but nothing presents itself. To cover my embarrassment I dip what remains of my rusk in my coffee, more cautiously this time, wary of its high solubility quotient, and am left with a tooth-shattering chunk gradually liquescing towards the point. I bite off the soggy bit and then quickly pop in the cruncher as well, hoping the two textures will mix and produce a chewable cud.

It is while my mouth is filled with this gunge that Oom Blik once again takes the initiative.

'*Ja-nee*,' he says. 'I don't know.'

'What is it that Oom Blik doesn't know?' I ask, my mouth at last clear of the remains of the rusk.

'I don't know,' he says, 'why Desirée ever married that ... that *man*.'

'Ag, Jeremiah,' says Aunt Dolly, 'we've been over that so often. The Lord moves in mysterious ways.'

'The Lord had bugger-all to do with it, and you know it,' he says fiercely. 'The devil, more likely. That man put a spell on her.'

'She was always so trusting, you remember, Pieter,' says Aunt Dolly. 'And I'm afraid he took advantage of that.'

'So you were opposed to the marriage?' I ask.

'Opposed? You bet we were bloody opposed!' Oom Blik interjects. 'We knew no good could come of it.'

'I tried to reason with her, but she wouldn't listen,' Aunt Dolly says. 'She was so in love with Hector, it was as your Uncle Jeremiah says, as if he put a spell on her. And she always had a mind of her own.'

'Are you convinced, then,' I ask cautiously, 'that Hector did kill Desirée?'

Oom Blik's yellowish-grey turns pink. 'Good God, man, do you doubt it for a minute? So who did it if that man didn't do it? Can you tell me that?'

'No. No, no, I just asked, because as you know, I wasn't here when it happened, so I don't know all the circumstances.'

'The circumstances are as plain as the nose on your face. He was jealous and so he killed her.'

'But jealous of whom?'

'Of everybody and everything. You don't expect rational thought from someone like that. He felt inferior, for all his airs and graces, and thought she was in love with every man she spoke to.'

'You know what a friendly girl she always was to everybody,

Pieter,' Aunt Dolly adds, 'without meaning anything by it. And I'm afraid they don't understand ordinary friendliness.'

'They?'

She gestures with her crochet needle in the general direction of the street. 'They, you know, *them*. And they say nothing makes people as insecure as not understanding.' She resumes crocheting, nodding her head sagely; then, abruptly, she looks up at me and declares almost vehemently, 'And I know, because Desirée told me herself, that there was never anything between her and that Dr Pretorius.'

'Dr Pretorius?' I ask. So there was something to Joachim's gossip about Henk Pretorius, after all.

'Come on, Dolly,' says Oom Blik, 'don't even mention it, it was just a rumour, people with nothing better to do with their time than sit on their backsides and chit-chit.'

Aunt Dolly, though, is clearly anxious to establish Desirée's innocence; I guess that she's had to deal with some neighbourly scepticism. 'Desirée told me herself, her words were, Henk's a good friend, but it's not as if he's in love with me or anything. You know, she lost a lot of so-called friends when she married Hector, so I think she was quite lonely, the poor girl. It's not as if Hector was good company for someone as cultured as her, a degree from Stellenbosch and all those books.'

I hope for more on the subject of Henk Pretorius, but she's jabbing away at her crocheting as if trying to eviscerate it.

'And where is Hector now?' I ask somewhat disingenuously.

'In Robertson, with his mother,' Oom Blik replies, 'under house arrest, *kamtig*. Awaiting trial in the High Court. Probably living like a king with his mother spoiling him rotten. You know how it is with these ANC types: one of these days he'll be released and get a hero's welcome and a 4x4.'

'You mean you think he might be found not guilty after all?'

'Who's to tell?' he demands angrily. 'Anything can happen in this bloody country, it just depends on who's on the bench.'

'So you never took to Hector?'

Oom Blik looks as if he's going to explode, but Aunt Dolly

forestalls him. 'Ag, Pieter, we tried, for Desirée's sake, we treated him like family, he used our bathroom and everything, I even invited his mother to tea, but you know, he didn't really understand our ways, the things that make us *us*, if you know what I mean.'

'Like what, Aunt Dolly?'

'Ag, little things. You know, eating your salad on a side plate, not putting your knife in your mouth, getting up if a woman comes into the room –'

'And he didn't like braaivleis,' Oom Blik adds darkly. 'Said he preferred his meat underdone, I ask you. I suppose he ate raw meat in the jungle with all the other terrorists.'

'And he didn't go to church,' Aunt Dolly adds. '*And* he didn't flush the toilet after he'd been.'

It occurs to me that by their criteria I'm almost as foreign to my native culture as Hector Williams, although I do generally remember to flush the toilet.

'But *personally* … did you like him?' I persist.

'*Like* him?' Oom Blik explodes. 'Good God, man, the fellow murdered our daughter and you ask if we *liked* him?'

'No, of course, I mean, before … before you knew he … you know. They say murderers are often very pleasant people.'

'Who says that?' Oom Blik demands.

'People,' I say. 'People in general.'

'Which people?'

'You know, just people in general. Psychologists, criminologists, people like that.'

'Yes, psychologists, criminologists, arseholologists, they haven't had their daughter murdered by a savage otherwise they wouldn't talk such absolute … elephant turds. *Very pleasant people*, my old boot up my backside. Is this what those English have taught you, that murderers are *very pleasant people*? I suppose they have tea parties in London for murderers, oh do meet my friend Jack the Ripper he's a very pleasant person, and please lick his arse while you're about it?'

'Jeremiah,' Aunt Dolly says, '*Please*. We don't talk like that.'

89

'I'm sorry,' I say. 'I realise this is a very painful topic. I didn't mean to pry.'

'No, you're family,' says Aunt Dolly. 'We understand that you feel with us. It's the press I can't stand, with their *kamtige* sympathy when all they want is a sob story.'

'Don't mention the press to me,' Oom Blik rages at me, as if I were the one who'd mentioned the press. 'Sanctimonious suckers-up, so sorry to hear about your bereavement, do tell us all about it and next thing there you are on the front page of the next morning's paper looking like dogshit because you haven't slept for two days and you haven't shaved and they've been asking you questions to upset you and then they call you *A deeply-grieving Mr van Blerk* so their readers can slobber snot and tears all over their Post Toasties. *Huh!*'

'Or the magazines,' Aunt Dolly adds. 'They offered us five thousand rand for "our story". They wanted photographs of Desirée as a little girl, and wedding photographs, "the couple in happier times", you know the sort of thing. And they published a photo of David.'

'David who?' I ask.

'No, I don't know David who, I don't think they had surnames in those days, just David, you know, the statue …'

'The murder weapon,' Oom Blik supplies.

'Yes, the … the weapon and as you know David hasn't got any clothes on and they published him full … full …'

'Full-frontal,' Oom Blik helps out again.

'Yes, full-frontal, so of course what did people think, they don't know it's culture, they just think Desirée had a statue of a naked man in her sitting room …' Suddenly, quietly, she begins crying. 'You'd think people would show some respect,' she sobs. 'Not for us, but for the dead.'

'*Respect*,' Oom Blik growls, wiping his eyes with the back of his hand. 'All they *respect* is the money they can make out of your story.' He gets up and puts his hand on Aunt Dolly's shoulder. She takes a handkerchief out of her sleeve and pats her eyes.

'I'm sorry,' she says, 'but I'm still not used to it. She was such a beautiful girl.' She sobs twice, and then says, 'You know, I didn't want to say anything, and I hope you don't mind – but you look so much like Desirée, it really gave me quite a fright when you arrived.'

'Oh,' I say, feeling somehow responsible for her distress, 'I'm sorry, I didn't know …'

'No,' she says, 'It's not your fault. But Desirée always looked more like your mother than like me, and you look like your mother, so …' she gestures vaguely with her hands, her crocheting lying forgotten in her lap.

'Perhaps I'd better leave,' I say. 'I'm afraid I've upset you.'

'Oh, it doesn't take much to upset me nowadays,' she says. 'I'm a terrible cry-baby.'

'Nonsense,' says Oom Blik, turning on me, as if I'd been the one to call her a cry-baby. 'You don't know how brave she's been.'

'I can see that,' I say, getting to my feet. 'I can't imagine what you've been through.'

'No, you can't,' he says bluntly. 'But you can try.'

I nod, oddly disarmed by this sally. 'Yes,' I say, 'I can try.'

'And come to see us again soon,' says Aunt Dolly. 'Till when are you staying?'

'I haven't decided,' I say. 'It depends.'

'On what?' asks Oom Blik. I'd forgotten how literal minded he is, what a stickler for a straight answer.'

'Oh, on other people, really. I hope to see several people, and it will depend on when they're available.'

I expect him to ask me which other people, but he just grunts, '*Available.* You make Alfredville sound like bloody London. We're all right here and *available* all the time.'

'Yes,' I say feebly, 'but I haven't contacted most of them yet.'

'Well, let us know when you're free for lunch,' says Aunt Dolly. 'I must at least feed my only sister's only son some decent *boerekos*.'

I have memories of sugary pumpkin, of greasy lamb, of potatoes baked in the fat of the joint, of overcooked cauliflower with a glutinous cheese sauce, of beetroot oozing purple vinegar, a sourish grated-carrot-and-orange salad, of a stodgy baked pudding with boiling hot apricot jam somewhere in its innards. My stomach turns at the thought, but valiantly I say, 'Thank you very much, that will be lovely.'

'Come on Sunday, then,' Aunt Dolly says. 'I'm sure Boetie will want to see you too.'

'Thank you,' I say. 'I'd like that. And how *is* Boetie?' I add, conscious that the belated enquiry hardly bespeaks avid interest in Boetie's welfare. I remember him as a thick-thighed, morose little boy; I imagine he's grown into a thick-thighed, morose young man.

'He's all right,' says Oom Blik. 'He's been taking over from me at the garage. That's why I can sit on my bum and have coffee and rusks in the middle of the day.'

'He's a very good boy,' says Aunt Dolly. 'I don't know what we would have done without him.' There is something anxious in the way she says this, glancing at Oom Blik, that makes me wonder if the exemplary Boetie is perhaps a source of discord.

I take my leave. Angelina sees me out. 'It's good to see you,' she says. 'It's not so lekker in the house with those two, I can tell you. Cedric and I keep each other company.'

'Is Cedric …?' I ask, not knowing how to ask it.

'Miss Desirée's dog, yes,' Angelina says. 'Missus doesn't like looking at him. She says he saw the murder.'

'I suppose he did,' I say, and leave.

CHAPTER 7

Wednesday evening

I meet Nonyameko at seven in the bar, as arranged. She arrives wearing a well-cut red linen dress and high-heeled sandals, and I wonder whether I'm underdressed.

'Do you think I need a jacket?' I ask, as she sits down next to me. Her perfume is a light, agreeable rose fragrance. 'I thought of wearing one, but it's so hot.'

She surveys me. 'I think you will pass muster in most of the establishments in Alfredville. Where are we going?'

'It's not as if we're overwhelmed by choice. But there is a French restaurant, or one with aspirations to being French, in the main street. Shall we try that?'

'Why not? But I want a drink first. It has been a trying day.'

'What tried you?'

'People.'

'Your patients?'

'No, they can be difficult, but they have reason to be difficult. I am talking of government people, overfed bureaucrats sitting in air-conditioned offices in Pretoria reciting their petty regulations at me as if it is holy writ, without any idea of the conditions that they are supposed to apply to. I spent forty minutes on the telephone just trying to get hold of one such and then she told me that government already had adequate programmes in place for ante-natal care and did not *deem it advisable* to extend their limited resources to *inessentials* like psychological counselling.'

I can't help wondering what kind of retort the overfed bureaucrat got from this formidable constituent, but I resist the temptation to enquire. Boris saunters up to take our order, and we both order a glass of Sauvignon Blanc, Nonyameko stipulating that it must be very cold. Boris grunts non-committally. He is in his remote phase again, not letting on that he's ever clapped eyes on either of us.

'So what do you do?' I ask. 'I mean, if government refuses to cooperate.'

'We get outside funding, usually foreign funding. But there is resistance in some quarters to what is seen as western condescension at best and neocolonialism at worst.'

'Heavens, what a comedy of ideological cross-purposes.'

'You may think of it as a comedy, but I assure you there is nothing amusing about its effects.'

'I suppose not,' I say, chastened but not really repentant. I don't believe that the comic potential of a situation is determined by its effects alone, but I can't see that Nonyameko is going to take readily to this perspective. 'Cheers, anyway,' I say as our wine arrives. It's going to be a long evening.

The restaurant, the Café Rouge, is small, with predictable red tablecloths and red candles on the table. I foresee a menu in bad French, and food to match. There are only ten tables in the restaurant, of which two are occupied. The inevitable Edith Piaf is moaning, heartbroken, in the background.

The waitress-cum-front-of-house-manager asks us whether we've booked.

'No,' I say, 'is that a problem?'

She looks at the list in front of her, which I can see is empty.

'I think we can fit you in,' she says graciously. 'Please follow me.'

She shows us to a table next to a window, and hands us each a menu. She strikes a match to light our candle, but Nonyameko holds up a hand. 'Please,' she says, 'it is hot enough. I don't think we need a candle.'

The waitress gives a suit-yourself shrug and walks off. Nonyameko glances at the menu, then calls the waitress back.

'There are no prices on this menu,' she says.

The waitress smiles in a slightly strained manner, and starts explaining that when one client is a man and the other a woman …

'Yes, yes, I know the reason,' Nonyameko says, 'but that is based on a totally sexist assumption, don't you think?'

The waitress regards her blankly; she doesn't look as if she'd recognise a sexist assumption if it bit her on the ankle. 'Do you want another menu?' she asks at last.

'Yes, please, one with prices,' Nonyameko says. The waitress takes the offending menu and retreats, shaking her head as if to say, What next? She does, however, bring a new menu, and we discuss the relative merits of Coque [*sic*] au Vin and Boeuf Bur-guignonne [*sic*], both of which seem rather heavy for a summer's evening. In the end we both settle for a salad followed by plain roast chicken; I order a bottle of Ghanta Pinotage. When it arrives I lift a glass. 'To ... what?'

'To your return to native soil,' she says.

'I'll drink to that,' I say. 'But I'm finding it a bit of a non-event, to be honest.'

'Oh? Why is that, do you think?'

'Does a non-event have to have a reason?'

She pretends to consider my question, narrowing her eyes, pursing her lips. Her face, though not conventionally pretty, has a very attractive mobility about it. Again I'm not sure whether her earnestness is an ironic affectation or a genuine lack of humour. 'Yes,' she says at length. 'Yes, I think something *not* happening may require explanation quite as much as something happening.'

'So you expect me to explain why my return to native soil leaves me cold?'

'I do not expect anything,' she says, lapsing into her mode of cool indifference again. 'But I should think you would want to ask yourself the question some time.'

'Okay, I might do that some time,' I say.

Unexpectedly, she laughs. 'That does not sound very convincing. But while you are about it, do you know why you are living in England?'

'Yes, I do. I went there in the eighties because I didn't want to go to the army.'

95

She nods. 'Fair enough. But you did not come back when there was no longer any chance of being conscripted.'

'No. By then I'd settled over there, all my interests were there. I'd studied at an English university, and I was working for an English newspaper – *The Independent*. I'd *become* English, if you like.'

She seems mildly interested. 'Do you have British friends?'

'Of course I have. I have a British partner, for God's sake.' Okay, so he's half Jamaican, and he's no longer my partner as of a week ago, but I needn't tell her that.

'And do your friends regard you as British?'

Christ, another interrogation. 'I really don't think they give it a thought.' So James calls – called – me the Saffer honky, but my new acquaintance wouldn't appreciate that.

'And if they were to give it a thought?'

Jesus, she's persistent. If she weren't a psychologist she could be an advocate, one of those you see in courtroom dramas reducing innocent witnesses to blubbering idiots. 'No, I imagine not,' I say.

She nods, pleased; I expect her to say, I rest my case m'lud, but instead she returns to the chase. 'And do you think they ever will?'

'Probably not. The Brits can spot a foreign accent fifty years on. But so what? Do I derive my identity from my friends?'

'To a large extent, yes, from your friends and other people around you. We are relational beings.' I suspect this is the psychologist going into explanatory mode. Then she tightens the thumb-screw one turn. 'Or do you think identity is some kind of incorruptible individual essence that you keep in a closet at home?'

'Is national identity the only kind of identity?' I ask, realising too late that by asking another question I've created a platform for her to pronounce from.

'It is the first one,' she says, duly occupying the platform. 'The others follow on from that.'

'I'm sorry, I just don't agree. I have a social identity, a sexual identity, a professional identity, a racial identity ... I even have a *name*, for heaven's sake. I have a bloody *passport* to prove it.'

She's unimpressed with this litany. 'And where, in the midst of all these identities, is the one you call yourself?' she asks.

'I could say I'm a relational being, if I wanted to take refuge in your jargon, but let's just say I'm the sum of all of them, the one that's summed up by my name.'

'And what *is* your name?'

'I've told you. It's Peter Jacobs.'

'Of course. Sorry. And that is Afrikaans Jacobs or Jewish Jacobs?'

'Jewish. That is, my father was Jewish, my mother Afrikaans.'

'And you are ...?'

'Neither one nor the other. I'm a British citizen.'

'That is nice. So at least the Queen thinks you are British.'

'Well, she should know, after all,' I say, determined not to be goaded by her manner. 'And you?' I ask. 'I take it you were at the forefront of the Struggle?'

She's no longer looking at me, answers as if she's lost interest in this conversation with this white man, honky, boer: 'The Struggle was democratic, there was no forefront. And I was very young. But I was a member of the ANC in exile, yes, stationed abroad. Umkhonto we Sizwe. The Spear of the Nation,' she explains.

'Thanks, I know what Umkhonto we Sizwe means.'

'No reason why you should. You were out of it.'

I decide to ignore this goad too, if goad it is. 'And where did you grow up?'

'Here, mainly.'

'Here? In Alfredville? When?'

'The first eighteen years of my life. Which, if you really want to know, was from 1970 to 1988.'

'Then we're the same age,' I say. 'I'd have thought you were a good deal younger.'

'Thanks. I am told black women do not show their age, at any rate not so white people notice. Assuming white people are interested.'

'And we grew up in the same town.'

'Hardly. You grew up in white Alfredville, I grew up in black Alfredville. They are two different places. Although my mother did come into white Alfredville to work.'

'Where did she work?'

'She was what was called a domestic. She worked for a woman called Mrs Viljoen.'

'Alie Viljoen?'

'I don't know. My mother was not on first-name terms with her. She called Mrs Viljoen Madam and Mrs Viljoen called her Gladys, although that was not in fact her name. Mrs Viljoen lived in Church Street, the big house with the gable.'

'Yes, that's Alie Viljoen. She had a daughter called Santie.'

'I know. I got to wear Santie's hand-me-down-down bloomers when she outgrew them. Which she did very quickly, fortunately for me.'

'Yes, Santie was a large girl. I wonder what happened to her.'

'If you had stayed around you would have known. She has become an actress – larger than ever, but very popular as the owner of a boarding house in one of the soaps, I forget which one.'

'And you? Did you matriculate here?'

'Yes, thanks partly to Mrs Viljoen, who paid for my school books. She was outraged when I left the country after matric to join the ANC. She told my mother that she had not paid for me to become a terrorist, and that I would come to no good. I went to see her when I arrived here last week, to show her what I had *come to*. She received me in the kitchen and asked me if I was happy now that Zuma was our president, and whether that was what I had fought for.'

'And what did you say?'

'I said that I was not happy about Zuma, but yes, I had fought for people's right to choose their leader.'

Our food arrives. The salad looks more promising than I'd dared hope for.

'And now,' she says, spearing an olive with her fork, 'now that we have established what I do and where my political allegiances lie, you can tell me what you are doing here in Alfredville.'

'Oh dear. I'd hoped you'd forgotten.'

'No such luck, I have a good memory. So, spill the beans.'

I hesitate. 'Can I trust you?'

She smiles. 'Trust me to do what? Not to sell your story to the *New York Times*?'

'Who says I have a story?'

'You have told me that you are a freelance journalist and you cannot give me any other reason for being in Alfredville, so since I am not a total half-wit, I assume that you are here to write a story.'

I wince. 'I suppose it is rather obvious. But you'd be surprised at how few people are interested enough to make the deduction. In any case, I must ask you to keep it absolutely to yourself, for reasons that will become evident when I do tell you.'

'I am used to keeping things to myself. I am a psychologist, remember?'

'Yes, but I'm not one of your patients.'

'Never mind, I shall pretend that you are. You can go ahead, discretion guaranteed.'

She sits back, putting down her fork and assuming an expression of rapt attention.

I take a sip of my wine, self-conscious. 'You're looking at me like a cartoon cat guarding a mouse-hole. If that's how you look at your patients, I'm surprised they tell you anything.'

'We call them clients, not patients. And I have never had complaints about the way I look at them.'

'Call me sensitive, but I suspect you're sending me up.'

'I assure you I am not. Please carry on.'

'Right,' I say, feeling thoroughly patronised. 'I suppose,' I nevertheless continue, 'you remember the case of Desirée Williams?'

She considers. 'Yes, I think I do. It was in all the papers. White woman murdered here in Alfredville by her black police-chief husband. But I don't know the details.'

'Then how much do you know?'

'If I knew more than that, I have forgotten – so assume I know nothing. I would rather hear something I know than not hear something I do not know.'

'Right.' I take a deep breath. 'Desirée Williams was born Desirée van Blerk, the only daughter of the former mayor of Alfredville, Willem van Blerk, known as Blik van Blerk, the owner of a garage in the town, prominent citizen, member of the church council.'

'I think I can see him: red-faced, thick-set, moustache?'

'Actually, you're wrong. He's as sinewy as a piece of biltong. But that's not really relevant, except in so far as the whole background is relevant. I know something of the background, because Desirée was my cousin, daughter of my mother's only sister.'

'So your interest in the case is personal?'

'It's also professional, but I suppose I wouldn't really have noticed the case if I hadn't known Desirée.'

'Did you know her well?'

'Not really. She was four years my junior, which is a considerable difference at that age. But there was something intriguing about her, even as a teenager. She gave one the impression of having ideas of her own, of being at odds with Alfredville. That appealed to me, I guess, because I identified with it.'

'She was a rebel?'

'Not openly. She was the apple of her father's eye, as they say: a sweet-natured, pretty girl who did well at school, was elected head girl of the local high school, then went off to Stellenbosch University, where she studied languages. I thought then that she'd never come back to Alfredville, but after four years come back she did, and started teaching English at her old school. She was a popular teacher, and did what was expected of her: coached netball, conducted prayer meetings, helped in the library. Her one indulgence, if it can be called that, was tennis.'

'Hardly a vice, I would have said.'

'True. But what was slightly irregular was that instead of playing on the school courts with the other teachers, she joined the town club, which some of her colleagues regarded as a bit uppity.'

100

'I suppose the tennis was better at the town club.'

'Indeed. But she was suspected of preferring the more varied company at the town club to that of her colleagues.'

'And that is a vice?'

'Not really, but it was noted against her, along with the fact that she spoke English in her classes ...'

'I thought you said she *taught* English?'

'And so she did, but her predecessor Mrs Brink, the wife of the principal, who incidentally taught me English years ago, used to conduct her English classes through the medium of Afrikaans, and nobody thought it was odd. Indeed, as I was saying, it was regarded as a bit eccentric of Desirée to insist on English.'

'So Desirée was after all not so popular?'

'She was popular among the children, but may have been a bit of an outsider among the other teachers. As I say, there was always an air of not fitting in about her, and her colleagues would have noted that against her.'

'Heavens, the poor woman.'

'Indeed. Small towns are supposed to have a warm heart, but they also have a very cold eye. Desirée, though, seemed impervious, and was, apparently, a popular member of the tennis club. She played a good game and was sociable.'

'So how does a woman whose worst sin is joining the wrong tennis club get murdered?'

Nonyameko has taken up her fork again and resumed eating, which takes some of the pressure off me.

'You think one needs to be a sinner to get murdered?' I ask. 'In South Africa you can get murdered for owning a mobile phone.'

'Even in South Africa you need a *reason* to get murdered, even if it is only a mobile phone. But I assume from your interest in the case that this is not a run-of-the-mill robbery-gone-wrong. So what *was* the reason?'

'I'm getting to it. First some more background, which is in fact inseparable from the reason. You see, at the tennis club Desirée met, among other people, the new chief of police, the station commander, one Captain Hector Williams. You may have met him in your days with the ANC. He was an MK member then, stationed in Moscow, London, all over.'

She nods. 'I never met him, but yes, he was quite well known. One of the relatively few Coloured cadres.'

'Yes. Now Captain Williams ...'

She holds up her hand. 'Excuse the interruption, but how do you know all this?'

'My mother no longer lives here, but she has stayed in touch with some of her friends and relatives here, and has kept me abreast of events in Alfredville. To be honest, I generally skip those bits of her letters, I mean, what do I feel for Alfredville, but this case interested me because of Desirée, and I've been reading up on it all. It was pretty well covered in the daily press and the more sensational periodicals.'

'In England?'

'Well, no. But I had the papers and periodicals shipped to me.'

'My, you really did take an interest. One might even call it a morbid interest. Why?'

'As I say, she was my cousin.'

She mulls this over, then asks, 'Are you that close to your family, even ... how many years after emigrating?'

'Twenty-two. And the answer is no, I'm not that close to my family. But my mother phoned me with the news, and then she came here for a few weeks after the murder to be with her sister, so she heard just about every extant detail about the murder and reported most of them to me. At first my interest was, as you say, personal, but then I started thinking that the story had ... possibilities.'

'Possibilities? So poor Desirée, having reached the end of her other possibilities, becomes a story opportunity?'

I stab at an unoffending chunk of tuna. 'Look, nobody holds it against Shakespeare that he used the tragic death of two young lovers as a story opportunity. It's of the nature of stories to deal with sad situations, and of the nature of storytellers to seek out sad situations.'

'Mm. And what can your story add to the extensive coverage

it has already had in the papers and sensational magazines you made a study of?'

'The press only covered the events. I want to find out what the facts *mean*, what they tell us about the possibilities or impossibilities of a non-racial South Africa.'

'Can you separate the facts of the story from the personalities involved?'

'You mean I'm going to end up with another Human Interest Story? Yes, that is a danger, that it will seem like just an unfortunate combination of personality types. Still, I think there is something more here than a bad marriage, some … some significant confluence of events,' I end lamely, hoping she'll accept my vague generality as legal tender.

I should have known better. 'That sounds very grand,' she says, 'but *what* particular confluence of events? You have not really told me how she came to be murdered, you know.'

'Yes, I'm sorry, I got sidetracked. I was saying about Hector Williams, then, that he returned to South Africa in 1991, and joined the police force. He made rapid progress, and after the dawn of the new dispensation, was appointed station commander of the Alfredville police station in 1996. He replaced Captain Blikkies Blignault, a man not noted for his good race relations.'

'I remember Captain Blignault. He had me locked up along with twenty of my classmates because there was pro-ANC graffiti on our classroom wall.'

'That's the man. Apparently he's now running a private security firm in Port Elizabeth. He was not much lamented, even by the white citizens of Alfredville, because he was widely suspected of being implicated in the sheep stealing that had become endemic in the district. The fact that the sheep stealing stopped abruptly when Hector Williams took over did much to recommend him to Alfredville. In fact, counter to expectations and predictions, crime actually decreased under Captain Williams, which, as you know, really bucked the national trend. Williams's critics said that his methods were brutal.'

'Do we know what these methods were?'

103

'Not in detail. But I gather they were what is called in other parts of the world *zero tolerance*. Still, most of the white community didn't feel all that strongly about tolerance anyway, and were only too grateful to enjoy pre-1990 levels of crime. And then, he proved to be presentable and personable; and, as I have said, he joined the hitherto exclusively white tennis club.'

'Unopposed?'

'Oh, there were objections. Several people threatened to resign, and a few of them joined the Riversdal tennis club and organised a lift club on Saturday afternoons, but apparently the Riversdal people complained that their courts were being usurped – they said "cluttered" – so the Alfredville commuters returned to home base. Hector turned out to be one of Alfredville's best players, though it was a matter of some conjecture where he could have learnt the game, having spent his youth, according to public opinion, being trained as a terrorist by the ANC. Perhaps you can enlighten me on that.'

'It is true that training camps were not exactly tennis camps, but the ANC in exile had access to the amenities of whatever country they found themselves in. Some people in fact lived quite well.'

'They must have, given the expensive tastes some of your leaders acquired in exile.'

Quite visibly, she decides to ignore the jibe. 'But about Hector Williams ...?'

'Yes. So, as I said, it was here, at the tennis club, that Hector met Desirée.'

'And they fell in love at first sight?'

'And they fell in love, but who's to tell whether it was at first sight? Some of the magazines wanted it that way. All I know is that about a year after they met, the two were married.'

'And when was that?'

'November 1997. Desirée continued teaching English at the high school, and as far as anybody could tell they were a happy couple. They had no children, and didn't really entertain. They were invited out to some houses, the more progressive or the more curious, but they didn't reciprocate. Still, there was no active hostility to the union, though there were a couple of incidents. Once, at a braaivleis, a drunken farmer, Pens Peltzer, pointedly went and washed his hands after Williams shook his hand. Williams ignored the slight, but on his way back to his farm that night Pens was stopped by a police car, taken to the District Surgeon for a blood test and arrested for drunken driving. He spent the night in a police cell along with Lappies Ontong, the town's official vagrant, who was sometimes locked up at his own request. Lappies asked to be released at 2 am, after Pens had been sick all over the cell.'

I look at Nonyameko, hoping that she'll relent into a smile, but she continues eating her salad with irksome single-mindedess.

'One other incident,' I continue, with the slight desperation of a comedian whose first joke has failed and now has to come up with another. 'At a school function Mrs Maria du Pisani, whose daughter Chantelle was in Desirée's English class, asked Desirée if it was "better" with a black man. Desirée said she'd not had any opportunities of comparison and there was only one way for Mrs du Pisani to find out.'

'And that was quoted in the press?'

'This particular story I had from my mother, who'd heard it from a scandalised Mrs du Pisani herself. As I say, my mother came to spend a while with her sister after the murder, and so got to meet, as she says, everybody that she used to avoid when she lived here.'

Nonyameko's face twitches, possibly with the effort of suppressing a smile. Then she composes her features. 'So the marriage ended in murder.'

'Yes. On the night of 25 October last year, while her husband was on duty at the police station, she was battered to death in the sitting room of their house in Victoria Street, not five hundred metres from the police station. Nobody had heard any sound of a struggle, and her pet Maltese poodle, Cedric, apparently slept through the attack. Indeed, when found by her husband, Desirée was sitting with the television remote control in her hand; she had evidently been bludgeoned from behind with a statuette, a copy of Michelangelo's David, which she had brought back from her overseas honeymoon with Hector.'

'I suppose you could call that a cultural weapon,' Nonyameko says.

I look at her, trying to discern some evidence of ironic intent, but she is busy removing the pip from an olive, and seems unaware of having just made a rather tasteless joke.

'Was that a joke, by any chance?' I ask.

She looks up impassively. 'Impossible. Political activists have no sense of humour. But please continue with your story.'

'Thank you. Yes, where was I?'

'At the end, or the beginning, depending on whether it is your story or Desirée's.'

'Yes, her death – let's say the point at which her story intersects with mine.'

'Becomes yours, you mean.'

'If you will. Anyway, Alfredville was aghast, not only at the death of Desirée, but at the idea that their hitherto safe town had proved to harbour its share of the violent crime so prevalent elsewhere. The police could find no evidence of a break-in, but the front door and the back door were unlocked and anybody could have walked in and out again without being seen. It was judged to be too important a case for the local police to handle, so detectives came from Oudtshoorn for the investigation. They complained that the scene of the crime had been contaminated beyond all hope of reconstruction by the local police, but they did manage to lift some fingerprints from a glass Desirée had been drinking from, which turned out to match those of Captain Williams. Further investigation found that a bloodstain on the bathroom floor, where the killer had presumably cleaned himself up, matched a mark on the sole of one of the shoes Williams had been wearing that evening. On the day before Christmas, Captain Williams was arrested for the murder of his wife.'

Edith Piaf has at last croaked herself into silence, but our relief is short-lived: the restaurant's sound system now oozes forth a treacly tenor, probably Andrea Bocelli or Helmut Lotti, lavishing himself all over 'O Sole Mio'.

'Jesus,' I say. 'I thought Piaf was intrusive.'

'Try not to notice it,' she says. 'And how did Alfredville react to the arrest?'

'As was to be expected. The white community shook their heads knowingly – *We knew it could come to no good* – and the black community suspected a racist plot. The man will come to trial in the High Court in Cape Town next month, but in the meantime, apparently, race relations are as bad as they ever were.'

'Excuse me, sir,' our waitress interjects, and I realise she's been standing there for half a minute waiting for an opening. 'Is everything all right?'

'My salad is fine, thanks,' I say, annoyed at the interruption. 'Yours?' I ask Nonyameko.

'Yes, thank you,' she says to the waitress, 'but do you think you could turn down the music slightly?'

The waitress visibly suppresses a sigh. 'I'll see what I can do,' she says, 'but there are people who are enjoying the music.'

'I cannot imagine why,' Nonyameko retorts, but the waitress pretends not to have heard. 'Or for that matter who,' Nonyameko says to her retreating back. There is now only one other couple in the restaurant, two bored-looking middle-aged men, who seem unlikely Bocelli fans.

'I thought you didn't mind the music,' I say to Nonyameko.

'I don't really, but you obviously do, and I am trying to have a conversation with you.'

'Thanks. The thing is, to return to Desirée's death: as I say, I'm not interested in the sensationalism; I'm interested in what this *means* in terms of racial attitudes in South Africa.'

'Whose racial attitudes?'

'I'd hope to have a representative sample of people, people not interviewed by *You* magazine, and to find out what they make of this.'

'And you think you are going to find out by going up to people and asking?'

107

'Credit me with some subtlety. This is not the first story I'm writing.'

'So you think you have some line on the story that is going to get it into *The New Yorker*.'

I flush with annoyance, partly because in fact I do have an angle that I hope will get my story into *The New Yorker*. 'I wouldn't call it a *line*,' I say. 'But the story does bear some interesting similarities to *Othello*.'

'You mean because a black man kills a white woman?'

'Well, a white woman he happens to be married to, the daughter of a high-ranking official of his home town, and he himself a trusted functionary of the state –'

'But was Othello not supposed to be insanely jealous or something?'

'Yes. So I want to find out who or what Hector Williams was jealous of.'

'Why are you so sure he was jealous?'

'Why else would he have killed her?'

'I don't know. A fight about finances. A fight about her choice of lounge curtains.'

'What I'm interested in is the kind of insecurity that, even after he's achieved total success, would still undermine his self-image to the extent that he's driven to kill. As with Othello.'

'Was Othello not driven by somebody else?'

'By Iago, yes, exactly. I'm hoping to find out if there was some such person in the mix, somebody who made it his – or even her – business to play on Williams's jealousy.'

'I cannot quite see why you assume that the police chief of Alfredville and his wife would feel obliged to follow Shakespeare's plot.'

'Please, that's not what I'm saying.'

'Then what are you saying?'

'I'm saying that there has to be an explanation for something as extreme as a man murdering his wife. To assume anything else is extremely racist, as you'll forgive me for pointing out.'

'Racist? How?'

'Well, if you discard the possibility that there has to be some very cogent reason for his murdering her, you're saying that he murdered her because he was black, as indeed much of white Alfredville no doubt is saying. Now *I'm* saying there must be another factor, possibly another person.'

'And you are going to find that factor or person?'

'I'm certainly going to try.'

'And it has not occurred to you that perhaps Hector Williams did not kill her at all?'

'Of course it's occurred to me, but for the moment I can't see who else could have done it. Nothing was stolen from the house.'

'And theft is the only motive for murder?'

'Well, either somebody killed her because he wanted something she had, or he killed her because he was angry with her. If we rule out the first motive, Williams becomes the most plausible exponent of the second – especially if we take into account the fact I forgot to mention, that he was missing from his job at the police station at the time of the murder, and can't provide a satisfactory explanation of his whereabouts.'

'Has he offered any?'

'He says he was called out to a cattle theft, but there is no record of any call reporting a cattle theft.'

'It is all pretty negative – no explanation, no call – was there not something positive?'

'Wasn't it Sherlock Holmes who solved a crime on the basis of a dog's *not* barking in the night?'

'Like, in fact, Desirée's dog?'

'Yes, I hadn't thought about that. So that's another negative.'

'You mean four negatives add up to a positive? I still prefer a real positive.'

'I've given you two: the fingerprints and the bloodstain.'

'You said yourself the crime scene had been contaminated. I am not sure those count as positives.'

'Here's a positive, then. The murderer, whoever he was, walked in without forcing an entry. Isn't it unusual in South Africa for a woman on her own at night not to lock the doors?'

'Excuse me, but that sounds like another negative. The door was not locked. But yes, I grant you, unusual, though perhaps not as much so in Alfredville as in most places. You have said yourself that crime is less of a problem here than elsewhere. Also, Desirée could have opened the door to the murderer. So that one is not all that significant.'

'Listen, please don't confuse the issue. I'm not here to write a whodunit, I'm here to write an account of a wife's murder by her husband.'

'So you have decided in advance what your story's outcome is.'

'Yes. The outcome is known; the story is in the why, not the who.'

'Okay,' she says. 'Well, I certainly hope you get your story.'

'Do you really?'

She considers. 'Yes, by and large. Remember, I am a psychologist. We also deal in stories.'

'Yes, only your subjects come to you. I have to search out mine.'

'So have you interviewed Hector Williams?'

'No, dammit. I left London at very short notice, but I did manage to get hold of his legal representative in Cape Town. Only, he said he'd instructed his client not to grant any interviews before the trial. I even tried phoning his mother – Williams is staying with her – but the old lady had been primed and duly put down the phone on me, after some choice vernacular abuse.'

'The murderer, or alleged murderer, would seem to be a pretty essential element of the story.'

'Please, don't depress me. I'm hoping, if the worst comes to the worst, that I'll be able to reconstruct his part in it. And of course, I'll attend the trial.'

'Mm,' she says sceptically. 'Well, I suppose you already have to reconstruct Desirée's part in it.'

'Exactly. And haven't we been taught that all truth is merely a construct?'

110

'Sorry, I am from the old school. I believe in the unconstructed true and false and right and wrong and even black and white. I was a revolutionary, remember.'

'How can I forget it?'

She laughs, at last, and the tightness of our conversation relaxes somewhat, the guardedness dissipating as the wine mellows the mood. The main course arrives, and we talk in a more desultory fashion.

'So, why did you leave London in such a hurry?' she asks.

'Did I say I left London in a hurry?'

'Well, you said at short notice, which is pretty much the same thing.'

'Oh, yes, of course. You don't miss much, do you?'

'I keep reminding you that I am a psychologist. We are trained to listen for significant incidentals.'

'Yes, well ... you've been well trained. The reason I left London ... well, more quickly than I'd envisaged, is ... well, a personal one.'

'Too personal to tell me?'

Half an hour ago I wouldn't have exposed any aspect of my private life to this woman's sardonic gaze; but there is something in the way she asks the question, something relaxed and yet engaging, that persuades me to lower my guard.

I take another sip of wine. 'Okay, I'll take my chance on that. The thing is, my partner of five years' standing – and I might as well go all the way and tell you that he's a man, a black man – broke up with me a week ago.'

'Oh dear. I am sorry. And was this totally unexpected?'

'Yes, although I should have seen it coming. He'd been expressing misgivings about the relationship for some time.'

'What kind of misgivings?'

'Oh, about what he saw as my lack of emotional commitment. He said it was like trying to have a relationship with a traffic light, all go one second, all caution the next and then total no-go. He said he was in a state of perpetual exhaustion trying to catch the green light before it changed.'

She smiled. 'You know that we call traffic lights robots in this country.'

'Yes. I remember. Thank heavens James didn't know that. I can just imagine what he would have made of that metaphor. The robot lover.'

'You still love him, don't you?'

'Do I? How can I tell, when I didn't even know if I loved him when I was living with him?'

'Isn't one supposed to realise the full value of something only when one has lost it? Or is that too much of a cliché for you?'

'Oh, I've made my peace with a quite a few clichés of late. I certainly miss James more than I thought I was capable of.'

'Enough to rethink the relationship?'

'It's not for me to rethink it. He's the one who broke it off.'

'And you are sure he won't rethink if you offer him a green light, so to speak?'

'I don't know. You see, the moment you ask me that, I wonder if I really want to.'

'The yellow light comes on, yes. I see what James meant.'

'Oh, you'd get on really well with James. You could discuss my emotional shortcomings at length.'

'Don't flatter yourself. Did you not say he was black? He and I will be discussing the proletariat revolution. Relationships are a bourgeois obsession.'

I snort. 'James is more bourgeois than I am. He went to Cambridge, and his father's a stockbroker.'

'The revolution has often been driven by the sons of the bourgeoisie.'

'This son hasn't driven any revolutions. Breaking up with me is the most violent thing he's ever done.'

'That is a good start, getting rid of the personal baggage.'

'Is that what you counsel your clients?'

'Touché. The revolutionary and the psychologist don't always see eye to eye.'

We finish our meal – we skip the dessert, the usual line-up of crème brûlée and ice cream – and go back to the hotel. I suggest another drink, but Nonyameko pleads an early morning.

'I hope to see you again,' I say, as we part in the lobby of the hotel.

'Oh, I am sure you will. How long are you staying?'

'I don't know. A week, perhaps. And you?'

'About that, too. It seems almost inevitable that we shall see each other.'

I laugh. 'I like your philosophical resignation!'

She laughs too. 'Rather that than outright avoidance, not so?'

'I don't know. I'll have to think about it.'

I go to my room and power up my laptop. There's a message from James:

Tried to Skype, but you seem to be out on the town. Alfredville must have more to offer than you anticipated. Or are you off à la recherche du temps perdu? *Glad, all the same, that you arrived in one piece, albeit without a mobile. I realised that you had in some way been separated from your phone when I tried to call you, hoping to catch you before take-off. The phone was answered by someone with, at a guess, an Eastern European accent. I said, 'But what are you doing with this mobile? It belongs to my boyfriend.' He replied, 'Your boyfrenn's asshole. You perverts should be in preeson. You theenk everythink belonk to you.' So now you know.*

Yeah well … the audition. Good news and bad news. To start with the bad news, they didn't want me for Othello. Turns out the whole cast's going to be black except for Othello, who's white. Set in Harlem, black gangsters, you get the idea. Changes the symbolic logic of the play, the director explained, Richard Pryce, you remember we saw his all-male Electra at the Donmar, bit of an Islington-OxCam pretend-proletarian-poofter but solid I think. Anyway, so it turns out I'm auditioning for bloody Iago! (That's the good news.) Not that I've got the part yet by a long shot but they said they'd get back to me and looked like they meant it. Richard (I'm practising the first-name thing, just in case) is thinking ('just thinking, mind') of casting Iago as a woman to change the sym-

113

bolic logic some more, and that Andrea Wilde woman, the one who was Berenice Sadie Brown in The Member of the Wedding, was also there so it's by no means home and dry. She'd kill for the part and guess who she'd kill?

Foul weather here, everything's slushy and everybody's got a cold and the Tube is like the deepest circle of hell. So enjoy the heat. I could almost miss you, if I allowed myself – an electric blanket's just not the same as a good man.

Hope the article's coming along according to plan.

As always, James.

As always, I snort to myself. What does that mean? And I could almost miss you – what a prince of magnanimity. I consider a reply, then decide against it. Never write an e-mail after ten at night, especially on a few glasses of wine. But I wonder why he tried to call me.

CHAPTER 8

Thursday morning 21 January

On Thursday morning I sleep late. I feel as if I'm still recovering from the flight, and there doesn't seem to be any very pressing reason to get up, other than going for a run, which I for once can persuade myself I needn't do today. I go in to breakfast at five minutes to nine, to the evident displeasure of Boris, who is directing clearing-up operations. He looks at his watch as I walk in.

'Morning, Boris,' I say. 'I take it I'm still in time for breakfast? It *is* till nine o'clock, isn't it?'

He treats me to a surly nod. 'Derek, stop clearing up those tables and see what Mr Jacobs wants for breakfast,' he says to the sole waiter, who is standing before the ornate mirror against the wall, prodding his upper lip with his index finger. I hope that whatever he's examining is not contagious.

I'm tempted to order as lavish a breakfast as the menu permits, but I don't feel like eating that much, so I order toast and tea and leave by ten past nine. Which does not prevent Boris from looking at his watch again as I leave. Poncy little queen, I catch myself thinking.

Back in my room, I write James an e-mail, carefully neutral, informative.

Dear James,

Sorry to have missed you last night. I was out to dinner – a rather exhausting affair with a fellow-guest at the Queen's Hotel, one Nonyameko Mhlabeni – also, as it happens, Alfredville-born, though, in the nature of things at the time, our paths did not cross, and she travelled widely all over the world during the Struggle in the interests of liberation. She now travels widely all over the country in the interests of

115

women's mental health, that is, under-privileged women's mental health (she's a psychologist). Anyway, pleasant enough company, though with a chip on her shoulder the size of a butcher's block. Liberation has not relaxed her, and she can be a strenuous dinner companion. Humour is not her strong suit – I suspect she regards it as a bourgeois ploy to defuse the revolution. She also is clearly suspicious of me because I've disowned my native land and gone whoring after foreign gods.

Other news is that my best friend from school, a chap called Bennie Nienaber – I don't think I ever mentioned him to you – turns out to be the town's main cop. I went to see him, and he was rather constrained – it's been twenty years, after all – but he did invite me to supper with his family this evening. So, what with one thing and another, I'm having a livelier time socially in Alfredville than in Maida Vale. When last did you and I dine out two evenings running?!

But, of course, I'm not writing to sound off about Alfredville, I'm writing to say wonderful about Iago – a more interesting role anyway than that old blusterer, Othello. Okay, you say the part's not in the bag yet, but I can sense you're optimistic, and you've never been optimistic without a reason. So I'm taking this as a positive sign. But keep me informed.
As always, Peter.

As always – what *does* that mean? But that's what he said, so that's what I'll say, and hope he's interested enough to wonder about it.

I decide to have a quiet day, reading one of the books I've brought along, and making notes of all the meetings I had yesterday. Bennie, Oom Blik and Aunt Dolly, Nonyameko – even if it's not quite clear yet how they'll fit into the fabric of my story, it does seem as if they're part of the pattern. My job – not to call it a quest! – is to trace that pattern, or perhaps rather, first to establish what the pattern *is*. It's a bit of a conundrum, in fact: how to place the details of a pattern in terms of a pattern that will only emerge once the details have been placed. It's like building a jigsaw puzzle without knowing what the final picture is going to look like. Of course, I have my Othello hypothesis to guide me, but that is proving to be at best a rough guide, at worst totally misleading. Rather accumulate detail, I decide, and see whether pattern emerges from that. It seems safe to assume, at least, that Hector Williams did kill his wife; but why he should have done so remains murky, in spite of Joachim's confident theories. A key figure in his theory, and apparently also in Aunt Dolly's frettings, is Dr Henk Pretorius. I will have to scrape up an acquaintance, but how? I look at my scrawled notes, not yet transferred to the files on my computer: 'Fairy: takes walk regular as clockwork.'

What are Dr Pretorius's hours? I could phone his surgery, but decide to walk there instead; it may also be possible to find out something about the man by examining his milieu.

His surgery is further down Victoria Street, in the opposite direction to the police station, on the way to the Rietvlei Dam. The building is pleasantly unostentatious, like most of Alfredville's vernacular architecture. It used to be somebody's house, but ever since I can remember it's been a veterinary surgery; or rather, has had a surgery in front, with the vet himself, in my day Albie Wessels, living at the back. You had the comfort of knowing, if your animal spent the night in the clinic, that help was close at hand if something should go wrong.

Dr Pretorius seems to have continued this admirable practice. A quick glance down the strip running along the side of the building confirms that Henk Pretorius has followed his predecessor's example in living behind the surgery. From the street I can see a fenced-in back yard with, as far as I can see, a well-maintained garden. An elderly station wagon is parked outside the garage. Lying in the sun next to the car is a black Labrador. As I pause to check out the yard, the dog lifts its head without getting up, gives a half-hearted bark in my direction, and goes back to sleep. If crime is a problem in Alfredville, the dogs haven't been informed.

A brass plaque outside the front door informs me that the vet's morning hours are from eight thirty to ten and his afternoon hours from three thirty to five thirty. Opposite the surgery is the Country Pumpkin Café. It has a convenient veranda, or stoep as it would be called here (unless it's become a *terrace* in the meantime), from where it would be a simple matter to see the comings and goings at the surgery and, eventually, Dr Pretorius's own departure on his walk. I have little idea of how I'll accost him, but it should be possible, in a place like Alfredville, to strike up a conversation without being taken for a con man or a pervert – 'Excuse me, but do you know where the such-and-such restaurant is?' Or 'Excuse me, do you know where I could buy a newspaper at this hour?' How to proceed from there, I'll leave to my instincts to decide once I have engaged my target.

Late afternoon, Thursday
From the stoep of the Country Pumpkin, where I'm lingering over a pot of rooibos tea with *My Traitor's Heart* open in front of me, I have a clear but, I hope, inconspicuous view of Dr Pretorius's consulting rooms. It is now five thirty-five. The Country Pumpkin is showing signs of wanting to close. A waitress is wiping the tables around me with considerably more energy than she has hitherto displayed in pursuit of her duties. Inside the restaurant a vacuum cleaner is relentlessly whining. Fortunately two schoolgirls, more thick-skinned than I, are loitering over their coke floats. They are discussing some vamp-in-training called Surina who by common consent flung herself shamelessly at poor Wouter Venter at some school function. As far as I can reconstruct the event from their indignant exchange, Wouter had no choice but to take Surina to the shooting range for a smooch, or run the risk of being labelled a wimp or worse. And this after Surina had sworn eternal fealty to my two neighbours just that afternoon, without informing them of her designs on Wouter. 'I'll *kill* her,' says the more belligerent of the two, sucking at her Coke float with such indignation that it slurps angrily in sympathy.

Though I suspect Wouter may have been less of a victim than it suits my neighbours to believe, I am grateful to him for providing me with another ten minutes' cover, not long after which Dr Pretorius, if he really is the man of habit of Joachim Ferreira's account, is due to venture out on his evening walk.

The last of Dr Pretorius's patients, an elderly man with a wonky-looking Dobermann, leaves – I know it's the last, because

I've been keeping tally of the comings and goings for the last forty minutes. Joachim's account of the vet's client demographic was accurate within the margin of error permissible in gross generalisations: of the ten patients who showed up in that time, eight were women, two of them with cats, four with dogs, two of them unaccompanied by any animal at all.

I squeeze another cup of rooibos out of the pot and wait. The schoolgirls seem to have exhausted the iniquities of Surina and the tribulations of Wouter: they have twice in the last three minutes said, 'Well, she's like, gross, is all I can say,' which sounds as conclusive as this conversation can by its nature ever be. Soon I won't have their presence to draw the fire of the waitress now banging closed the shutters facing onto the stoep where we're sitting. And if I'm to be at Bennie's for supper at seven thirty, I hope Dr Pretorius is as punctual as Joachim claimed.

I'm no longer sure that this method of approaching Henk Pretorius is going to work: would it not be simpler just to tell him that I'm Desirée's cousin and I'd like to talk to him? Perhaps even tell him that I'm writing an article and need his perspective on the affair? But not knowing Henk Pretorius, I have no way of predicting how he'd react. If, indeed, he did have some romantic interest in Desirée, or vice versa, he won't appreciate what he might see as journalistic prying. And, this way, if no opportunity presents itself, I needn't engage him in conversation just yet: once I know what he looks like, I can contrive to meet him later.

At last, just as the two schoolgirls get up to leave, someone appears from behind the surgery, a man with a dog, the black Labrador of this morning, but now considerably more exuberant. The dog is not on a lead, but keeps to the man's side, evidently well trained. The two of them set off in the direction of the dam; so far then, Joachim's outline of Pretorius's habits has proved to be accurate enough.

I take my time gathering my book and my notepad; by the time I leave the Country Pumpkin (the front door is slammed none too subtly as I leave), Pretorius is about a hundred metres down the street. He walks briskly, but stops every now and then for the dog

119

to have a sniff or a pee, rendering his progress desultory and my pursuit tricky.

As part of the protocol of inconspicuous pursuit, I have to make the most of such shop windows as are on offer in Victoria Street. I find myself peering earnestly at farm implements in the Co-op, and with equal intentness at faded photographs of passé hairstyles in the window of Chez Bettie. I examine with minute attention the ragged geraniums in planters on the stoep of the municipal offices (MUNICIPALITY/MUNISIPALITEIT/UMASI-PALA: the new dispensation has made the fortune of signwriters), the plants surviving precariously in a bed of cigarette butts and sweet papers and other detritus best left unidentified. I stoop twice to retie a shoelace.

In spite of my self-imposed distractions, I catch up on Pretorius when his dog finds a particularly attractive patch of grass; he makes no effort to cut short the dog's exploration and irrigation. From his indulgence of his dog I gather that he's a patient sort of person.

I can make out more of his appearance now. He's tall, thin, loose-limbed, with a gangling walk and a slight stoop, not altogether comfortable in his own body. He's dressed plainly, not to say drably, in blue jeans and khaki shirt, with leather half-boots. I can see his face only in profile every now and then when he turns to address his dog; from this distance it seems like a bony kind of face, with a fairly prominent nose and chin. The sum is more attractive than the parts: he has the kind of rangy weatheredness that women and some men find irresistible.

As I somewhat unconvincingly scrutinise the board listing 'New Specials' in the window of the Pop-in Shop (D'lite Cooking Oil, R7.95; Brenco Lentils, R6.50), he glances back. I'm watching him in the reflection in the glass, so can see him register my presence and take in my appearance. I suppose a stranger in Alfredville is not a common occurrence – although, I remind myself, there is a moderate throughput of tourists. He resumes his walk, and I, too, saunter on: now that he's spotted me, I'm careful not to match my pace to his: it wouldn't do to give him the impression

120

that I'm stalking him. And yet at some point I must make contact; I can't very plausibly follow him all the way to the dam to ask him where to buy a newspaper. Pretorius stops again next to a small patch of grass, as if to give his dog time for an inspection. But the dog seems not particularly interested, in fact, looks up at the man, clearly impatient to get going again, but too well trained to take the lead. So why is Pretorius holding back? Presumably he wants me to pass him; but why?

I amble on, turning over my options. Do I cross the street and find a pretext to speak to Pretorius? Do I carry on and hope some pretext presents itself? But I am now in danger of leaving my quarry behind: he could at any moment turn back and leave me standing in Victoria Street. I'll have to act soon if I'm going to act at all.

I pause in front of the window of Mr Price – an uninspiring display of children's underwear that it wouldn't do to be thought to be examining too avidly. In the window I see Henk Pretorius hesitate, inspecting his dog's ear in a professional but under the circumstances unconvincing sort of way. I decide that this is the moment to declare myself, and am just about to cross the street to his side when he apparently takes a similar decision. He crosses the street a short distance ahead of me, feigning unawareness, intent only on solicitously shepherding his dog across the street – a somewhat redundant concern, as there are no cars in sight.

He is now about twenty metres ahead of me, on the same side of the street. He keeps walking steadily but quite slowly. I either have to dawdle unconvincingly in front of the closed doors of the Ghanta Grocery Store or catch him up.

Since he has now made a decisive move, it's up to me to make the next, the crucial step of starting a conversation. I decide to ask him if there is a tea room nearby that will be open at this hour. I mend my pace, intent now on catching him up. But before I can do this, Pretorius stops. He turns round and waits for me to come up to him. He is staring into the late afternoon sun and for the first time I get a full view of his face. An ordinary-looking sort of chap, Joachim called him, and it's true that there's nothing flamboyant about Dr Henk Pretorius. But there's nothing ordinary about the mobile but firmly drawn mouth, the large but delicately formed nose, the intense blue eyes, the fine dark hair, cropped short. The ladies of Alfredville have a better eye than Fairy Ferreira.

I look at him, wondering whether he's going to tell me to stuff off, as his glowering at me suggests he might well do. Better get my introduction in before he does so.

'Can you …?' I start, at the same time as he says 'Are you …?'

We both stop, each waiting for the other.

'Am I …?' I ask, just as he asks 'Can I …?'

'Tell me whether …?' I say, as he says, 'Are you following me?'

His question catches me unawares. I hadn't expected him to seize the intiative. So I decide to come to the point, albeit obliquely. 'Only in a sense,' I say.

'In what sense?' he asks, a polite enquiry rather than an interrogation.

'I want to talk to you,' I say.

'About anything in particular, or are you just lonely?' He says this very dryly, but with a dash of irony that makes me decide I like Dr Henk Pretorius, in spite of his inconvenient conversational style.

'I do in fact have something particular to talk to you about,' I say.

He raises his eyebrows. There are brown flecks in his eyes. In the sunlight the end-of-day stubble of his beard glints on his cheeks and chin.

'Look,' he says, 'I don't mean to be rude, but I don't know you from Adam. What could you possibly have to talk to me about?'

He smiles as he says it, but he's clearly quite serious; I'll have to declare my interest, or part of it, at least.

'Will it reassure you if I tell you that I'm the cousin of Desirée van Blerk?'

'Desirée? You mean Desirée Williams?'

'Yes, yes of course. I knew her as Desirée van Blerk.'

'And you want to discuss Desirée with me?'

'Yes.'

'Why?'

'Well, you see, I used to live here, but I now live in London, so I wasn't here when ... you know ...'

He nods. 'When she died, yes. But wouldn't it be better to talk to her parents, who are, I suppose, your uncle and aunt?' He has a slight stammer, possibly more a certain diffidence in speaking English than a real impediment. Though correct, his English is strongly marked by an Afrikaans accent.

'Yes, I saw them this morning in fact, and will talk to them again, but I think there are things you can tell me that they can't.'

'I can't imagine why you think that.'

I decide to take the plunge. 'I can tell you if you meet me for supper.'

He seems unfazed by this. 'Am I really interested enough in finding out?'

'I think you are,' I risk. 'Or you will be when I tell you.'

'I'll be interested in hearing what you have to say once I've heard it?'

'Yes.'

'And if I discover I'm not?'

'You'll still have scored a meal.'

He considers this for a moment. 'I suppose a meal is a meal,' he says at last. 'Where do you want to meet?'

'You know Alfredville better than I. Where would be good?'

'There isn't a hell of a lot of choice, but the R62 Diner up in the main road isn't bad.'

'Good,' I say. 'Shall we meet there tomorrow ... say at seven?'

'Make that seven thirty,' he says. 'Liquorice needs his walk.'

The dog, hearing his name, looks up and wags his tail without very much hope.

'Don't you, boy?' he says, and the dog, now more optimistic, gets to his feet and looks up at the man expectantly.

'Well,' he says, 'till tomorrow, then.'

He starts walking away, then stops. 'Oh, and by the way ...'

'Yes?'

'You haven't told me your name.'

123

'Oh, I'm sorry. It's Peter Jacobs.'

The dog takes off exuberantly and the man follows at a slower pace. I stand looking after him. After fifty paces or so he looks round and waves. I wave back. He smiles, an amused, slightly perplexed smile. Dr Henk Pretorius is a very attractive man. I can see how he might have represented a complication in the Williams marriage.

I glance at my watch. Six fifteen. I'm hot and sweaty; if I want to shower and change before going to Bennie's for dinner, I'll have to get back to the hotel.

Thursday evening

I turn up at seven thirty, as directed, at the address Bennie's given me. It's a characterless sixties house in a newer part of town – not a candidate for gentrification or anything else except inconspicuous family living: corrugated iron roof, small stoep in front, steel-framed windows, Venetian blinds. Without having been inside I know what it will look like: three or perhaps four bedrooms separated by a passage, bathroom at the back, sitting room and dining room on either side of an entrance porch, kitchen behind the dining room, a bog-standard box divided into smaller bog-standard boxes. The gate has an old-fashioned sprung metal latch. I press back the wrought-iron catch. The gate swings freely on its wire hinges; it's recently been oiled. The garden is tidy and, by the standards of perennially drought-stricken Alfredville, lush. There are two peach trees, an orange tree, a patch of lawn with a small paddling pool; a border of agapanthus, over their best, running to seed. The outside light next to the front door is burning, insects circling it. The door has oblong frosted glass panes.

When I knock, a dog starts barking. The front door is opened by a woman whom I take to be Chrisna, with a wire-haired mongrel by her side. 'Okay, enough, Kerneels,' she says, patting the dog. He stops barking and sniffs at my shoes. 'Peter,' she says, extending her hand. She does not smile, but her voice has a certain warmth to it.

124

'Hello, Chrisna,' I say, shaking her hand; her handshake is as firm as a man's. In the thin electric light she seems pale, but her figure is compact and strong. Her features are emphatic: dark, slightly protuberant eyes, a nose that would have been too big had her mouth been less generously proportioned, a chin that holds its own more than adequately in the ensemble. Her hair is dark, tied back behind her head, not quite a ponytail, not quite a bun, and certainly not a chignon, a practical arrangement rather than a decoration. She's wearing a simple cotton dress, pale yellow, and flat shoes. A dutiful wife, uncomplaining, starting to show the strain of making do, scraping and saving to live decently on a policeman's salary.

'Come in. You won't remember me,' she says as she shows me in, switching off the outside light. A statement of fact, not a question. 'I was in standard six when you were in matric. But I remember you – the matric boys were our main topic of conversation in those days. And you were Bennie's best friend. I had a crush on him even then.' She talks fluently, possibly with a light pressure of nervousness. But her manner is completely natural, with nothing of the anxious hostess about it.

'And when did Bennie start noticing?' I ask half-jokingly, wanting only to relieve some of the tension.

She pauses in the hallway. 'Oh, only when he came back here,' she says, giving my question the serious consideration it neither deserves nor desires. 'I'd left school by then, and was working as a typist at the Co-op. I was very grateful to be delivered from that.' Her voice is low, a pleasing contralto, her delivery factual and emphatic.

She leads me to the sitting room, a tidy, unimaginative room, without much style, but also without the extremes of bad taste that I remember as the norm in Alfredville, everything, my mother used to say, looking like a prize from the tombola stall at the church bazaar. Here there are curtains instead of Venetian blinds, and an undistinguished kilim rug. The furniture is heavy, upright, more substantial than comfortable.

An old lady is sitting under a lamp, embroidering something

125

that looks like a large pillowcase or even, conceivably, a small shroud. She looks up over her glasses when we come in. 'You may remember my mother,' Chrisna says.

'Yes, I do. Mrs Rabie,' I say, pleased that Bennie has prepared me for this meeting. I do in fact remember Mrs Rabie more clearly than I anticipated. Her features have lost none of their point with age: the mouth still pursed as if in disapprobation, the eyes, in spite of the glasses, still peering accusingly. Despite the heat, she is wearing a jersey, a shapeless light-blue cardigan. I walk up to the old woman and extend my hand.

'I can't shake your hand,' she says. 'I'm working.'

'Mother is a great embroiderer,' Chrisna explains, not quite in apology, I think – in extenuation, perhaps. 'Have a seat. I'll call Bennie, he's reading the children a story.'

I sit down. The chair turns out to be even more uncomfortable than it looks. Kerneels leaps onto the sofa and starts licking himself. 'Sies, Kerneels,' Mrs Rabie says, but carries on embroidering. We sit in silence for a minute or two; I can't think of any topic of conversation that might engage the fierce-looking old woman. She's moving her lips as if counting stitches.

I use the opportunity to inspect the sitting room more closely. On a small bookshelf across from me, I recognise the spines of *Othello* and *The Great Gatsby*, our matric setworks. There is also, I notice with mild shock, my copy of *The Catcher in the Rye*, which I'd lent Bennie just weeks before our ways parted, and a copy of *The Outsider*, which I'd always nagged him to read – 'Preten-*shus*!' he'd mocked me. 'Who wants to read about some French psycho shooting a guy because his mother dies?' For the rest, the books are standard South African fare: some love stories, some André Brink, regarded as risqué in our youth, probably Chrisna's contribution to the family's literary holdings. On top of the bookshelf is a small music centre, with some CDs stacked next to it. On the pretext of looking at the painting on the wall above it, an uninspired watercolour of what I identify as Something-or-other-poort, I scan the titles of the CDs. Mainly Afrikaans music, some of which I vaguely recall from parties at the home of Alta Basson, one of our 'artier' classmates: Laurika Rauch, Koos du Plessis, and some names that are foreign to me, names that seem to have been chosen for their gauche folksiness: Valiant Swart, Koos Kombuis. Incongruously, there are 'Favourite Strauss Waltzes' and 'Opera 2007'; and, on its own in a double-CD set, the Bach Cello Suites – the reissue of the Casals recording.

Then, abruptly, Mrs Rabie says, 'Benjamin says you're from overseas.'

'Yes,' I say. 'England.'

'It's all one to me, those countries,' she says. 'Full of foreigners, I'm sure.'

'Well, yes, that's true,' I concede.

'Lots of foreigners are coming here now,' she continues. 'From Germany and Holland and Johannesburg. They're buying up all the houses and kicking out our people.'

'But I suppose they're paying the people that they're kicking out,' I suggest.

'You suppose, do you?' she asks, looking at me as if I've made an indecent suggestion. 'And what makes you suppose so?'

'Well, it's normal for the buyer of a house to pay the seller, I suppose.'

She fixes me with her blue glare. 'You suppose a lot. Are you here to buy a house?' she asks.

'No, absolutely not.' Her tone, as if suspecting me of an intention to molest children or trade in baby seal fur, compels me to exonerate myself. 'I've got a flat in London.'

'A *flat*?' she asks with infinite contempt. 'Who wants to live in a flat?'

'Actually, most people do, in London.'

'Yes, in London, of course. Like in Hillbrow. But I'm talking about white people.'

I'm saved the indignity of a reply by Bennie's entrance. He's changed out of his uniform into a short-sleeved khaki shirt and khaki shorts with flip-flops. He seems to be in good shape – no incipient paunch or double chin – though there is the same disconcerting deadness to his eyes that I noticed this morning.

He looks critically at my chinos and white shirt. 'I should have told you it's quite informal,' he says.

'This *is* informal where I come from,' I rejoin, and immediately regret what could be seen as an invidious comparison between London and Alfredville. 'I mean we don't have this kind of heat,' I try to cover up.

But if he's offended, he doesn't show it, just offers me a drink. I ask for a glass of red wine and he produces and opens a bottle of Ghanta Pinotage. The business of pouring drinks and establishing that Mrs Rabie disapproves of liquor but will have a glass of sweet sherry 'not to be rude' (the old woman has never before shown any disinclination to be rude, I should think) occupies us till Chrisna comes in with the children and introduces them to me. The little girl, named Lettie after her grandmother, looks eerily like her redoubtable namesake: she has the old lady's piercing blue eyes and determined chin; she even has the formidable frown. In due course she may develop the temper to match the features, but for the time being she lacks the authority to enforce her temperament. The little boy, Kosie, seems shy, which is surprising: Bennie was never shy, and Chrisna seems perfectly self-assured.

Chrisna has come to announce supper. We take our glasses, Bennie carrying the bottle, and follow Chrisna to the dining room, as tidy and featureless as the sitting room, except for a large antique sideboard, presumably an heirloom. Over it hangs a reproduction of a Canaletto. What aesthetic or sentimental aspiration could have suggested to Chrisna or conceivably her mother that Venetian canals belong in Alfredville?

The conversation at dinner is mainly a question-and-answer session between me and Chrisna, with her asking most of the questions. Bennie looks on, never supplementing her questions or following up on my replies. Mrs Rabie interjects something bad-tempered from time to time. The children are quiet; Lettie nudges her brother now and again when she finds something to criticise in his behaviour, corrections which he seems to suffer with equanimity.

128

Chrisna's questions are predictable – where I live, what I do for a living, how I find being back – and I give bland, non-controversial answers: I live in London, write for a living – she doesn't ask me what – being back is interesting, though I haven't really had time to form a more definite impression.

Then comes a question I did not expect: 'You were Desirée's cousin, weren't you?'

'Why, yes. How did you know?'

'Desirée was my best friend. At school she used to boast about her clever cousin Peter.'

'How odd. I wouldn't have thought she'd spare me a second thought.'

'Maybe you didn't spare her a second thought.'

'Not so,' I object. 'I was quite proud of my pretty cousin.'

'Yes, she was very pretty, wasn't she,' Chrisna says matter-of-factly. 'And she became more beautiful as she grew up. I take it you are here to see her parents? Have you seen them?'

'Yes,' I reply, pleased to be able to conform to expectations in this respect. 'Yes, I saw them today.'

'And how did you find them?'

'As is to be expected – pretty much devastated.'

Chrisna nods. 'Yes, it's not easy. Your Aunt Dolly took it very hard, and Oom Blik – well, he's very angry.'

'Of course,' I say. 'Losing a daughter …'

'Yes, but it's as if he's angry not so much about losing his daughter as about … well, the whole system that he thinks made it possible for Desirée to be murdered.'

'You might as well say, Chrisna,' Bennie cuts in, 'that he's pissed off with the whole police force.'

'Watch your language in front of the children, Benjamin,' Mrs Rabie says.

'Well, the fact that Hector was in the police …' Chrisna says, 'but that's only a part of it, to him it's the whole set-up … You know that he was voted out as mayor of the town just before the murder? But he may have told you all about it.'

'Not in detail,' I say. 'I didn't really want to pry.'

129

'It's all part of a plot to wipe out the white people,' contributes Mrs Rabie.

Chrisna has been casting curious glances at me from time to time. She notices me noticing, and blushes lightly.

'I'm sorry,' she says. 'you must think I'm rude. It's just ...' and she hesitates.

'Just ...?' I encourage her.

She blushes more deeply. 'I hope you don't mind my saying so, but it's really remarkable, how much you look like your cousin.'

'My cousin? Boetie?' I ask, disingenuously.

'Oh no, please.' Her distress suggests that I wasn't wrong about Boetie: he's not grown up into someone one would want to look like. 'No, I mean Desirée.'

After Aunt Dolly's remark, this comes as less of a surprise than Chrisna may think, but it still leaves me at a loss for a reply, and Chrisna becomes almost flustered in covering up what she now imagines may have been a faux pas. 'I don't mean ...' she says, 'I mean, making allowances of course for the differences between a man and a woman, you really do look almost uncannily alike.' As I still say nothing – what, after all, can I say? – she turns, I think almost in desperation, to her husband. 'Don't you think so, Bennie? Don't you think Peter looks just like Desirée?'

Bennie looks up from his plate, pretends to be studying my face – it's the longest he's looked at me since our meeting this morning – then says in an unhurried, emphatic way, as if pronouncing on the prospects of rain, 'No, Chrisna, I can't see any resemblance.'

Unexpectedly, Ma Rabies chips in: 'Then you must have your eyes examined, Benjamin. Anyone can see he looks just like that cousin of his. I saw it the moment he walked in.'

That may explain her rudeness to me, in so far as rudeness coming from Mrs Rabie requires explanation. No doubt she was among the townspeople who deplored Desirée's marriage.

Bennie glances at me. 'Well, there you have it, mother and daughter agree you look just like your cousin. Perhaps it's something only women can see.'

130

Lettie nudges Kosie and whispers something, and they both giggle.

'Lettie!' Chrisna says. 'Don't whisper at table!'

'I was just saying that I agree with you and Ouma, Mommy,' the child says in an ingratiating whine that I find irrationally irritating.

'As I said,' Bennie says, in an evident attempt at jocularity. 'What say you, Kosie? Are you at least taking sides with the men?'

Kosie blushes and nods, but doesn't say anything.

'We'll take that for a yes,' Bennie says, his tone becoming gentle, 'then we have a three-all draw.'

The meal is a simple affair of macaroni cheese and salad; I take it that the family follows the country habit of having their main meal at midday. Dessert is preserved quinces and custard. Lettie announces that quinces are sour and she doesn't like them; her mother patiently tells her that she needn't eat them if she doesn't like them. She accepts a helping nevertheless and finishes it before the rest of us.

After the meal, Chrisna excuses herself to get the children to bed. 'Will Daddy come and say good-night?' Kosie asks, his first audible contribution to the evening.

'Yes, boy,' says Bennie, 'but I have to go and check on something at the station first.'

'Will you be long?' asks Chrisna.

'Half an hour,' he says.

'Not longer,' she says. 'It's past their bedtime. And tomorrow's school.' Then she looks at me. 'That doesn't mean you have to go,' she says apologetically. 'I won't be long. Or maybe you can walk with Bennie to the station and then come back for another glass of wine.' She points at the bottle, but it's empty: Bennie has been drinking quickly, and I suppose I have, too.

'Is it time for the news yet, Chrisna?' Mrs Rabie interjects. 'I don't want to miss the news again.'

'Not yet, Ma,' Chrisna says. 'Not for another half an hour.'

'Thanks,' I say. 'But it's time for me to be off.' It's clear that my

131

presence is disturbing the family routines; and in any case, I don't fancy another tête à tête with Mrs Rabies.

'I'll walk with you,' Bennie says. 'Hang on while I put on some shoes.'

'Take Kerneels with you,' Chrisna says.

The evening has cooled down and the streets of Alfredville are grudgingly surrendering the heat they have built up all day. By midnight it will be almost cold, and then at six o'clock start heating up again, in the exhausting cycle of summer in the Little Karoo. We walk in silence for a minute or two, Kerneels happily running ahead and pausing whenever he comes across an interesting smell.

'You have a nice family,' I say after a while.

'Yes,' he says non-committally, and then, with a trace of his old irony, 'especially my mother-in-law.'

'Well,' I shrug, 'mothers-in-law ...'

But he won't let me off with a generalisation.

'She's had a hard life. Her husband ...' he trails off.

'What about her husband?'

'You may remember him. Albert Rabie, one of the church elders, had a face like a bad-tempered boot.'

'Yes, I do remember him vaguely. Very pious and proper.'

'Yes, that's him. Real prick. So anyway, the old hypocrite would go home from church and beat up his wife and children on the slightest pretext, just for the hell of it. Chrisna still has a scar on her head from when he slammed her against the kitchen cupboard.'

'Hell, Bennie, I had no idea.'

'No, of course you didn't,' he says drily. 'You didn't have much of an idea of anything.'

'Fuck you, Bennie,' I protest. 'You're not still playing the more-miserable-than-you game, are you?'

'I'm not playing any fucking games. I'm just telling it like it is.'

'Well, then, keep me and my presumed inexperience out of it. You have no idea, either, of what I know or don't know.'

132

'I don't suppose I do,' he says, but not very repentantly. 'So inform me. Do *you* have a mother-in-law?'

His question is more satirical than interrogative, but I decide to play it straight. Yes, I could say, I have a common-law mother-in-law; her name's Sadie Burke and she's Jamaican and a fundamentalist Christian and she's married to an Englishman called Colin and I'm living, or was until recently, with their son called James. Instead I say, 'No, I don't have a wife.'

'Oh,' he says. 'Why didn't you say so?'

'When was I supposed to say so?' I ask.

'When Chrisna asked you all those questions.'

'She didn't ask me that one, did she?'

'Do you always wait to have your arse licked before you volunteer information?'

'Well, I generally assume that people will ask what they want to know.'

'I didn't ask you.'

'You didn't ask me anything. Did you want to know?'

'Sure. In a general sort of way. To know where you're at.'

'Are you interested?'

He stops. 'Look, you want me to say I'm fucking fascinated with your private life. Well, I'm not, but, as I say, in a general sort of way, when you're talking to a bugger it helps to know where he's coming from.'

Where you're at, where he's coming from ... the clichés of our youth clot the air between us; they've lost the slangy ease of youth, now seem forced, inappropriate. Or perhaps it's just that I've moved off and moved on: I'm no longer *coming from* where I used to. But it's the most Bennie has said to me all day – and it's a relief to hear him lapsing into his old expletive-riddled style.

'Okay,' I say, as he resumes walking, 'that's where I'm at. Not married. No children. No dog, even.'

He smiles for the first time. 'You should at least get a dog.'

'Yes, I know, but it's difficult in London. You can't let a dog run free like here.'

'Oh, Kerneels doesn't run free, he checks on me all the time,

133

except when he's checking on Chrisna. He's her dog, really. Not so, Kerneels?' he says more loudly, and the dog looks back and wags his tail.

'Then he has the best of freedom and of domestication,' I say. 'Connection without restriction.'

'You could say that,' he says. 'He used to be a bit of a wanderer, but Chrisna had him neutered.'

'Oh,' I say. 'Perhaps not exactly the kind of freedom one wants.'

'Yeah, or the kind of domestication,' he says. If he's joking, his face doesn't register it.

'I suppose not,' I say. He doesn't reply and after a while I ask, 'And your brothers?'

'What about them?'

'Where are they now?'

'If you really want to know, they're all fuck-ups, although each one in his own way.'

'That's a bugger.'

'You can say that again. Petrus, the eldest, went to the army, joined the permanent force, and was shot on the border.'

'Not so much a fuck-up as a misfortune, I'd have said.'

'Yes, luckily that's what most people think. He was even given a military funeral. But he was shot by a friend in an argument over a zoll.'

'Oh dear.'

'You can say that again. And then the two youngest – Errol is in some kind of clinic for drug addicts, and Victor got his girl-friend pregnant and got married, then had an affair with his sister-in-law and was kicked out by his wife. I hear from him whenever he needs money.'

'Shit, Bennie, what a string of tragedies.'

'No, not tragedies. Just a mess. We're just one huge steaming mess of a family.'

'You're not a mess.'

'I've got a job and a family, you mean. Yes, it's better than the drug clinic. But I sometimes think I'm the biggest fuck-up of them all. At least the others don't hide the fact that they're a mess.'

134

'And you hide … what?'

'If I told you, I wouldn't be hiding it, would I?'

'Don't you think you could tell me?'

'Why? Because we were friends twenty years ago?'

'Yes, and partly also exactly because I'm not part of your story.'

'If I told you, I'd be making you part of my story. Forget it, I'm not going to spill my guts to you.'

We're in Victoria Street by now, walking past the house where I grew up and where Bennie visited me almost every day. It seems unnatural not to comment, and yet it's awkward to say something without seeming to reminisce.

'Our old house seems to be standing empty,' I say, slowing down.

He stops. 'You do know, don't you …?' he asks.

'That that's where Hector and Desirée lived? Yes, I know. I was just wondering what's happening to it now.'

'Well, technically Hector still lives there. But it was her house, really.'

'Yes, I know her father bought it from my parents when they moved away.'

'Yes, so it's quite complicated,' he says. 'The house was in Desirée's name. Normally Hector would inherit it, but if he's found guilty then he can't inherit, and it will pass back to her parents. But in the meantime nobody knows who it belongs to.'

'The garden seems cared for.'

'Yes, I get the gardener from the police station to come here. He used to do the garden anyway, when Hector was station commander.'

We start walking again. 'Were you … close to Hector?'

'Do you mean were we friends? Not really, but we got on okay. He was a nice enough guy, and a good cop.'

'And Desirée?'

'What about her?'

'Did you know her well?'

He looks at me as if gauging the reach of my question. 'Well

135

enough,' he says. 'She was Chrisna's best friend, as you heard. She visited us now and again.'

'With Hector?'

'No, he never came along, as far as I remember. Hang on, he may have come to supper once, soon after they got married. A kind of goodwill visit.'

'And did you visit them?'

'Now and again. From time to time. The house is close to the police station, so I sometimes dropped in with a message for Hector, or whatever, and had a cup of tea or coffee.'

He looks at me quizzically, a look I remember from twenty years ago; it's half-way between a challenge and an appeal. 'So why all the questions?' he asks.

'Well, she was my cousin, after all.'

'So is that why you're here?' he asks abruptly, without looking at me.

'Because she was my cousin? No,' I prevaricate.

'Then why exactly are you here?'

I take a deep breath. It seems monstrous to lie to Bennie, and yet I know from experience that people clam up when they realise I'm a journalist – those, at any rate, who don't start spilling their guts incontinently, and Bennie's not one of those. So I sidestep the question. 'It's a long story.'

'Give me a summary. You were always good at précis.'

'I think I'd rather tell you when we have time for more than a précis.'

We have reached the police station, where Kerneels is waiting for us. Bennie stops, his hand leaning on the iron balustrade of the little staircase. He doesn't answer immediately, apparently distracted by a motorbike snarling past, the only traffic in Victoria Street at this hour. Then he turns to me. 'Okay,' he says. 'When we have time. As we used to have.'

For a moment we look at each other, the past before us as an issue, a *discussible* issue, and to that extent a relief from the oppressive politeness that has somehow seemed an element of the stifling heat of the evening. 'Look,' I say, 'how about a drink when you've done here? At the Ladies' Bar of the Queen's,' I add with a smile, but he doesn't pick up the allusion.

'No go,' he says. 'You heard, I have to get back to the children.'

He puts out his hand; I shake it, though with a disconcerting sense of being fobbed off. He has retreated into politeness. Bennie was never polite. 'Cheers,' he says, and goes into the police station. Like a small lion, Kerneels lies down on the steps.

Going back to my room, I check my e-mail. There's a message from James.

Hey Peter,

Tried Skyping three times, but you're never there. Your home town seems to have pressed you to its bosom with a vengeance, what with old friends and new acquaintances. Beware the embrace of the past – it's a nostalgia trap, SpiderWoman and vampire all in one. As for the new acquaintance – beware politicised women, they're forever trying to form alliances with gay men. I was once dragooned into joining the Islington Women's Anti-Discrimination Cooperative. Being black AND gay, I was their posterboy for a while, but they lost interest when they discovered I'd been to Winchester and Cambridge, and that I actually Slept With The Enemy. (I'm not sure what they thought gay men did.)

Guess what? Yes, of course you've guessed it – I got the part! Yes, the Iago part.

Andrea got the Emilia part, which both of us had to pretend to be pleased about, since she'd obviously rather have had the female Iago, and I'd obviously rather not have had her breathing resentfully down my neck – I mean, after all, Emilia and Iago are supposed to be married, even though it's hardly a marriage made in heaven. But then, we'll fake it, we're actors aren't we?

Othello is to be Preston Gubbins, a fine figure of a man, but queer as a coot and as predatory as a ferret (what is a coot, by the way?); he gave me a very assessing sort of look, so I may have to watch my back. Between Emilia with her dagger out for me and Preston with … well, with a possible interest in me, my Iago may be an uncommonly pussy-footing sort of fellow.

Off to rehearsals, in my galoshes and three layers of overcoat. Spare me a thought as you disport yourself in the African sun.
  As ever,
  James.

I consider replying, but decide against it. If James thinks I'm having a grand old time of it in Alfredville, I am not compelled to correct him. I turn off my laptop and get into bed, making sure the mosquito net is securely tied up and tucked in.

CHAPTER 9

Friday morning 22 January

After my early-morning run and breakfast, I go looking for Joachim, as I will have to learn to call him, at the reception desk. Not relishing another interview with Boris, I'm relieved to find that the desk is now in charge of what I assume to be the regular receptionist returned from her holiday in Margate. This theory is lent plausibility by her tan, which is almost ferocious in its intensity, and is generously displayed by a turquoise halter top that may also, in its skimpiness, be a souvenir of Margate.

As I approach, the receptionist looks up at me and smiles, rather more hospitably than Boris ever managed or attempted. There's something to be said for the professional touch.

'You must be the gentleman in twenty-three,' she says, taking me in with one swift, practised scan. 'Mr Jacobs?'

'I am.'

'Welcome to the Queen's,' she says. 'I hope everything is to your satisfaction. I'm so sorry I wasn't here to welcome you personally.' Like all successful members of the hospitality industry, she manages to infuse the tired formulae of her trade with an air of sincerity; she really does seem if not inconsolable then at any rate gravely disappointed at not having overseen my arrival.

'Oh, everything's fine, thanks,' I say. I feel it incumbent upon me to console her. 'Boris sorted me out.'

'Well, that's fabb-elous then,' she says, her tone implying several degrees of reservation. 'But don't hesitate to ask if I can assist you in any way whatsoever.'

'Thank you, Miss …?'

'Mrs. Mrs Pakendorff. But call me Joy.'

Joy. Through several coats of make-up and a layer of middle-aged emollescence I recognise the lineaments of the Joy Duvenhage of my youth and of Bennie's youthful fantasies. The manner, too, now seems familiar, though here, too, an overlay of gentility has partly obscured what used to be a rather more forthright approach.

It's clear from Joy's demeanour that she doesn't recognise me – why should she, after all? I was an anonymous schoolboy who didn't make it with her twenty years ago, and she was the local hooker – though I gather that she has in the meantime acquired a degree of respectability along with a husband, unless Mr Pakendorff is as much of a prosthesis as I imagine the lavish bosom to be.

'Thanks, Joy,' I manage to say. 'I was actually looking for Joachim.'

'He and Boris went off *somewhere*,' she says, with a simper that doesn't really become her. 'Is there anything I can help with?'

Since all I'd really had in mind was to elicit, as inconspicuously as possible, Joachim's version of the recent events in town, I can't come up with a certifiable need. It occurs to me, however, that Joy is as likely as anybody to possess a version of these events, and that it might be worth my while to tap into that – even at the risk of having my motives misinterpreted.

'Not really,' I accordingly say. 'I was really just hoping to catch up on some local news. I used to live here a long time ago.'

'Oh?' she says, and a certain caution edges into her tone. 'How long a time ago?'

'More than twenty years,' I say. She seems on the point of following up on this, so I quickly continue. 'I've really lost all touch with the town. Have you lived here long?'

'Long enough,' she says non-committally. 'My late husband was the town clerk.' She dabs away an imaginary tear.

Casting my mind back, I manage to dredge up a memory of Mr Pakendorff, known locally as Pink Pakendorff, a small emaciated man the colour of a boiled shrimp. As a guarantor of respectability, he was an admirable choice, though it's difficult

140

to think of any other respect in which he would have been a suitable match for Joy. One can only hope that he expired in a transport of delight rather than from the rigours of matrimonial duty.

I make a polite, vaguely condoling noise. 'How sad for you,' I say. 'I'm afraid I never knew your husband.'

'He was a good man,' she says, a trifle too automatically. Then she asks, a sudden sharpness of tone suggesting that she has left behind nothing of her acuity in her ascent to respectability, 'What kind of local news were you hoping to catch up on?'

'Oh, anything really. I'm so out of touch that I wouldn't even know where to start.'

She smiles abruptly, an alarming display of very large very white teeth. The late Mr Pakendorff seems to have had a good medical scheme. 'Well, for local news you can do worse than start with me,' she says. 'I tell you, most things that happen in this town end up at the Queen's Hotel eventually – those that don't start here in the first place,' and she laughs raucously, before recalling herself and resuming her receptionist's air.

'That sounds promising,' I say. 'Perhaps I should buy you a drink sometime after work.'

She purses her lips in a show of hesitation. 'I don't normally socialise with the guests,' she says, 'but since you're an Alfredville boy I'll make an exception. Why don't you meet me in the bar this evening?'

'I'd like that,' I say, and then remember my appointment with Henk Pretorius. 'But I have a dinner appointment first. Can we make it after dinner?'

This time her hesitation is genuine. I guess that she had bargained on a free dinner. Then she relents, 'Well,' she says, 'I'm a girl of early habits, so long as it's not *too* late ...'

'Would nine thirty be too late?'

'Normally it would be, but since tonight's Friday night I'll make an exception,' she says graciously.

'I'll look forward to that,' I say. In truth I am rather apprehensive. Joy's new-found primness is about as authentic as the red-gold splendour of her hair. Though modesty compels me to reflect that I may not be quite the tender young morsel I was twenty-two years ago, I am not reassured by the smile that Joy bestows upon me as I leave. I think the word is *vulpine*.

Friday, too, I spend reading and transcribing my notes. So far my investigations, if they can be called that, have yielded few surprises, other than the unexpected figure of Dr Henk Pretorius, and, to a lesser extent, Cassie Carstens. As an object of jealousy, either or both will do, though my writer's instinct inclines to Dr Pretorius as the more interesting option. Desirée had all her life before Williams to flirt with Cassie Carstens: why should she all of a sudden after her marriage find him irresistible? Whereas Henk Pretorius was a new face, a fresh perspective: much more likely to appeal to a bored wife. Apart from anything else, though, Pretorius promises to be a pleasant dinner companion, which in Alfredville is an amenity to be cherished – as Desirée herself may have discovered.

Friday evening
The R62 Diner turns out to be a bit less utilitarian than its name suggests. The diner theme is admittedly applied rather heavy-handedly, with chrome and formica in unlikely places, but the menu, which is stuck diner-style into a holder on the table, does offer slow-food alternatives to the Ghanta-burger and the mushroom-and-marshmallow salad.

Henk Pretorius hasn't arrived yet. The only other people in the diner are a group of Dutch people who piled out of a Kombi and are unselfconsciously discussing their bathroom needs, which the single bathroom, apparently, is unable to satisfy promptly enough to avert catastrophe.

Henk arrives before the crisis is resolved in one way or another, and I am fated never to discover its outcome. He apologises for being late – 'Liquorice was chasing a mole, he wouldn't give up' – and sits down. In spite of the dog's delinquency, Henk has clearly

142

had time to shower and change: I can smell Radox, and his shirt is fresh from the wardrobe.

'Have you decided what to eat?' he asks, taking the menu I'd left on the table in front of me.

'I was hoping you could make a recommendation,' I say. 'As an inhabitant of these parts.'

He looks up from the menu, over the reading glasses he's taken out of his shirt pocket. 'Well, it depends on whether you eat tripe, because that's probably their best dish. But I know it's an acquired taste.'

I grimace. 'No, sorry. Some tastes you never acquire.'

'Try the lamb curry then. Good Karoo lamb. Malay curry, not too hot.'

'I'll go with that,' I say. The waiter appears, an awkwardly tall but friendly young man with dreadlocks and home-made sandals, and we order our food, along with a bottle of the by now familiar Ghanta Pinotage. 'Good choice,' our waiter beams patronisingly, and I feel absurdly pleased, though I know he would probably have said the same whatever I'd ordered.

As the waiter lopes off, an awkward silence settles on us for a moment, broken only by an animated Dutch discussion of the shortcomings of the Diner's plumbing. I decide to jump in right away. 'You must think this very strange,' I say, 'my wanting to talk to you about Desirée.'

'Not necessarily. You were her cousin. I take it you were told that we saw a fair deal of each other. You may think I know something about the circumstances of her death. That's understandable.'

The man is almost too accommodating, too bland. A bit of resistance might have generated some energy. 'I'm glad you find it so,' I say, not quite sure how to proceed from here.

Fortunately he now demurs. 'I do, up to a point. But what I don't altogether understand is why Desirée never mentioned you, if you were close enough to her to come out here now.'

So the man is not that gullible after all. 'Of course, I can't speak for Desirée,' I say. 'Actually, we'd lost touch ever since her mar-

143

riage; but I remained interested in her, and I was kept informed by my mother, who in her turn was kept informed by my Aunt Dolly, whom you may have met.'

He nods. 'Yes, I have – though not, in fact, through Desirée, but through Socks.'

'Socks?'

'The family cat. I thought you might have met her, she's such an institution in the family.'

'Ah, yes. I have actually met her, but I wasn't formally introduced.'

'She's quite a cat. You should get to know her.'

'I'll do that. In the meantime, I suppose I'm interested in whether Desirée was, well, happy in her marriage.'

'Yes,' he says pensively. 'But why?'

'But why what?'

'Why should you be interested in whether she was happy in her marriage?'

So he is not so bland after all. I calculate rapidly. It's very unlikely that he will have heard of the nature of my business in Alfredville – I've told nobody but Nonyameko – but he'll still want an answer to his question, and something tells me that generalised vagueness isn't going to do it for him. Henk Pretorius seems like the kind of person who would value openness and by the same token resent duplicity. This may be the time for honesty.

'Look,' I say, 'I don't really want all of Alfredville to know this, but, well, I'm a freelance journalist, and I'm writing an article on Desirée's death, more the political implications, what it means in terms of the new dispensation, that kind of thing.'

'And you think I may help you to work out the political implications?'

'Well, yes, that is … you see, although I'm trying to avoid a kind of human-interest story, the personalities of the people involved do sort of become relevant …'

'As they tend to do,' he interjects.

'As they tend to do, of course. And with Desirée – well, it's

144

quite difficult to find out what kind of person she was, and how this relates to her death.'

He smiles wryly. 'And you think I might be a willing source of information?'

'Well, I was hoping, yes, that you'd be prepared to talk to me about your impressions of Desirée.'

He plays absent-mindedly with the menu. Then he says, 'I don't suppose it can do any harm any more, as long as you don't name me as your source.'

'I won't if you don't want me to.'

'I don't. Alfredville is suspicious of outsiders, and would regard me as a traitor within the gates for talking to you.'

'I actually grew up here, if that's an extenuating circumstance.'

'I'm not sure. It might even be an aggravating circumstance – you chose to leave, you see.'

I hold up my hands. 'Right, I confess. I have sinned against heaven and am no longer worthy to be called a son of Alfredville.'

'And you want me to kill the fatted calf for you?'

'Please, I didn't mean for you take the parable that far.'

'Okay, then I won't fall upon your neck and kiss you either.'

'I can see you also grew up in the Dutch Reformed Church. All those Bible stories.'

'Yes, I was a star in Sunday school.'

'So was I. It's my only party trick in London, amazing the company with my knowledge of the Bible. They, of course, don't know the Old Testament from the Old Vic.'

We sit for a moment pondering our patrimony. Then he says, 'You've probably heard all sorts of gossip, including the suspicion that Desirée and I were, let's say, more than friends.'

'I must admit I have heard that, yes.'

'Then you must also have heard various other,' he clears his throat, '*brokkies*...?'

'Gobbets?'

'Yes, thanks, gobbets of gossip suggesting that Desirée was not exactly faithful to Hector.'

145

'I have, indeed.'

The waiter appears at our table brandishing the Pinotage for our approval. We go through the ritual of watching while he somewhat inexpertly opens it, then tasting it, and once again approving it, then waiting as he fills our glasses with painstaking care. By the time he's done I'm ready to tell him to shove off, but his bumbling inexpertise has something appealing about it, and I manage to thank him warmly enough to earn a 'You're welcome.'

'You were going to say …?' I prompt Henk Pretorius, though not in fact sure that he was going to say anything.

He takes a sip of the wine. 'Hell, this Pinotage can be rough on an empty stomach.' He pauses, and I wonder if I should prompt him again, but before I can do so, he continues, 'I think I was going to say don't believe everything you hear.'

'No, not everything. But how much?'

'How much can you believe?' He looks up from his glass. He's taken off his reading glasses and his regard is sharp, penetrating. 'Well, if you are told that Desirée Williams was quite a lonely woman, you can believe that.'

'But she used to be so sociable,' I risk.

He nods. 'She was. But after her marriage she was shunned by the good people of Alfredville, who don't really approve of unconventional behaviour.'

'You mean her marrying Hector.'

'Mainly that. But marrying Hector, well, that was just part of a general attitude, if you know what I mean, that pissed the people off, a kind of outsider attitude.'

'But Desirée was hardly an outsider,' I say. 'She grew up here.'

'Yes, she did, but when she came back from university she didn't really hide the fact that she was bored with Alfredville.'

'Why didn't she leave?'

'Yes, why not? At first, I think, it was a question of money: she was saving up to go overseas, and while she was staying with her parents she could save most of her salary. And then she met Hector, and he was everything that Alfredville was not.'

146

'Such as?'

'Well, he'd been a freedom fighter, he'd lived in London and Moscow and Prague, he could speak five languages and tell her marvellous stories about his experiences. So she fell in love.'

'And why did he fall in love with her?'

He looks at me, evidently considering his reply. Then he says, 'I'm not so sure that Hector Williams was in love with Desirée. Or let's say that he was attracted to Desirée less for who she was than for what she represented.'

'And what was that?'

'Well, think for yourself. She was a beautiful woman, she was the mayor's daughter ...' He pauses, twirling his glass.

'And she was white, is that what you mean?'

He makes a face, half humorous, half impatient. 'I don't know if that is what I mean. Why should somebody who spent ten years of his life fighting the white rulers of his country marry a woman because she's white?'

'Perhaps,' I suggest, 'marrying her was part of the spoils of war. It's an old enough tale: the victor gets to marry the daughter of the conquered chieftain.'

'Well, I suppose that's possible, even if Hector himself didn't really understand why he did it.' He looks at me quizzically. 'So you never met Hector yourself?'

'No. As I say, I lost contact with Desirée after her marriage.'

'Yes. Well, Hector is a very intelligent man, but he acts on instinct. His feelings always seemed quite close to the surface. I'm not saying they were superficial, just that if he felt something strongly, he'd blow up. He said what he thought, he wasn't scared at all, but I couldn't help thinking that all that confidence covered up a basic insecurity. I suppose I'm saying that he was – *is* a man who does not know himself very well.'

'You're sketching the profile of a man who could have killed his wife in a fit of rage when he discovered that she'd rejoined the enemy, as it were.'

'Am I? Maybe. But I'm not sure that she *had* rejoined the enemy, as you put it.'

147

I hesitate for a moment, then ask the question that I know will have to be asked. 'But weren't you ...?'

'Wasn't I what?'

'The enemy in question?'

He looks at me mildly enough: he seems not to be offended by my probing. Then, to my surprise, he laughs. 'Oh, come on, you don't really still think that Desirée and I had a thing going?'

'Still?'

'I mean, after I cruised you down the main street of Alfredville.'

It takes me a while to absorb this; part of what I have to absorb is the realisation that I've been extraordinarily obtuse. 'You were *cruising* me?' I ask.

'You mean you didn't notice? Well, actually,' he says, 'I thought you might be cruising *me*. Not that I was exactly running away.'

'But what ... what made you think I was cruising you?'

'Well, I had no way of knowing that you were after information rather than my beautiful body, so what else could I think? I only had the usual signals to go on. And even though you may not have been cruising me, your body language was telling me different.'

'Hell, that's a thing. I must tell you, though, that my body language was misrepresenting me and misleading you.'

'So you don't bat for our team?'

'I don't think of myself as a team player. But to the extent that I am, well, yes, I do bat for your team, but I wasn't actually batting when I met you. To tell you the truth, cruising is not really part of my repertoire.'

'Oh. Pity.'

'Well. Thanks.'

'You're welcome.'

'Good,' I say. 'And now that that's settled ...?' I trail off, hoping he'll take the initiative, but he calls my bluff.

'Yes?' he asks.

'Well, could we return to our original subject?'

'Of course,' he says, slightly too genially. 'But what was it?'

148

Henk Pretorius has abruptly become less cooperative. Could it be that he had consented to my interrogation only because he'd assumed I was of like mind and inclination, and perhaps even biddable and beddable? But no, that's too cynical.

So I say, 'Well, I seem to remember that you were implying that you were ... nothing to Desirée.'

'Not nothing, no. I hope I was a good friend to her.'

'And she to you?'

'Yes, she was. I was new to the town, and she was good company. And as I say, she was lonely, and she liked talking to me. But I think the excitement of being married to Hector wore off after a while.' He smiles. 'She used to say she was too much of a free spirit for marriage. She'd read about the old German *Glücksritter*, soldiers of fortune, and she used to fantasise about being one. But she lacked the courage; she wanted someone to go with her.'

'Like you?'

'She did suggest that we might make a good pair of *Glücksritter*, not being sexually or romantically involved, but I'd just bought my practice, and I didn't really fancy pushing off to unknown destinations in search of *Glück*. Anyway, Liquorice would never have put up with it. So no, I was no threat to the marriage, if that's what you're getting at.'

'But for Hector to have been driven to extremes, there must have been *somebody* who was a threat to the marriage, as you say.'

'Well, no, not really. All that was necessary was for Hector to *think* there was somebody. But ...' He hesitates. 'I don't want to get you over-excited, but it could help you to know that Hector's subordinate, a man called Bennie Nienaber, was in love with Desirée.'

I feel as if he's kicked me in the stomach, and it's all I can do not to scream – with shock, with bewilderment, with, unexpectedly, pain. Instead, I gulp at my wine, take a deep breath, and repeat, as calmly as possible, 'Bennie Nienaber in love with Desirée?'

'That's what I said. Do you know him?'

'I used to know him. In the old days, before I went away.'

'And you think it unlikely that he could have been in love with Desirée?'

'Not unlikely, I suppose; it's just so unexpected. Are you absolutely sure?'

'How sure can you ever be of something like that? But Desirée said *she* was sure. She said that Bennie was very insistent. And he was very jealous of her friendship with me.'

'So he could have told Hector that you were involved with Desirée in the hopes that he would put a stop to the relationship?'

'It is possible.'

'But not probable?'

'I don't know. Look, you asked me who Hector might have been jealous of, so I'm just guessing.'

'Are you being deliberately cagey, or do you just have an unusual capacity for entertaining a large number of possibilities?'

He smiles. 'Maybe one of the possibilities is the possibility that I may be deliberately cagey.'

There's something provoking about the man's refusal to be drawn. 'I share your predilection for a world of perpetual possibility,' I say, 'but don't you think that in our workaday world, possibilities need to be whittled down to at least a balance of probabilities? In fact, in a murder trial, I believe, the case needs to be proved beyond a reasonable doubt.'

'I know that, but you didn't tell me that you were conducting a criminal investigation into Desirée's murder.'

'I'm not, in any technical sense. But it's natural, isn't it, that I should want to get behind the few reported facts, to the underlying truth?'

He seems unconvinced by my appeal. 'I don't really know what you mean by natural,' he says. 'I was fond of Desirée, and I miss her. In an abstract kind of way I would like to see justice done. But it's not going to bring her back, and there's something, I don't know, disrespectful about all these speculations.'

I feel myself flushing. 'I'm sorry if I come across as disrespectful. You seemed willing to enter into my various hypotheses.'

'Was I? Well, maybe as you say, I share your, what did you call it?'

'Predilection for a world of perpetual possibility?'

'That's it, I like that, it makes my wishy-washiness seem impressive. But that's the opposite of what you're trying to do, which is to nail things down to just one certainty.'

'But don't you think that sometimes we need a clear answer rather than an infinite possibility?'

'I don't think we need anything, really, in this case. It's over and done with. If it's not over for you, I don't know, then you haven't told me the real reason why you're so interested.'

'I *have* told you. I'm interested as Desirée's cousin and as a free-lance journalist.'

'Well, I'm not Desireé's cousin and I'm not a journalist. So count me out of your investigation.'

We are both angry now. The conversation is going nowhere: the more I press for a definite opinion or impression, the more uncommunicative he will become. Fortunately the food has arrived, and we can relapse into silence fairly naturally, or, the social substitute for silence, exchange comments on the quality of the food. The waiter arrives to ask 'Is everything all right?' in the perfunctory tone of most waiters, and looks startled at the enthusiasm with which we both commend our meals.

'Tell me,' I say after yet another ruminative silence, attempting a tone of sweet reason, 'in your practice – I take it you have to make diagnoses?'

'Of course. All the time. Why?'

'And you have to act on those diagnoses?'

'Usually. Quite often my advice is to let nature take its course.'

'But even that is a decision, not so?'

'I suppose so. But why the cross-examination?'

'I'm just interested in your reluctance to commit to an interpretation, when your whole job depends on your ability to interpret and act on your interpretation.'

He puts down his knife and fork and uses his hands to punctuate his points. 'But don't you see, that's exactly why? It's *because*

151

I have to make diagnoses all day and often have to put down animals on the strength of my diagnoses, that I don't want to take decisions I don't *have* to take, and make choices I don't *have* to make.' He has been talking louder and louder, and the Dutch tourists are unabashedly listening in. 'Too many mistakes are made by people who are sure they've made the right diagnosis, and act on their diagnosis.' He pauses, and visibly moderates his tone. 'Sorry, I get onto my soap box sometimes. My point is just that we could do with a bit more tentativeness.'

'We wouldn't be here now if you'd been *tentative*.'

He smiles; he has evidently regained his good humour. 'Exactly. I thought that for once I was reading the signs correctly. And look what a mistake that's turned out to be.'

'Actually, you read the signs correctly. It's the signals you got wrong.'

He laughs. 'That's too complicated for me.'

'It's very simple. The signs correctly told you I was gay, so you assumed I was signalling an intention I didn't have.'

'Yet unlike me, you still got what you wanted? Well, who knows, in the long run that may turn out to be a mistake too.'

'I don't see how.'

'I mean, as in Desirée's case. She also usually got what she wanted, but without realising the cost to other people. She was not very aware of her effect on other people. She seemed to be quite self-sufficient, emotionally speaking.'

'And you think I may be?'

'Well, you seem to know what you want.'

'Without realising the cost to other people? Ouch.'

'Yes, I'm sorry, I didn't mean to score a cheap hit.'

'No, you've given me something to think about. Thanks for that.'

'You're welcome.'

We've finished eating and the bottle of wine is also empty. I'm pleased that we've arrived at a more cordial tone, and suggest coffee, but Henk pleads fatigue after a long day. I pay the bill, declining his offer to pay for his share. We part on mutual assurances that we must meet again. He offers me a lift down to the hotel, but

I want a walk to clear my head before my meeting – I shy away from calling it a date – with Joy Duvenhage-Pakendorff. I also need to get my head around what Henk's told me about Bennie.

As Henk Pretorius gets into his car, he says, 'And I'd appreciate it if you'd keep your knowledge of my sexual preferences to yourself. Alfredville isn't ready for a gay vet, I'm afraid.'

I laugh. 'So what keeps you here?'

'The animals don't seem to mind. So you can tell *them,* if you like.'

CHAPTER 10

Friday night

The pub, at nine thirty on a Friday night, is more active than I've hitherto seen it. Though Alfredville can hardly boast a dynamic body of young professionals popping in for a drink before a night on the town, it does have a certain number of commercially employed people, largely male, who seem to need to socialise with one another. Interspersed with these is a herd – I can't think of a more appropriate collective noun – of generally hefty youngish men in khaki and boots, presumably farmers come into town in preference to an evening of indifferent home cooking and bad TV. The atmosphere is sociable, though building up to the raucousness that I suspect will later prevail.

Joy has not arrived yet, so I take a stool at the bar and order a glass of wine. I'm relieved to find that Boris is not on duty tonight: I'm served by a barman I've not seen before, a large and taciturn man, for whom a grunt, modulated to the occasion, seems to do multilingual service for everything from *What will it be?* to *You're welcome.*

As Joy enters, a good ten minutes late, the response from the assembled company would have reassured me, had I had any doubt on the matter, that Joy has not become a stranger to her old haunts.

'*Haai Joy, my nooi!*' one patron shouts lewdly. '*Kom na my kooi!*'

The company vie with one another in composing ribald variations on the man's doggerel; Joy, with all the aplomb of a hardened celebrity, acknowledges the attention only with a gracious inclination of the red-gold splendour of her hairdo, then lavishes upon me the full brilliance of her formidable smile as she trips daintily across the heavy pile of the wall-to-wall.

154

'I hope I'm not late,' she says, brushing past me, slightly more closely than necessary, to get onto the empty stool next to mine. 'I find I have to freshen up after a day behind the desk.' To judge by the smell, she has freshened up by dousing herself in something heavily floral with an undertone of alcohol. She is still, though, wearing the halter top, unless she has a whole collection of them.

'Do you live nearby?' I ask, judging the question to be more innocuous than it could sound later in the evening; but the flutter of her eyelashes – reinforced, I notice, with a fresh slather of mascara – suggests that this distinction is lost on her.

'Oh, *very* near,' she simpers. 'I have my own apartment in the hotel.'

The taciturn barman is now in front of us. His grunt sounds to me like a sceptical response to Joy's claim, but Joy, who must be assumed to be more familiar with his gruntings than I am, takes it as an offer of service.

'Yes, thanks, Zadoc,' she says, 'I'll have what the gentleman is having.' She giggles at me. 'I always say don't have anything that your partner's not having.' Then, as Zadoc places a generously-filled glass in front of her, she says, 'Chin-chin,' tilts her glass perfunctorily in my direction, and downs her drink in what seems like a single gulp.

She puts the glass on the bar counter; Zadoc grunts accommodatingly and refills it.

'There, that's better,' Joy says, turning to give me her full attention. 'I see from the register that you're from Lunnon. Now tell me, what are you doing in our little town?'

'Well, as I said, I used to live here a long time ago, so I thought I'd just come and check out the old place.'

'Do you still know people in town? You must know *lots*, 'cause everyone's been here for ever.'

'Yes, actually I still do know one or two,' I say, in what I hope is a discouragingly dismissive tone. I don't want to divulge my family connections to Joy: it might just deter her from giving me her frank opinion on Desirée.

But Joy is not one to let up on a line of enquiry.

'Like who?' she asks.

'Like who?'

'Like who do you still know in town?'

'Oh. Well, Joachim, for instance. I was at school with him.'

'Big fucking deal. Was he always the big cream puff?'

'I really don't know,' I equivocate. 'I didn't know him that well.'

She sniggers. 'I'll have to take your word for that, won't I?' she says, and addresses herself to her glass again, though more demurely this time.

As the evening wears on, Joy's hold on respectability starts to slip, along with the straps of her turquoise top.

'So what exactly are you doing in Alfredville?' she asks again. She has reached the pedantic stage of inebriation and is looking at me as if she's not going to accept generalised vagueness again. Besides, vagueness is no way to steer the conversation in the direction I want it to go; so I opt for the almost-truth. Some people, I've learnt, clam up when they discover you're writing a story, others open up almost indecently. My guess is that Joy belongs to the open-uppers. It's a calculated risk, because I'd be blowing my own cover, and I'm inclining towards generalised vagueness anyway when she adds, 'It says on your check-in card that you're a journalist. So what are you journalisting about?'

This decides the matter for me: Joy is more lucid than her slipping straps would suggest, and she is clearly alert to what she suspects is evasion on my part. So I decide to come clean, or at any rate cleanish. 'I work for a newspaper in London,' I say, 'and they sent me to do a story on that murder of the policeman's wife you had here recently.' I bargain on the likelihood that Joy won't question the interest of a London newspaper in a murder in a remote corner of Africa: like most people, she probably assumes that what's big news in her home town must be big news universally.

I'm right insofar as she doesn't question that aspect of my

156

story, but she does ask: 'Haven't they had enough of bloody Desirée van Blerk yet?'

'You knew the victim, then?'

'Desirée *van Blerk* ? Bloody sure I knew her. I knew her *forever.*'

'Were you friends?'

'Friends? You must be joking – that little go-getter – you'd think butter wouldn't melt between her legs, but I can tell you, she had more than butter in there plenty of times, and it didn't belong to that husband of hers either.'

'Are you saying Desirée was unfaithful to her husband?'

She explodes and sprays the counter with red wine. '*Oops*! Now see what you made me do! Zadoc! Little accident over here! The gentleman's *very* amusing.'

For a moment, in her mirth, she seems to have forgotten my question, but then she chortles again and says, 'Was Desirée unfaithful to her husband? Does a cat yowl when you pull its tail?'

Although these are clearly rhetorical questions, Joy seems to be waiting for an answer, so I say, 'I'll take that for a yes, then.'

She laughs again. 'Bloody right you'll take it for a yes. Desirée van Blerk-Williams cheated her husband blind before he even *was* her husband.'

'But *after* he was her husband …?'

'D'you think a girl who cheats on her fiancé is going to stop when she gets married to him?'

'I suppose not.'

'No, I suppose not either,' she says archly, and for a moment I fear she's going to retreat into a belated show of discretion. But I needn't have fretted: Joy is now in full cry.

'I can tell you,' she continues, 'and for all I care you can tell your newspaper, she was having it off with Cassie Carstens two days before her wedding, and started again the day after she and her policeman returned from their honeymoon.'

'How do you know these things?'

She narrows her eyes, 'Why d'you want to know that? Don't you believe me?'

'Of course I believe you. I was just wondering how ... well, how widely known this was.'

'It was widely known in a small circle, you could say,' she explains. 'Cassie happens to be a particular friend of mine, so I had you might say *privileged information*. But word gets round somehow, don't ask me how.'

'So do you think Hector Williams knew about this?'

'He'd have had to be thick as a plank not to know about it. But then, he isn't exactly Africa's answer to Einstein, and they do say the husband is always last to know. But obviously he must have found out in the end.'

'Why obviously?'

'Why obviously? Because why else did he kill her if not because of jealousy?'

'You're convinced he killed her then?'

'Of course I'm bloody convinced! I mean, if he didn't, who did? Hell, man, she was wearing a gold Rolex when they found her, that Hector had bought her on their honeymoon. Who's going to go to the trouble of killing someone and then not steal anything? And her dog, that little yapper, didn't even bark. And anyway, there was no way it was going to work, a black man marrying a white girl, I could have told them that on their wedding day, except there was enough shit flying around anyway, so I kept my mouth shut.'

'You were at the wedding?'

'Yes, and you needn't look so surprised. I'm *somebody* in this town. My late husband did Blik van Blerk a few favours, and I must say this for Blik, he's kept up the connection. And old Dolly's okay, if you like them meek and mild. They didn't deserve a daughter like that Desirée, though they did spoil her rotten.'

'Was it a big wedding?'

'You mean if I was invited everybody must have been invited?' Wine seems to make Joy sensitive to insult.

'No, I'm just curious. A wedding between a black man and a white woman can't be all that common in Alfredville.'

'Sure, all that was common about it was the bride,' she says and chortles gleefully. 'And they say that Blik and Dolly tried to persuade Desirée to elope, or at least to have a quiet wedding in the Presbyterian Church, but Miss Meek-and-Mild Desirée dug in her heels and said she wasn't going to have a wedding like Clara Welthagen's, who was seven months pregnant before her boyfriend agreed to marry her, some people say bribed to marry her by Lukas Welthagen, and who didn't even have a wedding dress or a reception.'

'So Hector and Desirée …?'

'Oh, they were married in the Dutch Reformed Church with all the trimmings, I can tell you – two bridesmaids, the organ playing that thing, Handel's Largo, and Stienie Pretorius, who thinks she's a bloody nightingale because she once sang in an opera in Boksburg or Roodepoort or somewhere, singing "I'll Walk Beside You". And Dominee Albertyn looked as if he didn't really know what to say, I mean what *do* you say? but preached for ever on that text, "Thy people shall be my people", which a lot of people thought was going a bit far, I mean if people want to marry each other that's their business, but why drag their families into it as well?'

'And Blik and Dolly?'

'Blik managed okay, considering.'

'Considering what?'

'Well, considering that he'd sworn beforehand that he was just going to park Desirée at the pulpit and push off straight away. In the end, he handed over Desirée to Williams without making a scene or anything, but Dolly broke down and had to be taken out of the church by Maria van Schoor, that busybody who runs the farm stall. Then, at the reception in the church hall Dolly was crying *snot en trane* all over Mavis Williams, Hector's mother, who was also in tears. Then Boetie van Blerk, Desirée's brother, you know, got drunk and made a pass at one of the bridesmaids, Livona Williams, Hector's sister. She slapped him good and hard, and then Livona's boyfriend got the moer in and challenged Boetie to a fight outside.'

'So much for thy people shall be my people, then.'

'Bloody right. As they say, if you mix cow dung with ice cream it doesn't do much for the cow dung but it sure spoils the ice cream.' She laughs uproariously. I'm aware of smiling rather tightly at the old racist joke, but also not really wanting to make a stand about it. Joy's perspective is probably pretty representative of a large section of white Alfredville, though her uncharitable take on Desirée may owe something to her own precarious social standing in a town where Desirée, with whatever reservations, would have enjoyed a position of some prominence.

As if to confirm this speculation, Joy turns to me with something like a snarl and says, 'That Desirée – I can't help it, but it pisses me off that she carried on like she did, and everyone was too shit-scared to say anything and they treated her like some kind of royalty or something, but if anyone else even has *one* drink too many' – she flaps a labile hand at the glass in front of her – 'the whole fucking town carries on as if you've killed your grandmother and danced on her grave.'

'So what happened – at the wedding, I mean? Was there a free-for-all?'

'No, I'm sorry to say. I was quite looking forward to a good fight, but then bloody Hector Williams got up, dressed in full uniform, and he's a big man, and quite handsome if you like that type of thing, and he just stood there without saying anything, just looking at these young guys who were ready to moer each other, and I don't know, just *standing* there he seemed to make them feel spare or something and they went back to their seats looking like bloody fools. And Hector went to his mother, who by now was hysterical and telling Livona she shouldn't have slapped Boetie, and he calmed her down, and Livona too, who was still the moer in with Boetie but also embarrassed by the whole thing.'

'And Desirée?'

'Oh, Desirée sat there like a big white cat on a feather pillow, above the squabbling of all those common people. To tell you the truth, she looked bored right through the ceremony, even in church standing in front of the pulpit, when the minister asked her do you take this man, she looked as if she was thinking it over and then decided what the hell I've come this far I might as well.'

By now Joy has downed about four glasses of wine to my one, and she is beginning to cant over alarmingly in my direction, putting a hand on my arm to steady herself, and leaving it there. She fixes me with a slightly out-of-focus stare. 'But I could swear I've seen you somewhere,' she says.

'Well,' I say as lightly as possible, 'I did live here for quite a few years. But as I've said, I was at school. I don't think you would have noticed me.'

A momentary flash of honest lust flickers over Joy's painted façade. 'Oh I don't know, sweetheart,' she chuckles 'I notice most things worth noticing. *If* they're worth noticing,' she adds, giving me another lubricious once-over. 'And I'm sure you were worth noticing.'

There is something pensive in the way she says the last sentence. This is disquieting, because it may mean she's starting to make connections I don't want her to make.

And sure enough, 'Hey,' she says, 'weren't you …?'

But before she can complete her question, a muscular arm encircles her from behind; its owner gives me a perfunctory but insolent wink and blows in her ear. She gives a little shriek that is less alarmed than titillated. 'Now *who* can that be?'

'One guess,' her captor says, making a feint at disguising his voice. He is a big man, not unattractive, but coarsely featured and heavily built; I'd guess him to be in his mid-thirties, a farmer, probably.

'Cassie!' she shrieks. 'You know you shouldn't give me a fright like that!'

'I can show you something that will give you a bigger fright if you ask nicely,' he says, moving his arm down around her waist. He gives me another collusive wink. I attempt a smile, to pretend that I'm more at ease than I am, but I suspect it's a rather pained little smile. In truth, I'm relieved that Joy seems about to be taken off my hands before things get awkward; but I'm also irritated

161

with the man's calculated rudeness. He's staking out his territory as crudely as a baboon pissing on a rock.

'Chickenfeed doesn't frighten me,' Joy says, and cackles at her own wit.

Cassie joins in. 'No, right, chicks like chickenfeed, don't they?'

'Let go of me, Cassie,' says Joy, not very insistently. 'Can't you see I'm talking to this gentleman?'

'I can see you're talking to someone but I didn't know he was a gentleman.'

'That's because you couldn't tell a gentleman from your grandmother's parrot,' Joy ripostes. 'Cassie, this is Peter. He's from Lunnon.'

I put out my hand, awkwardly, because his hand is still clutching Joy's midriff. He extricates it and presents it to me as if it were a packet of soggy chips, which it disconcertingly resembles.

Facing Cassie Carstens head-on, I can discern, under twenty-years' accretion of brawn, the features of a boy some years my junior at school who had enjoyed a brief spell of notoriety through beating up anyone who dared call him Septimus, the name his parents had blessed him with. He was a formidable fighter even at thirteen, and for a while it became a popular test of courage or plain foolhardiness to go up to him and say, 'Hello, Septimus.'

I suppress an irrational urge to say 'Hello, Septimus,' and say instead, 'I'm pleased to meet you,' assuming he won't recognise me: he doesn't look like an attentive student of human physiognomy. But I've underestimated him. 'You're Peter Jacobs,' he announces bluntly.

'Yes, that's right,' I confess.

'I heard you were in town,' he says. 'I remember you. Weren't you Desirée van Blerk's cousin or something?'

'Mm. Yes.' I try to pass it off casually, as if of no moment, but Joy is not so befuddled as to let that pass.

'He's *what*?' she asks Cassie.

'You heard – he's Desirée's cousin.'

'Then why the hell didn't he say so?' she demands indignantly.

'Fucked if *I* know,' he says. 'He's standing right in front of you, why don't you ask him?'

'I'm not asking him anything,' she mutters bad-temperedly. 'He took advantage of me.'

Cassie looks at me, torn between male camaraderie and macho aggression. I don't think he's the chivalrous type who will feel obliged to defend Joy's honour, but I don't want to take the chance, so I shrug deprecatingly, hoping to imply that I have no idea what Joy is talking about.

Joy, though, sees the gesture, and interprets it correctly. 'Don't pretend you don't know what I'm talking about,' she snarls at me, then turns to Cassie again, apparently seeing him as some kind of adjudicator. 'He asks me all about bloody Desirée so he can write about it in his bloody newspaper and I tell him what I think of her not knowing he's her bloody cousin. I mean,' she says, now turning to me, 'I wouldn't go around bad-mouthing somebody's family, for God's sake, even if she does happen to be a stuck-up piece of no-good.'

'Look,' I said, 'that's exactly why I didn't tell you. I wanted you to give me your honest opinion, and I'm very grateful to you for doing so.'

'Well, I'm glad *you're* grateful,' she says, only slightly mollified, 'because I feel a prize arse.'

'I don't know why,' I say. 'I asked you for your opinion and you gave it. There's nothing to feel … a fool about.'

'It's easy for *you* to talk, you newspaper people have no feelings, as long as you get your story.'

'So, you're from the newspaper?' Cassie butts in. 'Which one?'

'I'm not really from any newspaper,' I say. 'I'm hoping to write an article about the background to Desirée's murder, not really a news story …'

'You mean like in *Huisgenoot*?' he asks.

I wince. The *Huisgenoot* is not *The New Yorker*. 'Not exactly. I'm more interested in the … social context than in the personalities.'

'So what's the social context?' Joy demands belligerently. 'You

163

mean like what she gave people for supper and who did her hair, like on *Top Billing*?'

'No, not that either, really. It's more a matter of, you know, what her murder means in terms of the new South African political dispensation.'

'You mean because she was married to a hotnot?' Cassie asks.

I sense that Cassie is testing me; he must know that he's used a grossly offensive term, and he's daring me to be offended. And if I pretend not to be offended, he'll also have scored a point.

So I try to sound airily neutral. 'If you want to put it like that, yes,' I say.

But he's not letting me get away with it. 'And how would *you* put it?'

'I think the term would be cross-cultural marriage,' I say, aware of falling into exactly the kind of pompous attitudinising that he's been trying to push me into.

Predictably, he snorts. 'Don't try to sell me horse-shit for hay,' he says. 'I don't care what *term* you use, bottom line is she married a hotnot and lived to regret it.'

'Not for long,' Joy sniggers again.

'Well, long enough to regret it. Anyway,' Cassie says with a leer, 'anything you want to know about Desirée, just ask me.'

'Oh I'm sure,' Joy bridles. 'You're a real *expert* on Desirée, aren't you?'

I resist the impulse to tell Cassie to stuff off. Instead, I remind myself that I'm here to collect information, not to pass judgement on my informants. So I say, 'I may take you up on that.'

'Thought you would,' he says. 'Any time you want to buy me a drink I'll tell you what you want to know. For old times' sake.'

'Just not now,' Joy says. 'I'm sick of Desirée van Blerk, if you want to know the honest truth. I mean, just because she's dead, that doesn't make her interesting.'

Actually, that is partly what does make poor Desirée interesting to me, but I can't say so. Fortunately, Cassie takes over. 'Of course you're sick of her,' Cassie says. 'You were sick of her before she died. Confess you were jealous because she smaaked me.'

'From what I heard, she smaaked anything in pants,' Joy returns spitefully.

'Hey, she didn't insist on pants,' Cassie roars, and guffaws.

'Sies, Cassie,' Joy says, suddenly prim. 'I don't think it's right to talk like that about a girl when she's dead.'

'Better when she's dead than when she's alive, eh?' Cassie says to me, winking offensively.

'Yes, sure,' I say, doing my best to blend into his idiot's idiolect. Between Joy and Cassie I have a pair of potentially irate interlocutors, and in their different ways they seem equally sensitive to presumed insult. 'So, what do you say to a drink sometime?'

'I say what I say to a drink any time – bring it on!'

'Tomorrow evening?'

'Ja, why not? This is where I spend my Saturday evenings anyway.'

'Now that Desirée's not around any more,' Joy carps.

'That's right,' Cassie confirms, impervious. 'So let's make it seven o'clock?'

I nod. 'Seven o'clock is fine.' Cassie will by then still be relatively sober, which may or may not be a good thing. He'll be, presumably, a bit more articulate, but also probably a bit more discreet. And to a feature writer, an interviewee's discretion is like holy water to a vampire.

'So, seeing that you two boys are so eager to buy each other drinks, who's going to buy *me* a drink?' Joy asks petulantly.

'I thought I'd been buying you several, but I'll gladly buy you another,' I say, but Joy isn't listening: her question was clearly aimed at Cassie Carstens. He makes a face. 'Hell, am I here for some kind of mopping-up operation?' he asks, good-humouredly enough, and gestures at Zadoc to refill Joy's glass. He has the good grace to look enquiringly at me, not quite offering, but implying that I am free to order myself a drink. I calculate that this is the moment to make good my escape.

'Thanks very much,' I say, 'but I want to go for a run early tomorrow morning. I'd better get to bed.' I put a couple of notes on the counter.

Joy is above noticing mundane details like money and doesn't thank me. Instead she complains, but without much conviction, *'That'*s not very complimentary, to be stood up for a bloody jog.'

'You haven't been stood up, sweetheart,' Cassie says, and I almost warm to him. 'I'm right here to stand by you.'

Joy giggles. 'Okay then, but make sure you stand *close* by.'

'Well, good night then,' I say, but neither of them notices.

CHAPTER 11

Saturday morning 23 January

As I'm about to go for my run, my phone rings. I hesitate before answering: I tend to be apprehensive about answering a door or a telephone. You never know who you're letting into your life.

I answer anyway. 'Hello, Peter Jacobs.'

'Hi Peter.' The voice is familiar, but slightly strained, and it takes me a moment to recognise it as Bennie's.

'Hi, Bennie. You're early.'

'Oh, no such thing as early or late for a policeman. Were you still asleep?'

'No, I was just going for my run.'

'Yes, that's what I figured. I've seen you running in the morning.' There's a short silence, which I'm at a loss to fill, but before it can congeal, he continues. 'I was wondering … I've got a late shift this morning, d'you think I could join you?'

'On my run?'

'Yes. Unless you prefer to run on your own.'

In fact I do, but Bennie and I no longer have the kind of ease that allows for that kind of frankness. And there is the chance that he wants to repair his previous failures of full disclosure. So I say, 'No, that would be great. Are you ready now?'

'Just about. Should we meet somewhere? In Victoria Street?'

'We could do that. Or why don't I come by your house? It's not much out of my way.'

'If that's okay by you?'

'Sure. I'm setting off in about five minutes.'

'Good, see you in about ten.'

'Make that twelve.'

'Twelve, then.'

In eleven minutes I arrive at the nondescript little house. I was expecting Bennie to be waiting outside, and I'm slightly irritated to find that he's not. I don't feel like being sociable at this hour with Chrisna, or, worse, Mrs Rabie.

I ring the doorbell. The door opens almost immediately. It's Chrisna, even at this hour neatly dressed in skirt and blouse, hair tied back in her unfussy style. Kerneels is in attendance, cautiously pleased to see me. He extends a diffident snout towards my bare knee. I put out my hand and he sniffs at it, then wags his tail. Apparently I've passed some screening test of which only dogs know the secret.

'Hello, Peter,' Chrisna says. I needn't have worried about sociabilities. Her manner, though perfectly civil, doesn't invite niceties. 'Bennie will be out in a moment. He couldn't find his running shoes.'

'No hurry,' I say, hiding my impatience as best I can. I don't like to be kept waiting. But then, if Bennie couldn't find his running shoes, he's probably not been for a run for a while, which makes his asking to join me all the more notable.

As if guessing my thoughts, Chrisna says, 'I'm glad you asked Bennie to go running with you.'

Instead of correcting this construction of the situation, I just say, 'Doesn't he run often?'

'Not enough. He works too hard. And when he's not working, the children ...' She trails off as if the needs of the children are self-explanatory.

'Of course,' I say.

'Bennie's so pent-up,' she says. 'He never lets go.'

'He was always ... very intense.'

'Yes,' she says, 'but not like this. This is ... *dangerous.*'

I'm too surprised at Chrisna's sudden confidence to come up with a suitable reply, and while I'm still trying to formulate one, Bennie appears, in somewhat makeshift running gear, an old T-shirt – it says Ghanta Half-Marathon 1995 – and running shorts that have seen better days. His Nikes, too, show the signs of long service. Poor Bennie, I think, running shoes must come a poor second to the needs of a growing family.

He kisses Chrisna goodbye, a casual, unthinking intimacy.

'Will you be long?' she asks.

'I don't know,' he says. 'That depends on Peter. It's his run. Will we be long?' he asks me.

'I usually run for about an hour,' I say.

'Call it an hour and a half,' he says to Chrisna.

'Not longer,' she says. 'Kosie needs new brakes on his bike.'

We set off down dowdy little Milner Street, and make our way into Victoria Street, just beginning to gear up for its Saturday morning bustle, which will cease abruptly at one o'clock, when Alfredville subsides into its weekend torpor.

'Where shall we go?' I ask Bennie.

'It's your run,' he says again.

'Just forget that it's my run and tell me where you want to go.'

'Okay, how about the dam?'

It's what I would have suggested, only I thought it might seem too deliberate an invocation of the old days: the dam used to be one of our most frequented destinations, after Kanonkop. And I wouldn't have suggested Kanonkop.

We run smoothly, in silence. Bennie easily matches my pace, in spite of his shorter legs. I'm slightly disappointed; I was hoping that after all these years I might manage what I never did at school: outrun Bennie Nienaber. As we approach the dam, he is still by my side, sweating, but not noticeably out of breath. He may not have run for a long time, but he evidently has natural fitness.

As if guessing my thoughts, he grins at me: 'Thought you were going to leave me standing, did you?'

'Oh, I could easily,' I joke. 'I've been holding back.'

'Okay bugger,' he says, 'you can stop holding back. Race you to the dam.' And he quickens his pace, breaking into what we used to call the rabbit sprint: the oddly uncoordinated whirl of limbs, arms pumping, legs seeming to wobble. For a moment I'm left standing; then I summon such resources as I have left, stretching my pace, trying to gain maximum advantage from my longer legs.

He reaches the dam marginally ahead of me. 'Okay, bean-sprout?' he says. 'You admit defeat?'

'Yes, but only just. You started ahead of me.'

'Yeah, bad sport,' he jeers. We stand catching our breaths, looking at the dam. It's still relatively full, even this late in summer, and the little island in the middle is smaller than I remember it. The sparse vegetation bordering the dam yields to a muddy rim, trampled by animals that come here to drink. It's not an inviting spectacle, and yet there is something appealing about the familiarity of it: in all these years almost nothing has changed. At some stage, apparently, somebody tried to build a jetty of sorts, but it has long disintegrated into a treacherous-looking pile of planks and poles.

'Do you feel like a ghoef?' Bennie asks out of the blue.

Ghoef. I haven't heard the word for twenty-two years. *Ghoef*, verb, to swim, *ghoef* noun, a swim, *ghoefies*, noun, a swimming pool. It was a dated expression, even then.

'We don't have cozzies,' I say, more to relish the term than because I really think bathing costumes are de rigueur in the Riet-vlei Dam.

'So who needs cozzies?' Bennie asks.

'The water looks bloody cold.'

'Oh don't be a moffie, it's not that cold.'

Moffie – another near-forgotten word, the ultimate insult of our youth. 'Do you want to swim to the island?' I ask.

'Do you think you can make it?'

'Oh, I can make it. I was wondering about you. You were never much of a swimmer.'

'I've improved.'

'Right then. I look forward to seeing your improvement.'

'And I'll be looking backward at you bobbing in my wake.'

We take off our running clothes. As I slip off my shorts and somewhat self-consciously stand waiting for Bennie, he inspects me unabashedly. 'You've put on some muscle. Not such a weed any more.' He used to call me beansprout because I was tall, pale and thin.

'I work out,' I say.

'You mean in a gym?'

'Yes, where else?'

'In the army a workout isn't something you would want to pay for,' he says.

'Yes, well, the army ...' I say, wondering if Bennie is intent on bringing home to me the decadence of civilian life compared with the army. He has now also taken off his running clothes. He, too, has developed more muscle; but somehow, as he bends down to take off his socks, there is something defeated about his wiry body, as if it lacks the impetus and force that used to animate it. But then, taking off socks is nobody's most dynamic activity. He straightens up and is for a moment again the compact lithe animal of old, sleek, contained, full-nerved; then he runs into the dark water. As the water deepens, he starts swimming, the same rather awkward crawl, more energy than style, but still, something otter-like in the quick darting movements. I reluctantly edge into the water; it's devilishly cold, and the mud seeping between my toes is unpleasantly intrusive. Better swim than walk, I think, and lunge into the dark cold. As I surrender myself to it, my breath is all but shocked out of my lungs, but I strike out, following Bennie, and my breath and circulation return to normal. I push myself, trying to catch up with Bennie; I used to be a better swimmer than he, and I've been swimming regularly at my gym in London.

Bennie is stroking evenly, but then he notices me following him, and with a defiant yell he pushes himself faster. I grin to myself: if that's the way he wants it, I'll give him a race.

I force my arms to go faster, try to control my breathing, try to settle into a kick rhythm and tempo. I gain on Bennie, but he glances back and redoubles his efforts. He's splashing too much, I think, he's wasting effort, I'm going to catch him up. But Bennie makes up in drive what he lacks in technique and he draws away from me again. I know that Bennie's advantage, as a sprinter, is in the quick burst of speed that his adrenaline-fuelled metabolism allows him. I can't compete with this, so settle instead into a slower pace, but with a longer, more regulated stroke, turning partly on my side. I consciously slow down my breathing, taking deeper, longer breaths, keeping my head as still as possible. I can feel my chest, my stomach, my back working, and as I settle into a rhythm, they seem to synchronise, my legs kicking in time with the grab-and-press technique my gym trainer has tried to teach me; grab the water and press down on it. Grab-press-kick, I go, grab-press-kick, rotating my body, resisting the temptation to look ahead to Bennie, because I know that lifting my head will slow me down. But the increased turbulence of the water tells me that I'm gaining on Bennie, that I'm moving into his private space. Through the rush of water in my ears I hear a shout, Bennie no doubt trying to put me off my stroke, but I ignore it and carry on, grab-press-kick, grab-press-kick, pretending my body is a tube, as I was taught. Bennie's legs are now to my left, then his torso, then his head, but I see these only dimly as I keep my head down, grab-press-kick, my heart thumping with each grab and press and kick, the pulse in my ear getting louder, my lungs battling to meet the demands I'm making on them, my muscles aching, grab-press-kick, but a feeling of near bliss spreading through my body, the endorphins kicking in at last, and an exhilarated light-headedness takes hold of me, making me feel as if I could go on forever, my body cleaving to the water and yet escaping its clutch, my hands grabbing huge volumes of water, thrusting them away from me, grab-press-kick, until unexpectedly my chest scrapes the bottom and I get to my feet, my toes squelching in mud. Bennie, seconds behind me, leaps out of the water and tackles me, and we both collapse into the shallow water. I flail around clumsily, but Bennie has his arms around my legs, and I get water in my mouth and nose.

'Bugger off!' I say. 'This isn't fucking rugby.' I kick my legs to release them, but he holds on tight.

'Hey! You're going to drown us both!' I sputter, trying to keep my head above water by means of an undignified kind of doggy paddle.

'So what do you think I'm trying to do?' he says, and lifts my

legs to dunk my head. I swallow a substantial part of the Rietvlei
Dam before I manage to surface again. I grab hold of his hair, and
pull with all my might.

'Let go, bugger,' I shout. 'Let go, or I'll pull your hair out by the
roots.'

He shifts the grip of his right hand and grabs me between my
legs.

'You reckon you're in a position to bargain?' he asks.

For a brief moment we lie in stalemate, my hand in Bennie's
hair, his enclosing my groin. But with only one of his arms around
my legs I manage to get to my feet, and he loses his grip. I leave
him lying in the shallow water and walk out onto the little island.

'Hey, bugger,' I say, trying to catch my breath, 'that was dangerous. You could have drowned us both.'

'Oh come on, you can't drown in six inches of water,' he coun-
ters, hopping on one foot trying to get water out of his ear.

'You can too,' I say, shivering as the hot sun strikes my cold
body. 'We should have brought towels.'

'And how would we have got them here, fuckwit?'

'I don't mean we should have brought them *here*, numbnut. I
mean so that we'd have something when we got back to our
clothes.'

'The sun will dry you in no time.'

'Yeah, and burn the hell out of us too.'

'Out of you, maybe, with your lily-white English skin.'

'You're not all that tanned yourself,' I say, pointing at the faint
tan line on his hip.

'I don't have time to lie around in the sun any more.'

So we stand in the sun, assessing each other's bodies, at a loss
for something to add to our inept interchange. I'm suddenly
self-conscious; the body that was once so familiar to me from
daily interaction and contact has hardened into something self-
sufficient, apart. There is a light covering of hair on his chest,
between the two small nipples, and the line of hair running from
his navel to his groin is more defined than it was, but the main
difference is in his bearing; Bennie, even in this frankest of

173

exchanges, is holding himself separate, is not, as it were, acqui-
escing to my inspection.

I feel very naked, standing there uncovered to Bennie's gaze.

'Hey,' he says, 'you've been cut.' He points at my groin.

For a moment I'm at a loss, thinking I've scraped myself on a
rock. I glance down. 'Oh,' I say, 'oh yes, that. The circumcision. It
was when ... when I started having sex that I discovered my fore-
skin was too tight. It started bleeding sometimes. Very inconvenient.'

He shudders exaggeratedly. 'Yuck. And so you had it cut off?'

'Yes. You could say my father won at last. He wanted to have
me circumcised by the rabbi when I was born, but my mother said
she wasn't having me mutilated for a religion I wasn't going to
grow up in.'

'How do you know that?'

'Know what?'

'That your mother said that to your father.'

'My mother told me.'

'Hell, I wouldn't have discussed my dick with my mother.'

There's something comical about his outrage, and I laugh. 'We
didn't *discuss* it, it just sort of ... came up.'

He erupts in laughter, the manic screech of old. 'It just sort of
came up? So how did you get it to go down again?'

'God, you're just as much of a pig as you ever were,' I say, but
I laugh too. 'So if you've quite exhausted the subject of my dick,
shall we swim back?'

'Sure,' he says, 'it never was much of a dick anyway.'

'Let's take it easy back,' I say.

'Okay, if you're scared I'm going to thrash you.'

'I'm not scared you're going to thrash me, I'm scared you're
going to drown me.'

'Sissy,' he says, and we start swimming back, relaxed, companionable, enjoying the contrast between the cold water and the hot
sun. Is this why I came back, to recover something of an easier
time, of simple sensations and conversations? To pick up with
Bennie something we lost long ago?

But I know this is sentimental claptrap. Simple sensations are no more to be recovered than lost friendships. And I didn't come back to see Bennie, I didn't even know he was in Alfredville.

'Come on, you're lagging behind,' he says, and with an effort I draw abreast of him. For a moment it looks as if he's going to push the pace and turn this too into a race, but then he relaxes, and we reach the bank simultaneously.

Clambering out, we're both shivering. Without towels, we have to wait for the sun to dry us, which won't take long. We find a rock and sit down side by side, slightly awkwardly, because there isn't really space for us both. I'm aware of our thighs touching, but don't want to move my leg.

The silence is massive; there are some noises that, citified as I've become, I can only think of generically as insect noise.

'You don't smoke any more?' I say, to break the silence, but also because it has occurred to me that the last time Bennie and I sought out the silence of nature it was to allow him to smoke.

'No,' he says. 'I stopped smoking after I got married. Chrisna didn't like it, you know, with children and all.'

'Do you miss it?'

'Oh, I did.' He smiles. 'I started when I was fifteen, remember? And I couldn't have made it in the army without smoking. They say giving up smoking is like losing a friend.' He pauses, perhaps reflecting on his choice of comparison. He picks up a stone and throws it into the water. 'But I suppose, like losing a friend, you get used to it.'

There's a tightness around his mouth that I recognise. In the old days, I learnt not to argue with Bennie when his mouth set in that expression: it was his way of defending himself, and any attempt to breach his defences would simply reinforce his resistance. Nevertheless, I press on. 'So you in fact don't miss it?' I ask.

He glances at me, as if trying to figure out what I'm driving at. To my surprise, his expression relents, and he says neutrally, even conversationally, 'Most of the time not. But there are times when I could kill for a smoke.'

'And then?' I ask. 'Do you have one?'

175

He shakes his head. 'No ways. I know myself. If I had one I'd start all over again. I'm an addictive personality,' he informs me as neutrally as if telling me that he's left-handed. 'I can do cold turkey but I can't do moderation.'

'You really do know yourself,' I reply, as lightly as possible.

'I've had time to get to know my fucking fascinating self. 'The army, police college … you spend a lot of time with yourself.'

'I'd have thought that would be the one thing you didn't have in those places – time on your own.'

'Oh, you're with other people all the bloody time, usually on top of them, but that's just it, you have to, I don't know, withdraw into yourself somewhere, if you know what I mean.'

I nod, not wanting to interrupt his train of thought. He carries on, 'And then, when you're sitting there or lying there or just *standing* there with all those other people, you realise how alone you really are, because they don't matter to you and you don't matter to them. Not really.'

I risk asking, 'Didn't you have friends in the army or the police?'

'I had friends, sure, to get drunk with or share a joint with and talk shit with. But I didn't feel any connection, really. It was just getting drunk or high and talking shit. It could have been almost anybody, only it happened to be Dawie Kriel or David Henry or whoever.'

I feel Bennie is reaching out, wants me to give him an opening to say what he wants to say; but I can't give him that opening, because I'm not sure that I want to take responsibility, and I don't want to come up with a reply to whatever he might say. I don't want to be blackmailed into sentimentality by my past, forced to deny my present in the name of an idealised past.

So I just say, 'I can imagine that must have been tough.'

And he says, 'Can you really? I mean really imagine what it was like?'

'Not in detail, I suppose.'

'Can you have any idea what it was like to feel every day that you might be killed, and then to start *wishing* that you'd be killed, that the worst was not being killed but the fact that it didn't matter a flying fuck, to yourself or to anybody else, whether you lived or died?'

Bennie turns to me, evidently expecting an answer.

'No, Bennie,' I say, 'I can't. I can't imagine what it was like. It must have been awful.'

'It's all right,' he says, 'I'm not asking for your pity.'

'I'm not giving you pity,' I say. 'I'm trying to understand.'

'Understand? What's to understand?'

'You. Why you should have felt that it didn't matter whether you lived or died.'

'Have you never felt that way?'

'No, I can't say I have.'

He snorts derisively. 'Count yourself lucky then.'

'But ...' I hesitate for a moment, not sure if I can venture that far. 'But you've ... settled down now, haven't you?'

'Have I?' he asks cryptically.

'Well, you seem happily married, you have two great kids ...'

'And that's supposed to make me happy?' he asks.

'Isn't that what most people want?'

'Is it what you want?'

'No, I suppose not, but ...'

'But what? But you're so fucking superior to *most people* that what's good enough for them isn't good enough for you?'

'No, of course not. But people want different things from life, and I ...'

'So if people want different things from life, why am I supposed to be happy with what *most people* want?'

'For fuck's sake, Bennie, I'm sorry I said anything. If you want the right to be unhappy, sure, go ahead.'

'Thanks, mate, I appreciate your permission.'

We sit in silence for a moment. Then he says, 'I suppose I'd better be getting back. I'm going on duty at one. And Kosie's bike needs brakes. What's the time?'

I get up and find my watch among my clothes. 'It's only nine thirty.'

177

He nods, but doesn't get up. I stand around indecisively, not wanting to be the first to start putting on my clothes. We both sense, I think, that to leave now, like this, would be an obscure kind of defeat. I walk up to him and put my hand on his shoulder. He twitches his shoulder but makes no attempt to remove my hand.

'Look, Bennie,' I say, 'I'm sorry. I expressed myself badly. It's just that … it's just that it's difficult to talk naturally after more than twenty years.'

'I don't know,' he says gloomily. 'After twenty years it should be easy. It shouldn't matter enough to be difficult.' His tone, having lost its belligerence, is reflective.

There's something awkward about my hand resting passively on his shoulder, like a dead fish on a slab, but to remove it now would seem pointed. So I leave it there, and say, 'I suppose so. But it does matter, doesn't it?'

'Does it?' he asks.

'Yes. It matters to me, that I've seen you again and met your family.'

He looks up at me. 'Big fucking deal,' he says, but something in his tone has relented. We stay like that for a moment in the hot sun, not speaking. My hand drops to my side.

'Better get going, I suppose,' I look upwards. 'The sun will start frying us.'

He gets up. 'Yes, you're turning pink already. But you always were a rooinek.'

'And you always were a hairy-back.'

He turns his back to me. 'So? D'you see any hair?'

'I was speaking metaphorically,' I say, 'but I wouldn't expect you to understand that.'

'Bloody right, I'm just a thick policeman,' he says, but he's smiling; we've reverted to the good-humoured insults of youth.

'Bloody right,' I say. 'Now let's get our clothes on. Tell me if you need help with your shoelaces.'

We dress in silence and run back to Alfredville through the gathering morning heat.

CHAPTER 12

Saturday mid-morning

When I get back to the hotel, a light is blinking on my phone. I retrieve the message.

'Hello, Peter,' a hesitant voice says, 'This is Henk Pretorius. I've been thinking ... there's something I didn't tell you last night that you may want to know. If you're interested, give me a ring this morning – after twelve, 'cause I've got surgery till then.' He gives his number. 'Bye then, hope to hear from you.'

Dr Pretorius sounds *tentative*, I think, smiling.

It's too late for breakfast at the hotel, and after my shower I get dressed and walk to the Country Pumpkin, *My Traitor's Heart* in my hand. Instead of their 'Full Farm Breakfast' (boerewors, kidneys, fried eggs and bacon – the mind boggles and the stomach quails), I order a coffee and a slice of their 'homemade' milk tart, another forgotten childhood taste, the bland gelatinous vanilla-ish custard and the light flaky pastry that was Angelina's pride and my joy.

The tart arrives. It's good, though I think Angelina would have had something to say about the consistency of the pastry. She always said that good pastry required cold hands – 'Like mine!' she'd say, thrusting her hands down my neck, to my squeals of panicky pleasure.

Behind me is a mother with her three children. Concentrating on my book, I'm not really listening to their prattle, the desultory exchanges of an indulgent mother with children asking questions not so much to gain information as to keep her attention; but gradually their conversation seeps into my consciousness.

'Mammie,' the little boy asks, 'why am I called Thysie?'

'That's your pet name. Because your real name is Matthys,' his mother explains.

179

'And why is my real name Matthys?'

'Because you're named after your oupa. He was called Mat-thys too.'

'Oh.' A short silence ensues, filled with the sound of cool drinks being slurped.

'Do I have a pet name?' one of the girls pipes up.

'Yes, my doll. We call you Emmie.'

'And my real name is Emmerentia?'

'Yes.'

'So am I named after my ouma?'

'No, you're named after me because your ouma was called Huibrecht and we didn't want to call you that.'

'Why not?'

'Because your ouma hated the name. Everyone called her Huibie and then she married a man called Hennie Hatting and so they were Hennie and Huibie Hatting and she said it sounded like whooping-cough.'

The children crow with laughter and chant 'Hennie and Huibie Hatting' at the tops of their voices until the mother silences them.

I try to turn round inconspicuously to inspect the little family, but the woman notices me and says, 'I'm sorry, I hope we're not disturbing you, my children can be so rowdy … what, Peter Jacobs! Can it really be you?'

For a moment I'm blank; the woman's face rings no bell, but then, mercifully, I make the connection.

'Emmerentia!' I say. 'Emmerentia Meiring!' I get to my feet and shake her hand.

'I'm pleased you remember me,' she says. 'I'm not as young as I was.'

'We none of us are,' I say, though in truth I hope I have aged better than Emmerentia. She was never slim, but what used to be a pleasing schoolgirl plumpness is now frankly fat; and the hair, which used to be shiny and abundant, is carelessly tied back in a loose bun. She is looking what she is, the mother of three lively children, and quite comfortable under the burden. The face has retained, under an extra layering of fat, its sweet-natured expression, and her dimples have deepened. She has let herself go, as they say, and seems not to be anxious to reclaim herself.

'So, what are you doing here?' she asks – the inevitable question.

'Oh, just passing through for a few days, I thought I'd come and check out the old haunts.'

She laughs. 'Hasn't changed much, has it?'

'Not very much, no. But the cafés are better.'

'Yes, and more expensive. We have you tourists to thank for that.'

'I hope I'm not a tourist,' I say.

'Well, visitors, then. Where do you live now?'

'In London.'

'Mm,' she says. 'Nice.'

'Yes.'

'And do you have a family?' she asks.

'No,' I say. 'No, I'm not married.'

She shakes her head. 'That's a disgrace. A good-looking man like you should have children.' Then she laughs. 'I can say that now. I always thought you were the most beautiful thing since Mel Gibson, but I was too shy to talk to you.'

'Thanks!' I laugh. 'In fact, I rather fancied you too.'

'Did you?' she blushes with pleasure, and for a moment the young Emmerentia glimmers through this heavier incarnation. 'What an opportunity missed. But you were always with Bennie Nienaber. No girl had a chance.'

'And you …' I point at the children, all three of them solemnly peering at me over their cool drinks.

'Yes, I obviously do have a family. This is Thysie, and this is Emmie and this is Hannetjie. Say hello, kids, this is Uncle Peter, he was at school with Mammie.'

There is a ragged chorus of mumbles from the children, and Emmerentia continues. 'Yes, I married Wikus Scheepers, I don't know if you remember him.'

'Ah, yes, I do.' And I do remember: he was my rival for the back seat of Bennie's Mosquito. A bit of a wimp, but a nice enough guy.

'Yes. We're running a guest house now, the Ghanta Lodge in Shepstone Street. You must come and stay with us next time you're here.'

'I definitely will,' I say, and go back to my coffee, oddly touched by the little interlude. It is inconceivable that this fat, fruitful woman could ever have been the object of my and Bennie's erotic fantasies. Or perhaps she was never their object, more their occasion – that is, we needed to share an erotic fantasy and she was its pretext. But then, the fantasies of adolescence are so diffuse, so unfocused; what is a fantasy but a story we tell ourselves of which the outcome is more important than the elements? Not to put too fine a point on it, the end is ejaculation, the means almost incidental. I smile to myself: closure, had we but known it, was our aim.

And if I'd stayed in Alfredville, I muse over the remains of my milk tart, might I have married Emmerentia or someone like her? Instead of which I have, or *had* until recently, James. Is it possible that the same person could conceivably have been equally happy or unhappy with Emmerentia and with James? Except, I wouldn't have been the same person, would I? Or would I? Ah, how our stories write us, I think, returning to *My Traitor's Heart*.

Just after twelve, I phone Henk Pretorius. He is slightly abrupt, possibly embarrassed, and I have to take the initiative.

'You said you had something to tell me. Shall we meet somewhere?'

'Yes, yes let's do that. Do you want to meet for lunch?'

'Actually, I've just had a huge slice of milk tart. Coffee, rather?'

'Yes, coffee's fine.' He hesitates. 'Why don't you come to my place? It's behind the surgery in Victoria Street.'

'Yes,' I say, 'I know. I was stalking you, remember?'

He laughs, a blessed release of tension. 'How could I forget? Come … when?'

'Now?'

'Now. The entrance is at the back.'

Henk's house is a characteristic old Alfredville house, dark and cool even in midsummer. The smell, too, is familiar, slightly dank and musty, whitewash and old wood and smoke. His sitting room faces the garden, a pleasantly higgledy-piggledy mix of flowers and vegetables. Three geese strut by self-importantly towards a small pond at the far end.

Liquorice, who met me at the door as ecstatically as if he'd been waiting all morning just for me, settles in his basket with a contented sigh.

'I'm getting the coffee,' Henk says. 'Or do you prefer tea?'

'No, coffee's fine.'

'Make yourself at home. I won't be long. Have a seat.'

'Thanks.' But I don't take a seat, preferring to be free to explore the room. James says I'm nosy, but I think it's natural to be interested in what other people have in their houses; it's often the most revealing thing about them.

Henk's sitting room, though, does not give much away. If I hadn't known he was gay I might have picked it up from a certain meticulousness – not tidiness, because the room is amiably cluttered, but the evident care with which each object has been selected: a woven rug over the old but comfortable sofa; a colourful near-abstract Little Karoo landscape; two carved African coffee tables; two of the ingenious wire sculptures that vendors sell next to the road. A straight unmarried man's house generally looks makeshift, awaiting the ordering hand of woman; a gay man's house is always already what it's going to be.

On one of the coffee tables, face down, is André Aciman's *Call Me by Your Name.* I pick it up: ah, yes, this is unmistakable, the tastefully erotic cover, a pair of bare shoulders, a shaven head half-buried in the folded arms.

Henk comes in with a tray of coffee things. 'Read that?' he asks

'No. It was very big in London, but I haven't read it. I never could figure out the title. It seems paradoxical.'

He puts down the tray, takes the book from me. 'It is. But it's quite simple really – the idea is that the deepest intimacy you can have with someone makes you want to fuse your identity with his and vice versa.'

'But would you *want* that – to fuse your identity with someone else's?'

'Well, Aciman makes it seem quite pleasant. I wouldn't mind trying out a bit of identity-fusing if it came my way, but I don't think it's going to happen any time soon in Alfredville.'

He starts pouring the coffee, seeming ill at ease. We busy ourselves with milk and sugar and all the pleases and thank yous that taking coffee with a stranger entails.

Then he says, 'I think I was a bit abrupt with you last night.'

'We were both out of sorts.'

'Yes, but all that about not wanting to pin things down. I had a reason for that.'

'You mean other than a temperamental reason?' I say, looking at him over the top of my cup.

'Yes. But you know, in general my temperament *is* more tentative than absolute.'

'You don't say. But what was your other reason?'

'There's something I didn't tell you, which I think you should know.' He looks at me almost pleadingly. 'If I tell you what it is, you'll understand why I didn't tell you.'

'Well, tell me then. I'm all for understanding.'

I say this with a smile, but he remains as solemn as a priest. Then he says, 'That evening that Desirée was murdered ...'

'Yes?'

'Well, they say she was murdered at about seven thirty ...'

'Yes, so I've heard.'

'Now, at around that time I was at the dam – you know the one outside town.'

'Yes, I've been told you often walk there.'

'Have you? Hell, they do keep tabs, don't they? Yes, well, I was there that evening. And, well, I saw Hector Williams there.'

'You saw Hector Williams at the dam? At seven thirty?'

'Or thereabouts. Yes.'

'What was he doing?'

'Nothing. Just sitting there, in the police vehicle. Of course, I couldn't make out what it was all about, but later I heard that he

184

said he was upset about something and had driven out of town. Well, that is true, because I saw him there.'

'But why didn't you say anything? And why didn't he say you saw him there?'

'Well, that's the thing, you see. He didn't see me.'

'Why not, if you saw him?'

'I was hiding.'

'From Hector?'

'Yes – well not from him personally, but from the police. You see, I wasn't alone.'

'Yes – so?'

Henk Pretorius takes a gulp of coffee, then puts down his cup and clasps his hands on his lap. 'And the person I was with is … well, still at school. So I didn't want it to be known that I was there with the person, and the person didn't want it to be known either because his – of course you knew it was a male person – his parents are very prominent and very proper and wouldn't like the fact that he's been meeting me at the dam.'

'I can imagine that, yes.'

'Not that I have any problems on my own account, I just don't want to embarrass the boy. So I'm telling you this off the record.'

'You mean you'd let Hector Williams go to jail rather than embarrass the boy?'

'I was thinking that I might come out with it if it seemed to be going badly for Williams. But if it came out that I was there with a boy, that would be the end of me, too.'

'Yes, I can see that. Fusing identities with schoolboys in public places is not something the law smiles on.'

'Yes, not to mention my clients.'

'But why are you telling me this, then?'

'That's it, don't you see? If I can convince you that Hector Williams is innocent then you can take it further and have the real culprit arrested.'

I shake my head in exasperation. 'Hey, just wait a minute, it's not as simple as that. What makes you think I'm a bloody private investigator?'

185

'Well, you were certainly asking a lot of questions. I got the impression that you were trying to get to the bottom of this business. So I thought you'd be grateful.'

'Hell, man, thanks for nothing. You give me information on condition that I can't use it, and then tell me I should, while I'm about it, find the real murderer, have him arrested, and let you off the hook.'

'But if you want to write about the murder – surely you don't want to have the wrong murderer?'

'Yes, but – oh *hell*!' I groan. 'You've just fucked up my whole story. It was all based on the premise of this black man murdering his white wife. It was going to be called The Othello Murder.'

'So you'd let Hector Williams rot in jail rather than spoil your story?'

We look at each other and start laughing. 'Fuck, we're a dreadful pair,' I say at last. 'The newshound and the pederast.'

'I'm not a pederast, I'll have you know. He's legal.'

'But I *am* a newshound, you mean?'

'You said it, not me. Besides, there's not much point in his being legal. He's found himself a girlfriend. Or she's found him.'

'So now he's batting for the other team?'

'For the time being. I'm not sure they'd want Wouter, though. Not much team spirit.'

'Wouter? Is that his name?'

'Oops, I shouldn't have given that away.'

'And the girlfriend is called Surina?'

He looks at me in amazement. 'How in God's name did you know that?'

'Call me clairvoyant. Or call Alfredville a small town. And let's hope she doesn't call him by her name.'

We laugh so loudly that Liquorice leaps up, rushes out and starts barking at the geese.

The atmosphere is now relaxed enough to allow me to ask a question I've been dreading to ask. 'But if Hector didn't kill Desirée ...?'

'Then what?'

'Then who did?'

'I didn't say that I knew who did it, I just said that I don't think Hector did.'

'Well, hell, she was killed by *someone*, wasn't she?'

'Yes, I think we can rule out suicide by statuette.'

'Okay smart-arse, so what's your theory?' I try to keep my tone light, to hide my agitation.

'What makes you think I have one?'

I get up from my chair and pretend to look out of the window at Liquorice drinking water from the goose pond. 'You're an observant and reflective sort of person. You must have some suspicion.'

'And as an observant and reflective person yourself, who do you suspect me of suspecting?'

I take a deep breath. 'Well, you did mention Bennie Nienaber,' I say, as lightly as I can. There is nevertheless a light quaver in my voice.

'I didn't mention him in the context of murdering Desirée.'

I turn to face him. 'You mentioned him in the context of being in love with her, which is not necessarily a different context.'

'Ai. What a view of love you have.'

'In a way, it's quite a romantic view. Isn't hopeless love one of the oldest causes of murder? The crime of passion?'

He disregards my flippant tone. 'So now *you* suspect Bennie Nienaber?'

'No, I didn't say that. I'm just exploring possibilities. Your kind of thing.'

'Yes, but you're still looking for a certainty, which I can't give you. For myself, if you really want to know, I don't think Bennie Nienaber killed Desirée, but it's not an opinion I'd want to defend in court under cross-examination.'

'Why not?'

'Because cross-examination is about the last thing a tentative person wants to face. But also because I don't think my criteria would be acceptable to a court of law.'

'And what are they, these criteria of yours?'

He hesitates. 'Well, in my job I have to judge quite quickly which animals are vicious and which are just timid or shy – you need to be able to tell the killers before they've shown their nature in action. Now, if I had to judge Bennie Nienaber as an animal, I'd say he's not a killer.'

'Can one extrapolate like that from animals to humans?'

'I don't know. But I do. And that's what I've come up with.'

'Do you know Bennie Nienaber?'

'Not well. But he brought their dog to me once, a nice little mongrel, after it swallowed one of Nienaber's bulky police issue socks, and I had to get it out. And there was something very gentle about Captain Nienaber. But that's not a scientific basis. I'm a vet, not a criminologist.'

Irrationally, I'm immensely cheered by Henk Pretorius's unscientific theory.

'Well, I certainly hope you're right,' I say.

'Why, what's it to you?'

An impulse of caution or reticence prevents me from confessing to my friendship with Bennie. 'As I said, I knew him in the old days. It's difficult to think of him as a murderer.'

'Yes, it's always easier to suspect somebody you don't know. And yet that person is known in turn by people who can't think of him as a murderer.'

'Desirée's parents knew Hector, and *they* don't seem to have a problem thinking of him as a murderer.'

'They wouldn't, would they? The real test would be talking to Hector's friends and relatives – which I take it you've done?'

'Not yet, but I'm hoping to do so eventually. His father is dead, but his mother lives in the vicinity, apparently.'

'And Hector himself?'

'Staying with his mother under a form of house arrest – there was some concern that he might interfere with the witnesses. But he refuses to speak to me before the trial, or else his legal representative has forbidden him to do so.'

'So your story is missing its main component.'

'Thanks. Yes, I suppose so, except that a story is what you

make it – I mean, you can choose the angle to determine the main component. To you, for instance, the main component is your having it off with Wouter next to the dam.'

He laughs. 'I knew I shouldn't have told you that. You news-hounds are all the same.'

Saturday evening

At seven I go down to the bar, prepared for a longish wait, or even for a no-show. Cassie Carstens wasn't exactly making a mental note of our appointment, if appearances are anything to go by.

But it would seem I have underestimated Cassie. He's already sitting at the bar, presided over by the inscrutable Zadoc. He has a drink in front of him which, unless he's a very fast drinker, he's had for a while.

'I'm sorry,' I say as I sit down. 'Am I late?'

He nods at me, without a word of greeting. 'No, you're not late,' he says. 'I'm early.' He points at his left wrist, which sports a large and battered wristwatch. 'This piece of shit I inherited from my father can't decide whether it's fast or slow or in-between.'

'Why do you keep it, then?' I ask.

'I told you, didn't I? I inherited it from my fucking father,' he says, as factually as is compatible with his choice of epithet. Sober, Cassie is relatively subdued, though I sense a latent violence in him even now. He's not somebody I would want to trifle with, and I can't help wondering at Desirée's courage, if that's the word for it, in venturing into a passionate relationship with this man.

I order a glass of Ghanta Pinotage from Zadoc; Cassie taps his glass with his index finger and Zadoc pours him a double brandy and Coke.

Cassie takes a large gulp of the drink, shudders lightly, then turns to me.

'That's better,' he says. 'Now a man can talk.'

'I'm very grateful to you for agreeing to talk to me,' I say, but my niceties are wasted on Cassie.

189

'Fuck grateful,' he says. 'I'm talking to you because I want to, not because you want me to.'

'I'm glad, all the same, that you want to talk to me.'

Cassie drains his glass, signals Zadoc for a refill, and fixes me with a truculent stare. The man evidently doesn't take kindly to professions of gratitude. He probably doesn't receive very many. 'Why? What's in it for you?'

'Well, as I explained, I'm trying to get as many perspectives as possible on Desirée's death ...'

'Perspectives? So I'm a *perspective*?'

Oh, hell. I wouldn't have taken Cassie Carstens for the sensitive type. They're the worst. 'No, not just *a* perspective,' I say. 'Obviously, as someone who knew Desirée well, your, er, account will carry a lot of weight.'

I've learnt that most people think their story is more important than other people's, and it does no harm to indulge that belief. Cassie, though, surprises me by snorting sceptically. 'Ja. I bet that's what you say to everybody.'

I suppress a groan. This is like seducing somebody who wants to be seduced but doesn't want to seem over-eager.

'No, why would I do that? I don't have time to listen to *everybody* banging on about their story.' I decide on a change of tack. 'But I'd understand if you felt you'd rather not talk about something so personal.'

This has the desired effect, as it usually does. 'I didn't say I didn't want to talk about it,' he mutters. 'I just didn't like how you said it.'

Another surprise – Cassie Carstens is fastidious about tone. 'Okay, I'm sorry,' I say, doing my best to strike a tone that's appeasing without seeming abject. 'I know it's difficult.'

Another miscalculation. 'Difficult?' he asks. 'What's so fucking difficult?' Cassie Carstens can't really take his liquor, it would seem, and has already hit the aggressive stage of inebriation, which in his case is merely an intensification of his normal mode. Experience has taught me that there's seldom a story to be had from this stage: any attempt to elicit it just aggravates the mood.

190

The only hope is to hang around for the maudlin stage, which tends to be more communicative.

So I order myself another drink, and pretend to a lively interest in the rest of the room, which is now filling up with what I take to be the Saturday night crowd: mainly single or at any rate unaccompanied men, generally overweight, loud without feeling, hearty without warmth. It's intensely depressing. I decide I'm not going to spend the evening here waiting for Cassie to open up; I'll drink up and go and see if Nonyameko is around.

But Cassie is as sensitive to silence as to fancied slights. 'So do you want to hear my story, or don't you?' he asks, the note of self-pity in his voice signalling the onset of the maudlin stage.

'Of course I do,' I say, trying to sound properly interested without being too avid. 'Whenever you feel you want to tell it.'

He nods. 'Look,' he says, 'I don't want to talk bad about the dead.'

A bit late for that particular inhibition to kick in. 'I understand that,' I say.

'And I want you to know that what they say about Desirée isn't true.'

'What *they* say?' So far, the main source of gossip about Desirée seems to have been Cassie Carstens.

'Ja. About her and me.'

'Oh, that,' I say. 'You mean it isn't true?'

'Depends on what you mean. *What* isn't true?'

I was hoping Cassie would tell me this. 'Well, that you and Desirée ...'

'Were having relations?' The old-fashioned phrase sounds almost quaint on his lips.

'Yes.'

'Well, that's crap.' He stares morosely into his glass, and I wonder if I should nudge him gently, but decide against it. You don't gently nudge a ruminating rhinoceros.

After another gloomy silence, Cassie volunteers, 'She wouldn't.'

'She wouldn't ...?'

'Have relations. With me.'

'But Joy ...'

'But Joy what? Ja, I know all the stories, I told them to her because they seemed to turn her on. Geez, women can be fucking weird. In any case, I didn't want people to think that I couldn't get what I wanted. And I wanted Desirée van Blerk, I wanted her before she married that terrorist, and I wanted her after she married him.' He bangs his now empty glass on the counter, but Zadoc is at the other end of the bar. 'Where's that fucking ....? To tell you the truth,' he says to me, fixing me with an unsteady stare, 'to tell you the absolute fucking rock-bottom truth, I was in love with Desirée ever since we were at school. We were in the same class, you remember?'

'Yes, I do remember, now that you mention it,' I lie. Cassie Carstens seems to have struck a nostalgic vein that may well deliver some useful information along with its gush of self-revelation.

'Ja,' he says unhappily, 'the same class all the way from sub A to matric, and I always loved her. All that time.' He sighs; the brandy is now distilling pure self-pity from the strange mix of Cassie Carstens's emotions.

'And did she know this?'

'Not at the time. I didn't tell her, she would have laughed in my face. She called me Septimus,' he adds gloomily. 'Septic Septimus.'

He succeeds in catching Zadoc's eye and orders another double brandy.

'So when she came back from Stellenbosch I thought now's my chance, because by then I'd inherited the farm and I was doing well for myself. The *Huisgenoot* had an article about me when I started the commercial hunting on my farm,' he says, with evident pride.

Commercial hunting: it figures.

'And Desirée?' I prod. Cassie seems lost in contemplating his own advantages.

'Oh, Desirée, she wasn't impressed at all. I asked her out a few times, and she accepted, but she kept on calling me Septimus even though I asked her not to, and I always thought she was laughing at me.'

'But you did see her often?'

'Oh, sure I *saw* her, I saw her every chance I got. And she saw me. But that was it. She didn't want me,' he repeats, as if considering this singular fact with amazement.

So, I reflect ruefully, it's going to cost me several double brandies just to discover that Cassie's story is in fact that there's no story. But he has another surprise up his sleeve.

'She didn't want me,' he says again, then adds, almost as an afterthought, 'But she did want me to take her away.'

'To take her away? Where to?'

'Cape Town. Joburg. Anywhere. Away from Alfredville. Away from Hector fucking Williams.'

'She told you this?'

'Of course she fucking told me this, how else do you think I knew it?'

'But when?'

'When? All the time. If you love me, take me away from here, again and again, Take me away from this dump, I'm not going to be your weekend whore while you look for a nice boeremeisie to wipe your children's noses and bums and cut up the animals you slaughter and shoot.'

'And why didn't you take her away, if you were in love with her?'

'Now you're sounding like her. Why not? Because I'm a fucking farmer, that's why, and my fucking farm is right here in Alfredville and there's no way I could sell it even if I wanted to. And what would I do in Cape Town or Joburg? Become a hairdresser?' he demands, evidently arguing once again with the dead Desirée. 'And then that last night ...'

'You saw her that last night?' I ask.

''Course I saw her that last night. I went there because I heard a rumour she was having it off with that short fart of a policeman.'

'Bennie Nienaber?'

193

'Ja, Bennie fucking Nienaber. They were saying in the bar that she was screwing him, and they were teasing me about it, Hey old Cassie, so what's the matter, is the policeman's gun bigger than yours, shit like that. So I got the moer in and went over to her place. I knew her husband was on duty that night because she told me I could come over if I liked. So I barged in – she never locked the front door – and I tuned What's this crap I hear and she said what business was it of mine and I schemed why was she giving Bennie Nienaber what she wasn't giving me and I called her a cock-teaser and some other things as well and I was totally the moer in and I, you know, when I get angry I get, you know, very worked up and I was standing over her and she noticed and she laughed like a fucking drain and said Septimus your sceptre is showing.'

Cassie looks at me as if to gauge my response. I try not to smile. My cousin seems to have had a robust sense of humour. 'I mean,' he says, 'how would *you* like it, having your hard-on laughed at?'

'I imagine it's tough, yes,' I say.

'Tough? It's fucking *humiliating*.' He pauses. 'So I slapped her.'

'You slapped her?'

'Ja. Not very hard,' he adds, as if in extenuation.

'And then?'

'She told me to leave and I said I don't know what and I left and went back to the bar, but before I got there I thought no, I couldn't leave it there, and I would go back and apologise.' He looks at me, evidently expecting to be praised for his magnanimity.

'Big of you,' I say.

'You're fucking right. Not that I thought it would do me much good, but still.'

'So you went back?'

'Ja, I did. But when I got there – well, I opened the front door without knocking and went in. You know, there's a kind of entrance hall before you get to the sitting room.'

'Yes, I know. I used to live in that house.'

'Did you? Oh ja, I remember, Jacobs the Jew chemist. Anyways, so I was in the entrance hall and I heard voices and I stopped and listened, and it was Bennie Nienaber and she was scheming him the same line she always spun me, If you love me so much take me away from here, and Nienaber, he tuned her back, What about my wife and children, and she spins him, So what *about* your wife and children when you come round here pestering me, why don't you think of them then? What about if I tell your wife that you've been here twice a week for the past how many weeks? And he got angry and started shouting at her, so I left.'

He looks at me lugubriously. 'I fucking-well left. Do you know what that means?'

It takes me, in truth, a few moments to realise what he's telling me.

'So you think that Bennie …?'

'What else? They were having an argument, he was pissed off, chances are she was pushing his buttons the way she pushed mine, so he killed her. And the worst thing is, if I hadn't left I could have stopped the bugger.'

'You *really* think Bennie Nienaber killed Desirée?'

'So what do you think, I'm just chaffing you? Of course I *really* think so. Don't ask me to prove it, but I'm telling you, I think so. I'm fucking *sure*.'

'What time was this that you saw Bennie there? They say she was killed at about seven thirty.'

'Dunno. Could have been seven thirty, my watch said some time after seven o'clock, but I've told you, the fucking thing runs to its own time. But it was close enough. I tell you, Nienaber did it.'

'But why haven't you told anybody?'

'So, I'm telling you now, aren't I?'

'Yes, but when they arrested Hector Williams, wasn't that the time to speak up?'

'Why? Do I care a two-cent fuck for Hector Williams? He's a terrorist, and if he didn't kill his wife he killed plenty of white people anyway. I feel fuck-all for Bennie Nienaber too, but I can sort of understand how the bugger felt. I mean, I slapped her, didn't I? If she'd worked my case any harder, who knows, I could have killed her. So as I say, I can understand. You could even say she sort of deserved it. You don't work a man's case like that without expecting him to cause shit.'

'But I thought there was pretty strong evidence against Williams – fingerprints and bloodstains and so on.'

'Ha!' he laughs mirthlessly. 'You've been out of the country for too long, boetie. You ever heard of fabricated evidence?'

'In a general sort of way, yes.'

'Well, in a general sort of way the police have become expert at fabricating evidence, to make up for not being able to get it in any other way.'

'But you can't know that this was what happened here.'

'Can't I, Mr Wiseguy? What would you say if I told you I *know* the evidence against Williams was fabricated?'

'I suppose I'd ask you how you knew.'

'And I could say that's none of your fucking business, but since you're paying for the drinks I'll tell you I know because I was told by the man who fabricated it.'

'And who was that?' I ask, dreading the reply.

'Nobody you know. One of the detectives they sent from Oudtshoorn to come and investigate. He got drunk here, right there where you're sitting, and told me. He said he didn't like doing it, but he was ordered to do it. By his superior.'

'But why would they want to frame Williams?'

'How must I know? But you take two white cops, they're investigating a murder, and here's a black cop, outranking them and putting on airs. Doesn't take much to say, You bugger, we'll get you. And so they got him. To be fair, the oke who spoke to me said they were convinced that Williams was the murderer, they just didn't have the evidence.'

'So they fabricated it.'

'So they fabricated it.'

'But … but don't you have a duty to tell the police what you know?'

He grins unexpectedly, lending an oddly boyish air to the

pugnacious features. 'You want me to tell the police that I know they fabricated evidence against the man they arrested?'

'Yes. Not the same policemen obviously, but ... there must be somebody.'

'Ja. Maybe there is a somebody. So why do you scheme I'm telling you all this?'

'I don't know,' I say, truthfully enough. 'Why *are* you telling me this?'

'So I can get the fuck out of the whole thing. So I can stop worrying what to do about it.'

'You mean that I ...?'

'Ja, it's your baby now. She was your cousin. So don't tell me about my fucking duty. *You* decide what to do with it. For me, it's overs, finished and klaar.'

He drains the last few drops in his glass. 'Thanks for the drinks,' he says.

'You're welcome,' I say bleakly.

CHAPTER 13

Sunday morning 25 January

I wake up with the nagging sense of an unresolved quandary. It takes me a moment to trace it to its origins: the trick Cassie Carstens played me. For a trick is surely what it was. He adroitly passed on to me the burden of deciding what to do with his suspicion. What he couldn't have known – not that it would have made any difference if he had known – was how truly diabolical his trick was: he was in fact challenging me to denounce my erstwhile best friend as my cousin's murderer, or otherwise be complicit in the conviction of an innocent man. Well, I think wryly, I wanted a story and I got a story; I'm knee-deep in the story.

Of course, Cassie Carstens might have planted his story in order to deflect suspicion from himself: he had as much reason as Bennie to kill Desirée, and I have only his word for it that he saw Bennie with her. But then, why would he raise the topic at all? No, it would have been simpler to say nothing. Which doesn't detract from the sheer unlikeliness of his story: Bennie could never kill anybody, could he? Or could he? Since I knew him last, he's been to the army, he's been through experiences I have no inkling of – what do I really know of his capabilities and capacities?

The day is once again blazingly hot, and I remain indoors for such coolness as the wobbly fan can provide, bringing my notes up to date, trying to make some sort of sense of them. I think of writing to James to explain to him, and to myself really, my sense of being embroiled in a story that I thought I'd merely come to report. But there is too much that needs explaining, the place that Bennie used to occupy in my life, and now seems about to reclaim against every inclination of my nature. I don't think I ever even told James about Bennie: in London, he seemed impossibly remote, a dim memory of a disowned past. And now it is James and our London life that seem dim and distant. The Maida Vale tube station with its perpetually draughty vestibule, the hay-fever-inducing plane trees in Randolph Avenue, our flat in Maida Mews with its two hours of sun in summer and pervasive gloom the rest of the year: these seem unreal, part of somebody else's existence, somebody to whom it is difficult to ascribe a name and identity. I myself, from this perspective, seem insubstantial. Can I really be so fickle? Or am I reverting to an older loyalty, which I have for twenty years tried to deny?

No, that isn't it either. Loyalty seems not to be a virtue I've been blessed with, or an inconvenience I've been saddled with. When I left in 1988, I missed Alfredville for about six months, I suppose; Bennie I missed on and off for a year or two. Then Alfredville and Bennie receded from consciousness in the welter of new impressions and experiences, the pressure of university life, the new friends and new anxieties, discovering and exploring my sexuality. I loved Sussex, the green landscape and the ram-shackle city: Brighton, with its seedy glamour, its down-at-heel worldliness, its louche pubs and pebbly beaches, its air of assignations and betrayals, its history of royal excess and petty crookery, was as remote from Alfredville as it was possible to be. The somewhat uncertain direction of my sexuality, too, seemed not to be a problem here, where everything was permissible and experimentation was encouraged. I discovered somewhat to my bemusement that I was, if not exactly courted, then at any rate in moderate demand, at parties and in pubs, both by women and by men. I found that I could give and receive pleasure to and from both, and decided that the fuss about sexual orientation was a hangover from a puritanical age when human diversity was regarded as subversive. As far as I was concerned, it was not yet necessary to choose.

As a South African, at a time when that country had sunk to its lowest point ever in international esteem, I would probably have been shunned by the more conscientiously left-wing students, had I not been known to have left South Africa in principled opposition to the regime, to avoid conscription into the apartheid army. For some reason this was regarded as an act of bravery, and I did not try to disillusion people who seemed to need this interpretation.

Moving to London after graduating with a creditable but not spectacular degree in English, I found a job with *The Independent*, then still a relatively young and vigorous paper – I liked its un-committed political line, and they seemed to like what I did. I was lucky in that at the time – 1992 – South Africa was undergoing its momentous and troubled transition to majority rule, and as a native I was deemed to have a more innate understanding of the forces at work than I in fact had. But I allowed the assumption to operate in my favour, and, being given assignments well in advance of my expertise, I slowly brought my level of real know-ledge respectably close to my level of imputed knowledge.

I worked for *The Independent* for ten years, and made a modest name for myself – enough to embolden me to strike out on my own in 2002, and since then I've made a reasonable living as a freelance writer. James was not the first person I'd had a relation-ship with, but at five years, it was my longest-lasting connection. He's younger than I am – he's thirty-three – and much more out-going. This is partly a function of his profession and perhaps partly of his background, an English father, Jamaican mother and six siblings of assorted genders.

But, as I've said, that part of my life now seems very remote. I can't really imagine telling James about going swimming with Bennie, for instance – 'You mean you went swimming starkers in some muddy dam in the middle of nowhere?' he'd say. 'Is this some kind of macho South African ritual?' And as for Desirée's situation – 'You mean the woman just sat there waiting for some man to *take* her somewhere, like some African Madame Bovary?' James has little patience with people who are passive victims of their situation, as he calls it. He couldn't understand that Desirée could have been a victim exactly of her determination not to be a passive victim. There is a lot about my life, I realise, that James never understood – or I about his, I imagine. It's almost a relief to think that it doesn't matter any more.

So in the end I write him a humorously anodyne account of Alfredville and its people, downplaying the murder and its ramifications, and overplaying the backwardness of Alfredville, perhaps to compensate for my temporary loss of rapport with my London life:

As for the 'story' I'm here to write, that is showing some promise. I may be onto something with plenty of 'human interest', not to mention the political angle that is de rigueur for all writing about South Africa. There is enough local colour to liven things up, though in truth the local colour is less lively in the flesh than it will, I hope, be on the page. I'm off to lunch with the relations – my mother's sister and family. Likely to be a heavy affair, both in terms of the home cooking – think plenty of meat and starch – and the company – again think plenty of meat and starch. I dropped in soon after my arrival and found them rather lugubrious. It's just my aunt and her husband and their thick son, who wasn't there when I called but is sure to be around to feed his face. Not exactly the Bloomsbury Group, nor even the Brady Bunch.

I send off the letter and go down to breakfast. Joy is on duty at reception, and gives me a frosty greeting. 'Good morning, Mr Jacobs,' she says in her best professional manner. There is clearly not going to be any fond reminiscing about Friday evening between the two of us.

'Morning, Joy,' I say. 'How are you today?'

'Thank you, I'm very well,' she says, the lacquered surfaces of her lips undisturbed by even the merest hint of a smile.

The momentary twinge of discomfort occasioned by Joy's coolness disappears when I find Nonyameko in the dining room, apparently just starting her breakfast. She looks up, sees me, and with a smile gestures at the empty chair at her table. I sit down.

'You're late this morning,' I say. 'Normally you've disappeared by the time I have breakfast.'

'That is because it's Sunday. Normally I work.'

'Of course. And normally I go for a run before breakfast.'

She makes a mock-impressed face. 'That is commendable.'

201

'It gets to be a habit, even an addiction. So there's nothing really to commend.'

'You look good on it, anyway.'

'That's the second compliment you've given me in five minutes. Is there something the matter?'

'On Sundays I try to take a charitable view of things.'

'You certainly dress in a more laid-back fashion,' I say; she's wearing a T-shirt instead of her usual business jacket, and from what I can see of her lower limbs she's wearing jeans. She is looking fresh and alert; her remarkable eyes are brighter than the eyes of anyone over the age of eighteen have any business to be on a Sunday morning. 'You are looking almost indecently good.'

'I always dress appropriately,' she says, adroitly avoiding the compliment. 'This is appropriate for the walk I plan to take after breakfast.' She hesitates. 'Would you like to come along?'

'I'd have loved to,' I say, 'but I'm supposed to be having lunch with my aunt and uncle in ...' I look at my watch, 'about three hours' time, which wouldn't give us much time for a walk.'

'I said a walk, not a hike. We could be back in an hour and a half. But if you'd rather not ...'

It gives me a strange frisson of pleasure to see Nonyameko so unsure of herself. I'm tempted to prolong the moment, but then say, 'No, I'd love to, really. I'll meet you in the lobby at half past nine?'

'Sure.' Then she reassumes the initiative. 'But let's have breakfast first.'

At precisely half past nine I'm in the lobby, trying to ignore Joy's pointed ignoring of me. When Nonyameko appears and walks up to me, Joy glances up from the pamphlet she's been studiously perusing, and a brief frown discomposes her features. If Joy is a reliable gauge, my return to Alfredville has not been a totally successful exercise in human relations.

We leave the cool refuge of the lobby and find that the morning is already blanching under the onslaught of the sun. I'm not sure that a walk is the best way of spending such a morning, but

I'm committed now, and Nonyameko seems unfazed by the heat.

'Good morning, *m'sieur dame*!' Vincent appears, as always, from nowhere.

'Good morning, Vincent,' Nonyameko says.

'Oh, you two know each other?' I ask, though I realise I shouldn't be surprised.

'But of course, monsieur,' Vincent says. 'I know everybody.'

'And you work even on a Sunday?'

'Ah, monsieur, what do I do if I don't work? I stand around. So now I stand around here and perhaps somebody will pay me for it.'

'We must find you a real job,' Nonyameko says, 'one in which you can sit down.'

Vincent widens his eyes and places a long finger in front of his mouth in a parody of discretion. 'Ah, madame, don't tell anybody, but I think there may be a *boulot* – a job – for me soon.'

'That is wonderful, Vincent,' Nonyameko says. 'What is the job?'

He shakes his head. 'No, it is still a great secret. Please do not say a word about it.'

'Okay, we promise,' she says. 'But I hope it is a good one.'

'It is an excellent one, madame,' he says as we walk off.

I automatically turn left, in the direction of the dam: Alfredville does not offer a wide variety of walks. But Nonyameko puts a restraining hand on my arm. 'No, let's walk this way,' she says, turning towards the road leading up to the R62.

'There's nothing there, apart from the main road,' I protest.

'Yes, nothing, apart from the road and about twenty thousand people.'

I feel myself flushing, partly from embarrassment, partly from annoyance. 'Sure,' I say, 'I know people are living there, but it's not exactly a scenic walk, is it?'

'So, when last did you take a walk through a township?'

'It's been a while.'

'Have you *ever* taken a walk through a township?'

203

'No.'

'Well then, be my guest.'

We walk up through the outskirts of the village, discussing Vincent.

'The thing is,' says Nonyameko, 'he is far too qualified for almost any job he could get here.'

'But why doesn't he go to the city and find something better there?'

'Well, he has a place to stay here, which is not so easy to find in the city. And then, you may have read about the attacks on foreigners in the cities.'

'Yes, I have.'

'So Vincent may not feel safe there. The more qualified you are, the more you are felt to be an outsider.'

We cross the main road and I enter the terra incognita of the township. Since it's Sunday, the streets are full of people idling away the day or otherwise finding some shared activity: children playing with cars made of wire; women plaiting each other's hair; men sitting on makeshift seats in front of ramshackle houses. Various species of music – I realise that I have no idea of indigenous South African music – compete for dominance from hidden radios or boom boxes, or, more likely, MP3 players. People look at us with mild curiosity; I'm the only white in sight, and Nonyameko's attire, though informal, is rather more citified in style than that of the locals. There's an amiable interchange of greetings and what I take to be small talk between Nonyameko and some of the residents, questions that she parries with a smile or a quip, followed by loud laughter, amid general and vociferous goodwill.

'They want to know what I am doing with a *bhulu*,' she says. 'They say you look as if you could give me lots of children.'

'Oh, I get told that all the time in England.'

She laughs, a mellow contralto. 'Yes, I'm sure.' Then, after a pause, 'Do you miss England?'

'Not really,' I say. 'Though I guess I would feel more at home on a Sunday morning in London than I do here.'

We have walked through the main part of the township and

are now in a desolate area, where some goats are grazing, a few children are playing with an old tyre, and a dog is sniffing at what seems to be a garbage dump. It's a scene of desolation, of neglect and decay, of heat and flies and stench.

'Hell,' I say, 'this looks like the cover of *Disgrace*. Why did you bring me here?'

'Why do you think?' she asks.

'Let's see. Perhaps you want me to say how terrible this is, so that you can tell me this is how the majority of people live in South Africa.'

'Why would I want to do that?'

'I don't know. But perhaps to make me feel uncomfortable about my own privileged status.'

She laughs. 'Just because you feel uncomfortable, you must not assume I am trying to *make* you feel uncomfortable. No, I really just wanted you to see where I grew up. Not everything I do is politically motivated. And this spot, terrible as it seems to you, is where I used to come when I wanted to be on my own. You can see the Swartberg from here.' She points to the horizon where, indeed, a mountain range masses in the haze, beyond range upon range of lesser hills. 'It made me feel that there were other places on earth, and that I could get to them.'

'And there were, and you got to them.'

'I did.'

'And now that you're back – could you stay?'

'I don't know. My mother is dead, my friends have left – and I suppose I am used to a more dynamic environment. But this takes its own kind of energy, people scrambling to make a living with fewer opportunities and fewer amenities.'

'So you could in fact come back?'

'Perhaps I could come back if I felt that there was some reason to. I would not come back just for the sake of coming back.'

'And if I said that was my feeling about South Africa, would you accept that?'

'Yes, I would. I do not really want to find you guilty of high treason, you know.'

'That's good to know,' I say. We stand there for a moment in the still sunshine. It's strangely peaceful here, and Nonyameko too seems to feel it, because she stands quite still with her face lifted to the sun. Or perhaps she wants me to experience for myself the immensity of space and light transcending the squalor of the immediate surroundings and the heat pressing down on us.

Then she opens her eyes and looks at me. 'Are you sorry you left when you did?' she asks me abruptly.

'I suppose I've been asking myself that question since I've been back, without really knowing I was doing so.'

'And have you come up with an answer?'

'No. I don't think there really *is* an answer. But I can see, I think, what I missed by leaving.'

'And what is that?'

'It's difficult to say, exactly. But going to England was such a safe option.'

'Are you saying you'd rather have been unsafe?'

'Given a choice, no. But the point is, I wasn't given a choice. My father decided for me that I wouldn't go to the army like all the other young men, and he decided for me that Sussex was the place to go.'

'Forgive me if I do not pity you for having had a protective father who deprived you of the privilege of joining the SADF. Would you rather have gone to the army and ended up coming in here' – she gestures towards the township behind us – 'in an armoured car to shoot kids?'

'No, I really wouldn't. Nor would I have wanted to go to the border to terrorise the indigenous population or be blown up by a landmine. And yet I wonder – I just *wonder* – whether an experience like that, or an experience such as you had, joining MK, whether it wouldn't have *changed* me in some way.'

'I am sure it would have, especially the landmine. It could even have traumatised or maimed you, as it did many young men and, for that matter, women. Would you have wanted that?'

'No, no, *no*. I think I'm saying that perhaps we weren't meant to be so damn *safe* all the time.'

'Meant? By whom?'

'Oh, I don't know, by whatever scheme of things is supposed to produce well-rounded adults, some *ideal* of growth.'

'I have not come across any such scheme that suggests that it is beneficial to the young person to grow up in an unsafe environment.' She says this in a deadpan way that I have come to recognise as, after all, her brand of irony.

'You're mocking me, and I know I may be talking the biggest rubbish, but you asked me how I felt about leaving here – so no, I'm not *sorry* I left, but I do feel that I missed something by leaving.'

'And you would have missed something if you had not left.'

'Of course, and I would have wondered about *that* for the rest of my life.'

'Then perhaps wondering is our natural condition.'

'What is it *you* wonder about?'

'Oh, me, I have given up wondering. The world is what it is, and I have to deal with it, or with the part of it that comes my way.'

'That sounds very mature.'

A slight frown signals her habitual earnest engagement with any proposition she's confronted with; then she visibly relents and smiles. 'Now you are mocking *me*.'

'Oh, I wouldn't dare. But tell me,' I say, emboldened by her more relaxed manner.

'Mm?'

'Don't you have a partner – a husband or a boyfriend?'

For a moment she seems about to repel this invitation to intimacy, but then she simply shakes her head, not looking at me, and says in an almost contemplative tone, 'No, I do not. I had one once, but he died. He was from here, too. We grew up together and ran away together to join MK. He was blown up by a car bomb in Bulawayo soon after.'

She turns to look at me. 'Since then I have not had anybody. I have been too busy,' she says with a laugh, evidently trying to lighten the tone.

'I'm sorry,' I say. 'I didn't realise ...'

'Realise what?'

'That the Struggle affected you so personally.'

'It affected everybody personally. The history of the Struggle is the sum of millions of stories.' She is obviously uncomfortable with this turn of the conversation. 'And many people lost somebody. But shall we go back?'

'Yes, let's,' I say.

'So,' she says, as we turn and start walking back, 'how is the story going?'

'I don't know whether to say it's going well or it's not going at all. Let's just say it's not going as expected.'

'Isn't that the mark of a good story?'

'Perhaps, from the reader's point of view. As the writer, I'd like a bit more control.'

'And in what respect is your story getting out of hand?'

'To cut a long story short, then ...'

'You need not do that, you know. We've got time.'

'Yes, but I'll spare you the cast list and back stories. In essence, my story has lost its punch line.'

'And what was the punch line going to be?'

'Well, you remember that I intended it to be an analysis of racial attitudes in a democratic South Africa, as highlighted by the murder of a white woman by her black husband.'

'Yes. The *Othello* scenario.'

'Exactly. Only now it seems that perhaps the husband didn't do it.'

'Mm. I seem to remember asking you what made you so sure.'

'Yes, yes, I remember, and I said that the evidence seemed fairly conclusive. And it did, too. Only now I've met someone who claims that somebody else did it.'

'And who is the *someone* and who is the *somebody else*?'

'Do you mind if I don't tell you just yet? It's all up in the air at the moment.'

'Sure. But are you going to bring it down to earth?'

'I'm hardly the person to do that. I'm just the writer, remember.'

'But you are not going to sit back and see an innocent man take the rap, are you? Just so as not to spoil the punch line of your story?'

I feel myself flushing. 'Of course not. But what's the alternative?'

'Do something. Go to the police.'

'It's not as simple as that. If you must know, the … person named by my informant is also a policeman.'

'Heavens, it's a closed shop, isn't it? So why can you not finger a policeman?'

'In the first place, he's quite a senior policeman, and I'd be asking his subordinates to act against him. In the second place, he's my best friend. That is, he was.'

She whistles between her teeth. 'Oh dear. You really have gone and mixed yourself up in it, haven't you?'

I can't escape the sense that she's enjoying my situation. 'Look,' I say, 'I haven't *mixed myself up in it*. It's still only a story.'

'In which you seem to be taking a leading part.'

'I'm not *taking* it. It's being inflicted upon me.'

'Whichever.' She seems to be thinking of something else. When I start to speak, she holds up a hand. 'Wait. I must tell you something and I am thinking how to do it.'

'As long as you don't tell me you also have a theory as to who killed Desirée.'

'No – no, not exactly.'

'What do you mean not *exactly*?' I almost shout.

'Well, call it not at all, then. But I do have some information that could affect your theory.'

'Listen, I don't *have* a bloody theory. All I have is other people's hunches.'

'Well, here's another one then.' She pauses; I'm surprised at her diffidence. 'What I am about to tell you constitutes a breach of professional confidence, and I would not normally do it. But I think in this instance there are considerations that outweigh professional ethics, so I am doing it. But please do not let it go any further.'

I nod. 'Of course.'

'As, for instance, in writing about it.'

209

'Of course,' I say, though I find myself tempted to ask, But what's the *point*, then?

She takes a deep breath. 'You know that I am dealing with the psychological problems of disadvantaged pregnant women.'

'I do. But what ...?'

'Be quiet and listen. One of my patients is a young woman called Sarah Augustyn.'

'From the name, I gather that she's ... not black.'

'She is Coloured. She was referred to me by the local birth control clinic because she was having anxiety attacks and asking for an abortion, which the clinic won't perform because she is six months pregnant. It took me a while to find out why she is so upset and why she wants an abortion. It turns out that she is, or was, Hector Williams's girlfriend.'

'Oh, hell. How recently?'

'Up to his arrest. The child is his.'

'Oh *fuck*,' I say. 'Poor Desirée.'

'Perhaps. Although that is not how Sarah sees the matter. And my concern is with Sarah, who is in a bad way.'

'Physically?'

'No, physically she is absolutely fine. But mentally she is very confused.'

'But why?'

'*Why*? The father of her child gets arrested for murdering his wife and you ask why she is confused?'

'I mean, why *confused*? I can see of course that she'd be upset or angry – but *confused*?'

'Basically because she does not know what to do. She says she does not want a murderer's child.'

'So she believes Hector did it?'

'She says she does not know what to believe. She is not allowed to speak to Hector himself, and she thinks it is more than possible that he did it, and what is more, that it was her fault.'

'How could it be?'

'Yes. That is the difficulty. Hector visited her on the night of the murder.'

'So he has an alibi?'

'No. He left her at six thirty. The murder took place at about seven thirty.'

'Yes, I know. I mean, I know that the murder took place at seven thirty. So she thinks he did it?'

'As I say, she doesn't know what to think.'

'But why does she think it could be her fault?'

'It seems that when he came to see her, she told him that she was expecting his child, and told him he had to leave his wife. There was an argument, and he left in a rage. But she thinks he may have gone home and confronted his wife and then had an argument and killed her. That is what is upsetting her. The thought that Hector could have killed his wife. She is in many ways a very conservative woman.'

'Not that you need to be conservative to be upset at finding out your lover's a murderer. But may I ask why you're telling me this?' I enquire, though I suspect I know the answer.

'Yes, you may ask. I am telling you because if it is true that there's a chance that Hector did not do it, then Sarah must be told. For the sake of her peace of mind and for the safety of her child. She is very emotional.'

'And you want to tell her what I've just told you?'

'No. I want you to tell her.'

'But why? You've been talking to her, she knows you and trusts you ...'

'That is the problem. I am not sure that she does trust me. She thinks I would do anything to get her to have the child – which is true, up to a point. I think it would damage her for ever if she had an abortion now. But I cannot convince her of that. As I say, she is very conservative. She does not really attach much value to a woman's opinion, I think, and a black woman at that. Whereas a white man ...' She sighs. 'Old habits die hard. You would not think she'd have much reason to trust white men, but there you are.'

'There I am, indeed. You want me to go to Sarah and tell her that I don't think Hector killed Desirée.'

211

'You can tell her that there is a good chance that he did not kill her.'

'And if he did kill her?'

'Then we will have seen Sarah through a very emotional time.'

'We?'

'Yes, *we*.' Again, I can't help noticing a certain savouring of my situation: the ex-pat has been corralled again.

'And when am I supposed to have this ... interview with Sarah?'

'As soon as possible. I am seeing her tomorrow morning. Can you talk to her tomorrow afternoon?'

'I suppose I *can*. I'm not sure that I *want* to.'

'Want is not an option.'

'Clearly.'

'Then there you go. I will tell her you're coming.'

'There I go.'

She takes my arm. She's much shorter than me, but we're a good fit. 'Let's get back to the hotel. You have to prepare for your lunch.'

CHAPTER 14

Sunday midday

I gird my loins for lunch with Aunt Dolly and Oom Blik. I've lost
the trick of dressing for Sunday lunch in Alfredville, indeed, have
never really had it. Our house, under my father's benign rule,
always favoured comfort over formality, and, unlike many of my
friends, I did not have to spend my Sundays jacketed-and-tied. A
certain minimum of decency was, however, required: though I
could dispense with shoes at home, I was not to appear barefoot
in public on a Sunday: 'Not because God cares what you wear,'
my mother said, 'but because the neighbours do.' My father,
though he was as little exercised about the neighbours as about
God, would not have gone without shaving, for instance, and he
never wore shorts on a Sunday, even though it wasn't even his
Sabbath. My mother, for her part, though she was contemptuous
of 'dressing up', was by nature neat and always looked her best.
At the time I thought there was something hypocritical about my
parents' humouring of the neighbours; now I think that they were
simply considerate.

But Aunt Dolly and Oom Blik were of another persuasion: they
dressed as they did everything, heavily and with an eye to effect.
Oom Blik, who was an elder in the church, wore his black suit all
day on Sunday, even while reading the *Sunday Times* on the back
stoep. (He would not have read it on the front stoep, because the
Sunday Times was regarded as 'liberal' by many of his neighbours.) Aunt Dolly took off her hat on coming home from church,
but kept on her church dress, stockings and shoes for the rest of
the day – also, according to my mother, her 'step-in', as corsets
were then called. This, in Alfredville in February, was a heroic
feat, assuring Aunt Dolly, my mother said, a place in heaven.

I, though, have no desire to earn a place in heaven by sweltering through a Sunday lunch, and I decide that a pair of chinos and a clean white shirt is all that the Lord and for that matter Oom Blik and Aunt Dolly could reasonably expect from me.

I turn up at ten past twelve; 'a little late, to give them time to put on lipstick,' my mother used to say, 'but not so late that the food gets cold.' I take with me a bottle of Robertson Shiraz that I bought yesterday as a respite from the Ghanta Pinotage.

The door is opened by Angelina, with Cedric in attendance. She makes big eyes at me. 'Morning, Master Peter,' she says. She shakes her head and in a conspiratorial whisper says, 'Everything is *deurmekaar* again here this morning. It's all a big mess again.'

'Why, Angelina? Is anything wrong?'

She looks over her shoulder as if expecting an eavesdropper. 'No,' she says, still in the dramatic whisper, 'nothing *wrong*, but the missis and the baas don't want Boetie to bring his girlfriend to lunch, and Boetie says then he's not coming to lunch, and they say it's an insult to you, and he says you've been gone for twenty years so you've got no business being insulted.' She smiles at me slyly. 'I'm sorry, Master Peter, but I'm just repeating what they said.'

'But what's wrong with Boetie's girlfriend?' I ask, with a guilty sense that I'm exploiting Angelina's evident itch to gossip.

'Ney, nothing, Master Peter' – she holds back for a moment with the dramatic timing of a small-town raconteuse – 'except that she is, you know, a Coloured.'

I try to keep my surprise from showing. Coloured girlfriends are not among the range of possibilities I'd imagined for Boetie van Blerk; but then, I've never really given much thought to Boetie and his possibilities. Angelina, evidently disappointed at my lack of response, continues. 'But that's not all. She's Hector's sister.'

'Hector *Williams*?'

She nods emphatically. 'Livona Williams. She's a nice girl, very decent. She works there by the Municipal Office.'

I remember now Joy Duvenhage's story about Boetie causing

214

ructions at the wedding by making a pass at Williams's sister. Apparently the flirtation has been more successful than the marriage.

'And Oom Blik and Aunt Dolly don't like it?'

She giggles. 'You must be joking. They've had the Williams family up to *here*.' She performs a slicing motion across her epiglottis.

'And so, is she coming to lunch or not?'

'If you ask me, she doesn't want to come, and I don't blame her either. Boetie's just being stroppy. And you'll see, he'll be at lunch. He likes making a scene.' She ushers me in, closes the front door behind us, and says more loudly, 'The missis said to show Master Peter to the best sitting room.'

The house has two sitting rooms, one for family use, the other for guests. Cedric's toenails click on the wooden floor as Angelina leads me into the guest sitting room. It's a gloomy room, cold even in midsummer. Heavy wooden chairs and coffee tables squat on ball-and-claw feet on the yellowwood floor, like malign exotic reptiles. A three-tiered chandelier is suspended from the high ceiling; like the furniture, it seems to harbour evil intentions, as if it could come crashing down and squash someone. On the walls are improbable landscapes, leaping cataracts and pellucid pools, in heavy gilt frames. A display cabinet houses a willow-pattern dinner service, an heirloom descended from my mother's grandmother, I remember. 'The dinner service was left to me in Ma's will,' my mother said one day. 'But Dolly can have it, she's got a daughter to leave it to.' I suppose it will go to Boetie's wife, now that Dolly no longer has a daughter. It can't be what Ouma Visagie had in mind, that her dinner service should go to Livona Williams, but then, what Ouma and her generation had in mind has long ceased to dictate events in South Africa.

'Sit down so long, Master Peter,' Angelina says. 'I'll tell the missis you're here.'

Missis presumably knows this already, having heard the doorbell, but protocol demands that she be informed with due ceremony before making her appearance. I hand Angelina the bottle of wine; she examines the label and says '*Robertson* wine.' I'd forgotten that drinking Robertson wine in Alfredville is tantamount to ordering Turkish coffee in a Greek restaurant.

I am kept waiting for about five minutes. I think I can hear muttered confabulation in the further recesses of the house, but the house is big and the walls are thick and I can't be sure. Clearly, the House of Van Blerk is in turmoil today.

At length, I hear Aunt Dolly's footsteps in the passage. She's walking slowly, as if reluctant to arrive at her destination. When eventually she does so, her face is grave, her manner formal. I suspect this is intended to signal that she has not officially forgiven me for not staying with them. I get to my feet to kiss her; she once again offers me her cheek. I suppress an impulse to tell her to stuff off then, and I brush her cheek – it's surprisingly cool – with my lips. She smells of talcum powder – liberally puffed on to counter the effects of the church service, a gruelling affair at all times, but particularly sweaty in midsummer.

'Oh hello, Pieter,' she says, her tone implying polite surprise at my presence.

'I hope I'm still invited to lunch,' I try to joke.

'Oh, but of course. Of course. It's just …' She tails off.

'Is anything the matter, Aunt Dolly?' I ask. 'If it's not convenient I can always come some other time.'

'No, no,' she says, vaguely gesticulating as if commending me to the landscape paintings. 'Now that you are here,' and again she stops, leaving her implication in mid-air.

We stand stranded in the middle of the floor, helplessly staring at each other as if just introduced by somebody we neither of us know. She doesn't offer me a seat or take one herself; I'm tempted to take the initiative and offer *her* a chair. Having time now to examine her more closely, I note that she is looking less washed-out than when I last saw her. She is, if not exactly elegant – she lacks the presence for elegance – then at any rate less conspicuously respectable, less corseted and confined, the hair less brushed, combed and sprayed, than I'd expected. She is wearing a simple black cotton dress – it occurs to me with a slight shock that she's probably in mourning, a custom I'd forgotten about – and the gloom of the room is kinder to her complexion and eyes than the bright sun of the back stoep. She is, I realise with a twinge of pity, a mother who has lost her child.

'Is Oom Blik ...?' I also gesture in the general direction of the landscapes.

'Jeremiah? Oh yes, he's here somewhere,' she says, then subsides into silence and vagueness again.

'And Boetie?' I persevere.

'Boetie. Oh, yes. Yes, he's here all right.' She gives a single, abrupt giggle, then looks shocked at her own levity.

Another silence settles around us, broken at last, to our mutual relief, by the tread of Oom Blik's black toecap-shoes.

'There's Jeremiah now,' Aunt Dolly says, and, 'Oh good!' I exclaim brightly, not entirely insincerely. I never thought I'd be pleased to see Oom Blik, but I'm almost overjoyed.

My joy is short-lived. Oom Blik, when he appears in the doorway, looks more lugubrious even than usual; he seems to be a shade or two yellower, although he is not wearing the black suit I was expecting. He is in fact relatively informally dressed in khaki, and the black toe-caps have yielded to regulation Grasshoppers.

'Morning, Oom Blik!' I say, still with my brightest manner. 'Or is it afternoon yet?'

'It's late enough,' he says. 'Dolly, when are we eating?'

He turns round without waiting for a reply; we hear his footsteps trundling towards the dining room.

Aunt Dolly and I are once again beached. 'Well,' she says after what feels like an interminable silence. 'I suppose we can go and join your uncle.'

We walk down the long passage to the dining room, our footsteps echoing on the wooden boards. As if decorum demanded it, we walk in step.

Oom Blik has already taken his seat at the long table. As we enter, he looks up and asks Aunt Dolly, 'Where's Boetie?'

She looks at me as if hoping I could tell her where to find their errant son. 'I don't know,' she says, when I fail to come up with a suggestion – the only suggestion that comes to mind being Let's forget Boetie and hope he doesn't turn up.

Boetie, when I last saw him, was six or seven years old, and entirely charmless, even as seven-year-old boys go. He was over-weight, but with none of that saving jollity that overweight people often adopt to propitiate a merciless world. A scowl was his default expression, as if anything more approachable might be sissy or even moffie. I was his senior by a good eleven years, and thus had little to fear from his truculence, but I was sorry for his coevals: he couldn't have been a pleasant person to share one's boyhood with.

So I'm not looking forward to a reunion with my long-lost cousin, and would not miss him at lunch – though he has unexpectedly acquired a peripheral kind of pertinence to my story. The murdered bride's brother and the murderer's sister – actually, it seems more than a merely peripheral aspect. Properly handled, it could form an effective climax to a sad story: tragically, if the lovers are forced to separate by their circumstances, or happily, if their love triumphs over their circumstances. A bit cheesy for *The New Yorker*, perhaps, but as long as I keep it factual, well, everybody likes closure, even *New Yorker* readers. Somewhat surprisingly, I am looking forward to meeting Boetie.

As we take our seats – Oom Blik of course at the head of the table, Aunt Dolly at the end, me adrift between the two of them at a table designed to seat twelve – Oom Blik says, 'Dolly, ring for Angelina.'

Angelina, having been rung for, duly appears. Oom Blik says, 'Tell Master Bertus that we're waiting for him.'

Angelina catches my eye and turns on her heel without saying anything. I look around for a bottle of wine, if need be the bottle that I brought, but a big jug of water with a few slices of lemon floating in it constitutes the liquid refreshment. Then I notice that there are no wine glasses on the table, and remember: Oom Blik is a 'recovering alcoholic'.

'What's the matter with Angelina?' Oom Blik demands of Aunt Dolly. 'Why is she so long-lip?'

'I don't know, Jeremiah,' Aunt Dolly sighs. 'We all seem a bit out of sorts today.' This last is half-directed at me, as if in apology.

'Speak for yourself,' Oom Blik growls. 'I'm not out of sorts.'

'Yes, yes, Jeremiah,' she says. 'It's just ...' and she does her vague gesticulation again, this time towards the unwieldy sideboard against the wall.

'It's just what, Dolly?' Oom Blik demands, as I knew he would. I'm surprised that Aunt Dolly after forty years of marriage hasn't discovered what I picked up in one meeting: Oom Blik never leaves a vague statement uninterrogated.

But she has her own way of dealing with the interrogation: she simply swathes vagueness in vagueness. 'It's just ... you know ...' she says, this time gesticulating with the other hand, at the garden outside the windows, as if proposing a larger context for her proposition.

'No, I *don't* know, Dolly,' he says, glowering at her. 'I wish you would call things by their name.'

'Yes, Jeremiah,' she says. 'It's only ...' and she trails off again.

'It's only what, Dolly?'

'It's only that I've forgotten what we were talking about.'

Oom Blik sighs heavily, seems to be on the point of speaking or perhaps even erupting, then visibly changes his mind and subsides into his seat. We wait in silence, the grandfather clock in the corner ponderously marking the passage of each slow second.

At length we hear unhurried footsteps in the passage. Boetie would seem to be wearing flip-flops, judging by the sound. I wonder if his wearing beachwear on a Sunday is part of his defiance of the moral order of the universe as proclaimed by Blik van Blerk.

Boetie enters, a study in serene arrival. He is dressed in shorts and a T-shirt. He takes his seat without acknowledging my presence, pulls his napkin from its ring – a piece of bone, probably cut from the horn of some animal – spreads it on his lap, and only then nods at me, as if taking a seat opposite a stranger in a railway carriage. I nod back, and say, 'Hello, Boetie.'

'Boetie, you remember Pieter, Tant Minie's son,' Aunt Dolly says, clearly embarrassed by her son's churlishness.

219

'Ma, I've told you not to call me Boetie,' he says. 'I'm twenty-eight years old, for God's sake.'

'Watch your language, Bertus,' Oom Blik contributes. 'It's Sunday.'

Boetie-Bertus rolls his eyes but says nothing. He is making a point of not looking at me, so I am at leisure to examine him. Of all the surprises I've had today, Boetie-Bertus is the most spectacular. The fat little boy has grown into an intimidatingly good-looking young man. Combining his mother's blue eyes with his father's black hair and dark complexion (except that what looks yellowish-grey on Blik looks olive-ochre on his son), he is extravagantly out of place in this dour dining room – and, I should think, in this aesthetically challenged little dorp. Now that he has lost his puppy fat, his mouth, nose, eyes, are all shaped with a strength and delicacy that Alfredville would be at a loss to do justice to. The harmonious disposition of his features, indeed, is at odds not only with his environment but also with his temperament, if his present behaviour is anything to go by. If Desirée shared her brother's good looks and bad temper, it's perhaps not surprising that she drove men – or a man – to extremes.

Angelina appears, bearing a tray. Another surprise: instead of the array of meat, starch and sweetened vegetables of old, there is a large platter of chicken pieces with what seems to be a mushroom sauce on a bed of pasta; also a salad, the latter a far cry from the iceberg lettuce and pale tomato conjunctions that used in their chill savourlessness to strike the keynote of family dinners *chez* Van Blerk.

'That looks excellent,' I say, glad to be able to enthuse sincerely. Aunt Dolly brightens briefly. 'Yes,' she says, 'it's a Chicken Terrazzini.'

'Tetrazzini,' Boetie mutters.

'Yes, Tetrazzini. Boetie made it.'

Surprise upon surprise. 'Oh?' I say, 'I'm impressed. Are you a practised cook?' I ask the dour young prodigy.

He ignores my question, and Aunt Dolly replies. 'Boetie, I

mean Bertus, spent a year at the hotel school after matric. He wants to start a restaurant.'

'And bugger the garage,' Oom Blik mumbles; this is clearly a source of discord.

'I'm sure we'll find a way,' Aunt Dolly says, without much conviction, and serves the chicken. Angelina takes charge of the salad. She serves Oom Blik first, then Aunt Dolly, then Bertus, leaving me for last. Nobody comments on this breach of etiquette, or perhaps here it is no breach: the family comes first.

Bertus takes his time, selecting bits of feta and asparagus from the salad, avoiding the cherry tomatoes. I am irritated with the leisurely pickiness of his actions, but can't help noticing the fine muscular definition of the arm, its slow grace a function of its strength. No gym in Alfredville: perhaps it's lifting engine blocks or whatever it is he does at the garage that keeps Boetie in shape. But his T-shirt was not bought at Pep Stores in Alfredville, unless Pep has acquired the DKNY franchise.

As he replaces the salad servers, Bertus meets my gaze at last. His eyes are almost shockingly blue.

'So, how's your *article* going?' he demands with a smile that reminds me, in spite of a perfect set of teeth, why I used to dislike him as a little boy. There's nothing friendly or even ingratiating about the smile: it's pure malice.

His question, crudely sarcastic as it is, has been cunningly calculated. To say 'What article?' is to invite him to tell the table exactly what article – and I have no doubt that he has, through the Alfredville grapevine, been given some version of my presence in town that's not going to please Aunt Dolly and Oom Blik.

So I say simply, 'It's going fine, thanks.'

But he's not going to let me off so easily. 'Cousin Peter is writing an article about Alfredville,' he informs the table.

Oom Blik says nothing, shovelling chicken into his mouth; but Aunt Dolly puts down her fork and says, 'Are you, Pieter? That's very nice.' Then she recommences eating daintily.

'Yes,' says Bertus, 'tell them what it's about, *Pieter*.'

I by now fortunately have the salad to occupy me, or what's

left of it after Bertus's depredations – mainly cos lettuce and cherry tomatoes – so I needn't reply at once. But when I do, it's lame enough. 'Oh, it's nothing really. I don't think you'd be interested.'

'Nothing?' Bertus says, with an infuriating air of polite interest. 'You call it nothing? And I heard it was all about Desirée.'

Oom Blik and Aunt Dolly put down their cutlery simultaneously. Aunt Dolly chokes on her food and starts coughing violently. Oom Blik demands, 'All about *what*?' Then, 'Where did you get this story from, Bertus?'

'Oh, they were talking about it at tennis yesterday. Everybody knows about it. But you tell them, Pieter. It's your story.'

Aunt Dolly is still coughing. Angelina puts down the salad bowl and goes to her. She makes her get up and gives her a hard blow on the back – a bit harder than strictly necessary, I think with some part of my mind that's not thrashing about like a drowning man. Aunt Dolly stops coughing, takes a sip of water, and sits down. She stares at me, her eyes red, a shred of asparagus dangling from her mouth.

'Wipe your mouth, Dolly,' says Oom Blik, then fixes me with his watery glare. 'What story, Pieter?'

'I'm writing something for an overseas periodical,' I say, hoping that they will be charmed by the magic formula *overseas*.

But Oom Blik is not to be charmed. 'I don't care if it's for the bloody Queen of England,' he says. 'Is it about Desirée?'

'It's really about the set of circumstances surrounding her death,' I try to explain. 'It's not about Desirée as such.' I cringe. *As such* is a phrase I detest.

Oom Blik would seem to share my distaste. 'Not as such? Then as whuch?'

'As I say, the circumstances surrounding …'

'Yes, yes, you've said that. I'm asking you to explain what you mean.'

'Well, the whole … demographic of Alfredville, and the way it has affected the responses to the murder and its aftermath.'

'So are we' – and he points with his fork at Aunt Dolly, stricken silent in her chair, and at Bertus, eating his chicken and salad as serenely as if he were dining at a table for one at the Savoy '– are we part of this *demographic*?'

'Well, yes, Oom Blik, but only in so far as everyone in Alfredville is part of the demographic. You see, I'm not interested in the first place in individual responses ...'

'So the feelings of your aunt and uncle, their feelings at having their only daughter battered to death, they're just part of a *demographic*?'

'No, no, of course not, Oom Blik. It's just that I didn't feel I could trespass on your grief and presume upon our family relationship ...'

'So if you're not trespassing and presuming at this very moment, what the hell are you doing here?'

'I'm ... having lunch with my uncle and aunt and cousin,' I reply, conscious of a certain lameness in being forced to reply to a rhetorical question.

'Count me out,' says Bertus. 'I didn't invite you.'

'And this lunch with your uncle and aunt and your cousin, is it also going to be part of your story, part of the demographic of Alfredville?'

'What is a demographic?' Aunt Dolly enquires from nobody in particular.

'It's the black-and-white mix, Missis,' Angelina, who has made no effort to leave, volunteers.

'Answer me, man,' Oom Blik says. 'Are you here to write about us?'

'No, Oom Blik,' I say. 'I'm not here to write about you and Aunt Dolly. I'm here to write about the political implications of an unfortunate human situation. The individuals involved are secondary to the larger issue.'

'And in the meantime you're eating our food, and bugger the larger issue. Well, I can tell you, you can get out of here and see if the larger issue will feed you *donnerse* Chicken Benzini and salad.'

'It's Chicken Terrazzini, Jeremiah,' Aunt Dolly says.

'Terrazzini *se moer*. Get out of here and don't come back, and if

223

you know what's good for you get out of Alfredville as fast as your matchsticks can carry you.'

'But Jeremiah,' pleads Aunt Dolly, 'he's my only sister's only son.'

'Well thank God for that,' Oom Blik says. 'I couldn't have put up with more than one.'

Aunt Dolly starts crying. 'And he looks just like Desirée,' she sobs. 'When I see him I miss her so much.' She grabs her napkin and buries her face in it.

Oom Blik gets to his feet and goes across to Aunt Dolly. 'It's okay, Dolly,' he says awkwardly; he has tears in his eyes. 'I know it's hard for you.' He pats her shoulder. He wipes his eyes with the back of his hand, then glares at me ferociously. 'Are you still here? Are you going or must I throw you out?'

I have no choice but to get to my feet and beat an ignominious retreat. As I leave I glance back. Bertus is still eating, but he glances up and gives me a beatific smile. 'See you around,' he says.

As I reach the front door, I hear quick steps behind me. It's Angelina, the faithful Cedric hard on her heels. 'Master Peter,' she says, 'I don't want you to leave without this.' She puts a plastic bag in my hand. 'I made them specially.' The packet contains six syrupy koeksisters.

'Thank you, Angelina,' I say, and kiss her cheek.

'Ag, it's sad,' she says. 'The missis was so looking forward to your visit.'

When I get back to the hotel, sweaty and hungry, I take a shower and try to read the newspaper I bought that morning. It's full of the ins and outs of another government scandal, over-empowered functionaries and their over-dressed wives over-spending state money on the over-lavish trappings of office. I don't have the stomach for the rest of the paper. I try to get Angelina's words out of my mind: *The missis was so looking forward to your visit*. I don't want to have to revise my assumptions about Aunt Dolly's attitude to me, on top of all the other adjustments I've recently been forced to make to my mindset.

I eat one of Angelina's koeksisters. I'd forgotten how cloyingly sweet they are, and yet how irresistible: the crisp outer layer crumbling deliciously and releasing the gingery syrup inside. Bennie and I used to steal koeksisters when Angelina baked for the church bazaar.

'Isn't it a sin to steal from the church?' I asked him once.

He considered this while selecting the fattest of the remaining koeksisters.

'I reckon not,' he said. 'If you think about it, what's the church going to do with the money it gets for the koeksisters?'

'I dunno. Give it to the poor, I suppose.'

'Well, then there's no problem. I'm poor, aren't I?'

'So?'

'So I'm saving the church the hassle of selling the koeksisters and then giving me the money so I can buy koeksisters.'

'That's very clever,' I said. 'But what about me? I'm not poor.'

'No problem,' he said. 'Be my guest,' and he handed me the last koeksister.

CHAPTER 15

Sunday evening

Towards evening, as it gets cooler, I go out for a walk. I've eaten all Angelina's koeksisters and have no appetite for dinner. In fact, I feel slightly nauseous. I take my camera, thinking to take photographs of our old house – 'the scene of the murder' – and such landmarks as might feature in my story, though in truth I have little stomach for that at the moment.

As I step out onto the sidewalk, Vincent materialises abruptly from behind a pillar.

'Hey, Vincent!' I say. 'You gave me a fright!'

'I'm sorry, monsieur,' he says. 'It was not my intention.'

He stands there, smiling his enigmatic smile, clasping his hands in front of him. Is he expecting another contribution, a kind of retainer while my car is standing unused in the back yard?

'I'm sorry,' I say, 'I don't have any money on me.'

He shakes his head, saddened, apparently, by my mercenary assumptions. 'I don't want any money.'

'Is there anything else I can do for you?' I ask, dreading a story of complicated distress, of bureaucratic tangles, sick children, lost identity documents.

He shakes his head again, another implied reproach. 'Thank you, monsieur,' he says. 'But there is nothing I desire, except to tell you something.'

Ah. In my experience every story has a purpose, if not a moral. But I have time to kill, and I am interested in Vincent's story – a kind of respite from the story I'm here to write.

'Yes, Vincent,' I say. 'I'm listening.'

He looks around us. At this hour of a Sunday evening, Alfredville is all but deserted: a few desultory loiterers stand around the

226

Cresta Café down the road, a police van drives by. The air is dusty and exhausted; the end of another summer's day in Alfredville.

'I must ask monsieur to meet me behind the hotel,' he says. 'It is not good to talk in public.'

I hesitate for a moment. I have been told that in present-day South Africa one doesn't lightly venture out of the public eye, especially with a relatively unknown companion. But Vincent – I feel as if I know Vincent, though I've really only seen him half-a-dozen times. Well, this is where I test my intuitive feelings about people.

'Right, let's go, Vincent,' I say. To get to the back of the hotel from the outside one has to walk around the block – not far, because the hotel is on the corner of the street, but still.

'No, monsieur,' he says, wagging a finger at me in a way that seems oddly Continental here in Alfredville. 'You traverse the interior of the hotel, and I meet you at the back.'

'If you say so, Vincent,' I say, and go back into the hotel. To reach the back door I have to walk past the counter, where Joachim and Boris are having one of their perennial altercations, apparently about a malfunctioning stapler. They are taking turns trying to get it to staple two sheets of paper together. There is already a small heap of mangled staples on the counter.

'I'm telling you, you fucked it up with those cheap staples you bought from that travelling salesman,' Joachim says. 'If I told you once I've told you a *thousand* times never to go for an unknown brand of staple.'

'So name me a world-famous brand of staple,' Boris says. 'You want Prada staples, for fuck's sake?'

The discussion seems set to last for a while. I walk past and wave, 'Evening, gentlemen,'

Boris doesn't reply, but Joachim lets go of the stapler and says, 'Well, hello stranger! Been out and about, have we?'

I stop, though loath to get involved in a discussion of my movements, especially with Boris glowering at me over the stapler, which he's now reclaimed.

'Yes, here and there,' I say, I hope dismissively.

227

But Joachim is not to be dismissed so airily. 'Here and there, mm, so I hear,' he says archly. 'Living it up with our Nonnie, I hear. Not to mention our Dr Henk himself.'

'Obviously news travels fast in Alfredville,' I say, trying to seem less annoyed than I am. Drat these small-town types, with nothing to do but scratch their own arses all day and squabble about stapler malfunctions. No wonder Desirée wanted to get away.

'Oh yes,' he trills, 'you can't get away with a thing here.'

Except murder, I want to say, except murder.

Vincent is waiting for me in the hotel's back yard. He pulls me in under an awning.

'There's no one watching, Vincent,' I say, uncomfortable at being drawn into a cloak-and-dagger fantasy.

'People watch all the time,' he says. His manner certainly suggests that, whatever the truth of his claim, he himself believes it; he is not so much nervous as hyper-aware of his surroundings – though this, I suspect, may be a survival mechanism brought from the Democratic Republic of the Congo. Democratic republics aren't what they used to be.

'Well, what is it you want to tell me, Vincent?'

'Yes. Yes, monsieur. I have heard it said, monsieur, that you have interested yourself in the death of the wife of the policeman.'

The very car guards proclaim it at the gates of the city …

'Yes,' I say cautiously, 'yes, I am interested in the subject, yes.'

'And you think the policeman killed his wife, yes?'

'Yes, isn't that what everybody believes?' I certainly don't intend sharing my suspicions with Vincent.

But apparently he's intent on sharing his with mine. 'I don't know what everybody believes, monsieur, but I know what I know.'

'What is it you know, Vincent?'

'I know who really killed the wife of the policeman.'

'How do you know that, Vincent?'

He points his middle finger and index finger at his eyes. In the gloom the eyes are very bright.

'Because I have some eyes. Because I see.'

'And what is it you see, Vincent?'

'I see, on the night the wife of the policeman is murdered – I see people going in and out of the house of the policeman.'

'Yes, I know, Vincent, it was a veritable open house.'

He looks at me uncomprehendingly. 'Never mind,' I say. 'I'm sorry I interrupted.'

'Yes,' he says with an air of hurt dignity. 'The house was open. But I continue. People come and go. The farmer. But he comes and goes before seven thirty. And the wife of the policeman is killed at seven thirty, *n'est-ce pas*?'

'So I have been told.'

'Yes. And at seven thirty I am walking up and down the street, because it is Saturday evening, many of cars to watch. And I look at my watch, because one man, the cow farmer, he said he is coming out of the hotel at seven thirty, then he gives me five rand. But the cow farmer does not come, and I walk past the house of the policeman. And I see in front of the house of the policeman ...' he pauses for effect, then pronounces emphatically, 'the *dog of the policeman*.'

This is so anti-climactic that I almost laugh. But that clearly would be a mistake, so I keep a straight face and say, 'Yes? But is that strange? For the policeman's dog to be outside the policeman's house?'

'No, monsieur misunderstands. I see the dog of the *other* policeman.'

'Which other policeman?' I ask, though with a sickening sense of certainty.

'The other one, the white one, the one who is the chief now.'

'Captain Nienaber?'

'*C'est ça*. It is him. His dog follows him everywhere, I know, I see them every day. And the dog, he waits outside. And on this evening, at seven thirty, the dog is outside the house of the wife of the policeman while the other policeman is inside' – he lowers his voice dramatically – 'killing the wife of the policeman.'

'But Vincent, how can you be so sure?'

229

'I am sure because I see the dog with my own eyes.'

'But did you see Captain Nienaber?'

'No, I did not, because then the cow farmer comes out and I go to his car for my five rand. And then somebody else wants the parking place and I have to show him and then I forget about the dog.'

'So you've got only the fact that the dog was outside the house …?'

He shrugs magnificently. 'But what more do you want, monsieur? The dog, he does not go to the house on his own, *n'est-ce pas*?'

'I suppose not.'

'So, there is somebody in the house, *n'est-ce pas*?' Vincent has now gone into courtroom mode, and I'm a recalcitrant witness.

'I suppose so, Vincent.'

'And that person, he is the owner of the dog, *n'est-ce pas*?'

'*Yes*, Vincent.'

'At the time of the murder, *n'est-ce pas*?'

'Yes, yes, yes, Vincent.'

'So the policeman, the other policeman, is in the house with the wife of the policeman at the time when she is murdered?'

'Yes, Vincent.'

'So why do you not believe me, monsieur?'

My shrug is a feeble shadow of his. 'Just because it seems so … so *impossible*.'

'Why impossible? Someone killed the wife of the policeman, *n'est-ce pas*?'

'Yes, of course, somebody killed her, but it just seemed somehow more … *plausible* that it was her husband.'

'Why, monsieur?' Vincent asks, now very politely. 'Is it because her husband is a black man?'

'No, no, of course not, Vincent. It's just … I don't know, a new idea for me to get used to.' I'm lying, of course, I've had all of twenty-four hours to get used to the idea. But also I'm not lying: there's a difference between what I still hoped might be Cassie Carstens's jealous speculation and Vincent's certainty.

'*Eh bien*, but when monsieur gets used to the idea ...'

'Yes, Vincent?'

'What is it that monsieur will do about it?'

He is looking at me still with his air of polite enquiry, as if asking me my opinion on the day's sporting events.

'What is it that you *want* me to do about it, Vincent?' I demand, irritated with being thus passed the buck. Yet again.

'I think, monsieur, that it would be good to tell the proper authorities, so that the proper steps may be taken.'

'Thank you, Vincent, that's a very helpful suggestion, but may I ask why you don't tell the proper authorities yourself?'

His face is a study in amused disbelief. 'Monsieur thinks that I, a kwerekwere, must go to the police and tell them I think the chief policeman murdered the wife of another policeman?'

'I can see that would be awkward,' I say. 'But, Vincent, why me?'

'Because monsieur knows the truth,' he says. 'And it is the duty of someone who knows the truth to make it known.'

'Thanks for the moral lesson, Vincent. But can't you see, I don't even live in this place, it's none of my business what happens here?'

'I do not live in this place either, monsieur. But I think our duty is not confined to our *arrondissement*.'

'There are those who would disagree with you. How about cultivating our garden?'

'Perhaps, monsieur. But I think Voltaire wanted to say that our garden is everywhere. But I think you know what your duty is. You are a good man.'

Disarmed, I stare at Vincent. I have never met a car guard on familiar terms with Voltaire. But more disconcertingly, I don't think I have ever been called a good man. And it feels like the heaviest burden anyone has ever saddled me with.

I take a short walk but am driven back to my room by my own restlessness, hoping that once there I'll be able to collect my thoughts into something more manageable. I take out my laptop, I make notes, trying to rearrange my meagre data in some way that leads away from Bennie as the prime suspect. But I've been over it all before, and again and again I come up against the recognition that I don't know Bennie, don't know what he's experienced in the twenty years since I knew him. And that whereas Cassie on his own and Vincent on his own could have been disregarded, together they make a stronger if unlikely pair – with nothing to counter them except Dr Henk Pretorius's quaint dog-centred theory that he can tell non-killers from killers.

At eight o'clock my phone rings. I don't want to answer it: it may be Nonyameko, and even her company would be a constraint tonight.

I answer anyway. 'Hello?'

'Hi. What you doing?'

It's Bennie; it's Bennie's old formula, that I'd forgotten: *Hi, what you doing?*

'Nothing much. Reading. Thinking.'

'You want to go for a walk? I'm just coming off duty.'

'A walk – now?'

'Yes, bugger. It's quite safe – I'm a policeman, remember?'

'Yes, I remember. So where do you want to walk?'

'Doesn't matter. Anywhere. Out to the dam or one of the koppies. I just want to get out.'

'Okay. Shall I meet you at home?'

'No, I'm still at the station. Meet me there.'

'Will do.'

I walk to the police station, as slowly as possible, turning over my options. Except I don't really have options. I have a strong suspicion that the person I'm about to meet murdered my cousin, but it's not the kind of thing that is easy to introduce into a conversation, especially not if, as seems likely, that person is fully armed. On the other hand, it's also quite difficult to imagine making small talk about other topics, with that suspicion lowering over the conversation.

Bennie is waiting outside – in full uniform, indeed. He greets me more warmly than before, shaking my hand and placing his left hand on my shoulder briefly as he does so.

'Thanks for coming, bugger. I didn't really fancy a Sunday evening at home.'

'Yes,' I say, 'I wasn't exactly having a wild time at the Queen's either.'

'Okay, let's walk, then.'

'Which way?'

'We've done the dam. Let's do Graskop for a change.'

We walk down Victoria Street, bereft of human activity on a Sunday evening, and turn off a side street that leads into the scrubby surrounds of the town. We pass quiet homes settling into Sunday evening, generally in the flickering gloom of the television set, here and there around a supper table – I even see a family with their heads bowed in evening prayer, a hefty family Bible on the table in front of the father – a vignette from my past, though never part of our own domestic practice.

Bennie also notices it. 'Not something you see often any more,' he says. '*Huisgodsdiens*.'

'Did you have it in your family?'

'You must be fucking joking. I don't think the old man ever prayed in his life. And if my mother ever prayed, it was that my old man would drop down dead. Which he eventually did, so maybe her prayers were answered after all. Only problem was she dropped down dead herself not long after.'

'You sound as if you didn't exactly mourn them.'

'No, I didn't. They did fuck-all for me except bring me into the world and then fuck me up.'

'You weren't a fuck-up, Bennie. You know that.'

'And if I wasn't, no thanks to them. But the thing is, Jakes, I was always made to feel a fuck-up by my parents – at any rate by my old man, and my old lady knew better than to disagree. So I grew up thinking I was a fuck-up and I was well on my way to being a fuck-up like my brothers.' He pauses. 'But then I met you.'

I'm taken aback by the sudden note of intimacy. 'You met me?'

233

'Yes, or have you forgotten that we met at some point? Basically, in the school piss-house.'

'Of course I remember. But I don't see how this relates to your being or not being a fuck-up.'

He withdraws into his more guarded mode, and I realise too late that I have inhibited a reaching-out on his part. 'No, you wouldn't see,' he says, 'because you've always taken for granted things that were fucking incredible to me.'

'Such as?'

'Such as a family where you don't get donnered because your father feels like it or bullied because your older brother has been donnered by your father and wants to take it out on someone – like just having a fucking family that seem to like each other. And then ...'

'Yes?'

'And being able to be friends with someone who takes you seriously.'

For some reason, Bennie wants to revisit our old friendship tonight. I am touched by this, but excruciatingly uncomfortable. So I say, merely, 'I took you seriously?'

He is not to be deterred by my meagre response. 'Yes – not that you knew it or anything, and I don't think I did either, then, but somehow, somewhere, I could feel that you believed in me, and so I could believe in myself too.' He pauses. 'And then you buggered off.'

'I'm sorry if you felt I was leaving you in the lurch.'

'I'm not telling you this to make you feel shit or anything. Yes, of course at the time I felt you were deserting me, and I was pissed off with you. But then I saw that I couldn't rely forever on some other bugger to make me believe in myself, and I sort of battled on.'

'And surely you made a very successful life for yourself?'

'You mean I got a job and a wife and children. Yeah, fucking jackpot, cowabunga.' Then he relents, and says, 'Well, I guess that is success, compared with what I could have had.'

'Of course it is.'

Inconsistently, this irritates him. 'Of course, my arse. Do you know how patronising you're sounding? There you are snug and smug in London, and you pretend you think it's *success* to spend my life in Alfredville.'

I know I'm sounding patronising, but I'm not used to dealing with such unmediated emotion. In London we wrap everything in irony. 'I don't think success is measured by where you spend your life,' I say. 'You can be a success in Alfredville and a failure in London.'

'That sounds really good. But I bet you don't really believe it.'

'So how do I prove to you that I believe it?'

'You could always move back to Alfredville.'

I look at him in the half-light of a street light to see if he's joking, but his face is blank, betraying nothing.

'Are you serious?' I ask.

'Sure I'm serious. I'm seriously testing whether you believe what you say, about being a success in Alfredville.'

As I start replying, without quite knowing what I'm going to say, he holds up his hand. 'Forget it, I'm not serious.' Then he stops walking and faces me. 'But tell me, bugger,' he says, 'why exactly *have* you come back?'

The question is so abrupt that it takes me a few seconds to adjust my mind to it. 'I thought everyone knew by now,' I say.

He grins mirthlessly. 'The police are usually the last to know. But knew what?'

'That I'm here to write an article about Desirée's murder.'

He doesn't say anything, just stands there staring at me as if seeing me for the first time.

Then he says, 'Shit, hey. An article. Fuck *me*.'

'Yes. Well, more of an *essay* really, about …'

He holds up a hand. 'Please, I don't want to hear any more. I might puke all over your shoes.'

'But I thought you knew, I thought everybody knew.'

'Well, then, you were wrong. I didn't know.'

'But what … what did you think?'

'What did I think? What did I *think*? I'll tell you what I

thought, bugger, in my bottomless stupidity. I thought you came back because you wanted, maybe, to see me? Is that so fucking difficult to imagine?'

'But I told you I didn't know …'

'Yes, you told me twice on that first day and then again later and I thought you were telling me so many times to hide the real reason why you came back, because I couldn't figure out why else you'd be back. So I figured that you'd come back to see me. Yes, I know it's pathetic, but that's the story I told myself, fuckwit that I am.'

'Hell, Bennie, I'm more pleased than I can say to see you, but you know, I didn't even know you were in Alfredville.'

'You didn't know? Your mother didn't tell you?'

'No, they'd left by the time you came back.'

'She didn't tell you that she met me in the street when she came back after Desirée's death?'

'No, she didn't.'

'Well, bugger me. I thought she'd remember. She seemed pleased to see me.'

'I'm sure she was. But my mother can be a bit forgetful at times.'

'Sure,' he says. 'And I'm a bit forgettable.'

'Oh, come on Bennie, stop feeling sorry for yourself. She had other things on her mind, she was here for Desirée's funeral, for God's sake.'

'I suppose so,' he says bleakly. 'Okay, then, so you're here to write an *essay*.'

'Yes, but …'

'But what?'

'I'm not *here*, as in here with *you*, to write an essay. I'm here because I want to be here.'

'Gee, thanks bugger, I'll remember that when you've fucked off again.'

'Hell, will you stop turning yourself into some kind of martyr because I left? People do leave, you know, they don't stay in the same place for ever, which doesn't mean they don't miss the people they leave behind, which doesn't mean they don't love them, which doesn't mean they're not bloody *lonely* much of the time. Who was it who said somebody who emigrates becomes a foreigner in two countries?'

'How the fuck should I know? I'm just the local cop. But I get the message – I'm supposed to feel sorry for you.'

'No, I just don't want you to feel sorry for yourself.'

His cellphone starts ringing, a tinny rendering of 'Eine Kleine Nachtmusik'. He takes the phone from his pocket, glances at the screen, then puts it to his ear.

'Hi,' he says, his face impassive.

'No ... no, I'm taking a walk.' He glances at me, scowls slightly. 'No, with Peter. ... I just felt like a walk ... yes ... yes ... I don't know, maybe an hour, maybe more ... Can't *you* do it? ... yes, yes, I know, but just this once, okay? ... yes okay, I'll be there ... half an hour ... yes, that's how long it'll take, I'm not going to run back. Yes, I know, I'm sorry, but that's how it ... mm, I know ... sure ... bye.'

He slips the phone into his pocket and shakes his head. 'Kids,' he sighs. 'Lettie and Kosie want me to come and read them a story. Chrisna says she offered to read to them, but they want me.' He's clearly angry, but there's a kind of pride, too, in his manner. 'And Chrisna's on one of her rampages, has been for a week, so you can't argue with her.'

'So, do you have to go back?'

'Yeah, I do. I'm sorry.'

'I'm sorry too.' And I really am, to turn back now. Bennie evidently invited me on a walk for a purpose. Did he perhaps want to confess? Or was he just trying to recapture something of our old friendship? Either way, he's been forestalled by Chrisna's phone call. But something tells me that the break is just temporary, that between us Bennie and I have arrived at some juncture, that the unfinished business of twenty-two years ago will be finished. In one way or another.

CHAPTER 16

Monday 26 January

The morning brings another letter from James, full of sprightly gossip about the rehearsals, the in-fighting, the tirades and the tantrums. Two days ago I would have relished the details, relished in particular James's sardonic wit, but today I read his letter without much interest. The petty intrigues of a group of self-involved actors seem very far away from the pared-down passions I'm confronted with in Alfredville. And after Bennie's bleak hopelessness, James's scintillation is just the tiniest bit irritating in its implication that nothing really matters over-much to the cultivated mind. I remember the dinner parties in Camden, in Earl's Court, in Highgate, with James the life and soul and me the dry husk, the tolerated 'partner' who presents the ritual bottle of wine upon arrival and then is heard from no more until he says, 'James, isn't it time we got going?' I remember the theatrical in-jokes, the clever put-downs, the carefully honed scalpelling of a rival's performance, all the cut-and-thrust of envy and Schadenfreude masquerading as bonhomie and camaraderie, the cherishing of good reviews from critics who next season, after a bad review, will be reviled, the veneration of the celebrity of the hour, the powerful predatory agent, the dead-eyed coke-raddled supermodel, the conceptual artist with a talent mainly for self-promotion, the foul-mouthed TV chef: all the chitter and chatter and twitter and tattle purporting to be Culture, the flotsam of a civilisation sinking under the weight of its own pretensions, of a city that bought its own baloney and is now bankrupt. What a wealth of talent selling out to what tatty rewards. And poor old Alfredville, with no concept of the glittering metropolis and its prizes – what is it but a downmarket version? Is Joy Duvenhage's resentment of

Desirée, in the scale of things of the heart, any more ignoble than James's distrust of Andrea? So the one will end up on the London stage and the other … well, who's to tell where Joy will end up?

I shake my head to clear it. Perhaps I'm just feeling excluded from the excitement of the new production, the interest, with whatever abatements, of new people, new challenges, the frenetic activity, the hilarious crises, the panic and the pandemonium, the mad rush of blood to the head, the inhuman schedules, the breakdowns and break-ups, the uncontrollable egos and the rampant libidos, the setbacks and the breaks, the relentless pressure and the blissful release when at last a new production is running, and running well. All of which I have experienced at second hand, through James, and have felt, even at second hand, to be a potent and addictive drug.

Whereas my day yawns ahead of me – not emptily, no – would that it did, because I dread another interview on the subject I'm supposed to be only too avidly intent upon interviewing people about. I'm starting to feel that if I could walk out of the sad story of Desirée's murder, I would do it without a backward glance. But I know I can't, any more than one can decide to walk out of the ocean when a strong current has swept one away; received wisdom has it that one's only chance of survival lies in surrendering to the current and hoping it washes one up on dry land.

At half past two that afternoon I walk up the steep little road just below the R62 that leads to the Coloured township: the substantial evidence that Hector Williams and Desirée's union was hardly trail-blazing. Relatively easily, I find the address Nonyameko has given me. The house is tiny but neat, a featureless cube with a corrugated iron roof, a steel-framed window on either side of the stable-type front door. I guess two, at most three bedrooms. The small yard is enclosed with a wire fence, along which a scraggy honeysuckle is struggling to establish itself. The gate is secured with a simple hook made of steel wire. The short gravel path runs between two flower beds, in which dahlias and zinnias (the names come back unbidden from my childhood) garishly bloom. A few chickens scrabble around, officiously in charge of their little patch of earth. The dominant smell, of wet soil under a dripping tap, of flowers and chicken dung, takes me unawares; another memory I didn't know I had.

The front door is ajar. It opens directly onto a sitting-dining room that takes up the whole of the front of the house. At the back, a short passage leads to the living quarters and kitchen. A radio – or TV, I suppose, but for some reason it sounds like a radio – is jabbering in the background, the over-charged histrionics of soap opera. I knock discreetly; there is no response and I knock again, more firmly. A small child comes to the door and stands staring at me with the dispassionate regard of the very young, to whom no one thing is stranger than any other. I smile at the child but he doesn't respond, merely puts one grubby knuckle into his mouth. I knock again, and the radio is turned down.

A young woman appears from a back room, smoothing her dress as she walks, or perhaps wiping her hands. Heavily pregnant, she moves with a kind of stately clumsiness. Hector Williams has good taste in women; Sarah Augustyn is strikingly beautiful. Her complexion is finer than the tough South African climate normally tolerates, and her features show lineaments of a more exotic origin than the stark African plains. What eastern isle was plundered of its people, what oceans crossed, what slave ship crammed with human cargo to bring her forebears to the Cape? And what wanderings brought them to this arid outpost, what couplings, enjoyed or endured, between what fortuitous blend of races, issued at last in this lovely young woman? Sarah, I am willing to guess, has not ventured beyond Alfredville and its immediate surrounds; but how far she has come to get here, and how many bitter generations have gone into the making of her!

The woman is looking at me strangely, as well she might: I'm staring at her in what must seem a very rude fashion.

'I beg your pardon,' I say, extending my hand. 'I'm Peter Jacobs.'

She nods, wipes her hand again on her skirt before placing it in mine: a cool, limp hand, not used to shaking hands.

'You can come in, Mr Jacobs,' she says at last. 'The doctor said you were coming, the woman from Joburg. I'm Sarah Augustyn.' Her accent is as unexotic as the Little Karoo itself, the broad vowels of South African English contained by the harsh gutturals and consonants of Afrikaans. It is an accent without music or mystique, but it has a melancholy resonance about it; a Creole redolent of dispossession and disenfranchisement, and yet assertive of its own identity.

I enter the room and Sarah conducts me to the sitting area, where two easy chairs and a sofa, overstuffed and gleaming in the style of instalment-plan stores like Lewis and Ellerines – literally household names from my youth – hold pompous sway.

I sit down on one of the chairs; Sarah sits down and the child sidles up to her, still regarding me unblinkingly. Then he looks up at her and asks in a loud whisper, *'Wat soek die witman hier?'* What does the white man want here?

'Shush, Jason,' she says. 'I'm sorry,' she says to me, 'the children have no manners.'

'That's all right,' I say, trying to smile at the stroppy boy. 'It's a fair enough question.'

'He's my sister's child,' she says, as if needing to explain his delinquency. 'I'm looking after him while I'm on leave. This is their house, my sister and her husband.'

'Where do you work when you're not on leave?'

'There by the Ghanta Co-op,' she says.

'Making wine?' I ask, half jokingly, but she answers very earnestly.

'No, I don't make the wine, I just help with selling it. I'm in retail sales, I do the tastings and help the clients to select the wine.'

'I see. That sounds interesting.'

'Yes,' she says, 'it's a good job. It's better than working in Pep Stores where I was before, more interesting. And you meet a better sort of person,' she adds with touch of grandeur.

'I'm sure it is – more interesting, I mean.' The problem with small talk is that once you're bogged down in it, it requires such an effort to wade out of it. I decide to take the direct route.

241

'Nonyameko tells me that you are very concerned about the father of your child.'

She shakes her head. 'No, I'm not *concerned*' – she tries out the word, then adopts it – 'about the father of my child. He can sort himself out. I'm concerned about my child, who will go through life and people will point and say there goes the child of a murderer and a murderer's whore.'

'Why are you so sure that your … that Hector is a murderer?'

'Because he murdered that Desirée Williams.'

'Yes, but why are you so sure that he murdered Desirée Williams?'

She looks down at the child, who is leaning against her leg, still glaring at me. 'Go and find your ball,' she says to him. Obediently, he trots off.

'Why …?' I ask again, but she interrupts me almost fiercely.

'Because he said he was going to kill her.'

'He said that? When?'

'That evening, when he was here. I told him that I was that way with his child, and he was all excited, he wanted a child because his wife, she didn't want a child, but then I said to him I said you want this child you get rid of that wife of yours and you marry me, I'm not a battery chicken I said, making a child for some other woman's husband because she's too lazy to have one herself. And he said How can I get rid of her, the house we live in belongs to her, everything we have we got from her father, and I said You're a big deal in the police force, I said the police are doing well in this country, and he said Not the honest ones, he said the only ones who do well are the ones who take bribes. So I said forget that, I don't mind being poor, I said I've got a job you've got a job and he said You don't understand I can't just leave Desirée and I said Why did you get married to her anyway … you see,' she explains, 'he was my boyfriend when I was very young, before he went off to fight with Umkhonto, the ANC you know the Spear of the Nation *kamtig*, and then when he came back we started up again but then he met that white witch and she, I don't know but I think she *toored* him, and he thought having a white woman with a university degree and all was some big deal or something, and she made a fuss about him big-time and so he married her, big church wedding Dutch Reformed *nogal*. I was the moer in and didn't see him for a long time, but then one day he came to the Co-op, he said to taste wine but I think it was to see me, and he kept coming until the people were talking and he said he was going to keep coming until I agreed to see him after work he said and so I did, and now you see what came of it with that spear of his.' She gestures towards her abdomen. 'Spear of the nation *se voet*.'

'But,' I say, 'on that evening ...'

'Yes, that evening he was carrying on much better about how he was going to adopt the child, and I laughed in his face and said You think your wife is going to raise your child by your Coloured *steek-stukkie* and he said She won't know and I said Oh yes she will because I'll tell her I said and if you think I'm going to give up my child to your madam you're thinking with your Coloured backside so just forget it. And that's when he said Well what can I do because I want the child and I want you, so I said It's simple if you want the child and you want me you'll have to get rid of your wife first I said and he said How am I supposed to do that and that's when I said Well you can always hit her over the head with something, I was just joking you know in a serious sort of way, I didn't know he would really do it, and God knows I didn't like Desirée Williams and I wouldn't have minded very much if she sort of sommer disappeared down a hole or some-thing but I didn't mean for Hector to kill her, not really, I mean just look at the mess now. But he said That's a fucking good idea – excuse the language, Mr Jacobs, that's the way he talks some-times – and went off and I thought he was just the moer in but then ... you know. And now I'm scared to have the child, and I know when he gets out of prison he'll come find the child and that mother of his, she's already saying I'm not fit to look after the child ...'

'Excuse me,' I say, 'but Mrs Williams – do you know her?'

'No, thank the dear lord *Jee*-sus the old lady lives in Robertson,

I think Hector bought her a house there to get rid of her otherwise she would have been on their necks all the time, she was sommer thrilled to have a white daughter-in-law and all those Van Blerks suddenly being nice to her and having her to tea, she thought she was in white man's heaven second class and she didn't want Hector to have anything to do with me but now she's singing a different tune because now all her so-called white friends have just dropped *her*, and the Coloured people that she was too grand for won't have anything to do with her *either* so she's saying how I can't look after a child when I'm working which is *fokken* funny because if that was true no Coloured woman would have any children.'

'But about Hector …' I say.

'Yes, Hector,' she sighs. 'I'll always have a soft spot for him and I suppose it's not every man who would kill his wife for his girl-friend, I mean that shows something I suppose but I'm *deurmekaar* because I don't want a murderer either, if he kills once he can kill again and in this country if you kill someone they put you away for a little while and then they let you go or you escape, so I don't want to have his child. But you know what's the worst is thinking that it was my fault that he killed her.'

'Why do you think that?'

'It's mos obvious, isn't it?' she says, almost indignantly. 'If I wasn't there he wouldn't have a reason to kill her. And then I went and told him to hit her over the head.'

'But apart from what you said to him, why are you so sure that he did kill her?'

'Because she was hit over the head,' she explains patiently. She clearly thinks I'm exceptionally obtuse. 'And because he left here at half past six and Desirée van Blerk was killed at half past seven and Hector can't tell anybody where he was between half past six and quarter to eight.'

'The thing is,' I say, 'there are other people too who could have killed her.'

She hesitates; it's obvious that she wants to believe me, but wisely doesn't want to do so on slender evidence. 'Ja, there's always plenty other people who can kill you, but Hector was the one who had a reason to kill her.'

'He wasn't the only one. I know of at least two other people with a reason for killing her.'

She looks interested, but then visibly pushes the thought aside. 'Yes, maybe, I'm not surprised, a bitch like that. But just having a reason doesn't mean they killed her.'

'Yes, true, but I happen to know that one of them' – I take a deep breath – 'well, I won't say I'm a hundred percent sure, but I'm eighty percent sure that it was him and not Hector who killed Desirée.'

She stares for a while at the scuffed carpet. Then she says, 'So the bastard didn't have the guts after all.'

This is so unexpected that I laugh. 'You mean you're disappointed?'

But she's also laughing. 'No, no. Not like that, you know. But it's something, hey, your lover murdering someone for you. It's like a play or something.'

'Yes, I can see that. But those plays never have happy endings.'

'And will you make a happy ending?'

'Please – I can't guarantee anything. I'm telling you what I think. Proving it is something else.'

'So have you gone and told the police?'

'No, not yet. It's … complicated. I must make sure of my facts first.'

'But you said just now you are sure of your facts.'

'Yes, eighty per cent sure, sure enough for myself –'

'And for me.'

'Well, for non-legal purposes. But I must be more sure before I go to the police. And that's why I'm asking you not to take any over-hasty decisions about your child.'

'So what if you're wrong and I'm stuck with the child?'

'I suppose you could always give it to Hector's mother.'

'Over my dead body.'

'Mm. I hope not.'

'Yes I hope not too, but hoping won't get you anywhere when your time's come, and there's one dead body already.'

245

'But if I'm right and Hector didn't kill Desirée, he'll be free to marry you and look after the child himself.'

This is the thought that she's not allowed herself to have. 'Do you *really* think so?' she asks. 'I mean like *really*?'

I'm faced with the responsibility of creating a hope that I'm not sure I can fulfil. 'I really *think* so,' I say.

Jason has returned and is tugging at Sarah's dress.

'Shush Jason, Auntie's talking,' she says.

'I have to be going anyway,' I say, thankful for the interruption.

'I'm sorry – I was going to ask do you want some tea?'

'Thank you, but no thank you. I have to get going.'

I get to my feet and so does she, with a heavy grace.

'Thank you Mr Jacobs,' she says.

'Don't thank me,' I say. 'I haven't done anything.'

'Yes, but you will, I can see it. I know you will.' As I take my leave, she says, 'Just wait a moment, Mr Jacobs.'

She goes into the back of the house and returns a few minutes later with a bunch of dahlias, hastily wrapped in damp newspaper.

'Take these,' she says. 'They're from the garden. My sister grows them to sell by the Co-op.'

'Thank you, Sarah,' I say, touched. 'They'll liven up my hotel room.' Though how I'm going to get a vase out of Boris or Joachim is another matter.

In the event, the vase is no great problem. The Queen's Hotel is, if nothing else, lavish of ornament, and there is in fact a large earthenware jar of uncertain function in my room, which admirably holds Sarah's colourful offering. Flower arranging is not my forte, but the lush flowers fill the jar of their own accord with a kind of ragged opulence, and the damp peppery smell permeates the room.

CHAPTER 17

Monday early evening

It occurs to me to speak to Vincent again, in the probably vain hope of finding a chink in his certainty. After all, he didn't see Bennie leave Desirée's house – but then, he didn't see anyone else leave the house either. I know all too well that it's a cinch to leave that house unnoticed: the back door opens into a back yard that opens into an alley running between two blocks, a relic from the days of the removal of night soil.

Still, I need to speak to him again, to test his certainty. I go downstairs and into the street, expecting Vincent to materialise, as he so unsettlingly tends to do. But the street and pavement are empty; I look up and down, but there's no Vincent anywhere. It occurs to me that I have no idea where he lives. I go indoors again. Joachim and Boris are standing behind the reception counter, for once not squabbling; indeed, they seem to be sharing some amusing incident, for they are both smiling. It almost seems a pity to interrupt their brief moment of harmony.

As I approach, they look up; Joachim's cherubic features dimple into a smile, a manufactured one very different from the one he was sharing with Boris, and Boris's smile fades into his usual deadpan.

'I wonder,' I say, 'if you happen to know where Vincent – you know, the Congolese car guard – lives?'

Boris chortles rudely and Joachim smiles more broadly than ever. 'Yes, I do just *happen to know.*'

'Is it nearby?' I ask, not very hopefully. I imagine Vincent lives in a cardboard shack in the depths of some informal settlement.

'Depends on what you mean by nearby,' Joachim says and Boris chortles again, or rather, sniggers. The man really is obnoxious.

'I suppose I mean walking distance,' I say.

Joachim's smile is now a smirk. 'Depends on how far you can walk,' he says, and Boris packs up.

'Look,' I say, 'why don't you just tell me where the man lives?'

'Okay, okay,' Joachim says, 'no need to get pissed off. It just tickles me that you don't know that Vincent lives in our back yard, right next to where you park your car.'

'Okay,' I say, 'so I didn't know. Nobody told me.'

'Maybe you didn't ask. Anyway, yes. That's where he lives, I let him have one of the staff rooms, now that we don't need such a large staff any more. I was sorry for the ou. I pay him a small retainer and the rest he makes from looking after cars.'

'I see.' Somehow I hadn't imagined Joachim as a Good Samaritan. 'So his room is next to the parking?'

'Right next to it. The only car guard in the country who sleeps next to your car.'

'Thanks,' I say, and turn to leave the two of them to their confabulation. But Joachim stops me. 'And incident-ally,' he says, with the coy inflection that I've learnt to tolerate if not love, 'I have big news.'

'Oh?' I say, my heart sinking. I can't imagine any news emanating from Alfredville, or anywhere else for that matter, at this stage being good news.

'Mm. You can congratulate us. We're engaged.'

'To be *married*?'

'Yes, what else, engaged like a public toilet or something?'

I look at Boris. I have often wondered whether black people can blush – James is impervious to embarrassment, so that's no test – and I'm intrigued to see Boris's melted-chocolate complexion acquire a distinct glow. 'But that's wonderful. Congratulations.'

'Thank you very much.' Joachim pauses archly. 'I must say, I wasn't sure that it was a good idea to get involved with a member of my staff, but then I figured what the hell if we can run a hotel together we can run a marriage, and saves me a salary on top of it all.'

'That does sound sensible, yes,' I say, 'But how does Boris feel about not getting a salary?'

'It's cool, bru,' Boris contributes. 'I'll make sure I get my cut of the profits.'

'Fucking sure you will,' Joachim says. 'We'll have to make a fucking profit first.'

'And when are you planning ...?'

Joachim giggles. 'To get married? I'm not sure, but maybe over the Easter weekend when it's not so hot any more.'

'So, what kind of wedding do you have in mind?' I ask.

'Oh, a white wedding, of course, can't you just imagine it, Boris all in white and me all in black, yin and yang checkerboard, much more stylish than the rainbow nation? And we can have Joy as bridesmaid for a bit of sex appeal. And we're going to invite all the Knersvlakte Ferreiras, they'll go anywhere for a free piss-up, and my mother will come all the way from Worcester in her mother-of-the-bride outfit, we'll get Errol Arendz to design it for her, and we'll have Dominee Albertyn in the Nederduits Gereformeerde Kerk, with a reception in the Kerksaal afterwards, koeksisters and tea for everybody ...'

'And what about my people?' Boris chips in. 'Where do they go, in the kitchen or somewhere?'

'Oh well, all your sisters and aunts, those of them who aren't dancing around with bare boobs and grass skirts, can serve the koeksisters and your dad from Matatiele in his leopard loincloth can slaughter a goat behind the Kerksaal and get drunk with Cassie Carstens and the boys passing around a calabash and' – he turns to me – 'can't you just see Boris in a cute little going-away number and a honeymoon at Groot Brakrivier in the ATKV rondavels along with all those nice couples from Gezina and Patensie, Frans and Sannie and Ewert and Johanna, all together around the braai at night singing camp-fire songs, "Laat die Vlamme Hoog Opslaan", with Boris helping us out with a little kwaito or maybe "Lethu Mshini Wami"?'

Boris shakes his head. 'You're one *befokte* white man,' he smiles.

'Well, I wish you both very well,' I say.

'Thanks hey, you'll get an invitation,' Joachim says as I leave.

Going out by the back exit I discover that next to my car there is indeed an outbuilding. I had noticed it, but assumed, in so far as I'd given it a thought, that it was some kind of store room.

Vincent is nowhere to be seen, and I go up to his door. It is ajar, and as I knock, it swings open. I step back, not wanting to barge in, but as there is no response from inside, I knock again at the now open door. There is still no response, but in the dusk I can see a figure lying on the bed.

'Vincent?' I say. 'Can I come in?'

Vincent doesn't reply; he would seem to be asleep. I push the door open all the way: an invasion of privacy, but at this hour of the evening Vincent is surely just dozing.

'Vincent?' I say again. 'Can I talk to you?'

He doesn't stir. He's lying on his back on the bed, one arm hanging to the floor. There is something unnatural about his stillness, and as I come closer, I see that his eyes are open.

'Vincent?' I ask again, but with a growing dread that he won't answer.

I look around for the light switch and find it next to the door. I flick it on; a single bare bulb glares down at Vincent's open eyes, a faint drool of spit on his chin. There is blood on the bedclothes; it is coming from a wound, perhaps two, in his chest. I force myself to grasp the hand drooping limply to the floor. It is not quite cold yet, though cold enough to tell me what I need to know. I turn around slowly. The shock has left me numb, unable to process the fact of Vincent's death, either emotionally or intellectually. Taking refuge in practicalities, I hurry back to the reception desk with my news.

The rest of the evening is a confusion of what seem to me some very inefficient procedures. Constable Hendrickse comes to take a statement from me. She has forgotten to bring a pen, and we have to borrow one from reception, where Boris is dealing dourly with requests for information from alarmed hotel guests.

'But,' asks one man, a gaunt and intense German, 'can you guarantee our safety in the hotel, if there are people shooting people?'

'Yes, you'll be okay,' says Boris. 'It's just xenophobic violence.'

'Xenophobic violence?' asks the German. 'You mean violence against foreigners?'

'That's right,' says Boris. 'That's what it means.'

'But we are foreigners too,' the German says, pointing at his wife, who's been standing in the background, manifestly bored with her husband's fussing, but now developing an interest in the conversation.

'I guess you are,' Boris says. I can see that he's tempted to leave it at that, but he apparently decides that the inconvenience of a panicky guest outweighs its entertainment value. 'But xenophobic violence is just for African foreigners,' he explains, 'people from the north who come down here. The local people think they take their jobs.'

'They shoot people for taking their *jops*?'

'They usually don't shoot them, they chop them up.'

'But how do you know it is just xenophobia?' the German woman demands.

'What else can it be?' asks Boris. 'That Congolese had nothing to steal.'

'I suppose that is in order then,' the man says.

I finish making my statement; it takes a while because Constable Hendrickse is meticulous to a fault. She cautions me not to leave the district 'until investigations have been completed.'

'How long is that likely to take?'

'Search me,' she says. 'Six days, six months, take your pick.'

'I'll take six days, thanks,' I say.

She doesn't enter into my spirit of levity. 'It takes as long as it takes,' she says sternly and leaves, taking the pen with her, to Boris's vociferous disgust.

'What's the country coming to, if the police come here and steal ballpoints?' he says.

'They practise on ballpoints,' Joachim contributes, 'so by the

251

time they get to be Commissioner of Police they're ready for the big time.'

'Please, what is a ballpoint?' asks the German, who has been hovering. 'Must we lock away our ballpoints?'

I leave before Boris has managed to explain what a ballpoint is.

After an early supper in the company, or at any rate sphere of influence, of the now-reassured German couple, I go to my room. I know I owe Nonyameko a report on my visit to Sarah, but I'm in no fit state to talk to her or anybody else. My mind is too full of the events of the day and their implications. I have as good as promised Sarah that I'll try, somehow, to establish Hector's innocence. Vincent's murder, too, I can't simply ascribe to xenophobia. As Boris implied, such attacks tend to be organised mob actions, rather than premeditated murder. I can't rid myself of the memory of Vincent's nervousness the last time we spoke, and of the police van driving past as we were speaking in front of the hotel. It seems inconceivable that his bright, argumentative presence has been snuffed out so easily.

But this is not the only spectre haunting me. I am alone in my room with my knowledge that I have in effect undertaken to turn my friend over to the police. Quite apart from the farcical problem of trying to find a policeman to whom one could turn over the town's chief policeman, there is the less amusing question of betrayal, of deliberately choosing to denounce a friend – indeed, *the* friend of my youth, and never since, I now realise, superseded. Yes, I know that every second that I spend trying to come to terms with my tender conscience is a second that an innocent man is deemed guilty; but the innocent man is a dim abstraction compared with the vivid presence of Bennie, as vital as always, and all the more appealing for having matured into gentle melancholy, the father of two children, husband to a doting if demanding wife. Whereas Hector – but unfortunately, having met Sarah, I can no longer pretend that Hector has no human appendages.

By about nine o'clock, I find the waiting intolerable and phone Bennie's home number, which is listed in the directory as

Nienaber, BJ. Chrisna answers. 'Is Bennie there?' I ask, after her usual somewhat brief preliminaries.

'No,' she says, 'He's just gone on night duty. Why don't you phone him at the station?'

'Thanks, I may do that.'

The voice at the other end of the phone sounds like Constable Hendrickse. She asks me for my business, and when I say it's private, she requests my name. I give it to her and, without any acknowledgement that she's come across it before, she says, 'You're going through.' The line goes dead: at least the South African Police Service (the erstwhile Police Force) does not inflict canned music on the waiting public. After an implausibly long spell of static silence, Bennie is there.

'Yes?' he says, businesslike, unencouraging.

'Hi, Bennie, this is Peter – Peter Jacobs.'

'Yes, I know. You were announced.'

'Of course. Listen, I was hoping we could meet for a chat sometime soon.'

There's a short silence. 'Sure. Only thing, I'm on duty, so if you wanted to come here?'

I take a deep breath. 'I was hoping to talk to you on your own.'

He takes it in his stride; if he's curious about my reasons, he's not about to say so. 'Sure,' he says again. 'I come off duty at six. Are you going for your early-morning run tomorrow?'

'Yes, unless …'

'No, that's perfect. I like some exercise after I've been on duty.'

'You mean you'd like to come for a run with me?'

'No, that's too complicated. Why don't I walk to Kanonkop and meet you there, say at six thirty? Or is that early for you?'

'No, that's perfect. I'll meet you there, then.'

'Good man,' he says, with a sudden warmth that makes my heart contract. 'I look forward to that.'

I mumble something and put down the phone.

Which leaves me with nine hours of wondering what to do, or rather how to do it. I've decided that the only way I can *address the situation* (I take refuge in euphemistic generality) is through

253

Bennie himself: that is, *confront him with my suspicions* and take it from there. Common sense tells me that the most effective way of *apprehending an armed murderer* is not to meet him in an isolated spot in one's running gear and confide one's suspicions to him; but some other inhibition prevents me from *turning him over to justice*, even if I knew who, in Bennie's absence, would be justice's representative in Alfredville – Constable Hendrickse?

On the spur of the moment I lift up the phone and dial Nonyameko's room. She picks up immediately.

'Hi,' I say. 'It's me.'

'Hi. I missed you at supper.'

'Yes, I'm sorry. Things are getting very complicated.'

'Too complicated to discuss?'

'Yes, for the time being.'

'To do with Sarah?'

'Only very indirectly.'

'But you did see her this afternoon?'

'Yes, I did, and I think I managed to persuade her that there's a good chance Hector isn't guilty ...'

'Good man.'

'And I think she won't take any rash decisions regarding the child just yet.'

'Very good.'

'Yes, but to make good on my assurance to her – well, that's the part that's complicated, and please don't ask me to explain, but ... well, if anything should happen to me, I just want you to know that I'm meeting Bennie Nienaber tomorrow morning at six thirty at Kanonkop.'

'All right. I take note of that fact, though I must admit I don't quite know what to do with the information.'

'Just hang on to it. You may not need it, and I sincerely hope you don't, but as I say, if anything untoward happens to me, you'll know.'

'Thanks, but I repeat: what am I supposed to do with the knowledge?'

'Pass it on to a competent authority, as they say.'

'If I can find one.'

'If you can find one. But chances are it won't be necessary, in which case I'll buy you supper tomorrow evening.'

'Are you sure you don't want to discuss it over a drink now?'

For a moment I'm tempted, but only for a moment. 'Yes, I'm sure. Or rather, I'm not sure I don't *want* to, but I'm sure I shouldn't. It may all just be a massive misunderstanding, in which case we can laugh about it tomorrow night.'

'And if not, I can cry about it on my own?'

'Oh, I don't insist that you cry on your own. You can call in Boris.'

'You know what, Peter? You can stuff off.'

'Thanks. Good night to you too.'

I switch on the fan and crawl in under my mosquito net, hoping that my waking thoughts won't pursue me into my dreams.

CHAPTER 18

Tuesday 26 January

I wake up to another unforgiving day, the sky even at five thirty steely with malign intent. The mosquito net has failed in its function, and I sport at least two fresh bites. It's the kind of day on which one gets up only because it seems preferable to staying in bed. Except I have another reason to get up: I am to meet Bennie on Kanonkop.

I have a quick shower and get into my running gear. A melodramatic impulse makes me pause at the door as I leave, wondering if this might be my last view of the drooping candles and the string-dispensing dog. But these objects are in themselves too banal to support my self-dramatisation. Sarah's flowers, on the other hand, have acquired a sinister poignancy. I close the door and go downstairs. I leave my key on the reception desk and let myself out by the side door of the hotel.

Victoria Street is deserted. No Vincent. In the first light of the sun it presents a gentler aspect than usual, the stark whites of the houses softened by a tinge of pink, the shabbiness of the commercial buildings mellowed into quaintness. It won't last more than ten minutes, but for the moment it's almost possible to feel as if one might miss Victoria Street.

I start running, and as I get into my stride, I feel the welcome sensation of my body adjusting to the exercise and tapping into its sources of energy. I run strongly, feeling as if I could keep running for ever, never tiring, never flagging, never turning back. I feel intensely alive, responsive to the breeze cooling the sweat on my skin, smelling the gardens hidden behind walls, hearing the sounds of early morning, somebody's rooster crowing up the sun, running, running, running.

In what seems to be a very short while, I reach the stony outcrop of Kanonkop. I climb to the top – not a very strenuous exercise – and sit watching the awakening town. This is where Bennie and I used to come on the Mosquito, where we came that last evening in January 1988, after we'd received our matric results. We'd decided that we needed to get drunk to celebrate our good results, so after supper I sneaked into the pantry, which doubled as my father's cellar, and stole a bottle of Ghanta Pinotage. I smuggled it out of the house under my windbreaker, which, in midsummer Alfredville, would have aroused suspicion if it hadn't been for the Mosquito.

'G'night!' I called to my parents, who were watching the news in 'the TV room', a poky little place off the dining room – my mother refused to have the TV set anywhere else, claiming it dominated the conversation even when it was switched off. Images of a car bomb explosion in Bulawayo flickered across the screen; a voice announced that two ANC guerrillas had been killed – 'terrorists' the newsreader called them, not bothering to hide his satisfaction as he treated viewers to a picture of the mangled, bloodstained vehicle.

'Will you be late?' my mother called, as she always did, and I replied, 'Yes, don't wait up,' as I always did.

'Are you two star pupils taking out those two girls again?' my father asked. I had told them about the date with Elrina and Gladys, but not the catastrophic outcome.

'Probably not,' I said, opening the back door – the Mosquito was waiting outside – 'Bennie and I will probably just chill.'

'You must tell me some day how one *chills*,' my father grumbled good-humouredly.

'Sure I will,' I replied, 'but right now I have to get going.'

'Enjoy yourselves,' my mother said. 'You deserve it.'

'And be careful on that buzz-bike,' my father added. 'I don't like you speeding around on the back of that thing.'

I left, feeling vaguely guilty at my duplicity. My parents would have given me the bottle of wine if I'd asked them for it; but then again, an officially sanctioned bottle of wine is so much less intoxicating than a purloined one.

'Drive slowly,' I said to Bennie as I got onto the back of the bike. 'I've got a bottle under my jacket.'

'Is that what it is? Thought it was a hard-on,' he said, and pulled off only slightly less aggressively than usual.

We parked on the far side of Kanonkop and climbed the koppie. Since it was night, we sat facing the town, as I'm doing now. Bennie took out his cigarettes and I produced the bottle of wine and my Swiss Army knife, which I'd not really had an opportunity to use since it'd been given to me the previous Christmas. The cork proved tighter than I'd expected, rather spoiling my nonchalant act.

'Here, gimme,' said Bennie, dangling his cigarette from his mouth. 'Let me show you how.'

'So, what makes you an expert?' I asked, handing him the bottle.

'Natural talent,' he said, extracting the cork, narrowing his eyes against the smoke in best gangster style. 'You're the clever one, I'm the practical one. Good team.' He passed me the bottle.

'I'll drink to that,' I said, taking a swig. It was all I could do not to choke as the acrid liquid hit my throat. But I was determined not to lose face in front of Bennie, and gamely swallowed the mouthful I'd gulped.

'Don't hog it down, bugger,' Bennie said. 'You're supposed to sip it. Here let me show you.'

It turned out, in fact, that sipping did improve the taste of the wine, and we sat for a while taking turns without talking, Bennie concentrating on his cigarette, me watching him out of the corner of my eye, taking surreptitious pleasure in his relaxed sensuous absorption, but dreading what I had to tell him. The wine was warming my insides pleasantly; gazing out over the sparse lights of Alfredville, the vast desert sky just starting to show its multitude of stars, the smell of Bennie's cigarette mingling with the night smells of Kanonkop – dry grass, dassie droppings, buchu – leaning back side-by-side against a rock still warm from the day's heat, our feet just touching, I felt a great sadness.

Bennie took a puff and a swig, and said, 'I suppose we'll be getting our call-up papers any day now.'

'Yes,' I sighed.

'Oh, c'mon,' he said, giving me a playful cuff and passing me the bottle. 'It won't be so totally shit if we're together. I've heard that they put people from the same town in the same regiment.'

'I suppose so,' I said listlessly, not wanting to go where I knew the conversation now had to go.

'What do you mean you suppose so? Don't you want to be in the same regiment as me?'

'Of course I do.'

'Then what's spooking you?'

'Listen, Bennie,' I said, taking a big gulp of wine and handing him the bottle. 'I've got something to tell you.'

'Hell, that sounds serious. What's up?' He laughed nervously. 'Don't tell me you've put Emmerentia up the pole.'

'No, nothing like that. The thing is … I don't think I'll be going to the army.'

He killed his cigarette on a rock. His hand seemed to tremble slightly, but he sounded calm when he said, 'You don't think? Listen bugger, haven't you heard? It's not optional, you can't say, Oh, now I think about it I'd rather not go to the army, thank you all the same for asking. You *have* to go. It's known as conscription, con-scrip-shun, and if you don't go you get sent to jail for six years.'

'I know all that,' I said, sounding sulky even to myself. 'I'm going overseas.'

There was a moment's silence. A cricket was sounding off not far from us. 'You're going *where*?'

'Overseas. England, to be precise.'

'Well, fuck *me*. So you're going overseas. Okay, so lots of people go overseas – but you'll be coming back, won't you?'

'That's the thing, you see. I don't think so.'

'You don't think *what*, bugger?'

'I don't think I'll be coming back.' I paused, then risked, 'I'm emigrating?'

'You're *emigrating*?' His aggressive tone modulated to something more vulnerable, more difficult to deal with. 'But … but you can't just *emigrate*. You need a passport … and, and … and all that stuff.'

'I've been getting a visa,' I said, almost eager to explain. It was easier to talk about practicalities than about motives and consequences. 'A study visa. My father was born in England, so it hasn't been that difficult. He wants me to go. He doesn't want me to go to the army.'

'So what makes you so special? Other people's fathers are *proud* for their sons to go to the army.' I knew that this wasn't true of Bennie's father – he'd at best be indifferent to Bennie's going to the army – but this was not the time to point this out.

'Yes, I know,' I said instead. 'But my father's different. He says he doesn't want his son to be killed for a lost cause.'

'A lost cause? So what does your father know anyway?'

'I don't know, Bennie. You can't argue with him. He says I'm his only son and he's not going to sacrifice me to the stupidity of the government.'

'So it's okay for me to be sacrificed because I've got three brothers?'

'No. That's not what my father means. He's just very sure that he doesn't want me go to the army.'

'So he'd rather send you to fucking England and never see you again?'

'I think he'd rather have me alive in England than dead on the border.'

'Yeah, and it's not as if you put up much of a fight, is it? You *want* to go to fucking England, don't you?'

'That's not true, Bennie. At least, not totally true. If I had my way, I'd stay here and go to the army with you. But I have to admit that I think England might be … well, it could be interesting.'

'Interesting, my arse. It's a fucking *island*, man. It rains all the time.'

This was difficult to take issue with, and I remained silent. He returned to the attack, on a different tack.

'So how long have you been plotting this?'

'Not *plotting*. Planning. A few months. Since June.'

'And you tell me now?'

'I didn't want to tell you before it was definite.'

'So it's definite, is it?'

'I heard yesterday I've been accepted at the University of Sussex conditional on my getting four As.'

'And you got five.'

'Yes. I'm sorry.'

'Don't lie. You're as pleased as a dog with two cocks.'

'I mean I'm sorry ... that I can't go with you.'

'Then why are you going to fucking Swussex?'

'Why Sussex? Because it's supposed to be a good university in a nice part of the country ...'

'I'm not interested in whether it's a fucking fairy palace in ... in *Disneyland* or a shit-hole at the arse-end of the world, I'm asking why are you fucking off?'

'Mainly because I don't want to go to the bloody army and fight in a war I don't believe in for people I despise.'

'You despise your own people?'

'I despise the government and the people who support them.'

'So you despise me.' He said this flatly, as a bleak fact.

'Do you support the government?' I countered.

'I don't know. No. Yes, if you mean would I rather have them than be taken over by the communists.'

'You've been brainwashed. We're not fighting against the communists, we're fighting against our own South Africans, people who just want their rights.'

'Oh *crap*! You're just too shit-scared to go to the army and fight for your country.'

'Sure I'm scared. But I promise you that if I believed in the cause I'd go.'

'So if you've got problems with the cause, join the fucking End Conscription Campaign and stand up for your principles.'

'And spend six years in jail for nothing? My principles aren't that strong.'

'Fucking sure they're not that strong. You haven't *got* any principles. You're too bloody holy to go to the army – but you're happy for *me* to go?'

'I'm not *happy* for you to go. That's your own decision. I'd much rather you didn't go.'

'Oh, you'd *much rather*. So what the hell am I supposed to do? Write to the fucking army and tell them Peter Jacobs would *much rather* I didn't go?'

'I don't know, Bennie,' I said. 'I don't know what you're supposed to do.'

'You don't know and you don't care. You've never cared, with your Jewish father and your British passport. All you care about is covering your own precious arse, fuck you Jack, I'm all right.'

'I do care, Bennie. I care for you, I wish I could take you with me, I ... I *love* you, Bennie, I'd take you anywhere if I could.'

'You *love* me? What kind of useless moffie talk is that? You *love* me but you bugger off to ... to fucking Sussex and leave me to go to the army on my own and what do you care if I get the shit shot out of me? Bugger-all! *You'd take me anywhere*! So how far will I get with my South African passport that's worth about as much as last week's movie ticket? And on what? My father's railway salary? We don't all have rich Jewish fathers, you know, some of us have to get places by the skins of our own arses.'

'Yes, I know, but that's not my fault, you can't be angry with *me* because ... well, because you don't have the means ...'

'I *don't have the means* – why don't you say what you mean, that I'm a fucking poor white and you want to get shot of me and your country all in one go?'

He was crying with anger; I put my arm around his shoulder, but he pushed me away. 'Oh, just *fuck off* to Essex and never come back. I never want to see you again anyway.'

He flung the bottle at a rock; he missed, but it shattered anyway. The night air was rank with the smell of wine.

'Please, Bennie,' I said. 'I don't want us to lose touch. I'll write to you and you'll come and visit me and ... we'll find you a job in England ...'

'Thank you very much, you'll find me a job cleaning shit-houses in old-age homes while you study at the Ooo-niversity of Swus-ssex. Shanks pal, but no shanks, and don't bother writing to me because I won't write back. As far as I'm concerned, you're as good as dead when you park your fat arse on that Boeing. In fact, you're as good as dead starting *now*.'

He got up and scrambled down the koppie. When he got to the bottom he turned round and shouted up the hill, 'Fuck you, Peter Jacobs! Fuck off out of my life!' Then he got onto the Mosquito Garelli and snarled off, leaving me to walk the two kilometres back to town.

My leg muscles are starting to tense up. I do a few stretches and walk along the top of Kanonkop. From here I can see, through the shimmer of heat already building up, the little town waking up to another day of work, of enduring the heat and the drought and the dust. Clouds are building up, holding out a promise of a thunderstorm later. An approaching billow of dust resolves itself into a police van. Bennie must have changed his mind about early-morning exercise.

He parks and gets out of the van. He is in full uniform, and his face is hidden in the shade of his cap. He's staring into the low sun, shielding his eyes, looking for me. I want to shout to draw his attention, but an odd impulse prevents me: there's something so intimate about looking at somebody who is not aware of being looked at. From up here Bennie looks small, vulnerable, even in the bulky uniform. Then he looks up and sees me. He waves, a sudden, spontaneous, joyful wave; he takes off his cap and scrambles up the koppie.

'Sjoe!' he says when he gets to the top. 'It's getting hot already.'

'Yes, this may not have been the best place to meet.'

'We'll be okay.'

We neither of us comment on the fact that this is where we parted twenty-two years ago. We find a seat, on adjoining rocks, facing the town.

'I had to come by van because I was late,' he says. 'They caught the bloke who shot that car guard.'

'Really?' I ask, trying not to seem as intrigued as I am. 'Who was it?'

'Arsehole called Wisdom Mhlabeni. Turns out it wasn't xeno-phobic violence after all – or I suppose in a way it was, but not your common township variety.'

'So, what was the motive?'

'Looks like Vincent – the car guard – who was actually a quali-fied lawyer, get that? – applied for the position of town clerk. But this Wisdom Mhlabeni had been eying the position for himself, and sucking up to our mayor, Mr Goodwill Mzweni, for months. Then, when Mr Mzweni let on to somebody that he was favour-ing Vincent's application, the somebody told Wisdom and Wis-dom paid somebody else a thousand rand to take Vincent out. I suppose the fact that Vincent was Congolese played its part, but at bottom he just got in the way of the wrong person.'

'And how did you find out who it was?'

'The murderer got drunk on the money and slept with his girl-friend's sister, so the girlfriend came and fingered him to the police. Of course, the killer lost no time in fingering Wisdom Mhlabeni, and he had plenty of witnesses to back him up. So it seems a fairly open-and-shut case.'

'Poor old Vincent,' I say. I'm thinking hard whether this affects my own suspicions regarding Bennie; but no, the possibility that he may have been responsible for Vincent's removal was always a very vague and far-fetched one, and this new development doesn't materially alter matters.

'You knew Vincent?' Bennie asks.

'Yes, he was the first person I met when I arrived here. He offered to look after my car.'

'Ja, he was a very dedicated car guard. Would probably have made an excellent town clerk.' He shakes his head. 'What a fuck-ing waste.'

Then he looks at me. 'So what's up, bugger?' he asks.

'How do you mean, what's up?'

'Well, you got me here to talk to me, didn't you?'

Here, now, in the broadening daylight on top of Kanonkop on

a workaday Tuesday, it seems unthinkable that I would confront this man, this brisk, likeable man, with my suspicions. Surely I must be wrong, Vincent must have been wrong, Cassie must be wrong, there must be some other explanation, as there was some other explanation for Vincent's murder.

So I say, 'It's just that I thought, on Sunday evening, that you wanted to say something that you didn't get round to saying.'

'So you're offering me an opportunity to say it?' he asks, with his crooked smile.

'Yes. Yes, it's just that I thought our conversation was incomplete.'

'You mean because I had to bugger off home before we could really have a conversation?'

'Yes. Yes, that's what I mean.'

'And you want to finish it.'

'Well, I did last night. Now it seems a bit silly, I suppose.'

'Why, what was it about last night that made you feel you wanted to talk to me?'

'Just my sense that you were unhappy and that you might want to, I don't know, talk about it.'

'Ag, I probably just had the Sunday evening morbs. I don't think there was anything there that you need to break your head about.'

He smiles again, and I know that Bennie, having once shown me his hurt, will not do so again.

Then he says, 'Or do you want to tell me again, just in case I didn't get the message the first time, that you're here to write an essay or was it an article on Desirée's death? Do you want me to say again what a fucking fool I was to think that you might have wanted to see me? If that's what you want, I can do it. I've got fuck-all pride, I can't really afford it. So go ahead, tell me what you want to hear.'

I'm taken aback by the sudden bitterness breaking through the fragile shell of cheerfulness. 'No, it's not anything definite,' I say. 'It was just a sense I had that you were unhappy.' I'm aware of repeating myself lamely, but for the time being that's my refuge from saying what I know I'll have to say.

265

'And you wanted to hear me say it again? Why? So you could feel good about fucking off again? Or do you want to put it in your essay? The poor oke, the local cop who got his balls caught in a padlock?'

Bennie is losing his composure, I'm partly relieved to see. If we are going to have some kind of a showdown, it's more likely to happen when he's agitated. So I say, 'No, it's not to do with my essay or anything like that. It's just that I thought that ... well, that things had happened to you since I'd left, and that you might want to talk about them.'

'You mean tell you about my miserable life since you left? Don't flatter yourself that you left me with my finger up my arse. I made my life. I made my life as best I could. I went to the fucking army and I served my time and I came back and I joined the Police Service and I came back here and I married and I had children. It's a life. It's my life.'

'Of course it is,' I say.

He turns on me. '*Of course it is!*' he mimics my words savagely. 'What do *you* know about it, fucking off to England, about my life? You don't know what it was like to sit here day after day and see the sun come up over Kanonkop and go down over Graskop, with nothing in between, and see nobody but the people beaten up and the people who beat them up, to talk about nothing but the way the country is going and who's going to win the rugby on Saturday.'

'But you could have gotten away – to Cape Town, to Joburg, somewhere with more to offer?'

'More to offer? What more to offer somebody like me? More beaten-up people, more beating up people, more talk about the way the country's going and who's going to win on Saturday?'

'But you had other interests. You used to read.'

'I used to read because you used to read. When I came back from the border, books and music just seemed meaningless, worse than meaningless, callous, if you understand what I mean, I had to force myself not to get paralytic every night like on the border so that we could forget the sights we saw and the deeds we did.

266

But I'd watched my mother go that way and my father go that way and I was fucked if I was going to go that way, but it was hard, Jesus it was hard. I was scared of what I would do, of what I knew from the army I *could* do. You have no fucking idea, the things they made us do, the things we made other people do, the things we made ourselves do.'

He sits brooding. He's placed his cap on the ground. In the brightening sun I can see a few grey hairs among the mat of black, still as thick as the last time we'd sat here. I don't dare say anything. I have lanced the boil: I must deal with the mess.

He sighs and picks up a pebble. 'And then she came.'

'She?'

'Your cousin, man. Desirée.'

'She came? What do you mean?'

'She came back from Stellenbosch, not long after I came back from the border.'

'And so?'

'This was before I was married. I started seeing her. And she'd read all these books, and she talked to me about them, and she played me music.' He takes a deep breath, then seems to break down into a kind of sob. 'She even *looked* like you.'

'Oh,' I say, not daring to say more.

He sits quite still for a moment, seeming to see something in the distance, on the road from Alfredville. I look, too. It looks like another early-morning runner, coming towards us.

'I was in love with her but I wasn't going to let on, because she sure as hell had bigger notions than Bennie Nienaber the fuckwit cop. But I knew she liked me, too, and I thought, maybe, but then Hector Williams turned up, also a cop, when you think about it, but full of stories of London and Moscow and places and the fight for freedom and all that shit, and she could think of buggerall else, though she was still *nice* to me and, we hadn't got serious, well, not from her side anyway. And then fuck me, she married him. And a while later I married her best friend.'

'On the rebound?'

He is calmer now, simply supplying information. 'I don't

know, it didn't feel like that. You see, Chrisna was always a good listener and good fun to be with, so when I was feeling shit about Desirée getting married I told her about it, and she listened very sympathetically and yes we did have fun and one thing led to another and the next thing she was pregnant and we got married.'

'Oh, I didn't realise …'

'No, why would you? But it seemed okay at the time, I wasn't exactly arse-over-heels in love with Chrisna, but we got along fine and I knew I needed some stability in my life otherwise I'd go down the drain one way or another. And I always wanted a family different from the mess I grew up in, and I wanted to be a better father than my old man had been, and a better husband. So it didn't seem like a big-deal tragedy or anything at the time. Nothing that millions of people don't deal with every day. And Chrisna was – is – a good wife and mother. Only …' He hesitates.

'Only?'

'Only she's never really forgiven me for the fact that I used to be in love with Desirée.'

'But that was before you married her.'

'Yes, but you don't know the first thing about jealousy if you don't know that it doesn't keep a fucking diary. Chrisna hated the fact that I'd been in love with Desirée once, and she wasn't going to let me forget it.'

'But Desirée was her best friend?'

'So that's supposed to make it okay? It made it fucking worse, if anything. Except she didn't seem to hold it against Desirée the way she held it against me. I suppose she reckoned Desirée wasn't in love with me, I was in love with her. *If* she reckoned anything at all: as I say, jealousy doesn't keep a cool head.'

'So you still saw Desirée?'

'She saw Chrisna, and she came to our house, and then after a while I started sort of dropping in when I knew she was alone, and we sat and talked shit, and I don't think she thought anything about it, except I couldn't tell Chrisna about it. And I felt lousy about that and always felt I had to make it up to Chrisna, which is why she sort of bosses me around now, as I'm sure you've noticed.'

268

'Well, yes, I've noticed that … well, that she sort of calls the tune.'

'She calls the fucking tune all right, she wears the pants, she's got me under her thumb – take your pick of the idioms. So anyway, this went on for a long time, me visiting Desirée, for fucking *years*, and I told myself there was nothing wrong with it, it gave me an interest apart from my family. Of course, I love my children and I think I love Chrisna, and I love my *dog*, but at times it still all seemed so *nothing*. And Chrisna – well, she's not that interested in sex, and after our second child we sort of stopped. She once said to me while we were having sex, Are you thinking of Desirée? And you know what, I probably was, because Desirée was driving me mad, but at the same time she was the only thing keeping me sane. I felt like my mother-in-law, angry, angry, fucking *furious* all the time, because life never gave her anything to be glad about, but I couldn't let it out like my mother-in-law, I had to be nice to my family, I even had to be nice at work because I saw what happened to my father when he let his anger out on other people and I've seen what happens to policemen when they let their anger out, so I kept a lid on it, I tried …' He stops.

'And then?' I ask.

He glances at me briefly, but he's tuned into his own mind, not really aware of me any more. 'And then, sort of gradually, Desirée started encouraging me to come round more often, and she seemed to understand that I felt more for her than just friendship. But she became, I don't know, as if she was playing a game with me, very lovey-dovey one day, very fuck-you the next. It was driving me out of my fucking mind. And I heard that Cassie Carstens was visiting her, and I was pretty sure he wasn't visiting her to read books and listen to music. But anyway, when she was nice she was very, you know, warm to me, so it was a real mind-fuck, but by now I was also you could say in love with her. So anyway, when she said we should run away together, on that Saturday evening, I … I went ballistic, man. I …'

He breaks down, shakes his head. I put my hand on his.

'It's all right, Bennie,' I say. 'You needn't carry on. I know.'

269

He removes his hand. 'You know what?'

'What happened that Saturday evening.'

'How the fuck can you know?'

'Well, I know someone who heard you having an argument with Desirée just before the murder, and I know someone else who saw your dog in front of the Williams house that evening.'

'Jesus,' he half-whispers. 'You've really been lining up your witnesses, haven't you?'

'No, it wasn't like that, I ...'

'And this spy of yours saw Kerneels?'

'Yes. At seven thirty when the murder took place.'

'He saw Kerneels in front of Desirée's house at seven thirty?'

'Yes.'

He sits still, staring at the ground in front of him, where a dung beetle is making its laborious way over the dry soil. He shakes his head, as if to clear it, then looks at me.

'Well, fuck me. And the fact that Kerneels was there – so what do you make of that?'

'That you went to visit her, had an argument, because you were torn between your duty to Chrisna and your attraction to Desirée ... and, well, then you killed her.'

He sits quietly for a while, picking up pebbles and tossing them in a desultory fashion. Then he picks up a bigger stone and hurls it as far as he can. He gets up from the rock, starts pacing, but the terrain is too rough for pacing, and he sits down again.

'So when did you come up with this brilliant reconstruction of the crime?' He sounds almost amused.

'I don't really know. But I've been blind. It's so obvious.'

'It wasn't so damn obvious to anybody else.'

'That's because they assumed that the killer must have been a black man.'

'No shit, Sherlock, and you know better?'

'I do now. For a while I also assumed what everybody else assumed, but then ...'

'What then?'

'Well, things started falling into place.'

270

'Except the motive, Sherlock. You still haven't told me why the hell I would have done this.'

'I don't in fact think that it was a premeditated murder.'

'Thanks, bugger, that's big of you.'

'No, I think Desirée overplayed her hand, pushed you too far. She wanted you to take her away, and when you said what you said about your wife and children she said Well what about I tell your wife that you've been coming here. And then you lost your temper.'

'And you think I kill people when I lose my temper?'

'No, that's just it – you're normally so controlled that when you let go, you let go all the way.'

'You've really figured it all out, haven't you? And you don't think you might just be wrong?'

'No,' I say. 'No, I don't.'

'And aren't you scared I'll kill you too, now that you've told me you know I killed Desirée? You must have noticed that I'm armed.'

'Yes. Yes, I am scared. But what's the alternative? Pretend I don't know anything and watch an innocent man go to prison?'

'You would rather see me go to prison?'

'I want to see justice done.'

'Whoo*wee*. And Peter Jacobs has come all the way from England to see that justice is done.'

'No, I didn't come back for that. But now that I'm here, this seems to be what I must do.'

'Big fucking deal. How brave.'

'Somehow I was never brave when other people were.'

'So you're making up for lost ground? You're going to show your bravery by turning me over to the police?'

'That's not what I want to do. I thought I'd tell you what I know and then leave it to you.'

He laughs again, a mirthless cackle. 'Hell, thanks, bugger. So either I get to turn myself in or I get to shoot you?'

'I suppose that's the choice, yes.'

'You leave me fuck-all choice, Jakes.' He takes his pistol from his holster and clicks off the safety catch.

'You will have some explaining to do,' I say. 'I've told someone that I'm coming here to meet you. And Chrisna will know that you were with me.'

'Oh, I think Chrisna knows who killed Desirée. But I'll leave the explanations to you. You were always better at them than me, in any case. Cheers, Jakes.' Then he puts the barrel in his mouth and pulls the trigger.

CHAPTER 19

Thursday evening 28 January

Dear James,
*I guess I haven't been much of a correspondent. To be honest, I didn't
really think you'd be that interested in what was happening to your ex-
lover in a remote corner of Africa. And then, for the last three days I've
been pretty much out of commission, the horror of which it is difficult to
commit to words even now, except that I think writing it down may
make it somehow more manageable. I choke up just thinking of it, for all
kinds of reasons, none of which I seem able to fathom with any clarity.*

*But to state the main fact as baldly as I can: my friend Bennie is dead;
shot himself; shot himself in my presence and partly, I suspect, as a
result of my doing. It's a convoluted story, but in its simplest form – and
I don't begrudge you the full story, only I'd rather give it to you face to
face and when I've figured it out for myself in all its ramifications – in
its simplest form, then, I have for a while suspected that my cousin
Desirée was murdered not by her husband, but by Bennie, who seems to
have been desperately or despairingly in love with her. I confronted him
with my suspicion and he shot himself – this was on a hillock just outside the village, quite deserted. From a practical point of view, this could
have been very awkward for me, had not a jogger who happened to be
running past witnessed the whole thing. So I have, if anything, been
treated with a consideration I don't think I really deserve – and that, I'm
afraid, I'm rather ungracious about, just because I find human company
a trial. An exception is the local vet, who, used to dealing with dumb
animals, doesn't feel called upon to talk at me, just took me for a long
walk as he would an unhappy dog – although in fact we were accompa-
nied by his extremely happy black Labrador. The walk seemed to do me
good, up to the point when I got some kind of a panic attack and had to*

be taken back to the hotel gibbering like a monkey. And then there's Nonyameko, my censorious veteran of the Struggle, who has also witnessed enough slaughter in her life not to slaver after the details of this one, while yet being surprisingly gentle with me. In fact, I suspect she's surreptitiously giving me trauma counselling.

I am trying to write this as collectedly as possible, but it's an effort just to sit still for long enough to get the words down. I have an urge to get up, but then find there is nowhere to go, and I sit down again. I have gone for numerous walks, but by now every street harbours some memory of Bennie, and he is everywhere and nowhere, and I'm driven back to my hotel room, which is the one place he never was. I have imaginary conversations with Bennie, recasting our last conversation in some way, tell him I'm sorry, that ... but what does one tell somebody whose death one has caused?

Somebody, moreover, that one has loved all one's life.

Yes, I know that sounds sentimental, when I haven't given the guy a thought for the best part of twenty years. You've teased me about my recherche du temps perdu, and of course there is something absurd about the notion of searching for (and finding!) a clue to the past in dusty little Alfredville. And yet that is what I have found: that I lost something years ago that I haven't been able to replace, and if that something isn't altogether Bennie, it is what he represented to me then, though I had no idea of it at the time: the unfettered exploration of life, the life of the senses, the unexamined joy of daily companionship in that exploration. And then, the unconscious knowledge that I was giving as well as receiving, that I, too, represented something to him that was worth having, and that in that way we supplemented each other. He admired and perhaps envied the things of the mind that my upbringing had given me; I marvelled at the quickness of the life in him, the easy translation of instinct into action, the passionate obedience to the whim of the moment.

And I returned to find that the joyful boy had grown into a troubled man, that his gift of life was not enough to help him cope with the complexities of adulthood. He tried to deal with them, the complexities, according to his lights, but something was missing, and what was missing was what I in my ignorance had represented to him, and had taken away from him when I left. So he went looking for that something, and,

274

finding it in my cousin, he destroyed it. And I, coming back, found what
had been missing from my life, and I destroyed it.

You will wonder how I know all this. I can only say that when you
have for three days and nights been going over the same ground, things
achieve a certain supernatural clarity.

I stop writing, blocked by the same inhibition that has been pre-
venting me from writing to James for the past few days. It is partly, as I've said to him, that to dwell on Bennie's death is to relive
it in all its terror – but only partly. There is also the fear that at
some level James cannot understand, cannot really be *expected* to
understand what I have only now come to understand myself, the
way the past has reasserted itself through Bennie, the claim that
Bennie's despair has staked upon my blitheness, and its violent
repelling of my invasion of the ground I abandoned so long ago.
How can James understand something that in its primitive inar-
ticulateness is so alien to him and his life in London, with its
default assumption that all experience is subject to ironic analysis? If I find myself balking at my own phrases, such as *joyful boy*
and *supernatural clarity*, how can I expect him not to wrinkle his
nose at them, as he does when he suspects any kind of solemnity
or pretension? So I end, lamely, on practicalities:

I'll leave here as soon as I've made all the declarations I have to make.
They've sent someone from a neighbouring town to run the cop shop,
fortunately a sensible and competent woman who won't keep me here for
longer than is absolutely necessary.

So things could be worse. One ordeal remains, which is to go and pay
my condolences to Bennie's widow – and two children. Spare me a
thought. How do you sympathise with someone on a death you've caused?

I hope things are more cheerful in London than here. Othello *was*
never like this.

Peter.

I look at my watch. It's six o'clock. I haven't eaten all day, but the
idea of food nauseates me. I get up, have a glass of water. I have not

yet put on clothes; the heat, in spite of the fan, has been intolerable, and there seemed little point in getting dressed. I look at myself in the mirror. I expect to look different somehow, my face to have registered the failure of some vital principle, the disintegration of substance and identity. But apart from the traces of sleeplessness, the black rings under my eyes, it is the same bland mask that faces me in the mirror; some saving impulse of routine has seen to it that I have washed, shaved, brushed my teeth, even gelled my hair, kept myself *looking*, at least, as if I'm in control of some part, the public part of my life. My body, too, though defenceless in its nakedness, shows no sign of the disintegration of my spirit.

Nonyameko must have come in from her long day at the clinic. I pick up the phone and dial her room. It rings for a long time and I am about to give up, almost in relief, when she picks up.

'Hello?' She sounds out of breath.

'Hi. It's me. Have I made you run?'

'Well, I was in the shower, but ...'

'I'm sorry.'

'I was going to say but it was time to get out anyway. How are you?'

'Not too great. Do you feel up to a walk?'

There is a slight hesitation. I guess that she is mentally rearranging her evening for my benefit, but my need, now that I have recognised it, is greater than my normal anxiety not to inconvenience, not to intrude, not to make claims, and I wait for her to say what I know she will say: 'That's fine. Do you want to go now?'

'As soon as you've got on some clothes,' I reply, with a conscious attempt at humour.

'If you insist,' she returns, gamely matching my tone. 'I'll meet you downstairs in, say, fifteen minutes?'

'That's great,' I say. And though that's an overstatement, I do feel marginally cheered by the prospect of her company. If nothing else, it gives me a reason to put on some clothes.

Nonyameko's hair sparkles with tiny drops of water; the matt velvet of her skin shines in the late afternoon sun. The heat has relented somewhat, and people are opening the windows and shutters they'd kept closed during the day. Garden sprinklers come on – irrigation is banned between 9 am and 6 pm – and the smell of wet soil freshens the stale air. Gathering clouds may promise a thunderstorm later, but the gardeners of Alfredville have learnt to distrust such covenants. As we walk past our old home I try to avert my gaze, somehow block out the house with all its associations, but I am assailed by the heavy perfume of the huge magnolia blooms on the old tree. Somebody is working in the garden; I suppose the house is being prepared for Hector Williams's return. Good Lord, I think, one of the results of my efforts is that Hector is now presumably the legitimate heir to the house Oom Blik bought Desirée. One more reason not to face the Van Blerks before leaving. But nice for Sarah and the baby.

We walk for a while without talking. I leave Nonyameko to choose our route. We go uphill, cross the R62, take an unsignposted dirt road that leads to a copse of ragged bluegums. Under one of the trees we stop and look back; there is kind of mellow beauty to the village now, which it lacks in the full glare of day. The unassuming buildings seem settled in their stony surrounds, the trees valiantly standing their ground in untoward conditions. Somewhere somebody is hammering away, metal on metal: perhaps a backyard mechanic resurrecting some rusty wreck. In the township behind us there is the barking of dogs, punctuated by the shrill shouts of children at play. A day like any other, a place like any other, but transformed by loss into a unique locality of grief.

'Shall we sit down?' Nonyameko asks, gesturing at a large rock under a bluegum.

'What about your clean skirt?' I ask. She is wearing the yellow skirt she'd worn the first time I saw her.

'It will wash,' she says wryly, and sits down. I sit down next to her. The rock is not exactly comfortable, but it is pleasantly warm, and there is something companionable in the shared discomfort.

We sit for a while in silence. Then she says, 'How have you been?'

'Not really well,' I say. 'I can't seem to blot out the memory of … all that. Vincent. And then Bennie, of course …'

'It would be unnatural if you could. Don't try to do it. Learn to live with it.'

I try to suppress a judder of irritation, but don't succeed. 'Isn't that a bit glib?'

'I suppose it sounds that way,' she says. 'I know that all grief is unique, but I also know from my practice and even my personal experience, that there is a common ground, and that comfort may be found there eventually.' She pauses. *Eventually,* she repeats. 'For the time being, accept your grief, don't fight it.'

'Oh, I'm not fighting it,' I say. 'I've pretty much caved in under its weight.'

'I know it feels like that. But I have seen caved-in people, and you are not one of them.' She smiles, takes my hand, looks at my nails. 'For a start, you are clean. And you had the strength of purpose to lift up the phone to call me.'

'Only so that I could collapse on top of you.'

'Well, collapse away, that is also okay.' She is still holding my hand and squeezes it lightly.

'The thing is,' I say, 'that I can't seem to make any plans. Nothing I might do seems to matter more than anything else. I should leave, I know, but I can't bring myself to do it.'

'Is that because there is something keeping you here?'

'No, that's too positive. It's that there's nothing to go to. I've tried to write a letter to James, and all it expresses is my inability to communicate what I feel.'

'But even that is something. To say I can't tell you what I feel is to tell the other person at least part of what you feel.'

'That's a very kind sophistry.' I hesitate. 'But perhaps there is something keeping me here.'

She looks at me. 'And that is?'

'The fact that I haven't been to see Chrisna. I can't leave without seeing her, and yet I can't bring myself to face her either.'

She lets go of my hand and picks up a pebble, rubs it clean between her fingers. 'Yes,' she says, 'I can see that it is necessary for you to see her. As long as you realise that she may not be able to offer you very much. She will have her own demons to deal with.'

'You're not making this sound any easier.'

'No, I do not think it will be easy. But in the long run it will help you to come to terms with your own grief.'

'You mean I'll have achieved *closure*,' I say.

She smiles. 'No, I shall avoid the term. But do go and see Chrisna.'

When I get back to the hotel I hesitate for a moment before powering up my laptop. Do I even *want* a reply from James? How is he going to deal with my outpouring, so different to the usual tenor of our conversations? Between the two of us we have had to deal with no misfortune greater than a blocked drain or, one cold winter, a burst water pipe. We don't have a vocabulary of disaster.

There is no e-mail from James; but as I sit staring at the screen, not knowing whether I'm relieved or disappointed, the Skype ringtone sounds. I click on the icon.

'James,' I say.

'Peter,' he says, and I am, after all, overjoyed to hear his voice, his warm baritone that sounds humorous even when he's serious. 'I've been trying for the last hour. Peter, how are you?'

'I'm … well, I'm dealing with it. It's been pretty shit, but I seem to be coping.'

'You seem to be coping? What kind of talk is that? Are you seeing someone? Have you got someone to talk to?'

'Yes. Yeah, as I mentioned, there's the local vet and then there's Nonyameko …'

'The shrink?'

'Yeah, though she prefers to be called a therapist.'

'Well, hell, whatever she's called, I'm glad she's there for you. Not sure what a vet can do for you, though.'

'I don't see him in his professional capacity. He's just a friend.'

'That's good, then. But listen, when are you coming back?'

'I don't know. There are still some things to sort out here, and then I promised my folks I'd get down there for a visit.'

'Under the circumstances, won't they understand that you might just want to get home?'

279

'They'll pretend to understand, but they'll be very hurt. They'll want to … I don't know, support me, console me, *parent* me.'

'And do you want to be parented?'

'No, not really. But I'm not sure that what *I* want is the main thing here.'

'Listen, my man, what *you* want is abso-fucking-lutely the main thing here. You've had one hell of a time, you need to think of yourself before anyone else.'

'Oh, I'm sure to do that, whatever else I do.'

'You're too hard on yourself.' There's a pause; something in his inflection has implied that he's considering another statement, and I wait for it. Then he says, 'Look, do you want me to come out there? I could easily do that, you know.'

'Hell, James, that's … well, that's a wonderful offer, but I couldn't do it to you. What about *Othello*?'

'Oh, bugger *Othello*. They'll just have to do without me for a few days. Shall I check flights and get back to you?'

'No, no, don't do that. I really appreciate it, but … no, it's really not necessary.'

'Who's talking fucking *necessary*? You're in pain and distress, you're my ex-partner, I can't leave you to be miserable in that godforsaken place with only a vet and a shrink to talk to. I'm coming out there.'

'That's … that's really great of you, James. But have you checked the weather reports?'

'I don't need to check the fucking weather reports, I can look out of the window and see the bloody snow for myself.'

'So how likely is Heathrow to be operating a normal service, even if you *can* get a seat on a plane?'

'I don't know, Peter, I really don't, but I'm sure as God not going to get a seat if I don't try. So I'm going to log off now and get onto the airlines and get back to you. Are you going to be around for a while?'

'Yeah, sure. I'm not going anywhere tonight. My social programme is quite open at the moment.'

'Right. Stay online.'

The call is terminated. I sit and stare at my room, at Sarah's flowers, now wilting, at the off-kilter candle in the candlestick, at the demented dog's-head string holder, the surreal props to a dismal drama, and I search for an emotion, for something other than a bleak indifference, even to whether or not James flies out to … to what? Support me? Cheer me up? Or just to become another practicality to worry about, how to get him from the airport to Alfredville, how he'll cope with Alfredville and then with my parents? And are we going to have to rehash our relationship, *reconsider* in the light of recent events? A week ago all I wanted was for James to reconsider and come back to me; but if he did so now, it would be out of pity, which even in my present state I can see is a rotten basis for a relationship. And I can't rid myself of the thought that, with the best will in the world, and with all the generosity of his impetuous nature, James is not really going to know how to deal with a tragedy as bereft of beauty and dignity as this one.

So that when, half an hour later, he calls back to say that Heathrow is experiencing severe delays and that all flights are jampacked, I feel only a wan kind of relief. I don't think I'm strong enough to be supported.

CHAPTER 20

Friday morning 29 January
At an hour when I know the children will be at school, I walk to Bennie's home. I did briefly consider phoning to arrange a time, but I was afraid Chrisna would simply refuse to see me. Though that would in some ways have been a blessed relief, I know also that I can't leave Alfredville, this time for ever, without seeing Chrisna. She has become for me an extension of Bennie; perhaps if she can forgive me I can tell myself Bennie has forgiven me.

The blank little house looks closed; the curtains are drawn, and the front windows are shut. But as I open the gate, I hear Kerneels barking somewhere inside the house, so somebody must be home.

I knock at the frosted-glass door. The barking comes closer, and a figure looms through the dim grey glass. The door opens and Kerneels comes bounding out. In the doorway, Chrisna stands looking at me with a face of stone.

'It's you,' she says dully. Her face is very pale. She is neatly dressed as always, her hair pulled back in her usual functional fashion. Her eyes seem preternaturally bright.

'May I speak to you?' I ask. 'Preferably on your own.' I do not feel up to Mrs Rabies today.

'You can come in,' she says. 'My mother is at her women's prayer meeting. They're praying for rain again.'

'I hope they're successful,' I say. 'It's very dry.'

'I don't know,' she says. 'If I were God I don't think I would listen to my mother.'

She says this in a flat, affectless way, leaving no room for pleasantry or for any reply at all. She leads the way into the neat sitting room and gestures towards a chair. I sit down. Kerneels jumps onto the sofa and Chrisna sits down next to him. He puts his head on her lap and peers at me as if suspecting me of evil intent.

Chrisna looks at me neutrally, as if we were two strangers facing each other on park benches.

'I want to say that I'm … more sorry than I can say.'

Her face remains expressionless. 'Sorry? Why are you sorry?'

'I'm sorry that … this dreadful thing happened. I didn't mean for it to end … like that.'

'Then how did you mean for it to end?' Her tone is calmly interrogative.

'I was hoping that Bennie would … confess, give himself up …'

'And go to prison for the rest of his life?'

'I'm sure there would have been extenuating circumstances.'

'You're sure, are you?'

'Yes, surely …'

But she interrupts me. 'It doesn't really matter what you're sure of any more, does it?'

'Yes, I can see that. I really only wanted to say how sorry I am …'

'Yes, you've said that. But I'm still wondering why you're sorry. They say Bennie confessed to you. That's what you wanted, isn't it?'

'Yes, but not … to kill himself.'

'Yes. Well, what we want isn't always what we get.'

Her tone is so final that it takes a renewed effort to carry on. 'I know what you must think,' I say. 'If I hadn't confronted Bennie with what I knew, he wouldn't have shot himself.'

'So you want credit for Bennie's suicide?'

'That's very harsh. I'm plagued by the possibility that I might have contributed to it.'

'That's something you'll have to sort out with your conscience. You know best what passed between the two of you before he shot himself.'

'I could tell you, if you wanted to know.'

She lifts her hand dismissively. 'No, I really don't. I knew you would take him from me. I just didn't know how.'

283

She says this so flatly that it takes me a moment to absorb the impact. I try to control my voice – I can feel it threatening to quaver – as I ask, 'Why do you think I wanted to take him away from you?'

But she's not listening to me; she's immersed in her own private hell, not interested in mine.

'I knew you were going to take him away from me,' she says again, then adds, 'Just as she tried to do.'

'She.'

'Yes. She. That cousin of yours. She didn't want him, not really, but she wanted to take him away from me.'

'But why? If she didn't want him herself?'

Chrisna is now like one hypnotised. I could ask her anything and she would reply, like an automaton. 'She didn't want me to have something she didn't have. She was always the one who had everything, and I was there to admire her, the plain one who made her look more beautiful, the dull one who made her seem more brilliant than she was.'

'But I thought you were best friends?'

'We were. Desirée liked having me around, and I liked being useful. She even tried to persuade me to go to Stellenbosch with her, but then my mother decided to retire and she needed a home and someone to look after her. So I stayed and got a job at the Co-op and looked after my mother. Desirée wrote witty letters from Stellenbosch, but I got tired of hearing what a wonderful time she was having, and stopped writing back. So I had only my job at the Co-op and my mother's company, with nothing to look forward to for the rest of my life. And then Bennie came back, a year or two after I started working, and we started seeing each other. And it was as if a new life was starting, he was so lively, so interested, so full of energy, he took me out and he made me laugh. And I was in love with him and I think he was in love with me but then ... then she came back from Stellenbosch, and put a spell on Bennie, and we were still friends, Bennie and me, but it wasn't the same, although I pretended it was.'

She sits for a while, rubbing the dog's ear between her fingers, counting her losses.

'And then, when Hector came and Desirée lost interest in Bennie, he came to see me again and we fell in love again and got married. And for a while it was wonderful, but then he got all moody and I knew he was seeing Desirée again.'

'So you knew that?'

'Of course I knew that, I'm not a fool like that Hector Williams, too full of himself to see what was happening right under his nose. But what could I do? I couldn't leave Bennie, not with two children and a mother to look after. All I could hope was that it would blow over, and that he'd come back to me and the children.'

'And did it blow over?'

'No, you know it didn't. And then, when he told me that evening, when I went down to the station to take him his supper, that he was leaving me to go away with ... with *her* ...'

'With Desirée?'

'Who else, for heaven's sake?'

'No, no – it's just that I didn't know he was planning to leave with her.'

'Yes, she persuaded him to get a transfer to Cape Town, a demotion, and to take her away. He had some idea that he could make money in a security business. So when he told me that evening ...'

'What evening?'

'The evening of Desirée's death,' Chrisna says, again with uncanny patience. 'So when I gave him his supper, I remember it was fish cakes and mash, and he said that he'd been talking to Desirée and he was going to leave me and the children to go to Cape Town with her ....'

'Wait a minute,' I say, 'please just stop. Are you saying Bennie was going to leave you for *Desirée*?

She looks at me at last, then looks away quickly, as if appalled by what she sees. 'Yes. I'm surprised that you're so surprised. Didn't he tell you he was infatuated with your cousin?'

'Yes, but I thought ... oh, damn what I thought. It's just that he didn't ... didn't say that he'd decided to leave with Desirée.'

285

'Yes.' She almost smiles, a flicker of feeling over the desolate features. 'You see, he wasn't as open with you as you thought.'

'But why then did he kill her?'

For the first time she looks straight into my eyes. The feeble smile on her colourless lips is now more pronounced. 'He didn't kill her.'

It's not entirely unexpected, this attempt to cling to a belief in her husband's innocence, and the thought crosses my mind that as an act of charity one might allow her that luxury. But that would make nonsense of Bennie's action; so, as gently as I can, I say, 'But he said he did.'

'Did he really?' She seems almost amused.

I try to remember our last conversation. 'Well, he didn't contradict me when I … suggested that he killed her. And he said that you knew who killed Desirée – which I thought meant …' I stop, overwhelmed by the enormity of what's dawning on me.

'You thought he meant himself,' she suggests, almost kindly. 'Yes, well. It turns out you were wrong on that score too. So, no, he didn't kill Desirée.'

'How can you be so sure?'

'Because I killed her.'

She says this with a kind of nonchalance, as if reporting some minor, perhaps even mildly amusing, mishap.

'But … but why?' is all I can think of asking.

Now, at last, she laughs out loud. 'Why? You ask me *why*? That woman who had every chance in life, who went away but chose to come back to save up to go away again, who married a terrorist because she was bored with Alfredville, then got bored with her terrorist and took my husband away, that woman who was going to take him away to Cape Town, where as sure as fate she would have dropped him as soon as she met someone more interesting – you ask me why I killed her?'

'Then it was … premeditated?'

'No, not really. Oh, there were plenty of times I thought of ways of killing her, but I never had the courage, I kept thinking about the children and my mother, so I couldn't do it. But that evening, when he told me he was leaving me, well, even then I didn't plan to *kill* her. I went ... '

She breaks down for a moment, as if she's got something in her throat, then clears it and carries on. 'Yes. Anyway, I went straight from the station to her house to plead with her. I said to her, Please Desirée, you have everything and I only have Bennie and the children, and she said, At least you have the children, I have no children, and I said, You have a husband, you can have children, and she said, And stay in Alfredville for the rest of my life looking after children, like you? And I said, Please Desirée, you can easily go away without Bennie, your father would pay to settle you in Cape Town, and she said, Oh, it's always easier with a man, and I said, Yes, until you're tired of him too, and she said, Nothing lasts forever, but for now he'll do. And then I got on my knees, I literally knelt before her, and said, Please Desirée, please just leave him to me, please just let go of him. And then she laughed and said, My dear Chrisnatjie, don't speak to me, speak to your husband, I can let go of him, but will he let go of me? And then she took the television remote and switched on the television and I got up from my knees. I was quite calm; I took an antimacassar and wrapped it around the statue of David and I killed her. And I'm not sorry. Except now I've lost Bennie anyway and I am left with my mother. Thanks to you.'

'But if he didn't kill Desirée ...'

'Yes?'

'Why did he kill himself?

'You're the writer, you figure it out. But I'll give you a clue. That first evening, when you had supper with us ...'

'Yes?'

'Afterwards he said to me, he said, You know it's funny, but that's the first person who ever believed in me and he's still the one man in the world whose opinion matters to me.' She says this with a sardonic smile. 'And I said, Yes it *is* funny, it's really hilarious, he left you twenty years ago and you still care.'

'I ... I had no idea,' is all I can say.

'No, of course you had no idea. You're like your cousin, you don't know what effect you have on other people, so you sail through life not looking back at the people you've left behind in your wake. But the people you've left behind don't stop feeling just because you've forgotten them.' She's not looking at me as she speaks; she seems to be following a train of thought that is leading her away from me, into some darkling territory of memory or imagination. But then, abruptly, she looks at me, and says decisively but calmly, almost conversationally, 'If you really think about it, in the end it was you who caused your cousin's death.'

My first impulse is to laugh. There is something so outrageous about Chrisna's claim, and yet so rational about her manner, that it causes a kind of moral dysfunction in my mind: there seem to be no grounds for appeal against a charge of which the form is so constrained and the content so excessive. But I don't laugh; I contain my rising hysteria by digging my nails into the palms of my hands, and I simply stare at her, trying to get a grip on reality, to make my way through the subterfuges of a disturbed mind to the kernel of truth that may be lurking there. Chrisna is looking at me … *politely* is the word that crazily comes to mind.

'Look,' I say, 'there's no way I can take responsibility for Desirée's death. That's just too far-fetched. But Bennie … yes. I can see … well, yes. But what was I to do? I honestly believed that he had killed Desirée.'

'You *honestly believed*.' Her contained fury erupts. She pronounces the words with a vehemence suggesting incredulity, outrage, but above all, contempt. Her passion distorts her normally placid features; red blotches break out on her pallid skin. Always rather plain, she is now startlingly ugly. Kerneels jumps from the sofa and lies down on the floor, looking at her apprehensively. 'And do you think,' she almost shouts at me, 'do you really think your *honest belief* made it okay for you to come meddling in our lives, Bennie's and mine? What gave you the right to come back here after twenty years? You abandoned Bennie when he needed you, and then, when he no longer needed you, you came back to torment him. And then you took it upon yourself, all unasked, to clear Hector Williams.'

'But would you really have had an innocent man go to prison for a murder that you committed?'

'Hector Williams was not an innocent man. He planted a bomb in a restaurant in Durban that killed twenty-six people.'

'That was for political reasons,' I sputter.

'Tell that to the mother of the two teenagers who were killed. Tell that to the husband of the woman in the kitchen who was blown to bits. But don't tell it to me.'

'And now?'

'Now what?'

'Now what do I do?'

'Are you asking *me* what to do? You, the hot-shot detective, are asking me, the murderer, what to do? You came here to find out what happened to Desirée. You've found out. Okay, now deal with it. Go and write a story about it.'

'But you told me this ... you needn't have told me.'

'I told you because I want you to know what you've done to us – you and your cousin.'

'Even at the risk of my going to the police and telling them what you've told me?'

'What?' She looks at me almost pityingly. 'Three days after you told the police Bennie told you he killed Desirée, you're going to go back and tell them sorry, you made a mistake, Bennie's wife has just told you *she* killed Desirée?'

'I could, you know.'

'And achieve what?'

'Justice.'

Chrisna Nienaber laughs again. It's not a pleasant sound. 'You think you'll get *justice* by turning me over to the police? Justice is what Desirée van Blerk got, and you know it. But no, you need to feel good about the mess you've made, so you want to call it justice. Go ahead, have me arrested – that's if anybody will believe you – leave my two children with my mother, tell the world you accused Bennie of murder and drove him to suicide. I suppose that'll make you a hero in England. *Home-town boy solves murder on second try.* Go ahead, do it.'

I want to explain to Chrisna that she's making a mistake, that I didn't accuse Bennie of murder, that he had more things to drive him to suicide than just my opinion of him ... but one look at her convinces me that there is nothing I can say to alleviate her anger or restore her loss. The animation of anger gone from her face, all that remains is arid inconsolability.

'I don't suppose that will serve any purpose,' I say, 'now that Bennie's dead and Hector's been released.'

'No, unless you want to get even with me.'

'Get even with you? For what?'

'For taking Bennie away from you.'

I have in the last few days had to adjust my mind to so many different interpretations that I try, momentarily, to accommodate this one. But I can't. Chrisna's anger or grief has evidently deranged her. 'Look, Chrisna,' I say, 'I didn't even *know* you were married to Bennie, I didn't even know *you*, I didn't even know Bennie was living in Alfredville, I'd just about forgotten Bennie, for heaven's sake – how could I possibly resent your marrying him?'

'Oh, you didn't at the time. But then you came back and found Bennie happily married and you started working on him to make him dissatisfied, taking him running, going for walks with him at night, going *swimming* with him, two grown-up men carrying on like schoolboys. I don't know what you did to him, but after Desirée's death he was more restful, and he would have settled again, but then you came, and he became all restless again. And with you even looking like her, it was like having her back. And you didn't rest until you drove him to his death, because you couldn't face that he was happy without you.'

She says all this with a kind of desperate calmness, her jaw set with the force of her conviction. I know that there's nothing I can say to correct her, that this crazy construct has become her reality, and that she's going to live in it for the rest of her life. Chrisna Nienaber is lucidly and coherently *mad*.

'Hell, Chrisna,' I nevertheless hear myself saying, 'why would I want to take over Bennie's life? I have a life of my own to lead.'

'You're living in a flat in London with someone you're not even married to. Do you call that a life?'

'It's what millions of people call a life.'

'It's not what I call a life. It's a life support system. It's like battery chickens who lay an egg every time they switch the lights on.' She gets up. 'Now please leave. The children will be back from school soon. Get out of my life and don't come back.'

She shows me out. Kerneels gets up and follows her.

I walk back to the hotel to check out and then to meet Nonyameko for a farewell lunch. I am drained, too devastated even to feel grief or shock or outrage. I have no volition, no identity even; I just feel empty, as if I never want to write another word. If all stories are arbitrary constructs, what is the point of writing stories? If Chrisna's story makes as much sense to her as mine makes to me, who's to say mine is more valid? Around me Alfredville is going its humble workaday way, perpetuating its pointless existence; but is it any more pointless than the same thing multiplied by millions, in London? Here the farmer's bakkie stinks up the main street; in London the Tube fouls the lungs of a million passengers a day.

As I get to my room, the phone rings. 'Peter? I'm glad I caught you in time. They said ...'

'Oh, Henk,' I say. 'Thank you for phoning. I appreciate it.' And I really do appreciate it, this sign that I am not some outcast from my kind, sentenced to banishment in the wilderness.

'Oh.' He sounds vaguely surprised. 'You're welcome. I just thought to say, well, let's not lose touch.'

'No, let's not. And Henk ...'

'Yes?'

'I think you must be a very good vet.'

'Thank you, but on what do you base that opinion?'

'One day I'll tell you the whole story. But you were right about Bennie Nienaber.'

'You mean ...?'

291

'He wasn't a killer.'

'Then who ...?'

'Who? I can't really tell you without going into a longer story than I have time for now. And to be honest, I'm not too proud of my part in it. And you were right about tentativeness. But one day I'll tell you the whole story.'

'How can you, when you're buggering off?'

'We'll see each other again. I know.'

He laughs. 'Don't count on my coming to London, no matter how well vets are doing there. I love all of God's creatures, but I'm not that great on Pomeranians. I'm staying put.'

'Well, if the mountain won't come to Mohammed ... but we'll see each other again.'

'Good. I look forward to that.'

'So do I. And don't fuse your identity too inextricably with that of some ungrateful lout.'

'I won't. I'll hold something back for you.'

'Please do. And thank you for your support the last few days.'

He snorts dismissively. 'You're welcome.'

I take my bags downstairs. Out of force of habit I avoid the lift, and when I get downstairs I'm sweating.

Joachim is on his own at the desk.

'So you're leaving us today?' Joachim asks, producing my bill, neatly itemised. I run my eye over it; on a cursory inspection, it seems in order. Joy, to give her her due, seems to be an efficient receptionist.

'Yes, I think it's time I left,' I say. 'Can't stay forever, I suppose.'

'Some of us do,' he says cheerfully.

'Yes, if I owned a hotel I might also stay.'

He laughs, pleased. 'It's got its advantages, the old hotel.'

'Is your car round the back?' he asks, as I pick up my bag and my laptop.

'Yes, it's still there.' As I turn round to leave, Boris materialises.

'Here, let me give you a hand with that,' he says.

For a moment I want to resist, then realise that Boris *wants* to

292

carry my bag, or at any rate wants to demonstrate a willingness to carry it.

'Thanks, Boris,' I say. 'But be careful, it's heavy.'

Outside in the sun-blasted back yard, I open the boot of my car and he places my luggage inside. I fumble for cash, but he holds up his hand. 'It's on the house,' he says.

'Thanks, Boris,' I say.

'You're welcome, bru,' he says. I put out my hand. He shakes it, the triple African handshake that I haven't really mastered.

'Come back,' he says.

'Sure,' I say. 'Some day.'

'You'll know where to find me,' he says. 'I'm not going anywhere.'

'Good man, Boris,' I say and get into the car and drive off.

I've arranged to meet Nonyameko in the R62 Diner. I have to resist a momentary impulse just to keep driving, for ever if necessary, just never having to face anybody again, never having to repeat the story that I now have to go and spill into Nonyameko's lap like some foul relic of a disastrous exploit. But where would I drive to? To my parents, to their uncomprehending, loving, claustrophobic concern? Back to James, for another doomed attempt at reviving a moribund relationship on the basis of my pathetic state? No, of all people on earth, Nonyameko is the one most likely to be able to offer me the refuge of simple understanding. So, at the T-junction with the R62, I don't take the left turn to Cape Town, nor the right turn to the coast; I stop at the Diner.

Nonyameko is there already, reading her JM Coetzee. When I enter, she closes her book and smiles at me.

'So?' she says. 'Have you taken your leave?'

I sit down. 'Yes,' I say, 'I think I have. Of my senses. *God*, I really have.' The waiter – the same gangling youth who'd served Henk and me – appears, and we order food. I have no interest in eating, and order the first thing that catches my eye, which is a Ghanta burger. I tell her about my morning. It takes the better part of twenty minutes, even in the laconic rendering I adopt so as not to start screaming, shouting, tearing out my entrails and generally impacting negatively on the tourist trade, of which there is a solid polyglot sample installed in the diner. I sense that there's a thin line between absolute control and a complete surrender to a horrific breakdown of reason. The thin line, I tell myself, is irony. Cling to it like Perseus clinging to Ariadne's clue in the labyrinth of the Minotaur, conscious of the terrible fate that awaits you if you let go. So I recount the events of the morning as I imagine Joseph Conrad would have told it, or Henry James, the horror kept in abeyance by the effort of lucid narration. I concentrate on the details of the story, try to remember every nuance of Chrisna's indictment, so as to cushion myself against its content. The food arrives – as I should have expected from the name, it's in fact an ostrich burger – and I eat it, without tasting it. I cling to my thin line of irony, and methodically plot a course through the labyrinth of my story, steering clear of the monsters of the mind.

'Phew,' Nonyameko says, when I've done. 'That is quite a story.'

'I suppose so. The thing is, I don't think of it as a story any more.'

'You mean you are not going to write it after all?'

'I'm not going to write it after all. It's not my story to write. It's Bennie's story, and Chrisna's story, and Desirée's story, and only then is it my story, and every story has its own truth and its own moral, and they all contradict one another. Or, in a different sense, it's too much my story to write. What a sorry tale of a stuffup. Has anyone ever meddled so ineffectually and yet so disastrously?'

'I can see the disaster. But why ineffectually?'

'Well, what have I effected that is of any good? Other than the release of Hector Williams, who is only a name to me, and who would have been released in due course anyway?'

'You persuaded Sarah to keep her child. I saw her today, and she is quite radiant.'

'I'm pleased *somebody*'s radiant. So, Sarah's child will not have

294

to grow up believing its father is a murderer. But what about Bennie's children?'

She shakes her head. 'No, I do not know about Bennie's children. What I do know is that it will not help much for them to discover now that their mother is in fact the murderer.'

'No, not even I would want to pursue justice that far beyond the bounds of mercy. If Chrisna's right, then by my meddling I killed Bennie as surely as she killed Desirée. So who am I to denounce her?'

She shakes her head. 'No, I do not think you can do that. It would be a futile exercise in abstract justice. But that does not mean that you should hold yourself responsible for Bennie's death. He was obviously a complex person with complex problems. And the suicide rate among South African policemen is terrible – I forget the exact statistics, but in the period 2000 to 2005 more than five hundred police officers committed suicide.'

I suspect that she is deliberately shifting the ground of our conversation to one of neutral fact, but I am not ready yet to take refuge in statistics. Bennie is not just one of five hundred police officers. 'To think,' I say, 'that I left South Africa originally not to get embroiled in the bloodshed and share in the guilt. And here I am embroiled up to my ears.'

She sighs. 'Embroiled up to one's ears. That is the condition of living here.'

'But I don't even live here.'

She smiles, evidently amused. I don't know why I thought she lacked humour. 'Perhaps you can regard yourself as an honorary citizen.' Then she asks, 'And what are you going to do now?'

'Apparently I'm free to go.'

'Free to go where?'

'Anywhere.'

'Anywhere is nowhere. Where do you want to go?'

'I don't *want* to go anywhere. But I'll head down to Knysna to see my folks. And then it's back to London, I suppose.'

'You suppose? Isn't that where your home is?'

'I suppose. But I'm not quite sure what that means any more.'

'Well, home usually means something quite specific!'

'Like …?'

'Like where you have your house, your job, your friends, the place where you know where to go if you need to buy a pair of shoelaces.'

'My home is a flat I used to share with James, and don't much fancy inhabiting on my own. My job is freelance journalism, which I can do anywhere I can plug in my computer. My friends were my and James's friends, who I suspect find him by far the more entertaining of the two of us.'

'And the shoelaces?'

'I never travel without a spare pair.'

'Wise man. So you're free to go anywhere?'

'As I said.'

'Even free to stay.'

'Even free to stay.'

'Will you?'

'Stay? No.'

'Why not?'

'You mean here in Alfredville? Exchanging gossip with Joachim and Joy? Visiting Oom Blik and Aunt Dolly? Sharing memories with Chrisna?'

'No, I would not recommend that. Not because of Joachim and Joy and Blik and Dolly, or even of Chrisna, but because of Desirée and because of Bennie. I do not think you want to share the rest of your life with two dead people.'

'Especially not since I was responsible for the death of one of them. Both of them, if you believe Chrisna.'

'And do you believe Chrisna?'

'No, not really. And yet, there's a weird logic to it, too.'

Nonyameko puts her hand on mine. 'I do not think you should assume responsibility for Chrisna's weird logic. She is dealing with her losses in her way.'

'And I have to deal with mine in my way. Except I don't know how.' And saying it, I can feel myself losing my hold on my composure, approaching the point I have feared, where irony breaks down and you look at the blood on your hands in horror. So I try to deal with it in my way.

'But don't worry,' I say, 'I'm very good at not assuming responsibility.' I try to escape her concern, because it's easier flippantly to assume guilt than soberly to think through its exact nuances. 'Don't be fooled,' I say, 'by next week I'll be telling people in London about my weird adventure in Africa.'

Nonyameko looks at me, her great eyes filling with tears, and she takes my hand in hers. 'Poor Peter,' she says. 'And you still do not know yourself.'

The waiter appears next to us. 'Is everything all right?' he asks, the ritual, universal question that almost requires no answer. But now, here, the question strikes me as both hilarious and tragic.

'No,' I say, 'everything is not all right. Everything is a fucking mess.' I try to laugh, but it emerges as a stifled kind of cry, as of a distressed animal. And then the shell cracks, my time-hardened carapace, defence against feeling too much and showing too much, and I am left exposed on some desolate shore, delivered over to the furies that attend on human misfortune or misdeed. I cover my face with my free hand, and feel my body shaken with a violence of emotion I've never allowed myself, a flood of inarticulate horror overwhelming me. I'm dimly aware of a hush in the restaurant, the tourists ceasing their chatter, the waiter frozen in embarrassment next to the table. I seem to be making a scene, and force of habit tries to draw me back into the realm of expected behaviour. But, more strongly than habit, I feel the relentless pull of loss, of the losses I have caused and the losses I have suffered, the drift towards annihilation that nobody and nothing can stay. But I hold onto Nonyameko's hand, for all the world as if I could thus anchor myself to some saving vestige of identity, as if her grasp could keep me from being swept away into oblivion.

GLOSSARY

ATKV: Afrikaanse Taal en Kultuurvereniging (Afrikaans Language and Culture Association)

Baas: Boss; old-fashioned form of address for a (white) male employer

Bakkie: light pick-up track

Befokte: fucked-up; often used as a term of grudging admiration

Biltong: beef or venison cut into strips and cured

Boeremeisie: a young Afrikaans woman (literally, farm girl)

Boerekos: home cooking

Boerewors: farm sausage, a traditional spiced sausage much favoured for braaivleis (q.v.).

Boetie: little brother; a common form of address for the son of the family

Braaivleis: barbecue, barbecued meat

Bywoners: sharecroppers

Deurmekaar: confused, haywire

Dominee: reverend, a Dutch Reformed minister

Donnering, donnered: beating up, beaten up

Dorp: town, village

Gatvol: fed-up, very irritated

Haai Joy, my nooi! Kom na my kooi!: 'Hey, Joy, my girl! Come to bed with me!'

Huisgodsdiens: family prayers

Ja-nee: literally, yes-no; an expression of philosophical resignation and sometimes satisfaction: well, there you are then

Kamtig: supposedly, professedly

Kamtige: pretended, alleged

Kerksaal: church hall

Koeksister: a syrupy pastry, twisted into a double spiral

Koppie: a stony hillock

Kwaito: a form of township music, an indigenous form of hip-hop or house music

Kwerekwere: derogatory term meaning African from outside South Africa

Laat die Vlamme Hoog Opslaan (song): Make the flames flare high

Larney: posh

Lethu Mshini Wami (song): Bring me my machine gun

Longdrop: pit latrine

Missis: Madam, form of address of servants to the woman of the house

Moer: to beat the hell out of; pissed off (the *moer* in); expressing disgust (*se moer*)

Moffie: a homosexual, also used as a contemptuous term for a weakling

Morsdood: dead as a doornail

Mos: a word that adds emphasis (an intensifier); thus 'You're *mos* family' would mean 'You're family, after all?'

Nee wat: No, not on your life, never

Nogal: on top of it all, in addition

Oke: chap

Oom: literally uncle, though often used as a respectful term and form of address for an older man

Ouma: grandma

Poort: literally a portal; here a narrow pass through mountains; often part of a place name

Rooibos: literally redbush, an indigenous herbal tea

Rooinek: literally redneck, a derogatory term for an English-speaking South African

se voet: no ways, don't you believe it

Sies: an exclamation of disgust

Snot en trane: snot and tears

Sommer: simply, without further ado

Soutpiel: Literally salt prick, an allusion to the belief that English-speaking South Africans straddle the Atlantic, having one foot in England and one in South Africa

Spiff: elegant

Steek-stukkie: a 'bit on the side'

Tuine en Tossels: Gardens and Tassles (a TV home decorating show)

Verkramp: rigidly conservative; during apartheid, an Afrikaner Nationalist who opposed liberal trends in government policy, particularly those relating to racial questions

Volk: nation, people

vreet en suip en snotpik: stuff themselves with food and booze and pick their noses

Vrot: rotten

Witblits: literally white lighting, a colourless home-brewed brandy

Zoll: a marijuana cigarette, a joint

ACKNOWLEDGEMENTS

I am grateful to my usual band of readers: Lou-Marie Kruger, Lars Engle, Stephanus Muller, Christine Roe, Arnold van Zyl, and my agent, Isobel Dixon. I appreciate their interest and I benefited by their advice. They are not to be held responsible for those instances where I disregarded it.

Thank you to Deon Meyer, with whom I had an illuminating conversation about police procedure. Once, again, the mistakes I persisted in are all mine.

I owe an immense debt to my editor, Lynda Gilfillan, for her tireless and meticulous fine-combing of my text, and her tactful correction of my excesses and imprecisions. The novel is much better than it would have been without her intervention; no doubt it would have been even better had I not in a few instances persisted in my error.

Readers of Antony Altbeker's fascinating account of the Inge Lotz murder, *Fruit of a Poisoned Tree*, will note that I've appropriated some details of that case to my use. This is not meant to imply any correspondence between the protagonists in that case and my own characters, who are all, with the exception of Liquorice the Labrador, fictitious.